KITTY in the CASTLE

by

David Bramhall

Walnut Tree Books

Second edition 2022

Kitty in the Castle

KITTY in the CASTLE

When that the tide is in full fludde
There will arise and suck oor bludde
The lothesome Wyrm that lie and slepe
Beneath Crayle's lofty kepe
But when the tide doth run and wane
He'll hie him to his hame agane
To sleep untille a maiden's hand
Shall banish hym from all thys land

Anon.

I

Kitty polished her glasses and leaned back in her seat, feeling pleased with herself. It was a fine and grown-up thing to be travelling by herself, her suitcase in the rack above and her book unopened on the table. The train rocked gently and hummed to itself as the countryside fled past, green fields mostly, with the occasional copse of trees sheltering some grey-roofed house or farm. Level crossings shot by with a brief nee-naw of sirens, and stone bridges boomed back at her.

This wasn't one of the great London expresses with ten or twelve coaches and a diesel engine howling at each end, but the local train from Edinburgh south to Newcastle, only three coaches but a sleek and speedy thing all the same, slowing and stopping at little local stations, Cheswick and Goswick, Buckton, Beal, Lucker and Christon Bank, where a few people got on or off. Soon she would have to do the same, and the cheerful conductor had already come swaying down the centre aisle to remind her that hers was the stop after next. She stood and reached down her suitcase in readiness. She presumed someone would be at the station to meet her, perhaps her friend Marcia though she hadn't heard from her. She smiled to herself, imagining Marcia's grumpy face on the platform, and the grudging smile with which she would welcome her only friend. Kitty was friends with Marcia mainly because no one else was. It was her cross to bear, she thought, feeling smug.

This wasn't Kitty's holiday really, for they were going to stay with some of Marcia's distant relatives who must be quite posh for they lived in a castle, Castle Crayle by the sea. Kitty imagined it was a large house with a fancy name, rather than a proper castle with battlements and a moat. People didn't actually live in castles any more, did they? It was going to be wonderful all the same, she thought, even though Marcia was quite annoying. The term at boarding school that had just ended had been very tiresome, for Marcia had a new hobby. All last year she had eagerly collected ridiculous words like 'fazackerly' and 'snoot', then tried to use them in her school work. She gave herself three points if the teacher didn't notice, and four if they marked it wrong and then had to give way when confronted with Marcia's

Everyman Dictionary of Obscure Words and Phrases proving it was correct. That had been at least halfway intelligent, but now she had decided to see how many jaffa cakes she could eat under the desk during lessons without being caught, and when she inevitably did get caught, she had claimed that Kitty put her up to it for a bet so they had both got detention. Kitty had kept quiet about it, treasuring the feeling of being hard done by, her virtue unjustly victimised. She would get Marcia back sooner or later, possibly during this holiday, and justice would be served. As the train slowed for the last stop before her own, she gazed out of the window and mused happily about apple-pie beds, or a quick soaking in the sea ... yes, that would be best, for fat, lazy Marcia hated physical effort or discomfort above all things.

She wondered how her family were, all scattered and far away. Mother would be on the plane by now, flying across the Atlantic. That was an odd thought. And here Kitty was rushing southwards, all on her own. She would have liked to phone her mother and say "I'm on the train, I'm all right," but there probably wouldn't be a signal up round the Arctic Circle, thousands of feet up. Wasn't it odd that we say "I'm on the train" when it's "I'm in the car"? You'd never say "I'm on the car", but in both cases you walked through the door and sat down. Could you say "I'm in the train"? Kitty thought you probably could, which was even odder.

Mother was flying to America to be important for three or four weeks, while her older sister and brother were also doing adventurous things, beautiful Ellie with a summer job at a holiday camp wearing shorts and a blazer and entertaining small children until her university term started in September. All the other staff would fall in love with her – boys always did. Stocky, reliable Jake was on tour in France with his school rugby team. That was the reason she was here on this train, the reason why she had to make this delightful journey by herself though she was only twelve years old, and the reason why Marcia's invitation to join her at Castle Crayle had been so convenient. Her mother had flatly refused Kitty's offer to stay home in Perthshire and look after herself. She had no father, not any more. He had died several years ago in a car accident in Germany while serving with the army. Kitty still missed him more than she would ever admit, but briskly dismissed the thought from her mind and gathered her things together, ready to get off.

The train came smoothly to a halt and the doors slid open with a hiss. A kind man on the platform took her suitcase from her and she thanked him with a smile and a flash of her glasses. She looked around. The platform was empty. Perhaps Marcia was waiting outside in the carpark, just to be annoying? She tugged her suitcase behind her on its squeaky wheels, through the ticket office and out into the yard beyond. Still no sign of Marcia. Perhaps she was late, probably on purpose. But Kitty refused to be annoyed; it was just too nice a day for that. She settled herself on a bench to wait, her suitcase at her feet and her rucksack beside her. Overhead the sky was a soaring blue stitched with tiny flecks of white, seagulls wheeling far above. In front of her the sky lightened, speaking of the sea only a few miles away, and the sun was warm.

Several trains passed through the station behind her, mostly just roaring through without stopping. A few cars came and went, depositing passengers, and one or two people arrived and stood near Kitty until taxis came and collected them. Kitty sat happily enough, but still no one came for her.

After an hour and a half she decided that enough was enough, and she should shift for herself. If she was grown up enough to be trusted with the journey from Pitlochry to Edinburgh, then finding the right stopping train to Newcastle and getting off in the right place, she was surely grown up enough to make a decision like this. She waited until a car with "Taxi" on its roof arrived to deposit passengers for the train, and spoke to the driver.

"Do you know Castle Crayle?" she asked.

The man grinned. "Why aye, man. Everyone knows Castle Crayle. Is that where you're going, pet?"

Kitty had never been called "pet" before. "Yes. I'm going to stay there, but no one's come. Can you take me? And how much will it cost? I don't have all that much money."

"Howay, pet, it's nobbut three or four mile. How does two pound sound?"

Two pounds sounded fine to Kitty, Mother had actually been quite generous with her spending money. The taxi driver put her case in the boot and ushered her into the back seat as though she was royalty. She sat in the middle feeling like the queen, and was tempted to practise regal waves as they drove, but thought the man might look in his mirror and see her. They soon left the town, though it was more of a village, really, and reached the countryside. The road twisted and turned, up and down through broken country of bare hills and sheep. Only in the little valleys were there any trees, and those were poor, stunted things that huddled together to shelter from the winds that in winter must be merciless. Although you couldn't see it, somehow you knew that the sea was close. In front of them the sky grew brighter and brighter as they got nearer to the coast, and as they reached one particularly steep summit the view opened up and there in front of her was the ocean itself, blue and flashingly brilliant in the sun. Even from this distance she could see the fringe of blinding white where it met the shore.

And there, away to the right, was ... surely it couldn't be? But the driver gestured towards it, and said "There you are, pet, there's your castle!"

She had been wrong, quite wrong. It really was a castle, a proper one with towers and battlements. It humped on a great spur of rock that rose from the sea, and sprawled some distance with curtain walls that rose and fell to follow the contours of the rock. In its centre rose a single tower, from this distance squat and forbidding but probably tall enough. Kitty was entranced. This was wonderful, she was going to stay in a real castle! She could walk the battlements, and climb the tower to gaze out to sea like a fairy princess looking for her lover to return from a quest. He would be bronzed and battle-hardened, and he would look up to see her waiting with her long hair blowing in the breeze, and stand up in his stirrups and wave. She imagined troops of horsemen trotting up the winding grey road that led through the village clustered at the castle's skirts and round to where there must be a great gate, probably with a drawbridge and a portcullis. They would be coming to welcome the prince's return with feasting, minstrels and jousting.

But instead of gay knights in armour, what wound up the road was a string of cars with their roofs glinting in the sun, and as the taxi joined the queue and rounded the end of the battlements, what faced them was not a grand gate and sentries with halberds, but a car park and a wooden hut with a ticket window and a list of entry prices.

The driver got out and handed Kitty her suitcase, took his money, called her "pet" once again and drove off with a cheerful wave. She waited in line at the wooden hut, and when her turn came said to the lady inside the window "Please, I don't need a ticket, I've come to stay. How do I get in?"

The woman looked at her doubtfully. "First I've heard of it," she said, "paying guests, now, is it? First I've heard. This isn't a hotel, or at least it hasn't been so far."

"I'm not a paying guest, I'm a friend of the family. Well, a friend of a friend, anyway."

The woman still looked doubtful, and Kitty heard the man behind her in the queue mutter "How much longer?"

The woman picked up a phone and had a brief conversation with someone. Kitty thought that when she put the phone down she'd be all smiles and say "Oh, that's all sorted, you're very welcome!" but all she said was "Wait here, someone'll come and speak to you," so Kitty moved out of the way and stood to one side, feeling conspicuous. This wasn't quite the welcome she'd expected. Where was Marcia?

She polished her glasses again and stared round. Above her the grey walls loomed, made of great irregular blocks of stone. Bushes clustered at their foot, and here and there straggly growths of buddleia sprouted from the mortar, some of them quite high up. Bumble bees flew here and there, visiting the lilac-coloured flowers. Behind her spread the car park with seagulls strutting about glaring with their mad yellow eyes, and beyond that a view across sand dunes to the sea. A little way out she could see black rocks and a small island with a white building on it, the waves breaking and spray being flung high in the air.

"Can I help you?" said a voice behind her. She turned to see a severe-looking young woman with a clipboard in her hand. She wore forbidding horn-rimmed glasses, and a businesslike grey trouser suit. Her hair was scraped back and tied in a bun with a red clip which was her only spot of colour.

Kitty held out her hand. "I'm Kitty Younger, I'm expected," she said, "I've come to stay."

The woman didn't take her hand, but looked down at her clipboard. "Well, I'm afraid you're not expected at all," she said bleakly, "I'd have known if you were. That's my job, going forward. Who did you arrange this with?"

Kitty felt rather dashed. This wasn't what she had looked forward to at all. "With Marcia," she said. "That's Marcia Belchambers, my friend. She's a relative of ... well, I'm not sure who. The owners, I suppose. Is that you?"

The woman laughed shortly. "Oh no, I'm staff. I'm Sir Lancelot's P.A."

"What's a P.A.?"

"Personal Assistant. I'd better take you to see Lady Sybil, I suppose. Perhaps she arranged this without telling me, she does that sometimes. Well, quite a lot, actually. Moving the goalposts ... come this way."

She turned abruptly and marched through the small entrance gate. Kitty thought it might have been nice if someone had offered to take her suitcase, but pulled the handle up and dragged it after her, rattling and bouncing on the cobbles. They passed across a courtyard where groups of tourists stood and looked up at the tall buildings around them, and through a door with a sign saying "Private, no admittance". Inside, steep stairs rose into the darkness and Kitty had a hard job dragging her suitcase up. By the time she reached the top, the woman had disappeared. A broad corridor stretched in both directions with tall leaded windows at each end and many doors. Kitty stood, uncertain where to go.

Then one of the doors opened and the woman was beckoning her impatiently. Kitty hurried along the carpet, thankful for a smooth surface.

"Leave that case outside," the woman said shortly. "Lady Sybil, this is the little girl."

"Well bring her in, bring her in, don't stand there fidgeting at the door!" said a sharp voice, and Kitty was ushered into a broad, sunlit room with more tall windows and a view of the sea. There was a great stone fireplace at one end, and thick carpets, and many armchairs and sofas scattered around.

"So," said the voice, "you claim to be staying here, I understand? What makes you think that? Who are you, exactly?"

The voice came from a thin-faced woman with a proud jutting nose and eyes rather close together. Her grey hair was elaborately coiled, she wore heavy make-up, and the whole ensemble reminded Kitty of an animal, a sharp-featured animal with rather too many teeth, a weasel or a badger perhaps. Evidently this was Lady Sybil, and Kitty did not find her at all welcoming.

"Please, I'm Kitty Younger, Marcia's friend. I'm supposed to be meeting her, and stay here with her for three weeks. Where is she?"

"Not here," said Lady Sybil. "That's all off, she's not coming. Mumps or something, she's ill in bed. I can't think why Trinket didn't tell you that downstairs."

"Lady Sybil, I didn't know," said the P.A. "I never heard anything about it."

"Well you should have made it your business, you useless creature! You're supposed to be in charge of the day-to-day stuff, aren't you? Fancy not knowing who's staying here and who isn't! I don't know what we pay you for!"

Kitty bristled. Even though she didn't know the woman Trinket, and didn't really like her so far, this sounded pretty harsh. She expected Trinket to explode with indignation, but she just stood there looking pale and biting her lip.

"Lady Sybil, is Marcia still at home, being ill, is that it?" she asked. "Only no one told me. All I know was that I was to take the train and I'd be met at the station. Which I wasn't, I had to take a taxi."

Lady Sybil looked over her nose. "You're remarkably pert for a child that's in the wrong place. The cheek of it, turning up out of the blue and standing on the doorstep demanding to be accommodated, what do you think this is, some kind of doss-house?"

"I was invited ..." began Kitty, but Lady Sybil would hear none of it.

"No, that's all off. We don't know who you are, we don't know who your people are, and we don't make a practice of taking in every waif and stray who presents themselves making demands. Trinket, get rid of her. Phone for a taxi and send her back where she came from!"

Kitty was aghast. She knew adults could be remarkably unpleasant – she had an English teacher at school who was living proof of that. But this complete lack of hospitality was something she hadn't met before.

"I can't go home," she said stoutly. "I don't have enough money for the train ticket, and there's no one in when I get there. My mother's in America, my brother's in France and my sister's working in Somerset."

"What about your father? Can't he look after you?"

"Not really. He's dead."

She expected the usual condolence one received on this news, sometimes meant and sometimes just out of politeness, but Lady Sybil didn't even manage this.

"So, let's get this straight," she said, glaring. "Your mother put you on a train and sent you off to stay with complete strangers who know nothing about you or her, and flew off to America? And she thought that was all right, did she?"

"Of course she did!" said Kitty, her anger rising. "She knew where I was going, she knew I could manage the journey on my own, she knew I was staying with my friend Marcia Belchambers who's been to our house and everything, so of course she thought it was all right. It's what normal people do!"

Lady Sybil rose to her feet, her eyes blazing. "How dare you lecture me?" she said loudly. "Out of the goodness of my heart I agreed to let my cousin's daughter come to stay and bring a little friend, only to be let down at the last minute, my kindness thrown back at me ... and now some strange little ... tramp or whatever you are ... stands and lays down the law in my own home! Do you know who I am?"

This was like a red rag to a bull for a combative girl like Kitty. "I do know you're ..." she began but Trinket put a hand over her mouth. "Don't!" she hissed in Kitty's ear, "you'll just make it worse!"

Kitty tried to say "You might be scared of her but I'm not ..." but couldn't get the words past Trinket's hand.

"Lady Sybil," Trinket said, "please consider ... if you throw the girl out with nowhere to go, what'll it look like for the Castle?"

"Yes, what'll it look like?" Kitty finally managed to blurt out.

"I'll go to the police! Reckless endangerment, that is, and probably child abuse!"

Just then the door opened and a tall, distinguished old gentleman entered. True, he was dressed in a rather eccentric fashion with camouflage trousers, carpet slippers and a red velvet waistcoat, and true, his chin receded and there was a certain slack-mouthed weakness about his face, but he carried himself with dignity and was imposing at first sight.

"Ah, Sir Lancelot!" said Trinket. "There's a bit of a problem. This girl ... erm, Kitty Younger is it? ... has arrived expecting to stay for a holiday with Marcia Belchambers, your ... that is, Lady Sybil's cousin's daughter ..."

"But Marcia isn't coming," interrupted Lady Sybil, "so there's no need for her to be here at all. So she's got to go!"

"But Sir Lancelot, I've just been explaining to Lady Sybil how bad it would look, throwing a child out on the street ..."

"A child who just barged in here making demands on our hospitality, and we know nothing about her ..." interrupted Lady Sybil.

Sir Lancelot peered down his nose at Kitty. "Younger, is it? Would that be the Youngers of Leckie? Sir James is a friend of ours. Or perhaps you're the Youngers at Auchen Castle? I was at Eton with Julian Younger. Excellent chap."

"I don't think so," Kitty said. She had never heard of these people.

"So, she's nobody," said Lady Sybil spitefully, "Trinket, phone for a taxi!"

Trinket turned to Kitty, and said almost kindly, "Look, would you go and wait outside while I talk to Sir Lancelot about this?" and she pushed Kitty to the door and closed it behind her.

Kitty loitered in the sunlit corridor, watching the motes of dust floating in the sunbeams from the window. She walked around the pattern of the carpet, which led her on a labyrinthine route down to one end of the corridor and then back. She counted the doors (five one side and six the other) and wondered what lay behind them. She was tempted to look, but thought she shouldn't push her luck in the circumstances. She could hear the voices behind the door, sometimes rising as Lady Sybil became enraged again, sometimes falling. Now and then she could hear Trinket trying to be reasonable, and thought she probably wasn't as bad as she had seemed at first. She was certainly scared of Lady Sybil, and Kitty didn't blame her.

Eventually the door opened and Trinket came out. Closing it behind her, she said softly "Well, so far, so good, you can stay. Finally we're singing from the same hymn-sheet. Sir Lancelot didn't like the sound of the adverse publicity if it got into the papers. Which I would have made sure it did, quick and dirty. I didn't say that, mind you. Come this way!"

She led Kitty to the end of the corridor and through the last door. This opened onto another, broader corridor at right angles to the first. This one wasn't carpeted, and was dark and poorly lit. On the walls were pictures, people from a bygone age staring down from their ornate frames as the two passed. There were more stairs, and another corridor, and then a very winding set of stairs that smelled of old stone and ... something else, possibly wee, Kitty thought. Or cats. Up and up they went, turn after turn, with narrow doors opening off every so often.

"This is my room," announced Trinket, "and yours is directly above. I think it's been made up. Probably the servants knew you were coming even if I was out of the loop. They always seem to know things before anyone else, goodness knows how."

"Are there many servants?" asked Kitty. She hadn't seen one yet. She wondered if they wore uniform.

"Not many. Cartilege the butler, Mrs.Cott the Cook, two maids, the groundsman ... any other jobs, I get contractors in. That's part of my remit, what I bring to the table, you might say. Here's yours!"

The steps up to Kitty's door, off the main stairway, were so steep you had to use your hands as well as your feet. Once the narrow creaking door was open, the room was delightful. It was quite big, and completely round. It plainly filled the whole of one floor of the magnificent central tower of the castle. There were four windows, rather small, one in each quarter so Kitty thought they must face North, South, East and West. Two beds had gay coverlets, and a table and two chairs stood in the centre with a chest of drawers against the wall. The floor was oak planks, uneven and uncarpeted. This, Kitty thought, was a most suitable room in which a love-lorn princess might languish and be hard done by.

Trinket was all business, though, and plainly not interested in princesses or love. "Now," she said briskly, putting a pen to her clipboard, "this can be your room, and the bathroom is two floors down underneath mine. My name's Miss Trinket, and I'm in charge of business here. I don't want to let the grass grow too long on this, I need to drill down and take some details, so I can cascade any relevant information. Your name is Kitty Younger?"

"Yes."

"Younger, Kitty ..." said the girl, writing. "Do you have a middle name?"

"Yes, Jessica. But it's Kitty Younger, not Younger Kitty. That sounds as if there should be an older Kitty, and there isn't. There's only me."

"That's the way it's done, at the end of the day," said Trinket, smiling brightly as though to brook no argument.

Kitty thought that sounded stupid, but not worth an argument. Instead she said "I don't know your name, though. You know mine, but I don't know yours."

"Oh ... er, I told you, it's Miss Trinket."

"But you must have a christian name as well."

"Er, yes ... it's Melody. Miss Melody Trinket."

"Melody Trinket, that's a lovely name. What's a Personal Assistant? Is it like a secretary?"

"Well, yes. I manage Sir Lancelot's diary, make his appointments, see that he has all the paperwork he needs for every meeting, that sort of thing. Generally make sure all his ducks are in a row."

"Oh, where does he keep his ducks?" Kitty asked politely. "Does he have many meetings? Who with?"

"I don't think Sir Lancelot's business affairs are any of your concern."

"Can I call you Melody? I expect you'll call me Kitty."

"I don't think so. You're a child, but I'm ... well, best to keep things on a business footing, I think, that's what I prefer to bring to the table. Now, sign here, would you?" Miss Trinket held out her clipboard and a pen.

"What for?" Kitty said, taking the pen and peering at the document on the clipboard. "Oh, I see. I'm signing to say that you've shown me my room and told me where the bathroom is, and what time is supper."

"Dinner."

"It's supper at home. I don't understand why I have to sign, though. I've never had to sign anything when I've stayed at my friends' houses. It seems a bit odd."

"Well this isn't your friend's house, is it? The bottom line is, it's a business, so things have to be done in a businesslike manner. We don't want anyone to say I didn't welcome you properly."

Kitty said nothing, feeling rather bemused. If this was a welcome, she didn't think much of it. She looked more closely at the paper. At the bottom was the dotted line where she had to sign her name. There was nothing underneath it. "Bottom line?" she said, "there isn't one, is there?"

"Just sign here," Miss Trinket said. Kitty wrote 'K.Younger' and put a flourish underneath, and Miss Trinket took the pen back and marched towards the door.

"But you didn't actually tell me what time is dinner?"

"Oh, yes, so I didn't. It's at six, so you've got an hour to settle in. We don't dress for dinner."

"You mean you eat it in the nude? Eeuw, that's gross!"

"No, silly girl, I mean we don't put on any special clothes, we just go as we are."

"And where is it?"

"Find your way back to the main corridor ..."

"The one with the carpet, where Lady Sybil's lair is? I mean her room, sorry."

"... and just follow your nose, you'll find the dining room easily enough."

She left, but Kitty thought there was just the trace of a smile lurking at the corners of her mouth. Melody Trinket's relationship with the English language seemed rather tenuous, but she might be redeemable after all. Kitty liked a challenge.

What she really wanted was to explore this wonderful place, but that could wait until tomorrow. Instead she busied herself unpacking her suitcase and putting her clothes in the chest of drawers, and went down to investigate the bathroom. The spiral stairs were dark and treacherous, so she had to leave her bedroom door open to give a little light. Then she dragged one of the chairs round so she could stand on it and look out of each window in turn. One looked inland – she guessed that must be the west window – towards green and purple moorland. Over there must be the station at which she had arrived. The south window looked over a jumble of roofs and then the curtain wall and the carpark. The east one gazed out to sea, and there was the little group of rocks and islands she had seen before. The largest had one small white building at its centre, and she wondered if someone lived there. It would be terribly difficult getting on and off it in a boat, because the waves were bursting in spray all round.

The last window looked north, and here she thought was the most interesting view for beyond the huddle of lower buildings and the surrounding wall she could see the village of Crayle spreading on either side of the road before it turned inland towards civilisation. All the buildings were of the same grey stone as the castle, some with black slate roofs and some with red tiles. They were of all shapes and sizes, grown up higgledy-piggledy over many centuries. She could see a couple of larger roofs facing each other across a central green, one of which seemed to have a sign in front so it was probably an inn. She hoped there would be shops to make a visit worthwhile; if Marcia had been here she would already have been planning an expedition to hunt for sweets and cake.

She found that this window had a catch. It was stiff and took a lot of effort but eventually she was able to move it and push the window outwards for it was hinged at the top. Immediately she was enveloped in sound, the moaning of the wind from the sea, the cries of the seagulls that wheeled above the castle, and the gentler sounds of pigeons flapping and squabbling among the roofs below. Once there was the distant rattle of a powerful motorbike accelerating inland, and a faint clanking sound drew her attention to a yellow digging machine at work on the edge of the village amid a cluster of white vans and other machinery.

After a while she decided it must be supper time – or dinner time, she told herself – so she closed the window again and climbed down. Suddenly she was hungry. She hoped there might be chips.

There were not chips, though. Instead there was mashed potato and greens and a piece of grey meat that was hard to cut because the knives were blunt. Dinner was served by a gaunt old man who said little. He wore a black suit and bow tie and a white shirt with little wings to the collar. He moved slowly and in little jerks, and when he handed her plate his hand drooped and she was afraid her meal would be served in her lap. This must be Cartilege, the butler, she decided, and wondered if he had been here for hundreds of years, as old as the castle itself.

She had found the room easily enough, almost opposite Lady Sybil's. It had been simple to spot because as she approached, a big, pretty girl in maid's uniform came out. She smiled at Kitty and bustled off down the corridor. That was the first smile Kitty had seen since she arrived.

There were no smiles inside the dining room, however, and Kitty slipped into a chair beside Trinket. No one corrected her, so she must have chosen the right one. Lady Sybil sat at the end of the table, poker faced and silent. From the corridor there was a rustle of fabric and Sir Lancelot arrived, followed by a cloud of skirts and bustles, a smell of lavender and a faint twittering. He sat at the end opposite his wife, acknowledged no one, and busied himself shaking out his napkin and arranging it in his lap.

Behind him the cloud of fabric resolved itself into three extraordinary ladies, dressed as for a bygone age in layers of lace and flimsy flowered skirts, with ribbons and bows and tinkling bracelets and brooches. They curtseyed and trailed in after Sir Lancelot, fluting softly like a little flock of insubstantial birds, their feathers fluttering. They seemed, to Kitty, like creatures who had been beautiful once and were still lovely until you looked closer and noticed the wrinkled necks, the heavy lipstick and the strands of grey hair that escaped the lace caps. Rather pathetic, she thought. And harmless. You could brush them aside with one puff.

They sat down opposite Kitty and Trinket, a process which took some time as they dusted off their seats and got in each other's way. Once seated they smiled and bobbed and fidgeted in constant movement, their heads turning this way and that but their gaze vacant as it passed over Kitty. If they wondered who this stranger at the table was, they showed no sign of curiosity. Their faces were heavily made up but even this could not hide the wrinkles and sagging dewlaps. There was a lot of eye shadow, and always the faint twittering that did not seem to contain any actual words or meaning.

As the ancient butler began to carry plates of food from the long sideboard to the table, Kitty looked at Trinket and made a face of enquiry. Trinket leaned closer and whispered "Sir Lancelot's sisters ..."

But Lady Sybil looked up sharply and said "Trinket, it's rude to whisper. What are you saying?"

"I was just telling our guest ..." a snort from Lady Sybil ... "about the three Ladies ..."

"Well don't. If there are introductions to be made, Sir Lancelot or I will do it. Lancelot?"

Sir Lancelot dragged his vague attention back from wherever it had lodged, to the table. "Oh, ah, yes ... my dears, this is a guest who is staying with us for ... for a while, I understand. Her name is ... her name ... I've forgotten her name ..."

"I'm Kitty Younger," Kitty said brightly, "how do you do?"

This brought a fresh burst of twittering.

"These are my sisters," Sir Lancelot said, "the Lady Drusilla, the Lady Clorinda and the Lady Pamilia."

"How do you do?" said Kitty politely, "I'm pleased to meet you."

"Charmed ..." simpered Lady Drusilla, bobbing. And "... charmed ..." repeated Clorinda more softly, and "... armed ..." whispered Pamilia almost inaudibly. It was like the fading echo of a footstep in the hall, the sigh of the wind round some great cloister, or the forgotten cry of a distant owl in the night. Kitty thought the sisters were so insubstantial you could probably see right through them if the light was in the right place. There would be layer upon layer of filmy fabric but when you reached the centre there would be no one there at all.

The meal was eaten in silence, though once Lady Sybil said sharply "Lancelot, did you speak to Baggott about the pigeons?"

but received only a grunt in reply. Kitty sawed at the meat but eventually gave up and ate the mashed potato instead, which was quite nice with the gravy. She looked round the table and saw that others had done the same. The three sisters pushed and prodded their food with forks, but however hard she watched Kitty did not see anything actually getting as far as a mouth.

Lady Sybil clattered her cutlery into the centre of her plate to signal that the main course was over, and Cartilege drifted from his eyrie near the sideboard and began clearing up. Kitty was becoming alarmed at the silence. She thought if this went on much longer she would lose the power of speech entirely, like the Sisters.

She cleared her throat and made an effort. "I like your dresses," she said politely to the Sisters opposite. "What is that material they're made of?"

"It's organdie," simpered Lady Clorinda. Wonderful, Kitty thought, they can speak after all.

"Yes, it's organdie," agreed Lady Drusilla.

"... mm, organdie," whispered Lady Pamilia, "we always wear organdie ..."

"... ever since we were children ..."

"... children," sighed lady Drusilla, "we used to be children, you know."

"But then we grew up, you see."

"And then we weren't children any more."

"But we still wear organdie ..." Lady Clorinda simpered again.

"Yes, organdie," agreed Lady Drusilla.

"... mm, organdie, we always wear organdie ..." whispered Lady Pamilia, her voice fading away as her store of conversation was exhausted.

The Sisters, it seemed, had shot their bolt, and dessert was served. It was jam roly-poly with hot custard and was excellent. It helped to fill the void left by the first course, and Kitty would have liked seconds but thought she'd better not ask. She tried to catch Cartilege's eye and give him a meaningful glance, but he refused to look at her. At length Lady Sybil and Sir Lancelot rose to their feet in unison. Not a word or a glance was exchanged but their timing was perfect. Kitty wondered how that was done.

Telepathy, perhaps, or some secret signal with a buzzer under the table? However it was done the meal was plainly over.

Lady Sybil went back to her room, and Sir Lancelot stalked up the corridor with the Sisters rustling and twittering behind him. Trinket also left. Kitty wondered what to do. Perhaps she might make herself useful? She started to gather the dessert bowls and take them to the sideboard, but Cartilege glared at her with a look that plainly said she should leave his work to him and not interfere, so she also left the room and made her way back to the tower.

There seemed to be no electric light in her room – in fact, no way of making light at all. She would have liked to read, but had to content herself with another round of the windows. The seagulls had all gone to roost somewhere as the day faded, but the pigeons could still be heard clattering and scrambling among the roofs below. In the east window the sea was turning a purplish colour as the sun left it, but in the south the breakers were still white on the shore as it ran away towards distant Newcastle.

She undressed and got into one of the beds, then got out and took the coverlet from the other bed as well. She would sleep with the window open so she could hear the sea and feel the cold wind, but still be warm and cosy in bed. Feeling sleepy, she closed her eyes and concentrated on listening. Once a door slammed far below, and the wind whined round the window frame. Far in the distance she heard a car, and then a piping shriek which she knew for a Little Owl. She thought about the beautiful princess mourning in this room, longing for her love to come back and free her. She wondered if there were any ugly princesses, or were they all beautiful? Perhaps you weren't even allowed to be a princess if you were plain and skinny and ginger, and wore spectacles. In any event, it wasn't much of a life, was it, walled up in a tower with no one to talk to? Perhaps she was better off being Kitty after all.

If she really were a princess, she'd probably get so frustrated she'd try to escape by knotting her bedsheets and climbing down from one of the windows. Pretty risky, that'd be. She knew that throwing yourself out of a window, or being thrown out by someone else, was called 'defenestration'. Wasn't it strange that

English had a word for defenestration which hardly ever happened, but none for 'the day after tomorrow' which came round regularly?

She snuggled into the bedclothes and pretended to be a small animal in its burrow. Outside the owl was calling closer now. It had been a funny day. In a way she hated it here and wanted to go home, but in a way she liked it and didn't. It was weird about the English language, and how words that seemed to be identical in meaning were actually not. If you invited someone to your cottage in the forest it sounded cosy, but if you lured them to a cabin in the woods, they were going to die. She turned over and dug deeper into her burrow. She was just deciding that she would never, ever in her life wear organdie, when sleep overtook her.

II

It was the wind that woke her. She lay warm in bed and wondered why it sounded so different, moaning and whining at the window like a monster wanting to come in. Looking at her watch she found it was too early for breakfast. She didn't know what time breakfast was, but it couldn't possibly be as early as seven o'clock, surely? Eight o'clock, or eight thirty, that was a proper time for breakfast, so she had time to kill. It was nice in bed, but she felt restless and decided to get up anyway. She went down to the bathroom, then dressed and looked out of the window.

She could see that the sea was angry beneath a cloudy sky, in places brilliant green where the sun broke through, and in others a dark, vicious grey. The breakers on the beach to the south were impressive, and she thought she should go for a walk there after breakfast to savour their fury. There was almost unbroken foam between the islands and the shore, and the islands themselves were nearly invisible in a welter of white spray flung high in the air as the waves crashed onto the rocks. The rhythmic thud as the rollers hit the beach could be heard all the way up here, and the open window shook so wildly with the gusts that she decided she had better close it.

She wondered if she could get out at the top of the tower. Perhaps there was a door? She left her bedroom door open for the light, and groped her way up the next spiral. There was one more floor above hers, a narrow door almost invisible in the gloom, and the stairs led past it. At the top she found herself in almost total darkness, and felt around with her hands. Up this high the noise of the wind was louder even through the layers of stone, and a gusty draught led her to one final door, a door that shook under her fingers as she felt for a handle.

Why do we have 'fingertips' but not 'toetips'? she wondered as she ran her hands over the rough wood, but then she found the handle and turned it, and the door flew open and almost knocked her down the stairs. The light flooded in and she could finally see where she was. Peering over the top step she could make out the crenellated parapet of the tower, and a floor of dark lead sheets with ridges where the sheets joined. Over her head grey clouds scudded by, seeming so close she could reach up and touch them. Carefully, buffeted by the wind, she crept on hands and knees towards the parapet, kept her body down and inched forward to look through one of the gaps where, she supposed, in the old days archers would have hidden and shot at the enemy below.

Around her all was sound and fury. The chill wind thundered in her ears and whipped her hair so it stung her cheeks. She put one hand to her glasses, fearing they'd be pulled from her face and go hurtling into the void below. As she carefully stood up, holding on to the stone wall in front of her, the wind tugged and flapped at her skirt and threatened to upset her. It was hard to see clearly, partly because of the wind and her own hair in her eyes and partly because a patch of sunlight had reached her tower and she was dazzled, but leaning through the gap she could see seagulls around her, crying harshly in their excitement as they rode the wind with outstretched wings, almost motionless, twitching their tails this way and that, glaring from their mad eyes. Below, groups of pigeons huddled in sheltered corners of the roofs, not daring to take to the air in case their fat bodies might be caught and dashed to the ground. If that happened, Kitty thought the wicked gulls would seize their chance and tear them to pieces.

She crossed the roof to the other side, crouching to keep out of the wind as much as possible and stumbling on the uneven floor. Here the wind was right in her face, so she put her hands over her eyes and peered out to sea through the gaps. The welter of ferocious water, mostly white with foam, stretched half a mile out to sea and lines of enormous breakers marched towards the shore, rearing up at the last minute and falling onto the beach or the rocks with a thunderous noise that was clear to hear even at this distance. The carpark was almost empty at this hour, and she wondered if any visitors who did come later would imagine that while they gazed at the antiquities and searched for toilets, up here she had been engulfed in a savage glory they could never guess.

Pushing herself off the parapet she stood upright, the wind snatching at her like a living thing and plastering her dress against her thin body. Then a capricious gust got under her skirt, filling it into a bell shape and she hastily pushed it down in case it lifted her up in the air like a parachute and carried her high in the air, her legs kicking uselessly, and swept her helplessly downwind over the roofs of the village with the gulls for company, the world's first flying girl. She dropped to her knees and crawled back to the head of the spiral stairs, laughing with the excitement of it.

She had a job to shut the door against the wind. It took almost all her strength to push it closed against the blast and make sure the latch caught, but as she did so she was suddenly plunged into darkness and quiet, not total quiet because the wind was still a living presence on the other side of the door, but the dark, dead air closed around her like a blanket, folding her in a clammy embrace, the flying girl safely grounded. As she felt her way backwards from step to lower step, it got quieter and quieter and by the time she reached her own bedroom door all was peaceful again. Only in her mind did the wind still wrench and tear at her clothes and boom in her ears, a memory that she thought would stay with her for days.

That had been an adventure, she thought, but adventures make you hungry and it was probably time for breakfast. She made her way down the stairs, along the stone corridor where the portraits still glared down, and into the dining room. The room was empty but there was a smell of bacon. Had she missed it? Surely not? She looked at her watch – it was barely past eight o'clock. On the table places were set, and a big teapot, and racks of toast and pots of butter and jam, but there was no sign of Cartilege or any other servant, so she poured herself a cup of tea, found the sugar and milk, and took two pieces of toast.

It took four pieces smothered in marmalade to satisfy her hunger, and as she had almost finished the last one the Sisters arrived, twittering gently and milling around. She said "Good morning!" to them but none of them took any notice. Apparently it took every ounce of their tiny concentration to pour themselves tea and butter small slices of toast, which they sipped and nibbled, twittering unintelligibly to each other all the while. Then as Kitty had decided that she could manage one more slice and another cup, they rose and drifted out again, leaving most of their food untouched.

There were brisk footsteps outside and Lady Sybil appeared.

Instead of sitting down, she went to the sideboard and lifted the lids of several silver bowls. Over her shoulder she said "Now, young lady, let's get one or two things straight. I'm not having you making a nuisance of yourself. You are not to bother Sir Lancelot or me under any circumstance. In fact it might be best if you stay below stairs between meals. You may talk to the staff, but not to Cartilege or Trinket, they're too busy."

Kitty could almost feel her hackles rising. "I'd have thought the other servants would be quite busy as well," she said truculently. "Is this how you usually treat guests?"

"You're not a guest, because as far as I'm concerned, you weren't invited. And don't be pert."

"I don't know what pert is. If I'm not a guest, what am I?"

"An encumbrance!" snapped Lady Sybil.

Behind her a voice muttered "Mm, charity case, I suppose ...".

Sir Lancelot had entered, and made a halting progress across the carpet. He paused in front of the sideboard and rattled the lids. "Mm, that's it, charity case, that's what you are, confounded nuisance. Damn, there aren't any kippers."

Lady Sybil sniffed. "I'll speak to cook. In fact ..." she glared at Kitty, "that's a chance for you to make yourself useful. Run down to the kitchen and tell Mrs.Cott that Sir Lancelot wants a kipper."

Kitty rose from her seat, looking regretfully at her own last slice of toast which she had buttered and spread with marmalade but not eaten. The glory of the wind and the sun still thundered in her mind and here she was talking about kippers.

"No, no, it's all right," interrupted Sir Lancelot, "take too long. Can't hang about, things to do. I'll have ..." he looked around vaguely, "... other stuff instead. Eggs, that's it, eggs. Where are the girls?"

"Child, ring the bell," ordered Lady Sybil.

"No, I meant Drusilla and ... the others," said Sir Lancelot.

"They've already been and gone," Kitty said helpfully. Not that you'd notice, she thought to herself. She felt furious not so much with Lady Sybil as with herself. How stupid had she been? There were scrambled eggs and sausages under those lids, and bacon and probably kedgeree and devilled kidneys, whatever they were, and she hadn't looked and had to make do with toast!

Ah well, she'd know tomorrow. She resolved to get there early again, and make a feast before anyone could stop her.

When she got to the entry courtyard to start the walk along the beach she'd promised herself, she found that the clouds had beaten the sun and it was raining hard. There were still no cars in the carpark, and probably wouldn't be any today – the wild weather would put the tourists off. Kitty could see the miserable lady in her kiosk, reading a magazine and looking fed up. Squalls of rain blew in from the sea and marched across the cobbles with a hiss, and even standing in the doorway she got wet because the wind picked the water up and blew it horizontally. She went inside and closed the door. The walk was off.

She wasn't sure what to do now. Here she was on the first day of a holiday, and she was lonely and bored already. She knew no one, everyone seemed rather hostile so the chance of making any friends seemed small, and she couldn't even occupy herself by walking or going to the beach for a paddle or looking round the village because of the rain. The only thing was to go up to her room, wrap herself in a quilt and read her book, and she was getting near the end of that and hadn't brought another. She wondered about finding Melody Trinket and asking if there was anything she could help with. Melody did seem at least half human ... well, more like a quarter actually, but you had to warm just a little to anyone who was scared of Lady Sybil. Kitty wasn't, but she felt sympathy all the same. On the other hand she'd been specifically told not to bother Melody Trinket. She had no problem about being thoroughly defiant when necessary as several of her teachers had learned to their cost, but it did seem a little early in the day to start.

She trailed miserably up the stairs again, and wandered along the carpeted corridor, treading softly in case Lady Sybil heard. The portraits stared down at her. It seemed that every corridor and room was lined with them, and she wondered who all these people were - or had been, for most of them wore very old-fashioned clothes indeed. Their eyes followed as you passed, and she had the strongest feeling that when you'd gone they would look at each other and pass unspoken messages, raise their eyes to heaven in derision or give each other sinister winks, and as you walked on further the paintings hanging there would smirk behind your back, for they were all in on the secret.

She passed the entrance to the spiral stairs up the tower and kept going into regions unknown. When she came to a door, she listened to see if anyone was inside. Then she tapped softly just in case, and tried the door. Peeping round she found it was a large meeting room, with a long table down the middle and chairs either side. At the front was a whiteboard. If you took a good run-up and threw yourself on the table on your stomach, you might be able to slide all the way to the other end, but it did look a bit dusty. You'd have to polish it first. Otherwise, this was not at all interesting. Weren't castles supposed to have armour and treasure and things like that?

The next room was also a disappointment, a sitting room with leather armchairs that plainly hadn't been used for a long time, thick with dust. The next door opened into a store cupboard where old chairs were stacked up, and an ancient vacuum cleaner and shelves of cleaning products and dusters. This was going from bad to worse. Here she was, drifting around feeling sad and lonely. The weather was being beastly. Her host and hostess were beastly too. There were no tourists to talk to because of the weather, Melody Trinket was not particularly encouraging and out of bounds besides, and although the maid last night had smiled, she didn't know where the servants were to be found. She was missing her family and would have liked to phone Mother or Ellie, but she knew they'd both be busy and besides, she didn't want to admit defeat. Things were grim, but she was tough, wasn't she?

She wondered whether she should just run away. She had enough money for a taxi to the station, and what she hadn't admitted to Lady Sybil and Trinket was that she had her return train ticket in her rucksack. So she could get back to Pitlochry easily enough and they'd probably be pleased to see the back of her, but when she reached Pitlochry Station she'd still be several miles from home. She'd have to walk all the way over the hill to Strathtay dragging her suitcase, and it was a rough track through the forestry. And when she arrived, the house would be silent and empty and locked. She hadn't got a key but she could break in, there were tools in the shed. But there wouldn't be any food, and although the Land Rover would be in the barn she couldn't drive it to the shops. She had a rough idea how to do it, but the policemen in Pitlochry, nice though they usually were, would probably take a dim view of a twelve year old driving a Land Rover down the main street. Besides, her holiday money wouldn't be enough to last for three weeks till Mother got back.

Her musings had led her to a broad space, rather more grand than anything she had seen so far, and at the far end a magnificent stone staircase curved up to a sort of veranda at one end. She tripped up the stairs rather more cheerfully, for this was more like the kind of castle she had imagined. This was the sort of staircase a princess would use, coming down in her finery to dance at a grand ball perhaps. At the top she was faced with a pair of fine glass-paned doors, and through the glass she could see shelves, and books. This was a library, where she might find something interesting to read. This was more like it.

She pushed open one of the doors, and listened. There was no sound so she slipped in. On all sides she was surrounded by tall sets of shelves lined with hundreds of books, mostly great heavy things with ornate leather bindings and the titles in gold leaf on the back. There was a smell of leather and dust and ancient sunlight. She went along one shelf, examining the titles. They were not encouraging at first sight ... *'The Annals of the Northumberland Livestock Association 1887-8'* and *'A History of the Second Northumberland Regiment in Twenty Volumes'* and *'A Digest of the Land Archive 1913-14, Volume Three'* were not immediately inviting.

A small sound caught her ear. Peering round the end of the bookcase she realised she was not alone as she had supposed. At the far end of the room a figure was moving about, stooping and doing something on a table. It was Sir Lancelot. Beside him in a row on a chaise-longue sat the Sisters, gazing at him in rapt attention. Kitty wondered whether to withdraw quietly, but before she could do so he turned and saw her.

"Ha! The little charity case! Come to see my collection, have you? Come along, come along, you might as well learn something while you're here! Come here, girl!" he called. He didn't sound too angry, so Kitty obeyed.

"I'm sorry, I didn't know anyone was here ..." she began, but he paid no attention.

"This is a real treat for you, girl," he said proudly. "You see before you the third largest collection in the world! Only the Smithsonian in America and a reclusive millionaire in Argentina can rival this lot. This is my life's work!"

"His life's work," said Lady Drusilla, faintly proud.

"Life's work ..." echoed Lady Clorinda.

"... work, yes," whispered Lady Pamilia.

All round that end of the room were not bookshelves but glass-fronted show-cases, and tables with glass tops with things displayed underneath. There were thousands of small objects, and thousands of neatly-written slips of paper with each one.

"What are they?" she asked.

"Why, moths of course! The third largest collection in the world, and some might say the best, for quantity is not everything. Almost thirty thousand specimens, every one identified and catalogued and authenticated. Come, come, come and look!"

"Yes, come and look," said Lady Drusilla.

"Look, yes," muttered Lady Clorinda.

"... authenticated ..." Lady Pamilia whispered.

Kitty moved closer. She had to admit, there were an awful lot of moths, most looking remarkably similar. They were mounted on cream card, each one with a pin through it, and a label with tiny writing in Latin to identify it.

"Moths!" proclaimed Sir Lancelot, "most fascinating creatures! Properly they are *Lepidoptera*, but not butterflies for they are generally without clubbed antennae and mainly nocturnal. They evolved long before the butterflies which are mere late-comers. Moths have been around for 190 million years, and there are over 160,000 different species so even my enormous collection is a drop in the ocean! They have great economic significance, mostly negative, sadly, though of course we are all familiar with the wonderful exploits of the Silk Moth, *Bombyx mori*, which produces 200 million pounds' worth of silk every year. Nor is all silk produced by *Bombyx mori*: there are several species of *Saturniidae* that also are farmed for their silk, such as *Samia cynthia*, the Chinese oak silkmoth or ..."

"But they're all brown," Kitty interrupted, feeling the need to stem the flow. "Why do you kill them? Wouldn't it be better to take photographs and let them go?"

"Why would I do that? They're going to die soon anyway. The lifespan of a moth is short, all I'm doing is making it a little shorter. No harm in that."

"... no harm in that ..." breathed Lady Clorinda.

"... harm in that ..." whispered Lady Pamilia.

"... in that ..." sighed Lady Drusilla.

"I have conducted more than a dozen expeditions to various parts of the world in pursuit of obscure moths," Sir Lancelot continued, "and have to my credit the discovery of more than forty variants hitherto unknown to science. My regular contributions to serious publications such as 'Lepidoptera Quarterly' and 'Moths & Butterflies Review' have earned the respect ..."

But Kitty had heard enough. "Sir Lancelot, this is fascinating, but your wife has warned me not to bother you or interfere with your work, so I think it would be wrong to take up any more of your time."

"Oh! Well, I ...."

"But there's just one thing I would ask, if you don't mind? Do you think I might have a look round your library, maybe look in some of the books, if I don't disturb you? That would be so kind!"

"Well, er ... yes, I suppose so ... but I'd be happy to show you some of my collection ... did you know that the *mopane* worm, the caterpillar of *Gonimbrasia belina*, is a significant food resource in South ... "

"No, no! It would be wonderful, but I know Lady Sybil wouldn't approve. As I am a guest, I must respect her wishes, mustn't I? But thank you, thank you for showing me the collection, and I promise to take great care of your books!"

With that, Kitty withdrew, heaving a secret sigh of relief. That had been a close shave, and now she had the run of the library. Surely there must be something interesting here? A history of Castle Crayle, for instance, she wouldn't mind something like that. Preferably not in twenty volumes, though, and small enough to slip in her pocket when no one was looking.

'Castle Crayle is located on a remote outcrop along the sea-battered coast of Northumberland,' she read. 'It was built by Edward, 3rd Earl of Pembroke, in 1312. Prior to Pembroke's arrival the lands were controlled by Simon de Montfort in the middle of the 13th century whose primary residence was Kenilworth Castle in Warwickshire. After de Montfort was killed at the Battle of Evesham in 1265, Henry III gave the lands to Edmund, Lord of Embleton and younger brother of Edward I and father of Thomas. Following Edmund's death, the lands passed to Thomas, Earl of Lancaster. In 1307, Edward II, cousin of Thomas, took the throne to become King of England. However, his devotion and favouritism towards the deplorable Piers Gaveston did not sit well with the Northern barons ...'

Kitty grunted. This was not exactly fascinating. Who cared about all these old nobles with their disputes and their plotting? What she wanted to know was what had actually happened at the Castle, how did the people live, what did they eat, could they keep warm in the winter, how did they pass their time ...? Real things, real lives, not history like they taught you at school.

Besides, the book was heavy and dug into her legs as she sat on the wide window-sill of the library. Bookshelves ran away on either side of her window towards the centre of the room, and at the far end she could hear Sir Lancelot moving about and muttering to himself, and every so often a faint twittering from the Sisters as they watched him. Kitty had already looked him up – she knew that he was a Baronet, Fossett of Castle Crayle, or more fully 'Sir Lancelot de Verdon Hereward d'Arcy Fossett of Castle Crayle, 8th Baronet', and that his wife was Lady Sybil Fossett. She knew that his sisters weren't really Lady Drusilla, Lady Clorinda and Lady Pamilia, but had no titles of their own at all. She had read that when he died, his wife would become plain Lady Fossett.

She laid the big book aside and took up the much smaller one she had found nestling on the shelf beside it. This was entitled 'Northumbrian Castles' and had a picture of a picturesque ruin on the front. Looking inside she found that this was Dunstanburgh Castle, further down the coast. She leafed through and saw that Castle Crayle had a chapter all to itself. This was more like it.

She sighed, and laid her head against the window. Outside she had a closer view of the building that huddled against the walls of the great tower where she had been that morning, and the rain-swept courtyard where yesterday tourists had wandered. It was nice to be here, dry and warm while the storm blustered outside. She wondered about Marcia, miles away at home in Hampshire. Was she still in bed, being ill, or had she recovered and was now convalescent? Either way she would be dreadfully grumpy. In a way Kitty was pleased she wasn't here. They weren't being very friendly in the Castle, but Marcia wouldn't be much better. She was a trying friend at the best of times. They had been growing further apart this last term or two. Not that Kitty had a new best friend, not at all, but just that she was beginning to find Marcia very tiresome, despising her greed and being outraged sometimes by the depths of the girl's malice towards her teachers and the other girls in the school. Kitty found most of the teachers bearable - not Miss Hevesham, obviously, but all the others, and there were plenty of girls who were nice enough. Not very intelligent, to be honest, but you couldn't dislike them for it.

She mused on, and wondered about those girls at school. They were mostly thick and she wasn't, and they knew it. So most of the time, they did what she told them - or rather, they found that they agreed with her suggestions, was the way she preferred to express it. Was that normal? Did the same thing happen in other schools? Would the same thing happen when she was grown up and out in the world, would everyone do what she said then? And what did this mean? Did it mean she was really special? Because she didn't feel special, not particularly. She just felt like her. And if the other girls did what she said, it was only because she was a bit quicker than they were to work out what needed to be done. Probably they'd arrive at the same conclusion if she just gave them a bit more time, and then she wouldn't need to tell them, it would just be a bit slower, that's all. She resolved to be less bossy, and to give people time to work out that they agreed with her and do what she wanted anyway, because she was right.

'Come on,' she scolded herself, 'this is no way to behave, mooning about and wasting good thinking time', and applied herself to her little book. *'There has been a castle at Crayle since early Saxon times,'* she read, *'and probably long before that as people took advantage of the great mound of rock to build themselves a safe stronghold. Once it would have been built of boulders, turf or wood although this would have to be brought from inland for there is little useful timber in the neighbourhood. The present edifice dates from the 1300s, erected at vast expense by the ambitious Earl of Pembroke.'*

Kitty wondered about the Earl of Pembroke. Pembroke was in Wales, wasn't it, so what was he doing building a castle at the other end of the country? She knew, because they had done it in History at school, that nobles owned estates all over the place. They either inherited them from their fathers, or got them by marrying some poor girl from another noble family, or had them given by the king for services rendered. They must have been like kings themselves, ruling over hundreds and thousands of poor people. Was this how Sir Lancelot saw himself? Did he still think he was a sort of king, and everyone had to do what he said? But he was only the eighth baronet, so his family hadn't been up to much in the 1300s. They must have got hold of Castle Crayle much later on. Perhaps they sucked up to whoever was king at the time, and got given it. Pretty nice present, then, to be given a whole castle. Kitty wouldn't mind being given a castle, even if she had to do some serious sucking up to get it.

'After 1610 when the English and Scottish crowns were unified, the need for strong castles in Northumbria was less and Crayle passed into common hands and fell into disrepair. Only during the 19th Century did its fortunes improve and successive owners carried out restoration and improvements. At various times the building served as a prison, a hospital and a boarding school.'

Wow, thought Kitty, a boarding school, like her own? How romantic, to be at school in a castle instead of a boring old place like Haslemere House School. But how miserable, too, for the poor girls who must have suffered terribly in the winters in these great barn-like rooms and corridors, all cold stone walls and draughty windows and no central heating. In fact the only heating must have been from coal fires in the big fireplaces in some of the rooms – she could see one at the far end of the Library now, near where Sir Lancelot was working. She imagined the evenings with the girls clustered close around one such fire, their fronts warm enough but their backs freezing as the winter storms raged outside and sucked most of the heat up the chimney.

The storm today wasn't a bitter winter gale, but a summer one, and it was passing. Sunbeams began to pattern the floor in front of her, and the glass at her back was warm. The sun had won after all, and though the wind still blew, overhead the clouds were scudding inland and blue sky was spreading from the East. She should go out. The waves would still be crashing on the beach, and the gulls would be wheeling and crying. She would go out and let the wind blow away the cobwebs. She put the heavy book away on its shelf, tucked the little one under her dress and stole furtively out of the Library.

By dinner time Kitty was in an altogether firmer mood. She had enjoyed a glorious walk along the shore to the south, dancing and shrieking at the waves as they beat on the shore and smashed themselves into towers of glorious white spray, and chasing the seagulls. She had found sweet little flowers blooming among the rocks, and picked a little posy for her bedroom. She had hoisted up her dress and paddled, chasing the receding waves and then running away from the next one. She hadn't dared to try and swim, although she could, quite well. It was far too rough for that, and besides her father had been very firm about never swimming alone. But the temptation was great, and in the end she compromised by taking her dress off and paddling more deeply in her knickers, confident that she was unobserved for there was no one else on the whole broad sandy curve of beach. When she got back to the Castle, there were only a few cars in the car-park, a few hardy tourists, and she ran through the gate, across the courtyard and into the private door, well aware that she must look a sight with her dress wet, her hair in a confused tangle, her glasses encrusted with salt spray and her skin reddened by wind and sun. She felt wonderful, wild and confident, and gave not a second thought to the reproving looks she would probably get from Lady Sybil and Sir Lancelot. She would have a bath to wash the salt off, and then it would be almost time for dinner. And she would "dress for dinner" - she would wear her jeans, and they could like it or lump it!

There was something of an atmosphere round the dinner table. As last night, the meal was largely silent, only disturbed by Cartilege shuffling round the table and clinking plates as he served shepherd's pie and carrots. The food was nice enough, though Kitty could have eaten twice as much. Melody Trinket sat beside her looking pale and withdrawn. Kitty found herself glancing sideways at her, wondering what had upset her.

"Trinket, pass the gravy, would you?" said Lady Sybil abruptly. "Can't you see we haven't had it up this end, you useless creature?"

Kitty bristled. She'd have been furious to be spoken to like this. She leant sideways and whispered "Why do they call you that? Why don't they say 'Miss Trinket'? They're not very polite!"

Trinket didn't reply, but made a little "Sshh!" mouth at her.

But Lady Sybil hadn't finished. "Trinket, have you sorted out that man with the stained glass yet?You need to find someone else, someone who actually knows his job!"

"But I thought this man is the only one in the country who understands this sort of stained glass?" says Sir Lancelot, "isn't that what you told me?"

"Yes, but he isn't getting on with it, is he? Trinket, why isn't he getting on with it?"

"Your Ladyship, he's already finished the first ..."

"Yes, but I went up there this afternoon and I couldn't see any change from yesterday. He'll have to go. Trinket, why haven't you replaced him already?"

"Your Ladyship, I ..."

"Just do it, woman! Isn't that what you're for? You're paid to run things, so get on and run them. Because if it's beyond you, I shall do it myself, and then we'll look for someone else."

Trinket said nothing, but her cheeks were pale and her eyes red and moist. Kitty thought she was trying hard not to cry. Kitty stood up and began to collect the plates together, meaning to be helpful, but Lady Sybil snapped "Leave those, child! What do you think we have a butler for?" Kitty sat down again.

Sir Lancelot chuckled. "You better watch out, Cartilege! Girl's after your job, he! he!"

Cartilege glided behind the chairs, reaching over and picking up the plates. As he passed he accidentally on purpose kicked the leg of Kitty's chair, rather hard.

Trinket looked down at her plate. Kitty thought she might be about to cry. She thought to distract attention, cleared her throat and began "I went for a walk this afternoon, along the beach. The waves were really ..."

"Don't interrupt!" barked Lady Sybil. "How dare you interrupt me?"

"You weren't ..."

But something unforeseen was happening. Lady Drusilla stirred. "You might be wondering," she said dreamily, looking straight at Kitty, "why we speak so seldom?"

"Yes, you must be intrigued, no doubt. We are very quiet, it's true," murmured Pamilia.

"Surely that's ..." Kitty began, but Drusilla interrupted.

"The answer to your question is ..."

"I didn't ask ..."

But Drusilla was not to be stopped. "The answer to your question is that when we were little ..."

"Tiny," muttered Clorinda.

"Infinitessimal," added Pamilia.

"... when we were little, I say, we were taught not to say anything unless we had something interesting to say. That is, if we had nothing interesting to say, we should remain silent. Do you understand, child?"

"I'm sure that's very, er ... I didn't actually ..." said Kitty, but Pamilia interrupted.

"I had something interesting to say once," she said wistfully.

Drusilla snorted. "And what was that, pray?"

"I don't know. I've forgotten it."

"Did you say it? You didn't, did you? How like you – the one time you have anything worthwhile to share, and you keep it to yourself."

"What was it about?" asked Kitty helpfully, "or can you remember what you were doing at the time?"

"None of your business!" snapped Drusilla. "We can manage without you poking your nose where it isn't wanted, thank you very much. What are you doing here, anyway?"

"She's stealing things," put in Clorinda. "Stealing things and then blaming it on us!"

"I never ..." blurted Kitty, outraged.

"Where are the fish knives?" said Drusilla suddenly.

"Where are the fish knives, where are they?" echoed her sisters.

"SHE's got them!" Drusilla cried, pointing at Kitty, and her sisters pointed too.

"She took them, she stole them!"

"We saw her, she gathered them up and put them down her dress! She's a thief!"

Kitty looked at them with disgust. "The fish knives are on the sideboard, I can see them from here," she said evenly.

"And who put them there?" hissed Clorinda, thrusting her pointy face forward.

"Yes, who put them there?" repeated Pamilia.

"She did, that girl! She stole them, and hid them on the sideboard!"

Lady Sybil rapped on the table again. "Enough!" she snapped. "Trinket, I think the child would be happier eating in the kitchen with the servants. I can't think why you brought her here."

Kitty could feel herself flushing, a hot feeling as the blood flowed through her cheeks and forehead, at the insulting way Lady Sybil was speaking over her head.

"Excuse me, " she said coldly, "do I not get a say in this? I am a guest, after all."

"You're not, though," snapped her hostess, "guests are invited, and you weren't!"

"I was, Marcia said ..." Kitty began, but Lady Sybil was in full flow and not to be stopped. "You're not a guest, because I didn't invite you! Guests are people one knows, people one's been introduced to, or people whose family one knows or who you went to school with. But we don't know you from Adam. We don't know who your people are, or anything. You just turned up, without so much as a by-your-leave, expecting us to turn the entire household on its head to accommodate you! Go down to the kitchen now, you can finish your meal there."

Sir Lancelot was shaking with silent mirth as Kitty rose, feeling her face scarlet with indignation. "Guest," he snorted, "guest, she says? Invites herself, then complains that she's a guest! Preposterous!"

"Preposterous," agreed Drusilla, and her sisters echoed, "yes, preposterous ..." and "Guest indeed! Oh no, not a guest, dear me no ..."

Outside, the pretty maid was just approaching, bearing a tray of dessert.

"Please, where are the kitchens?" Kitty asked. "I'm to take my meals down there in future, it seems."

The girl smiled kindly. "Lucky you," she said, "you'll get much better fed than up here with the old fossils! Wait until I've taken these in, and I'll show you the way."

As the maid went into the dining room Kitty could hear Lady Sybil's shrill voice, still raised and in full flow. The maid came out, grimacing over her shoulder.

"I don't know what you said to set her off, but I bet it was a belter! She's in a rare old bate, the auld cow. Come along, this is no place for decent human beings. My name's Charity, and my ma's the Cook. What's yours?"

"My name or my mother?"

"Both!" giggled Charity, setting off at a trot.

"I'm Kitty, and my mother's in America for her job, so I'm marooned here. There was supposed to be my friend Marcia, but she's ill."

"Little chubby creature, always grumpy? Steals biscuits?"

"That's Marcia."

"Aye, pet, I mind her. You could find better friends than her, I'm thinking."

"She hasn't got anyone else. It's an act of charity, really."

Charity gave a hoot of laughter. "By, you're a caution, you are, pet! Come on, it's down here!"

Mrs.Cott, Charity's mum, was a jolly, red-faced smiling woman and her kitchen was warm and steamy and welcoming. "Now sit you down at the table, hinny," she said, "and how far did you get with your meal before the old crow kicked off?"

"I'd had most of the shepherd's pie, but no dessert," Kitty said hopefully.

"But you could do with a bit more pie, I shouldn't wonder?"

Kitty nodded, beaming, and tucked into a second plate of shepherd's pie flooded with gravy. Somehow it tasted better down here. "Aye, ma puts a little something in our gravy that them others don't get!" whispered Charity, and helped herself to a plate.

Kitty ate happily, and then demolished a huge bowl of yesterday's roly-poly and custard.

"Well," she said, sitting back, "I'm so happy I can't tell you! Thank you very much, that was really lovely. And it's really lovely down here," she added, looking round. "Are you sure you won't mind having me in here? I don't want to be a nuisance?"

"Why, bless the bairn! A nuisance, how could you be a nuisance? Another mouth to feed's no problem at all in a great kitchen like this, pet. You'll be family, now, won't you, along with me and the girls an' old Baggott? Charity pet, they'll have finished upstairs, you'd better go and fetch the dishes."

"Aye, no peace for the wicked, as they say!" Charity grinned and hurried out.

"Who's Baggott?" Kitty asked.

"Why, he looks after the grounds an' that. And there'll be Mr.Cartilege as well, but don't you mind him. He's a miserable old boggart, just ignore him."

"Do you all live here?"

"What, in the Castle? Bless you, no. Cartilege has a cottage in the grounds, and Baggott has another, but me and the girls live with Mr.Cott at home in the village. But ..." she leaned closer and put an arm round Kitty's shoulders, "you treat this like your own, pet. If you get peckish in the night, you pop down here and help yourself. Just keep out of Cartilege's way because he tells tales, that one. Baggott's all right, though, he's one of us. There's a big tin of biscuits under the counter over there, and there's always cheese and stuff in the fridge."

"Your little fat friend knew where the biscuits were, all right!" put in Charity, coming in the door. She was empty handed. Kitty wondered where the dishes were.

"Has she been here often?" she asked.

"No, just the once. I don't think she enjoyed it very much, but she went through a lot of biscuits, an' no mistake!"

Kitty thought about this. Was it possible, she wondered, that Marcia's illness was just a little convenient? Had she really wanted to come here, or had she involved Kitty and then baled out on purpose? She put the idea aside. It didn't really matter much either way. 'It is what it is', she told herself, 'I'm here and I can make the best of it,' and thought that might not be too difficult now she was banished below stairs.

She gathered up the dirty dishes from the table and carried them over to the sink, ran the hot tap, found a squirt of washing-up liquid and a dish-mop and began washing up as she did at home.

"Ee, our mam, we're going to like having this one around, I can tell!" laughed Charity.

Mrs.Cott chuckled. "Why, our lass, I could tell that soon as I looked at her. Proper little lass, she is, an' bonny too."

Kitty felt embarrassed, but secretly pleased. "Charity, where's a tea towel?" she asked.

"Never dry them up, pet, just stack 'em an' they'll dry themselves overnight. But I'm not Charity, I'm Faith!"

Kitty gaped at her. The girl was grinning broadly, and just at that moment the door opened and Charity came in laden with a tray. Kitty looked from one to the other. "Oh, I get it!" she breathed, "you're twins!"

"Aye, no flies on you, pet!" laughed Faith. "Twins we are, an' twins we've always been. Mind ..." she leaned closer and lowered her voice, "we make sure her Ladyship never sees us both at once. That's our little game. She's no idea, an' we're not telling!"

Full of food and cheer, and feeling more optimistic than she had since she'd arrived, Kitty took a Thermos of tea and a plate of biscuits up to her room and settled into bed with her book about the castles. Faith and Charity had given her some candles and candlesticks and matches, and one now stood on the bedside table casting a cheery light in the dim room.

She was already halfway through the chapter on Crayle, and had reached a section entitled *'Legends and Myths about Castle*

Crayle'. By leafing through the rest of the book she found that it wasn't only Castle Crayle that had legends and myths. Every castle in the book seemed to have a rich store of folklore. Witches and boggles, redcaps, 'queer fwoak', braags and gyests abounded, every kind of eldritch creature of the night. The wind moaned softly at the window and sent a shiver down her spine, but she grinned at her silly self and settled deeper into the bedclothes.

Crayle's eldritch creature was, it seemed, a Worm or Wyrm. By flicking from chapter to chapter she was able to work out that there had been a number of legendary Worms in County Durham and Northumberland, the Laidley Wyrm at Bamburgh, the Linton Worm, the Lambton Worm and several others. They seemed to be a kind of dragon, smelled disgusting, did a lot of writhing and coiling, ate maidens and generally behaved rather badly.

Crayle's Wyrm even had a poem to itself ...

'When that the tide is in full fludde
There will arise and suck oor bludde
The lothesome Wyrm that lie and slepe
Beneath Crayle's lofty kepe
But when the tide doth run and wane
He'll hie him to his hame agane
To sleep untille a maiden's hand
Shall banish hym from all thys land'

Kitty closed the book and blew out the candle. This was most satisfactory, she thought, an actual castle with an actual dragon, an actual bedroom in an actual tower ... and Mrs.Cott had said she was bonny.

III

Next morning Kitty remembered her resolution to get to the dining-room early and make a feast before anyone else arrived. It was tempting – she wasn't supposed to be eating in there, but if she was quick she could probably get away with it. It would serve them right, to arrive to find half the sausages eaten. In fact, she could probably do it, and then go down to the kitchen and get an entire second breakfast. That was the sort of thing Marcia would do, though, and she didn't want to do anything Marcia would do. Surely she was more grown up than that?

Instead she went back to the store room she had found yesterday, searched on the shelves for some soft rags and furniture polish, and went next door to the meeting room with the long table. Here she spent half an hour dusting and polishing the table to a high shine, so that if she was bored another day and the weather was bad, she could always come here and practise sliding. She would have to find a store of cushions or something, in case she got so much speed up that she shot off the end of the table and crashed into the fireplace. For the first time since the end of term she wished she had some of her other friends from school with her – two or three of them were daft enough to enjoy such a game.

Down in the kitchen Mrs.Cott and the twins welcomed her warmly and set before her an enormous plate of bacon, eggs, sausages, mushrooms and black pudding. There was cold milk to drink, and toast and marmalade after. When she had nearly finished, a black cat sauntered in and sat in front of the cooking range, blinking at her.

"Phew!" she gasped, sitting back. "I think I'm in heaven! That was wonderful, thank you. What's your cat's name?"

"Why, I don't think she has one," said Charity. "We just call her 'cat'. And she's not ours, not really, she just comes and goes as she likes. I suppose she keeps the mice away, because we never see any."

"Oh, you can't have a cat without a proper name, surely?" Kitty said, kneeling on the floor in front of the cat. It blinked at her without expression but graciously consented to be scratched behind the ear. "I think her name is 'Perkins'. She looks like a Perkins to me."

"But that's a man's name."

"Not now it isn't, it's a cat's name. This cat. Perkins? Perkins? What about it, Perkins?"

The cat just blinked, and stretched, and then scuttled quickly out of the door again.

"There, she's happy now she's got a proper name," Kitty said, getting up. "Now, what can I do?"

She spent nearly half an hour putting the cutlery away in a marvellous wooden drawer quite five feet wide and lined with beautifully made wooden compartments for every size and shape of spoon, knife and fork.

Mrs.Cott came in and started taking things out of a larder, eggs and flour and stuff. There was going to be baking. "Is it a pie?" Kitty asked her.

"Aye, lass, steak and kidney for this evening. Though what it'll be like I really canna say. Her Ladyship always insists on buying the cheapest cuts of meat, stuff I wouldn't give the cat if it was me. I'm not a bad cook, but even I can't make a silk purse out of a pig's ear."

Kitty remembered the tough meat at her first meal. "My mother makes steak and kidney pie," she said. "Jolly nice. Do you put mushrooms in? She does."

"Me too. What do you call your mother?"

"Just Mother, nothing else."

"Mm. People call me Ma. Ma Cott, I am, so that's what you ought to call me."

"All right, thank you, I will. There are things in here I don't even know the name of," she said, holding up a sort of wedge-shaped silver spatula. "And there are three different sorts of fish knife. Do you know, Sir Lancelot's sisters said I stole the fish knives, and they were sitting on the sideboard all the time?"

"Aye, pet, we heard about that. Even Cartilege was a bit fashed about it, the miserable old coot. You want to keep clear of those old harpies, though. They're dotty but they can be spiteful."

"So can I. I put salt in Miss Hevesham's cup of tea once, and she took a big swallow and went all red. She didn't know it was me, though. Well, she probably suspected. She shouldn't be drinking tea in class anyway. Why does Sir Lancelot put up with them?"

"Because they're probably the only people who take him seriously, I expect. Otherwise they're a waste of space."

"And organdie. They're a waste of organdie. Would you wear it?"

"I would not. Now, here's Faith with the dirty dishes. Faith wouldn't wear organdie either. She likes a bit of leather, and a fisherman's smock!"

She winked at Kitty, and Faith banged the tray down on the table, grinning. "I do not," she said, "Charity's the one who fancies a bit of rough, not me! Will you look at this lot? They've hardly touched anything, and it'll all go to waste. That could have fed most of the families in the village for at least a day."

Kitty went to the sink and picked up a dish-cloth, but Ma stopped her. "Nay, lass, never you mind. You'll be doing my girls out of a job, you will. Why don't you go off and have some fun?"

Fun was in short supply, though. Kitty decided to explore a bit more. So far she'd seen the dining-room and Lady Sybil's lair, and the Library, and the sliding room and a store room, but there must be lots of other places to explore. She wandered up to the top corridor and stood listening. She put her head round the door of the dining-room, and saw Cartilege by the sideboard. He was fiddling with some dinner napkins with his back to her, so she quietly withdrew and pulled the door not quite shut in case it made a noise. She paused outside Lady Sybil's room and could hear faint noises inside and a radio playing softly, so she crept on.

At the end of the corridor another door stood half open. She looked in. It was a large room, with very little furniture and a lot of blank wall space. A desk held a laptop computer, the screen showing little stylised castles bouncing from side to side and glancing quietly off each other, a mug containing several ballpoint pens, a telephone and a small pile of papers all tidily squared off. There were several filing cabinets in a straight line. Melody Trinket stood at an open drawer in one of them, riffling through the papers. Moving closer Kitty could see that every drawer was marked with a neat typed label, *'Invoices 05/04/2016 - 04/04/2017'*, and *'Planning - Events'*, *'Personnel A - J'* and *'Personnel K - Z'*. She wondered if there were any personnel whose names began with 'Z'. She certainly hadn't come across any.

Melody Trinket glanced up but said nothing, so Kitty sat on the corner of the desk and watched her.

"This is my office. Why are you here?" asked Melody Trinket eventually.

"We all have to be somewhere," Kitty replied. "I'm here because I was supposed to be on holiday with my friend Marcia, only she's ill. You know that."

"I meant, heads up, why are you here in my office?" said Miss Trinket. "What do you want?"

"Well, world peace and an end to poverty and Global Warming would be a start."

"But those things are hardly going to be found in this office, are they, so why did you come in here? Just to be annoying? I'm trying to get some joined-up thinking here."

"I'm bored. And Lady Sybil said I have to make myself useful." This wasn't true, but she thought it sounded reasonable. "What can I help with? I'm quite good at sharpening pencils. And putting things in alphabetical order, perhaps I could do some of that? Are there actually any Personnel under 'Z'?"

Miss Trinket closed the drawer of the filing cabinet with a bang, and sat at her desk. She hit a couple of keys on the computer and the little flying castles vanished, to be replaced by a blank white screen. "Look, I don't have enough bandwidth to play nursemaid," she said crossly, "I'm swamped as it is. Could you get off my desk?"

Kitty smiled and tried to look friendly, but didn't move. "I have no idea what you're talking about," she said, "except the last bit, obviously. Where's your pencil sharpener?"

"I don't use pencils. This is supposed to be a paperless office."

"So how come there's a pile of papers on your desk, and those cabinets are full of them?"

"I'm talking best practice. Sometimes a new idea doesn't have the legs you might wish. Once I've squared all my own circles I intend to reach out to my colleagues and persuade them to pick it up and run with it."

Kitty looked at her, fascinated. "No, still nothing," she said, slipping off the desk, "it's like a foreign language. Shall I come back later, when you've found the sharpener?"

"Whatever," said Miss Trinket, tapping at the keys and peering at the screen. "Let's rain-check that, all right?"

Kitty glanced out of the window. "Looks sunny enough to me. I think I'll go down to the beach. Why don't you come? We could paddle."

Just for a moment a wistful look passed across Miss Trinket's face, but she scowled at her computer and tapped even faster. Kitty slid out of the door and closed it behind her.

She thought that had been a fairly satisfactory overture on her part. Melody Trinket hadn't actually been nasty. She had just talked gibberish, but wasn't actively hostile so far as you could tell. Kitty thought she seemed like an unhappy person, and wondered why she chose to work here. Personally she couldn't imagine working anywhere she wasn't welcome and valued – she'd just pack her bags and go somewhere else.

And, thinking of going somewhere else, it didn't seem to be actually raining so perhaps she should go outside? There was an awful lot of castle to explore. Probably some tourists would be out there already. She could wander around with them and pretend to be a tourist too. She hoped none of them asked her any questions though, because she probably wouldn't know the answers.

Down in the courtyard there were tourists, right enough, but Kitty couldn't blend in because they all seemed to be Japanese who had come on a coach. They had lots of cameras and wore a sort of uniform of anoraks and long shorts. They had very white legs. One Japanese person seemed to be the leader, because he carried a sign on a stick which he held up in the air so they could see where he was. They trailed after him, snapping randomly with their cameras, and every so often he would stop and harangue them in Japanese – at least, she supposed it was Japanese, how would she know? Mother had been to Japan once, last year, on business. She went away on business quite a lot. This let her make quite a lot of money, Kitty thought, but made it necessary for some of that money to be spent on sending Kitty and Ellie and Jake to expensive boarding schools. It must be strange to have a mother who you lived with all the time, all year round and not just in the holidays. Kitty thought it would be nice, but all her friends at school were in much the same boat.

Speaking of boats, she had reached some stairs that led up to the top of the castle wall which was quite low at that point, and she could look out to sea. Just between the island and the rocks a little boat was ploughing gamely along with a white bow wave – a bone in its teeth, Kitty thought that was called. It had a tall wheel-house painted yellow, and the rest of the boat was blue. A man stood in the wheel-house, steering presumably. Another was on the deck in front, bending and stooping and every so often throwing something over the side. Kitty knew what they were doing, they were setting crab pots, each with a weight to hold it down to the seabed and a buoy to mark its position. Tomorrow they would come back and lift the pots and see if any crabs had crept inside. These they would take back to port and sell, and spend the money rollicking and roistering in the pub and drinking beer. Kitty knew all about fishermen.

It must be nice, she thought, to be out on the shining sea rocking up and down, and see the green and grey land from a different angle. She would like to go out on a boat. Perhaps she could find where the harbour was, and strike up a conversation – before they started roistering, obviously. They might invite her to go out with them next day. But she'd better not tell anyone, not even Ma, because grown-ups didn't approve of that sort of thing. But this train of thought did lead to a decision. The day seemed set fair, so she would go back to the kitchen and ask Ma for a picnic to take out, and then go off and find the harbour, and eat her picnic on the beach.

Ma thought it all sounded an excellent idea. While Kitty ran up to her tower to get a jumper and a towel in case she went paddling, Ma made a package of cheese sandwiches, cake and an apple with a bottle of milk to wash it all down. Happily Kitty packed these into her rucksack and sped off into the sunshine. She made her way down towards the beach, which meant winding her way by little tracks up and down and round about through the sand dunes, clothed in coarse sea-grasses and patches of gorse. Eventually she reached the proper beach, sliding down the last steep bank of sand on her bottom, then marched north towards where she imagined the harbour to be, as it was the direction of the village.

The harbour was, when she found it, a bit of a washout. It was nice enough, as harbours go, just a curving wall of weed-hung stone and a couple of sheds. Old boats lay about near the sheds and along the top of the wall, their paint flaking in the sun. At the top of the beach was a big machine, all giant cog wheels and a drum of cable, and a big handle to wind round and haul the boats out of the water. It was old and rusty but there was fresh grease on the cogs so it probably still worked.

In the circle of water embraced by the wall some small boats bobbed at their moorings, none as big as the fishing-boat she had seen earlier. But there was a sad lack of activity, no gnarled old sea-salts sucking their pipes and yarning away on an up-turned boat, no busy fishermen landing their catch, no laughing dinghy sailors hauling their sails up, just water and the stone walls and the boats bobbing quietly by themselves. It all smelled of salt and fish and seaweed as a harbour should, but once you'd looked at it and smelt it, that was all there was to do.

So Kitty walked back along the beach, admiring the bulk of the castle looking faintly grey in the distance with the curving sands and the breaking waves in the foreground. She went a little way into the dunes and found a comfortable nook of sun-warmed sand, sheltered from the wind, and set out her picnic.

Hunger satisfied and feeling rather sleepy, she lay on her towel and looked up at the sky. Some people, she thought, would be here and feel the wind and hear the waves and listen to the buzz of the insects and say that it was all proof of God's existence. Miss Hevesham certainly would – she frequently explained to her classes that everything you saw around you was proof of God, but Kitty couldn't see it. The fact that things existed didn't prove anything so far as she could see. Here in the dunes, keeping out of the wind, warmed by the sun, hearing the rattle of dry grass-stalks and the rustle of sand-grains sliding downhill, with bees buzzing and a dragonfly passing with a clatter of wings, she thought the explanation was something else entirely.

What it all proved was that there are three big things: the land and the sea and the sun. Those three things cause everything else. It's the sun that creates the wind, and it's the wind that makes the dunes. It's the land that nourishes the plants and the sea that waters them and the sun that makes them grow. It's the plants that nourish the bees and butterflies, and the sun's wind that carries them across the land. And it's the bees and butterflies that nourish the dragonflies and the birds ... and so on, and so on. She closed her eyes and drifted off.

She was startled awake by the harsh cry of a seagull sweeping close overhead. She raised herself and looked round. The sea was still in its place, beating on the sand, and the sun still shone, and the castle still loomed in the south. She lay back and resumed her musing. If things are so simple, she thought, the interaction between sun, land and sea, why shouldn't the same thing be happening on lots of other planets like this?

Was that so unlikely? All that was needed was a star, which is a sun if you live near it, and some land and some water, and the whole thing would work a hundred times over. Why not? Why should there not be, a million light-years above her head, some little alien girl lying on her back in the warm sand, gazing up at Kitty and thinking the same thoughts? And because she and the little alien girl, with her purple skin and three eyes and several legs, were thinking the same thoughts, that made them close, closer than she was to Marcia who never thought about such things, but had a head full of boys, jaffa cakes and spite. Marcia was supposed to be her best friend, but her real best friend was a purple alien whose name she wouldn't be able to pronounce even if she knew it.

Pleased with this philosophy though slightly annoyed at the way Marcia kept pushing herself in where she wasn't wanted, she lay back and waved her legs in the air. They were a bit thin, she thought. Marcia, butting in again, said that thin legs were really beautiful and the height of fashion, though she didn't take it as far as actually limiting her daily intake of jaffa cakes. Kitty gazed critically at her legs, silhouetted against the sky. They were thin all right, but they didn't look particularly beautiful to her. They just looked skinny, with knobbly knees. She felt the warmth of the summer sun on her skin, and looked at her arms to see if they were brown yet. No, they were still white with little fair hairs blowing in the wind, and hadn't started to get brown at all. Only the freckles had deepened, rather a lot of them, so she looked a bit spotty. Oh well, brains before beauty, people said. She knew she had the brains, but why couldn't she have a bit of the beauty as well? Was that too much to ask? It wouldn't hurt anyone, would it, if she were a bit prettier, like her sister Ellie? It wasn't as if there was only so much pretty to go round. If she used some of it up, no one else would have to go without.

Perhaps she could just bully people into thinking she was beautiful? She managed to bully them into most things, so why not that? After all, there were plenty of famous celebrities who weren't very good looking, and they were still famous. Grace Jones, for instance, or Paloma Faith, or that lady who played the Ice Queen in Narnia. Or Camilla Parker-Bowles who looked rather like a horse but was nice and was practically an actual queen. It was probably just a question of make-up. She would have to learn how to do really clever make-up, and then everyone would think she was beautiful. You could probably get special fat make-up to put on your legs so they wouldn't look so skinny. But if it was made of real fat, you'd have to scrape it off every day or two and replace it, or it would start to smell. Nothing worse than smelly legs, she thought, clambering to her feet.

She picked up her towel and her bag, and scrambled down the face of the dunes to the beach. She left her things halfway down, tucked her dress into her knickers hoping no one was around to look at her skinny legs without their fat make-up, and waded into the surf. The water was cold and made her shriek, and the waves were still quite big. They rose as they approached the beach, and began to curl first in one place and then the curl spread in both directions until there was a wall of water rearing up, poised, and you could see the sunshine through it and all the little bits of seaweed hanging there, and then it fell with a crash into a welter of white foam and rushed hissing towards you. It hung there a moment while some disappeared into the sand, and then the rest of it rushed back again to join its fellows, tugging at your feet.

Kitty watched this delightful process for a while, then threw caution to the winds, ran back up the beach, lifted her frock over her head and ran back into the sea in her undies, screaming with joy and the cold. She went in up to her waist, and let the next wave break all over her, knocking her over and sweeping her up the beach. Then she scrambled to her feet and did it again. The third time she went in a little further and the wave picked her up off her feet and carried her backwards and broke all over her, rolling her and getting sand in her hair.

In sudden panic she ran back up the beach, collected her frock and wrapped her towel round her, teeth chattering. Under cover of her towel she shrugged her underclothes off, rung them out and shoved them in her bag, then managed by various contortions to get her dress over her head so she looked decent to the casual glance. Then she set off back up the beach towards the castle, walking rather quickly and not looking back. Somehow the glorious afternoon felt soured, and as if on cue a cloud covered the sun and she shivered as the beach darkened. Even when the cloud passed and the sun returned, she hurried on, intent of getting home and into her room and into the bath. The afternoon was spoiled.

It was spoiled because that last time, as she waited for the wave to lift her and roll her back, she had seen something, just for a moment, something she hadn't expected. The wave had reared up and started to curl, the sun had glinted through the glass-green heart of the water in front of her with the skeins of weed hanging inside, and just as it hung poised to break, a face had looked at her. A dark face, with two liquid black eyes and a slightly puzzled expression, hanging in the face of the wave and gazing in wonder at this white inhabitant of the dry world. Then the wave broke and it was gone.

It was a seal, she told herself. It hadn't looked like a fish, it was too big. It wasn't a crab or a lobster for they didn't have big eyes that watched you soulfully. It might have been an illusion, a piece of beach debris, a bit of wood fallen from a ship or some plastic cast aside by a tourist, but there had been eyes, and puzzlement. Stop being silly, she told herself. The only thing that looked at you curiously from big black eyes was a seal. It was a seal, seals don't hurt you, they just look. You saw a seal, how lucky was that? Nine times out of ten you visit the beach and see nothing, and here she was spotting a seal on only her second visit. It was a seal, that's all.

Bathed and sand-and-salt free, in clean dry clothes with her hair brushed and glasses polished, Kitty felt firmer. It had been a seal. Seals swim in the sea. That's all, it had been a seal. Firmly she took her stolen – well, borrowed really – book and went back to the Library. Sir Lancelot was there, and the Sisters. She didn't disturb them, but returned the book she had finished with, and began to hunt for others. 'Natural History' yielded nothing of interest, 'The Supernatural' didn't seem to have a section in this collection, but 'Myths and Legends' was more fruitful. She found three books that looked promising, left them on a shelf near the door to collect on her way out, and walked quietly to the top of the Library where Sir Lancelot puttered among his moths.

"Excuse me, Sir Lancelot," she began, "I'm sorry to intrude, but ... well, you're a man of science so you might be able to help me ..."

The Sisters' twittering stopped, and they stared at her from six dead eyes.

"Well, what is it, child?" said Sir Lancelot, not looking at her. He had laid a number of identical moths on a sheet of card and was preparing to stick little pins in them.

"Sir Lancelot, I read ... well, heard a story ... I'm sure it's just a silly superstition or something ... but they were saying there used to be a monster here, a worm or some sort of dragon. Do you know anything about it?"

"She said monster," said Lady Clorinda.

"No, she said worm," Lady Drusilla said tartly.

"... it was dragon ..." breathed Lady Pamilia.

"Why would I know anything about it?" asked Sir Lancelot, his face close to the card, concentrating on his pinning. He had his mouth open and his tongue out in concentration, and Kitty thought he was in danger of dribbling on his specimens.

"I thought that as Castle Crayle has been the home of your family for so long, there might be some family history about it."

"There isn't," he said absently. "Never heard of it. What's it called?"

"I don't know. Just The Wyrm. It was in a book."

"All sorts of things in books. Being in a book doesn't make 'em true. Read a book once about a girl who fell down a rabbit hole and talked to a caterpillar. Absolute rubbish. Caterpillars can't talk."

"Can't talk ..." sighed Drusilla.

"Not caterpillars ..." answered Clorinda.

"... rubbish ..." echoed Pamilia.

"Oh, I do agree, Sir Lancelot," said Kitty smoothly. "Obviously a girl couldn't fit down a rabbit hole in the first place. Only I found a book that contained this legend about a Wyrm, so evidently someone must have taken it seriously or they wouldn't have bothered to write it down."

Sir Lancelot grunted, and stabbed with a tiny pin. "Obviously someone seriously thought a girl could talk to a caterpillar, or he wouldn't have written that down either. What does that prove?"

Oh ho, Kitty thought to herself, you're not as stupid as you look, Mr.Fossett? Out loud she said "Well, thank you for your help. I'm sorry to have bothered you."

As she started to withdraw, he said suddenly "There was Mercy Cott, though. That's the only thing I ever remember being said."

"Mercy Cott?"

"Yes. Mercy Cott. That's the cook's name, Cott, isn't it? You'd better ask her."

"Who was Mercy Cott, Sir Lancelot? What happened to her?"

Sir Lancelot straightened up, looked down at his card of moths and went "tsk" with irritation. "Damn me, that's not straight. Got to start again now. What did you say?"

"Mercy Cott. What happened to her?"

"What? Oh yes, Mercy Cott. Damn me, I'm going to run out of pins. Something ate her, I think. That's all I can remember. Ask cook."

IV

"Who's Mercy Cott?" Kitty asked next morning, taking her place at the broad scrubbed table. The kitchen was bright with the sunlight that slanted through the windows, glinting off the copper pans hanging on the walls, and heavy with the smell of frying bacon and fresh bread. Ma Cott put a plate in front of her and sniffed. "There is no Mercy Cott," she said shortly.

"But was there one?"

Ma turned away and busied herself at the sink, and did not immediately reply. At last she turned and regarded Kitty seriously. "Ask me no questions and I'll tell you no lies," she said. "Eat your breakfast. Sun's out, it's too nice a day to be frowsting in here. Go on, eat up and get on with your holiday!"

Kitty sensed that she ought not to persist, and dug in.

It was indeed a lovely day, warm and fresh with fluffy little white clouds drifting overhead and the smell of the sea in the air. She walked down the winding drive towards the village while the first tourist cars of the day made their slow way up towards the castle. She had drawn a blank with Ma Cott and wasn't hopeful about the Library. How do you search a thousand books for one simple name? It would be easy enough if she had access to the internet, but the only computer she had seen was the one in Melody Trinket's office, and she didn't think Melody would allow her to play with it. She set the problem of Mercy Cott to one side and looked for a shop.

The village began with small houses on either side, old-looking with their front doors opening directly onto the pavement on one side, and on the other straight onto the road itself for the pavement was on one side of the road only. They all had brightly painted front doors and colourful window-boxes. She passed only one or two people on foot. One smiled, but the others ignored her as they passed. There was a steady string of cars grinding their way up to the castle. She thought that on a day like this she probably wouldn't have the beach to herself. Many of the cars had children in the back, and she spotted towels and beach toys.

As the road broadened into a central square – or rather, a central triangle with more cars parked at right-angles to the road with their front wheels on the grass – she spotted a shop. It had many baskets and racks of postcards and buckets and spades outside, and proclaimed itself to be "Crayle Post Office, Grocery & General Supplies". She went in. The shop smelled of soap, mainly, and was like a small supermarket. One or two ladies browsed with wire baskets on their arms. At the back were the glass screens in front of the Post Office part. A tall, dark man with a bushy beard was serving a customer, counting out bank-notes and muttering to himself.

She wandered round until she came to the magazines, and beside them a shelf of books which a sign claimed were of *'Local Interest'*. They were mostly thin books entitled *'Castles of the North'* and *'Along the Northumberland Coast'*, *'Birds and Animals of the North-East'* and *'What to look for on the shore'*. Down at the bottom were some more serious volumes. It didn't look as though anyone had shown any interest in them for a long time, for they were dusty and piled any old how on the lowest shelf. She crouched down and picked through them. There were one or two that interested her for a moment, one about Bamburgh and Dunstanburgh Castles which were both further down the coast, and another *'General History of Crayle and its Castle'*. This looked interesting and she pulled it out. It was quite old and probably second-hand for the corners were dog-eared and one of the end papers had been roughly torn out. It was illustrated with black and white photographs from a bygone age, dull and fuzzy. Inside the fly-leaf was pencilled the price, 10/6d which she thought was 55p in modern money. That seemed reasonable, she would buy it. Mercy Cott and the monster might be in it.

At the counter she waited until the bearded man had finished with his Post Office customer. "Please," she said, "it says 10/6d inside. That's 55p isn't it?"

The man took it from her and looked inside. "That price is years out of date," he said crossly. "It's three pounds."

"But it's in very poor condition," she replied, unabashed. "Look, the corners are all turned down and there's at least one page missing. It's not worth three pounds, is it?"

The man paused, evidently not used to being checked. "It's

three pounds, take it or leave it," he snapped.

"I'll leave it then," she said, and turned to leave.

"Two pounds fifty!" he said behind her.

"One pound fifty," she said without looking at him.

He sighed and dropped the book on the counter. "Two pounds and that's my last offer," he said.

She smiled at him with her most winning smile. "But Mr. ... sorry, I don't know your name? It's only going to gather dust for another twenty years, isn't it? I'm probably the first person who's shown any interest in all that time. Wouldn't you rather get rid of it?"

At last he smiled, a rather predatory smile that had little friendship in it. "You're a forward little madam, aren't you? Do you live here, I don't recognise you?"

"I do and I don't. I'm staying at the Castle for a few weeks. I'm Kitty Younger, how do you do?" She held out her hand.

He took it briefly. His own hand was cold and rough to the touch. "Dashwood Belhatchett, pleased to meet you. All right, one pound fifty and there's an end of it!"

Pleased, she took her purse out of her rucksack and paid him, and thrust the book inside her bag.

"Thank you," she said, "nice to have met you!"

He just grunted. And nice doing business with you, not, she thought as she left the shop. They might have introduced themselves but she could hardly count him as a new friend. But at least she had a book that looked slightly promising.

Belhatchett's seemed to be the only shop in the village, but as she wandered around the central triangle and wondered where to go next, it came as something of a surprise to realise that two or three doors down from the Post Office was another door that stood open, and was plainly a shop of some kind though it had no sign to tell you what. She peered in through the door, and saw a dark, passage-like space almost filled with ... well, stuff, she thought. It was hard to tell just what you were looking at, but the walls were festooned with things and more enigmatic shapes hung from the ceiling. She made her way carefully down two steps and looked around her. There was a strong smell of ... something? Something sweet, incense perhaps?

Around her was an Aladdin's cave of colour and smell,

bundles of herbs, small artifacts carved from aromatic woods, clothes and scarves in exotic colours. Joss sticks burned in the corners and so filled the air with scent that it was thick and cloying and hard to breathe. Once you took a breath in, it tickled and you had to cough to get it out again. As she entered she brushed against the open door and set off, not a doorbell, but an antiphony of sweet chimes that in turn set off other tinkling bells sounding one after the other into the darkness at the far end of the shop.

Along the walls among the herbs and trinkets were packages containing mystic crystals and bottles of green and purple water that claimed healing properties, and aroma therapy oil and every kind of unlikely remedy for every imaginary ailment. Kitty was fascinated, and slightly repelled. Over her head hung little collections of sticks and scraps of fabric, tied into fantastic arrangements with coloured threads and beads and ... were those animal bones, tiny ribs and skulls of little dead creatures? This was weird, but somehow not frightening, just a bit daft.

"Hello?" she called, "is anyone in?"

There was a shuffle of footsteps, and from the darkness at the back of the shop emerged a woman, quite young, with huge dark eyes made even large by layers and rings of dark eye-shadow. She was beribboned and festooned with little things that rattled and rung as she moved, with coloured scarves round her hair and her neck and waist. She wore leather sandals that Kitty thought would probably still smell of the animal they were made from. Her hair was in dreadlocks with pins and combs holding the great mass in place, and she was smoking, holding a home-made cigarette awkwardly in two fingers. She drew at the soggy end of it then looked at it as though she expected it to change suddenly into a magic wand of mysterious narcotic wonder, instead of a rather sad, misshapen screw of rather suspect brown leaves.

"Hallo dear," she said, "can I help?" Her voice was unlike her appearance, for she sounded kind and really quite normal, and certainly not from around here because there was a twang of the south in it, more like the people Kitty had heard at school in Haslemere.

"Hallo," Kitty said, "I'm just nosing about, really, not looking for anything special. I saw your door and wondered what you were selling."

The woman chuckled. "Well, there's a question and no mistake. You're welcome to have a look round. You don't have to buy anything if you don't want, it's always nice to see a new face. You local?"

"Not really. I'm just staying here for a bit, up at the Castle. Do you know anything about the Castle?"

"No, not me. I'm not from around here, as you might have guessed. What's your name?"

"Kitty. What's yours?"

"Blue-Sky Lovechild. But most people call me Sky."

Kitty stared at her for a moment. "Yes, but what's your real name?" she said eventually.

"Denise Watkins," the woman shrugged. "But I prefer ..."

"... but it's not a matter of preferring, is it?" Kitty said sharply. "Never mind what you want to be, it's what you actually are that matters. That's what my dad says. Used to say, I mean."

"Why used?"

"He died."

The woman looked genuinely upset. "That's sad, poor you," she said. "Would you like a cup of tea?"

"Yes please, if you're having one. I'm sorry, I sounded a bit rude, what I said."

The woman turned away and busied herself with a teapot. "That's all right, you were probably right. I've always run away from stuff, me, and kept trying to be somebody I'm not because I didn't like what I actually was."

"What were you, then? Yes, one sugar please."

Sky or Denise handed her a cup. "I worked in a supermarket, then in the benefits office, and then I was out of work, and then I got married and then I got divorced and then I had a bit of money so I came here. On the whole, here is best. Not perfect, but the best I've managed so far."

Kitty looked round her. "It's certainly ... varied," she said. "Whatever are those things in the ceiling with the bones and stuff?"

"Dreamcatchers. You hang them over your bed and they catch the bad dreams and let the good ones through."

"And that works, does it?"

Sky grinned sheepishly. "What works is what you believe works, I suppose. Personally I believe in not eating cheese just before bedtime, that works for me. You'd be surprised how many people buy them, mind. They're one of my best sellers, along with the cantrips."

"Which are the cantrips?"

Sky showed her some little assemblages of knotted cords with shells and dried flowers and grasses woven in, and small pieces of carved wood or stone. "They protect you against boggles and witches and the dark forces," she giggled slightly, "things that go bump in the night!"

"Do they work?"

"Well, I haven't seen a single boggle since I came here. Mind you, I sleep with a big torch beside me and a rounders bat under the bed!"

Kitty laughed. "Yes, I expect that'll do just as well! Have you heard of Mercy Cott? Or a worm that lived under the Castle?"

"Yes and no. I don't know anything about a worm, but I have heard the name Mercy Cott. The Cotts are the oldest family round here. There used to be lots of them. There aren't so many now, but there's Mr. and Mrs.Cott, and they have two daughters and one son."

"I know them. At least, I know Mrs.Cott, she's nice, and so are her daughters. I don't know the men though."

"The son Billy is a fisherman. He works on the *Mercy*, that's a fishing boat, with Billy Brannicle."

"I've seen it. So they're both called Billy, that must be confusing? And the boat's called the *Mercy*? That must mean something. I knew there would be something."

"I don't know. All I've heard is that there was a girl called Mercy once, a long time ago, hundreds of years probably. And she disappeared. That's it."

Kitty put down her cup. She was finding the rich atmosphere a bit much and felt dizzy. "I'd better go," she said, "I've taken too much of your time already. Thank you for the tea."

"It's been a pleasure," said Sky. "Why don't you pop in again sometime? Perhaps if it's raining – there won't be many customers then, and I'm always happy to chat. You could come to lunch if you like. I live upstairs. Do you like tofu?"

"I don't know. What is it?"

"Blowed if I know. It's supposed to be good for you, though. Here, I've got something for you." She fumbled in her pocket. "You seem to like mysteries, so here's a mystery for you to think about."

She held out a small piece of something flat and grey. "You find these on the beach sometimes, and I've no idea what they are. Pretty though. I was wondering whether to try and sell them."

Kitty took it from her. It was a couple of inches long, and roughly diamond shaped. It was dark grey and looked like stone, but you could bend it slightly in your fingers. It felt strong, though. The surface was marked with intricate lines and swirls, pretty patterns that might have been carved into it by some minute craftsman. When you held it to the light and tilted it, it sparkled slightly and you got glimpses of colours as it turned, pale greens and pinks. It was, as Sky said, very pretty.

"Well, that's a mystery all right," she said, slipping it into her pocket. "Thank you, it's lovely. And I will come again."

It was a relief to come out into the sunshine again. She stood looking around at the houses and the grassy triangle. There were still cars passing, and she thought the grumpy lady in the ticket hut must be keeping busy. A few yards up the pavement a group of boys were lounging about, one sitting on the bonnet of a parked car. They shouted and hooted and pushed each other, and threw cigarette ends in the gutter. As she approached they all turned and looked at her. One muttered something, and the others laughed. They did not part as she came up, but stood blocking her path.

"Who are you?" said one rudely.

"None of your business," she said evenly. She wasn't intimidated, she had faced far bigger enemies before.

"That's not very polite," said another. "You're on our turf now, you should show a bit of respect."

"Respect has to be earned," she said. "What's respectable about you, exactly?"

"We'll show you," the first one said. "Come up the alley and we'll show you something to respect."

"Shan't. Make me." She set her feet and made sure her rucksack was firm on her back. She wished she had a stick or something.

But behind her there was a footstep, and over her shoulder appeared an extraordinary figure, a tall shabby man with staring eyes and an incredible variety of clothing, a filthy cloth cap on the back of his head, a chequered shirt under a black tail coat, and trousers that looked as though they were made of old curtains. On his feet were enormous wellington boots.

"Giving you grief, are they, the scallions?" he said. His voice was remarkably cultured with no trace of local accent. "You be off, you rabble," he said to the boys, and slowly they backed away, then turned and ran, shouting rude words over their shoulders and hooting in derision.

"Worthless rabble," he said to her. "You keep away from them, young lady. Stay out of dark corners."

"Thank you," she said. "I'm Kitty, who are you?"

"Nidd," he said shortly. "I'm Nidd. Watch yourself," and he nodded and strode off, his wellingtons making loud farting noises as he walked.

Well, this is my day for meeting new people, she thought as she crossed the grass and took the little lane that seemed to lead towards the shore. Dashwood Belhatchett, Blue-Sky Lovechild and Nidd. Doesn't anyone have a normal name round here? It would be a relief to meet someone called Smith or Johnson.

The cottages ended and the lane led across marshy land with tussocks of tall coarse grasses among which sheep grazed, searching out the short sweet tufts and raising little spurts of water where they walked. The lane was no longer paved, but had deteriorated into twin muddy tracks with grass in between. The breeze from the sea was warm and smelled fishy. In front of her the harbour appeared, and just rounding the end of the jetty was the blue fishing boat. She ran along the top of the jetty to watch it come in.

On the foredeck one of the two fishers stood, a coil of rope in his hand. He was a nice-looking young man, bare-chested and tanned by the sun and the wind. His hair was scraped back in a pony-tail. As the boat nosed gently into the wall, he held it up to her and called "Catch!", and tossed it at her. She grabbed at it with both hands and held it.

"Just loop it round the bollard!" he said, and she saw the iron bollard set into the cobbles of the wall, dark and smooth with use. She wrapped the rope twice around it, and tossed the end back to him.

"Thanks!" he said, climbed up on the boat's rail, put his hands on the jetty and vaulted up. "See, this is what you do." He took the rope off the bollard again, made a loop in it with each hand, then tucked the front loop behind the other one and dropped them over the bollard, tugging it tight.

"That's a clove hitch, isn't it?" she said. "I never saw anyone make it like that, though."

"Aye lass, that's the sailor's way of it. You're the little lass from the Castle, aren't you? Kitty, is it?"

"Yes. How do you know that?"

"I'm Billy Cott, Faith and Charity's brother. Here, Billy," he called down into the boat, and the other man came out of the wheelhouse. "Here's the canny lass Faith was talking about. Come and say hallo!"

The other Billy clambered up and shook her hand. "Billy Brannicle, I am," he grinned. "I'm the brains of this crew. How do you do?"

"I'm well, thank you. I saw you out yesterday. You were setting crab pots. How do you manage if both of you are called Billy?"

"It's no problem. If I call out 'Billy!' he knows I'm talking to him, and when he shouts 'Billy!' I know he's talking to me."

"What about when other people call you?"

"Well, we just guess, mainly. Though some call us Big Billy and Little Billy."

"But you're both the same size, pretty much."

"Not in every respect. He's got a bigger bum than me!"

Billy Cott snorted. "But I've got a bigger ..."

"Billy, manners!" interrupted Billy Brannicle, "you're talking to a bairn, remember!"

"That's all right, I don't need a picture drawn," Kitty smiled, "I'm a canny lass, mind!"

They laughed at this, and she asked them about seals. Oh yes, there were seals here, they said. Seals came every year, sometimes hanging round the harbour for scraps. Occasionally one would manage to haul itself on one of the small moored boats and lie there basking in the sun. But just at the moment there were no seals, not that they had seen. Hadn't been for several weeks. Why, had she seen one?

She said no, not really, she just wondered. But they had crabs to unload and pack into crates for the van to market in Newcastle, and she didn't want to get involved with them for she was a bit frightened of the claws, so she said goodbye and left them to it.

She took to the beach to walk back towards the castle, but didn't go in the water this time. As she left the harbour one of the white vans appeared, bumping up the muddy track, and parked. A man got out, wearing overalls, and started poking a long stick into the ground and making notes on a clipboard. She wondered what he was doing. Something to do with drains, perhaps, for the council. But surely there weren't any drains out here? She trudged happily on, taking Blue-Sky's gift from her pocket. She turned it over and over in her hands. One side was smooth, but the other had the pretty patterns and gave off colours in the sunlight. Perhaps if she walked at the edge of the water and kept her head down, she might find some more.

She found that there was another way into the castle when approaching from this direction. Through the dunes and up to the north end of the walls, she found a low door which stood open, though it had a second gate of latticed wood across it. She pushed the lattice aside and squeezed through the gap. Inside the wall, she was at the end of the castle she hadn't visited yet. The broad open space before the buildings was mostly down to grass, but there was the occasional bed of small shrubs, and a gravel path that ran along the inside of the wall with a garden bench to sit on every so often. Some faced across the grass to the buildings, and some faced outward but offered only a view of the stones of the surrounding wall which couldn't be very interesting. Near the buildings a man was working. He had a wheelbarrow full of tools.

"Come and give us a hand, would you, pet?" he called as she approached. "Could you hold the other end of this tape? I got to measure!"

Obediently she put down her bag and held the tape. He measured this way and then that, and put little sticks in the ground to mark what he had measured. He was an old man, wearing gardening clothes with boots and a brown apron.

"There!" he said, grimacing and holding his back as he straightened up. "There, that's the first step done. You must be the girl Kitty, I'm guessing? Bound to meet up sooner or later, my name's Baggott."

He was ruddy faced and keen eyed, and seemed friendly. She remembered Ma Cott describing him as 'one of us'.

"Pleased to meet you, Mr.Baggott," she said. "What are all these buildings, and how can I get into them?"

"You can't, miss. They're all sealed off, see?" He explained that everything on the north side of the old tower was ruinous and dangerous, and the Fossetts could never afford to repair them, so fifty years before they had been sealed off with brick and stone and mortar, and left to rot. "Everything to the south of the tower is open," he said, "that's where 'er Ladyship has her room, and the dining room and that, and the Library and then the kitchens down below. But this end, nothing doing, I'm afraid, pet."

"Thank you for telling me," she said, "I just wondered. There's such a lot of castle, isn't there, and I haven't seen even half of the bit that's open. I'll have plenty to explore. Can you tell me about Mercy Cott?"

"Well, bonny lass, I can and I can't, see?" he said, pulling out a tobacco pouch and starting to roll himself a cigarette. "There's a story, but no one don't know the truth of it."

He led her over to one of the benches and sat down, puffing on his cigarette. "See, pet, the Cotts are the oldest family round here, by many a hundred year. There have always been Cotts at Crayle, and still are. Good people, mostly. But many years ago – I think it must have been two hundred years at least – they had a daughter, Mercy, who was something of a beauty. And she disappeared. No one knew where she'd gone, and never a sign of her did they find though they searched high and low. But there was gossip that she'd been ... how to say? ... involved with one of the Fossetts, a lad named Roland, the Sir's son. And he disappeared as well."

"Well, that seems obvious, doesn't it?" Kitty said. "They ran away together. Very romantic."

"Well, no, it wasn't as simple as that," the old man said. "This is all just stories and rumours, you understand, no one really knows. But there were stories that they didn't go together, and that she maybe drowned herself."

"Sir Lancelot told me something ate her," Kitty said.

"Ate her? Haddaway with you, that's nonsense! No, no, what could eat a great lassie?"

"A monster? Like a worm?"

He chuckled. "Well, hinny, do you believe what you like, I can't stop you. But there ain't no worm, nor ever was. If there was some monster eating girls, don't you think it would have taken more than one, and we'd hear tell of it? It wouldn't last very long on just one girl, would it, it'd have to come back for seconds? Just stories, that is, all of it. Now," he said, rising, "I got to get on. Holes don't dig themselves, and I don't want to get wrong off 'er Ladyship. And don't you go nebbin' round that north end. Those buildings aren't safe, even if you could find a way in. Which you won't."

So far this had been a good day for meeting new people and learning things, Kitty decided. And it wasn't over yet, for that afternoon she was the unsuspected witness to a distressing scene. She had gone up to the top corridor, thinking that she might go and make a nuisance of herself to Melody Trinket, and generally have a nose about (nebbin', she told herself, that had been Baggott's word for it). She even wondered if somewhere among the filing cabinets there might be plans of the castle she could look at. She was dreadfully curious about the north end, though she had been warned off. There's nothing like a good warning to make you curious, she thought.

Melody's office was deserted when she reached it, which was good. She was just about to investigate the lower, unlabelled drawers of the filing cabinets when she heard raised voices, and a door slamming open.

"Look, young woman, don't defy me!" Lady Sybil was yelling, "you'll do as you're told or you're out on your ear, and you can whistle for a reference! Anyone who comes asking about you, I'll make sure they know how useless you are, that you're not to be trusted, and you're incompetent and sulky, and you'll never work again. Do you understand?"

The voices were getting closer. They were coming here. Kitty ran across the room and slipped underneath the desk. There was a space for someone's knees, and a board across the front. She wouldn't be seen unless someone actually came round the desk to sit down.

Melody Trinket was doing her best to stand up for herself, which surprised Kitty. "Lady Sybil, when I arrived I was told to prepare a Business Plan to improve the earning potential of the Castle, and that's just what I've been ..."

"I don't care what you've been doing, and I don't care whether you think you know best or not, because you don't! You can tear your Business Plan up and swallow it for all I care, it's irrelevant! You hear me? What you will do is send out a new mailing to the mailing list, with the alterations I have dictated, and you'll do it today! I shall check at dinner whether you've finished it, and if you haven't you'll get no dinner off me, and you'll not sleep until you've finished, is that clear? I'll not have this defiance!"

"But it's only three weeks since we sent out the last one ..."

"Nevertheless, young woman ..." Kitty could imagine Lady Sybil drawing herself up to a considerable height, "... you will do it again. You will mail every travel agent, and all the coach companies – not Charlie's Coaches, I'll not have them on the premises again - and all the tourist information offices within fifty miles ... no, wait, make that a hundred miles ..."

"But I don't know the addresses more than fifty ..."

"Then find the damned addresses! Find them, and do it now, you hear? Tear up your pathetic Business Plan and buckle down to the work you're given, or you'll not eat or sleep under my roof again until it's done! Now then!" and footsteps rang across the floor and the door slammed.

Kitty listened. She heard a high keening sound, and then sobs burst out, and a thump as Melody fell to her knees. Kitty climbed to her feet, went round the desk and found the young woman crouched with her head in her hands.

"Bad day?" she said.

Trinket stiffened and raised a tear-stained face. "Did you hear all that? Where were you?"

"Under the desk. The woman's mad, isn't she? Why do you allow her to bully you like that? Why don't you just leave? Would you like to borrow my hankie? It's almost clean, I only wiped my glasses on it."

Trinket took the hankie and blew her nose on it. "Thanks," she said, with a great shudder. "I can't leave. She won't give me a reference, so it'll be impossible to get another job. I'll have to stack shelves in a supermarket or something, and I used to have the beginnings of a good career."

"What were you doing before?"

"I was PA to the Chief Executive of a plastics factory in Birmingham. I was good at it. Am good at it, I mean."

"So why did you leave Birmingham?"

Trinket got to her feet and leaned against the desk, the hankie to her eyes. "Don't do that," Kitty said, "you just blew your nose on it. Haven't you got any tissues?"

"Top drawer. Thanks. I left because there was some   ... awkwardness. My boss changed, started dropping hints about ... well, just hints. Then I had to go with him on a business trip to Glasgow, and when we arrived at the hotel I found that he had only booked one room for both of us." She drew a shuddering breath, but at least the tears seemed to have stopped. "Normally I booked the hotels, but this time he'd insisted on doing it himself, and then I realised why."

"So you had to share?"

"Well, no, because I went and found another hotel for myself. But that's what he seemed to want. It made for a bit of an atmosphere for the rest of the trip."

"That was very silly of him. Suppose you snored and kept him awake? Did he know whether you snore or not? Erm ... why are you looking at me like that?"

"I don't snore, as far as I know," said Melody. She was indeed looking at Kitty rather strangely.

Suddenly Kitty's eyes grew wide and she put her hand over her mouth. "Ooooh, I get it!" she said, "silly me, I didn't think! He wanted ... well ... I mean, didn't you like him?"

"Not one tiny bit. He was short and fat and had a face like a frog."

"So you left?"

"Yes. He gave me a passable reference, not glowing, but adequate. And I answered an advert, and got this. I thought it would be interesting, and challenging, and something of a step up. I looked forward to it."

"But? ..."

"It's been a disaster. They pretend I'm a guest but they treat me like a servant. The real servants don't understand, they get upset when I try to give them orders though it was in my job description. They laugh behind my back, I think."

"I doubt that. I've met them, they're nice."

"Well Cartilege definitely looks down his nose at me."

"It's quite a nose. What's the stuff about a Business Plan?"

Melody explained that when she started, she was told to prepare a Business Plan for expanding the activities offered at the Castle in order to increase its revenue and make it a successful and profitable business. Easy enough, she had thought, for someone with a business degree and some experience. But every effort she had made was met with indifference by Lady Sybil. "It's as though she doesn't really want the Castle to make a profit," she said, "and Sir Lancelot isn't interested in anything except his moths so he's no help. I'm supposed to be running a business, and instead I'm being used as a filing clerk and ... every day there are these rows and I don't think I can stand it any ..."

Kitty could see the tears coming again. "Would you like a hug?" she said suddenly.

Melody Trinket looked at her for a long moment, her face working as though many emotions were chasing each other behind it. "Actually ..." she said shyly, "yes, I would," and she buried her face in Kitty's shoulder and sniffed deeply. Kitty patted her back consolingly.

"Oh now, look what I've done," Melody said forlornly, "I've made your t-shirt all soggy. And I'm supposed to be the grown-up here, not you ..."

Kitty took her by the hands and looked sternly into her eyes. Without her glasses, Melody's eyes were rather weak and, at the moment, very watery. "Every girl needs a hug now and then, and a bit of a weep."

"But I'm twenty-four, and you're ... what, eleven?"

"Twelve. That's not such a difference. And I've been around a bit. I was hunted by wolves once."

"You what?" Melody gave a sort of half-laugh, not believing.

"It's a long story. And I stabbed someone, too."

"I don't believe you," she laughed shakily, then looked hard at Kitty's face. "No, wait, you're telling the truth, aren't you? That's awful!"

"No it wasn't, he really needed stabbing. It was him or me, and I liked me better." Kitty stood up, suddenly businesslike. "Right, now let's sort you out. I don't need sorting, but you do. First, how about we print out these letters and get them into their envelopes and out of the way? I'll take them down to the post office if we can finish before it closes. That'll be one less thing for Lady Sybil to pick on, and she might let you have your dinner. And if she doesn't, I'll take you down to the kitchen and you can share mine. Don't worry about Mrs.Cott, she'll understand, she's nice and she knows what Her Ladyship is like. They call her The Old Crow ..."

That evening Kitty retired to her room with a sense of satisfaction at a day well spent. She had met some ... interesting people ... some who she might regard as friends like Blue-Sky Lovechild and Baggott and the two Billies, and some she wasn't so sure about, Dashwood Belhatchett and those nasty boys and the weird man Nidd. And she'd made one proper friend, she thought. Melody Trinket was quite nice really, and she was having a terrible time and needed Kitty's help. Kitty might be only twelve, but she knew already that helping someone else makes you like them better. That was how she'd been able to put up with Marcia all this time. It ought to be the other way round, being helped ought to make them grateful and like you in return, but somehow it didn't work like that. The mailing had been completed, and she had been able to take a ruck-sack of envelopes down to the Post Office just before it closed. She hoped that Melody had been able to survive her dinner without further upset.

Now, it was time for a bit of cosy bedroom research, tucked

up with a cup of cocoa and some of Ma's biscuits. She could search her new old book for information about the worm and with a bit of luck there might be mention of Mercy Cott as well. And what made bedtime just a little more entertaining was that Perkins had waited for her at the foot of the stairs and followed her up to her room. She left the door slightly ajar in case the cat wanted to get out in the night, and climbed into bed.

As she opened her book, Perkins leapt onto the bed and sat on her stomach, blinking. She tickled the cat behind the ear and was rewarded with a purr.

"This is nice," she said. "You do smell of fish, though, Perkins. How is that? Have you been down to the harbour? That's quite a journey for a cat, I would have thought. Where have you been to get so fishy?"

The cat said nothing, just blinked and purred, and when Kitty woke in the morning she was gone.

V

The three strangers looked quite out of place, standing in the sunlit courtyard next morning in their long coats and shiny black shoes. Kitty had been on her way to find Baggott when they stopped her.

"Young lady," the little one said, "you look as though you belong here. Perhaps you can give us directions?"

He was hardly any taller than she was, neat and dapper. He held himself very straight so that his shoulders hardly moved when he walked towards her. His black hair was slicked back and greasy, but the errant breeze had picked up a strand of it so he looked as though he had a crest like a cockatoo. Behind him was a giant of a man who, though he wore a similar long coat, looked entirely different for he was huge and blocked out the sun. He loomed, Kitty thought, loomed and looked down at her as though she were a beetle he could crush with his enormous shoes and not even notice he'd done it.

"I can try," she said, undaunted. "Who are you looking for? Miss Trinket? She's in charge of the business."

"Not her, no. Our business is with Lady Fossett. Where might we find her, is she at home?"

The third man stood a little apart. He was much older, a pink-faced man with a fleshy nose and grey hair that was just a little long. He had shifty eyes and carried a large brief-case.

"Probably," she said, "she generally is. Shall I show you the way? Who should I say you are?"

"My name is Medulla," the little man said, "and these are my associates, Professor Crust and Mr.Cockley Knowes."

"How do you do?" she said, not offering to shake hands as she hadn't enough for three.

"And what might your name be, young lady?" asked the fleshy-nosed man. His mouth smiled but the rest of his face didn't. As he was the one with the brief-case she presumed he was Professor Crust, while the man-mountain must be Knowes.

"It might be Kitty Younger," she said, "well, not might be, it is. I'm staying here for a few weeks. Would you like to follow me?"

She led them in a little crocodile across the courtyard, Professor Crust behind her, then Mr.Medulla taking tiny, quick steps, and Cockley Knowes hulking along at the rear. Knowes had to duck to get in the door, and blocked all the light as he did so. Up the stairs they went, and emerged into the carpeted corridor. Cartilege was just coming out of the dining room and stood in front to stop her.

"What are you doing here, miss?" he said. His voice was creaky from disuse. She had never heard him speak before. At the dinner table he had never spoken, just murmured something indistinct as he put the plates down. "What are you doing here? You've no business ..."

"Visitors for Lady Sybil," she said stoutly, "important visitors. I'm showing them the way."

"That's my job. You can go."

"Shan't. They asked me. You can announce them if you like, though. I expect that's your job too, isn't it, announcing?"

He stared at her, his mouth working. He looked as though he'd like to slap her, and she got ready to duck, but he only said "What names?"

"Mr.Medulla, Mr.Knowes and Professor Crust."

Cartilege turned away and walked to the door of Lady Sybil's lair. He rapped on the glass with his knuckles, then opened the door and held it open. "Mr.Ma ... some gentlemen to see you, your ladyship."

Kitty led the way. Lady Sybil was just rising from a sofa, and stared at her. Before she could speak, Kitty announced "Mr.Medulla, Mr.Knowes and Professor Crust have come to see you. I brought them up."

Lady Sybil looked daggers at her, but quickly wiped the frown off her face and advanced towards the guests with a hand outstretched. "How nice to meet you at last, Mr.Medulla. Do sit down, gentlemen ..." She waved a vague hand towards the furniture. Mr.Medulla took his coat off and handed it to Knowes without looking at him. Professor Crust also took his off, and threw it on an armchair. They sat down, but Knowes remained standing just inside the door, his arms folded.

Kitty also sat down, in an armchair so deep that her legs wouldn't reach the floor but stuck out in front. "Not you, child," said Lady Sybil, trying to keep the venom out of her voice but not entirely succeeding, "why don't you go down and ask Cook for a tray of coffee and biscuits? You'll be quicker than Cartilege."

Kitty was tempted to reply "Because I don't want to, and it's his job" but didn't quite dare, so she shoved herself off the chair and trotted off to the kitchen.

The message delivered, she returned to the top floor and went into Melody's office. Melody was tapping at her computer and greeted her with a wan smile.

"How did it go last night?" Kitty asked her. "Did you get your dinner? Was she amazed you'd got it all done?"

Melody gave a last tap, manoeuvred the mouse and clicked to save her work, and sat back. "Yes thank you," she said. She may have got her dinner and her bed after all, but she still looked pale and her eyes were dark with either tiredness or tears. "I think she was a bit surprised when I said it was all done, but she didn't make a fuss. So thank you, you were a big help."

"What are you doing this morning?"

"Going through my Business Plan."

"I thought she wasn't interested?"

"She isn't, but it's the right thing for me to be doing and I was told to do it, so I'm not going to throw it away."

"Good for you. Who are the visitors?"

"What visitors?"

"There are three men with Lady Sybil now. I showed them the way."

Melody shrugged. "I know nothing about it. She never mentioned it to me. What sort of men?"

"The leader is a little man called Medulla, and there's a Professor Crust, and a very large man called Cockley Knowes. I think he's a sort of minder for Medulla, he doesn't say much. They're in there drinking coffee at this minute. Can I look at your Business Plan, or is it a secret?"

"I know nothing about any meeting. That's typical, that is. I suppose you can, if you want. It's not very interesting for someone your age."

"I think I should be the judge of that," Kitty laughed. "You'd be surprised at the things I find interesting. Come on, show me!"

She had rather expected to see something headed *'How to make loads of money out of a castle'*, but what she read on the computer screen was a little drier than that. The document started with an account of the current activities at the Castle, which was mainly letting tourists walk round and gawp at stuff. It listed the assets, which was mainly one castle, a wooden hut and some garden tools. Then there was a section about how much they charged the tourists and why they couldn't charge any more because people wouldn't pay it.

Then she got to the real nitty-gritty, the section where Melody had listed other activities that could be introduced. This was much more interesting. She read ...

'(a) school visits - school groups of any size welcome though larger groups should be asked to break down into smaller groups of no more than 12, schools asked to ensure they bring enough staff. Offer one free adult place for every twelve pupils with additional adults at cost. All pupils 5-16 to be charged £3. The Castle not suitable for groups of Under 5's.'

"That sounds perfectly sensible," she said. "Can't argue with that. But this next bit, *'(b) corporate hire'*, what's that? I don't know what that means."

"It's when a company hire a place for a day, and use it to invite customers and guests from other companies to meet and have a grand meal and drink champagne and listen to speeches about how wonderful the company is. Sometimes they organise activities, games, perhaps a bit of an entertainment show, that sort of thing. They pay quite handsomely."

"Who'd cook the meal, though?"

"Well, if our own kitchen couldn't cope, you can always bring in outside caterers."

Kitty thought for a moment. "You'd need loads of tables and chairs and other stuff. Where would you store it? And you'd need a lot of people to put it all out – Cartilege and Baggott couldn't do it all."

Melody laughed. "You're quick, aren't you? How old did you say you were? Thirty-five?"

Kitty grinned at her, and read on.

"'(c) self-catering accommodation', that's like a gîte, isn't it, where people stay for a holiday and do their own cooking? We had one in France last year. You'd have to spend a lot of money putting little kitchens in, and extra toilets and stuff."

"Yes, capital outlay, that's called. My next step would be to work out how much it would cost, but there isn't any capital to spend as far as I know," Melody said, leaning and reading over Kitty's shoulder.

Kitty read on. The next section described *'(d) weddings – offering a unique venue, fairy-tale location, miles of breathtaking coastline providing a spectacular backdrop for the most important day. Licensed to hold civil ceremonies and partnerships in the grandeur of the Kings Hall, rebuilt as the Castle's centrepiece in the 19th century, rich teak panelled walls, ornate ceiling and overlooked by beautiful stained-glass windows. Ceremonies also in the Cross Hall, crowned by light from the soaring windows and surrounded by works of art. Seat up to 150. We offer … a suppliers list, in-house catering, accessible guest parking, services of a wedding planner included.'*

"Brilliant!" breathed Kitty. "Where are the Kings Hall and the Cross Hall? I haven't seen them yet?"

"I made that bit up, to be honest. I haven't quite worked out where all this would happen."

"The place at the bottom of the Library stairs could be the Kings Hall," Kitty suggested, "it's big enough, and it has some stained glass windows."

Lady Sybil would have hated the next bit, *'(e) picnic area, toilets, stall selling ice-creams and teas'*, and *'(f) accessibility adaptations'* would probably cost a lot of capital outlay, making the Castle suitable for people in wheelchairs.

Melody said "I showed that to Sir Lancelot because we ought to be doing it soon anyway, and he said if people couldn't be bothered to avoid falling off ladders or crashing their motorbikes, he didn't see why we should make special arrangements for 'em!"

For *'(g) filming and photography location'* Kitty suggested they might invite someone to make the next Harry Potter film in the Castle. *'(h) cafe and/or upmarket restaurant'* would be another expensive project, but Kitty had a couple of suggestions of her own.

"It wouldn't cost much to make a play area for children," she said. "You could have a treasure trail, and big bricks for them to build their own castles. You'd have to make the bricks of something soft in case they hit each other with them. And when we went to see the Bayeux Tapestry you could hire a set of earphones that told you all about what you were looking at. You could do that. And you could hire actors and give shows, people in period costume, and jousting and pony rides and ..."

"Stop, stop, stop!" Melody cried, laughing. "These are all good ideas, but they're not interested so it's pointless! And there's something I haven't told you. This is all a complete waste of time."

Kitty looked at her with amazement. "What do you mean? Surely they'll see sense eventually? These are all brilliant ideas!"

Melody shook her head. "Doesn't matter how brilliant they are, and it doesn't matter whether they see sense or not. See, this whole place is just a monstrous white elephant. Half of it's falling down, it all needs massive amounts of maintenance, and there just isn't any money. Lady Sybil spends money like water – she's mean enough when it comes to wages and food and day-to-day stuff, but if she decides she needs a new car or something, the sky's the limit."

"But the tourists, there are loads of them? All I see every day is cars arriving and more cars?"

"Oh yes, public admissions are doing OK, but they're very seasonal. Come September the whole thing grinds to a halt and the place will be deserted. As for all these ideas I've had, there aren't enough bedrooms to be a hotel or a conference centre and there isn't the money to add more, there's space for several gîtes – well, more like flats really – but creating them would be expensive. The kitchens are antiquated and would need completely rebuilding to do any serious catering for the public. There aren't enough toilets ... there's room to do all these things, but every time you come back to the same thing: there's no capital. And the banks won't lend to Sir Lancelot as his business record is disastrous: whenever he comes into a bit of money, it seems he spends it mounting an expedition to darkest

Venezuela, hunting moths."

"Oh. Well, yes, that is a bit of a problem. Still, it doesn't do any harm to have ideas up your sleeve just in case there's a change of heart, does it? Lady Sybil might drop dead tomorrow, and you'd come into your own."

"That's a bit bloodthirsty."

"I know, but you can dream, can't you? I bet you could wind Sir Lancelot round your little finger if you tried. I'd help, I can be jolly persuasive. And speaking of persuasion, why don't you come to the beach with me this afternoon, and we could paddle? You'd be entertaining a guest of the Castle, which must be part of your job description."

Melody looked tempted, and glanced wistfully out of the window at the blue sea sparkling in the sun. "Entertaining, yes, I suppose I could stretch things that far, but paddling would be too much, I'm afraid. You go and enjoy yourself. Come and see me tomorrow!"

Kitty thought she would make her way to the beach by the little wicket gate at the north end. She might run into Baggott on the way, and ask him some more questions, he was the most informative person she'd met so far. And she meant to walk along the shore to the harbour and ask the Billies whether Perkins had been visiting them. It seemed an awful long way for a little cat, but she could think of no other explanation for the smell of fish. She had seen what food Faith and Charity put down for the cat, and it hadn't been fish.

Walking across the north lawns she spotted Professor Crust standing near the derelict buildings, looking thoughtfully at their foundations. The walls rose from a sort of pedestal of rough stone, part of the great stone outcrop on which the entire castle was founded. He turned and saw her, and waved energetically.

"Well, young lady, Miss Younger wasn't it? And what do you do around here? Are you part of the Fossetts? Are you a little Lady Fossett in the making, perhaps?"

He seemed friendly but Kitty didn't think he was really. There was something mocking in his tone.

"No," she said, "I'm nothing to do with them. I'm just staying here for a bit. They don't really want me, but they're stuck with me so that's tough."

"Aha, I sense discord in the Castle. Not quite the happy family, then?"

"Not quite. But some people are nice. Mr.Baggott is, I'm looking for him."

"Well, let's us be friends as well, shall we? I know your name is Kitty, so I'll call you that and we shall be the best of ... erm, buddies! You may call me Wilberforce, for that's my name, Wilberforce Crust, B.Sc. and bar. I was just looking at these buildings. What's inside, do you know?"

"Not really. They're all derelict, apparently, and you're not allowed in because it's dangerous. The family can't afford to have them repaired."

He looked at her musingly. "Ah well, probably just as well," he said softly to himself. "Probably be best just to knock 'em all down and have done with it. What interests me ..." he was addressing her now, not just himself ... "is what lies underneath."

"Underneath? How do you mean? Oh! ... you don't mean the Worm, do you? Do you know about the Worm?"

"The Worm? Why .. yes, of course, one knows the stories ... what have you heard?"

"Just that there was supposed to be a Worm, or a sort of dragon, living under the Castle, and once it came out and ate someone."

He laughed, a sort of sneering laugh that she didn't like the sound of. "I believe there are such stories at many places in this corner of Britain. There's certainly a similar legend at Bamburgh, and several more further south. Makes you wonder if the old story of Saint George and the Dragon didn't start round here somewhere."

"So if it wasn't the Worm you were talking about, what was it? What's interesting about under the Castle?"

"Why, human remains, you know, and artefacts, tools, cooking utensils, that sort of thing, that might give an idea of what human activity there has been in the past."

He put his hand on her shoulder and walked her slowly across the grass. "I'm an archaeologist, you might say, and we're doing a bit of exploration all round here, to see what we can find. Fossils, and so on, you know."

"Is that what the men in white vans are doing, poking sticks into the ground?"

"Oh, you've spotted them, have you? And there was I thinking we'd been so discreet! There are no flies on you, are there, Kitty Younger?"

"And have you found anything?"

"Well, just minor finds so far, you know. The odd shard of pottery, fish bones, that sort of thing. The jawbone of a primeval porpoise, fossilised shark teeth ..."

Kitty thought for a moment. "It doesn't sound as though there's much you can deduce from things like that, is there? I mean, people put things in pots, fish live in the sea and we're beside the sea ... so what? Did these people eat the Primeval Porpoise?"

He gave a little chuckle. "Oh no, no, the Primeval Porpoise would have lived millions of years before there were any people to eat it. Just some leftover from the Ordovician Era, perhaps. Interesting, but hardly significant. Now, I must go and rejoin my friends. It's been most pleasant talking to you. Enjoy the rest of your day!" and he strode off towards the other end of the Castle.

No, the Billies said, they hadn't been having visits from any cats. Besides, the Castle was a good mile and a half from the harbour, and no cat with a comfortable kitchen to sit in would attempt a journey like that just on the off-chance there might be the odd fish-head lying about. So that was that theory knocked on the head. But Kitty was sure her nose hadn't been mistaken last night – Perkins had definitely smelt fishy.

Billy Brannicle walked her to the foot of the jetty while Billy Cott fussed over his crab pots.

"When are you going to come out for a trip with us, canny lass?" he asked, and they discussed a suitable day and time.

"But we'll have to find a lifejacket for you, and we don't have one that's small enough. I'll ask around in the pub. Someone'll have something we can borrow."

"I expect I ought to have wellingtons, too, and I haven't," she said.

"All right, pet, I'll see what I can do. Now ..." he paused and gazed innocently round at the harbour, "how are Faith and Charity? See much of them, do you? Have either of them mentioned me at all?"

Ho ho, she thought, I can see where this is going. Billy Brannicle fancies Faith. Or Charity. Or both, which is an interesting thought. Or perhaps he can't tell the difference? Out loud she said "No, I'm afraid I haven't heard anything. I do see them most mornings though, so is there any message?"

"No, no," he said lightly, "just making conversation. See you soon!"

On the long walk back up the beach Kitty kept an eye out in the surf for fish bones or the remains of the Primeval Porpoise. Perhaps it had been the Primeval Porpoise that had stared at her out of the wave? She glanced nervously at the breaking waves, but they were much smaller today. There wouldn't be room for the Primeval Porpoise, unless it was a very tiny one.

The wet sand just out of the reach of the waves was smooth and dark brown, but patterned with little spiral heaps where, she knew, worms or shellfish were hiding under the surface and pooping out sand as they sifted for food. Sometimes people scooped them out with nets, and ate them if they were shellfish or used them as bait if they were worms. She wondered what it felt like to be a worm, lying snug under the sand and sucking up the grains and pooping them out again, saving any fragments of food they contained. It must be a peaceful existence, until the men came with their net. There wouldn't be much to think about, just suck and poop, suck and poop, ooh, there's a juicy bit, suck and poop until you died. And then your children – who you didn't know, as they came from eggs or even a tail section you'd dropped ages ago and forgotten about – would carry on the job without you, and their children after them.

So it had been for millions of years, probably, millions of years of just sucking and pooping, and none of these diligent little workers ever thought about the larger picture. They never wondered about the stars, or algebra or première league football or thought that life might be better. And things changed so slowly. She knew, because they'd done it in school, that it took millions of years for even the smallest change to come over a species. Certainly, one millennium some little worm might develop fingers and crawl out of the sand looking for something to pick up and learn to juggle, but by then the sun would be practically dying and the winds would have stopped and the waves wouldn't break but just flop lifelessly on the beach, and the worm would find the whole thing a bit pointless and wonder why it bothered.

She knelt down on the sand, and spoke to one of the little worm casts. "Hallo, little worm? Can you hear me? Have you evolved ears yet? I am the Great God Kitty, speaking to you from the World Above, and I am here to tell you ... that it's all pointless! Give it up, you're going nowhere!" and then she stopped because there, right in front of her half buried in the sand, was something she recognised. She stopped being a Great God and became a girl again, and scraped with her fingers to free it. It was another of Sky-Blue's grey tiles, just like the first, smooth on one side and delicately patterned on the other. She washed it in the sea and held it up to the sun, and watched the pretty colours playing on the tiny ridges. Then she walked on, keeping her eyes down.

By the time she had to leave the beach because she'd reached the wicket gate, she'd found two more. They rattled gently in her pocket. As she walked up the sand and into the dunes she no longer had the beach to herself because there were little knots of people camped with bright wind-breaks and towels and bags, and children frolicking and screaming in the shallows.

After the wind and the sun on the beach and the screams of the little children, it was very peaceful in the Library. Sir Lancelot wasn't here for once, nor his sisters. She had the place to herself. She wandered up and down between the shelves, examining the titles of the books. She had decided to learn a bit more about archaeology. Somehow she felt a little uneasy about Professor Wilberforce Crust. Something he had said did not quite ring true, but she didn't know what.

Ah, here was something! *Archaeological Exploration in North East England – a brief exposition'* couldn't be all that brief, the book was enormous. It took all her strength to pull it down from the shelf and carry it to her eyrie in the window. It was lavishly illustrated, but with little black and white pictures that she thought were engravings or woodcuts. They were very charming, though. An awful lot of them were about Hadrian's Wall, with pictures of little Roman soldiers in their skirts, which must have been dreadfully chilly in these Northern winters. It was a subject she thought was probably quite interesting, but she wanted to concentrate on the coast where she was. After an hour or so of browsing, looking at pictures and reading the captions which said things like *'Grain jar (?), c.150 A.D., Vindolanda, P.Sterchis'*, she had reached one conclusion. Archaeology was about the remains of human activity, not about fossils or prehistoric relics, Primeval Porpoises and such. There wasn't a single fossil in the whole book.

Right, she thought, that's Archaeology sorted. What about the fossils? What was that called? She put the book back on the shelf, not without a struggle and having to stand on a chair, then ran down the stairs and up again to Melody's office.

"Melody, what's the study of fossils called?"

Melody looked up from her work, startled. She seemed to be adding columns of figures. "Oh, I'm not certain, "she said, "is it Palaeontology?"

"Yes, that's it!" Kitty shrieked. "I just couldn't remember it! Thanks!" and she dashed out of the door and back to the Library. As she bounded down the stairs two at a time she passed Cartilege who shouted "Hey!" at her but she ignored him.

"Palaeontology, Palaeontology ..." she muttered, scanning along the shelves. "There's everything else here, so surely there must be something ... where would it be? Near the Archaeology, or the History? That's where I'd put it. Or is it a science? I'm not sure I've seen any science in here at all. Science is a bit modern, isn't it, and most of these books are ages old."

At last, by kneeling on the floor and crawling slowly along peering at the books down in the shadows on the very bottom shelf, she found something. It was not a very exciting-looking book, rather mildewed and tattered, but it had the word 'fossil' in the title, *'The Fossil Record Explained by an Old Fossil'*.

"Ha ha, funny joke," she said to herself. "Eugh, there's a

spider in it. Get out, you silly creature!"

Brushing herself off, she rose and went back to her nest, hoping the spider wasn't following.

The book was slim and obviously only intended to give an introduction to a vast subject. The illustrations were very poor, fuzzy black and white photographs from a previous age. It was difficult to make out what any of the supposed fossils were. But in the back there was a useful table that showed the various palaeontological ages. It started with the Precambrian, which it said ended about 542 million years ago. During the Precambrian, which included about 90% of the Earth's history, the oceans and the atmosphere were formed and the first life began, bacteria first, and then the first multi-celled creatures.

Next came the Cambrian Period, flashing by in a mere 54 million years, with the seas filling up with invertebrates which Kitty thought must have been jellyfish and such. There was a nice description ... *'Carboniferous rocks yield brachiopods, crinoids, corals and plant remains. The seas were filled with corals, sea lilies and brachiopods, and vast deltas including swamps crowded with giant tree ferns. Brachiopods are marine animals that have existed for 550 million years. They have a pair of shells which they can clamp shut for protection or open slightly to filter the water, though not directly related to modern bivalves. Crinoids are echinoderms related to starfish and sea urchins. They are spiny, five sided and have a calcium carbonate endoskeleton (also called sea lilies from their resemblance to plants)'.* This was interesting and she might have spent more time here, but she was after mammals, because she was absolutely sure that porpoises were mammals, not fish. They breathed air.

Vertebrates, fish with backbones, arrived in the next period, the Ordovician, though the land remained barren so far. Wait a minute, she thought: hadn't Professor Crust used that word? Yes, he had, he'd said that the Primeval Porpoise was probably left over from the Ordovician Era. But the Ordovician wasn't an Era, it was a Period. And during it the land was barren, so no animals. And weren't porpoises mammals, animals who had developed on land and then gone back in the sea later on? So he'd been talking nonsense. She leafed on through the table, and found that the first mammals didn't evolve until the Triassic, a mere 250 million years ago. Huh, mere newcomers! she thought. And how many millions of years did it take for the porpoises to decide they didn't like scuttling about on the land but would be more comfortable in the sea?

She shut the book with a snap. She thought she'd hang on to it - it was interesting because it showed that Professor Crust didn't know what he was talking about. If he was searching for fossils he wasn't an archaeologist, and if he was searching for human relics he wasn't a palaeontologist, so what was he? And if he was a palaeontologist, he was a really bad one who didn't know his periods or his porpoises. So was he just pulling the wool over her eyes because she was a child who wouldn't know better? If so, he needed to think again. And if he was neither a proper archaeologist or a proper palaeontologist, what was he, and what was he doing here?

She felt very pleased with herself. She had spotted a mystery, and solved it. Well, half of it, anyway. She would reward herself with a little relaxation, looking for the Worm and Mercy Cott. She had brought her book with her, the one she had bought from Mr.Belhatchett. She settled happily back into her window seat.

She was disappointed about Mercy Cott. She could find no mention, though there was a sentence or two about Roland Fossett who had disappeared like Mercy. If she had been eaten, as Sir Lancelot said, perhaps Roland had too? As Mr.Baggott had said, it would take more than one girl to satisfy a hungry wyrm. The book used that spelling, 'wyrm', and she thought that was better so she would adopt it.

There was a brief passage about the Linton Wyrm that lived just north on the Scottish border, which 'would terrorise the nearby countryside, destroying most anything in its path – livestock, farmland and locals. No one dared approach the beast or its den, until the story made it to the local laird of Lariston, one William or John de Somerville. Somerville went to that place that all others had deserted. When the Wyrm emerged, Somerville urged his horse forward, shoving his lance – cleverly tipped with a burning peat – into the worm's mouth, causing a fatal injury.'

The Laidley Wyrm from nearby Bamburgh was a more complicated story, because different versions had it that the wyrm was really an enchanted princess who could be turned back into a human by kissing the wyrm. Kitty thought that seemed rather unlikely, she preferred the Linton story. Then the book talked of the Lambton Wyrm from County Durham, slain by Sir John Lambton who *'after consulting a local Wise Woman, donned armour bedecked with razor-sharp spikes and vanquished the worm, whose body was cut to shreds by the barbs'*. Plainly being a wyrm was a fairly short-lived career choice in those days.

Having spent nearly two pages setting the scene by describing these other wyrms, the book was strangely reticent about the Crayle Wyrm. No one was definitely eaten by it, it seemed to have destroyed no crops or livestock, and in return no one had killed it. Perhaps it had been a vegetarian wyrm? It had simply been there, apparently, and now was not.

But then she found something wonderful. There, almost at the end of the Castle Crayle chapter, was another poem about the Wyrm of Crayle, a whole poem in old-fashioned language. Well, that proved it, didn't it? Stories and rumours were one thing, but two whole poems? She was delighted.

'Ye windes do blowe sae wilde and high,' she read aloud,
'Ye waves do toss and rore,
But deepe and darke and quite I lie
Behint ye angrie shore.

Behint ye sand and neath ye stane,
I sleepe five hundred yere
And dreme of fleshe and blud and bone,
Of sacrifise and fere.

For down ye yeres ye fyres of hell
Beneath ye waters cribbed and tame
Do wait till men shall brake ye spell
And loose agen dred Hades' flame.

Tho few remmember me today
Ye days of fire will come agen,
I'll rise in wroth and hunte mine prey
Amonge ye world of men.'

For a moment everything around her seemed to fade just a little. The sunlight through the window dimmed, the colours of the floor and the bright backs of the books were suddenly muted, the faint sounds of the wind and the gulls outside and the children calling from the beach were silenced and the blood no longer pulsed in her ear. Just for two seconds, the world paused, and then the colours returned and things resumed their normal pace. She closed her book and put her feet to the floor. Everything was normal. But just for that moment, she felt she had sensed another world, a world that lay behind and beneath, that waited down the weary years ... and just for that moment, twitching in his long sleep, the Wyrm had stirred, and the world had stirred with him.

VI

"Why does your nose run and your feet smell?" Kitty asked, closing the door behind her.

Melody looked up from her computer screen and made an exasperated face, but you could tell she didn't mean it. "My feet don't smell, I don't think," she said.

"How do you know? I mean, you wouldn't necessarily notice, would you? They're at one end and your nose is at the other. How come 'fat chance' and 'slim chance' mean the same thing? Shouldn't they be opposites?" Kitty perched on the corner of the desk.

"Have you come for any particular purpose, or just to be a nuisance?"

"Just to be a nuisance, I think. What are you doing?"

"Accounts."

"Oh." Kitty was silent for a moment. "Is that like maths? I'm quite good at maths at school. What does "quite" actually mean? Because if you say something is "quite nice" it means it isn't actually all that nice, only a bit. Yet some people say "that song is quite wonderful" which means it's very wonderful indeed. So what does "quite" mean?"

"I don't know. It's confusing, isn't it?"

"Quite. Would you like to come to the beach?"

"Yes, but I'm busy. You go for me."

"You're no fun. Where do you keep all the money?"

"What money?"

"All the money people give you to come and see the Castle."

"There isn't all that much, actually. Not actual cash. Most people pay with their credit cards so it just gets into the Castle account automatically, and then I have to add it all up. If there is any cash, I take it to the Post Office and pay it in."

"Do you like Mr.Belhatchett?"

"Not particularly."

"Nor do I. Can I help with anything?"

"Not really. I do it all on the computer. I've got to transfer some money to Lady Sybil's private account. She wants a thousand pounds, just for her own spending money. That'll wipe out any profit we've made this week. It's no way to run a business."

Kitty thought about this. "Couldn't you just say no?"

Melody laughed shortly. "You're joking! You've seen what she's like. I'd get the sack."

"Not if you controlled all the money."

"Sorry?"

"I mean, you do all this on the internet, don't you? Moving money around and so on? So why doesn't she do it herself?"

"She doesn't know how, and she's too lazy to learn. And Sir Lancelot hasn't a clue."

"So when you get into the bank account, you must have to put in a password or something. Who knows the password?"

"Just me, but Lady Sybil has it written down somewhere. And Sir Lancelot, if he remembers where he put it."

"Then change the password so you're the only person who can get in. Then they can't sack you because they won't be able to get at the money. They'll need you. You'd be in charge."

Melody thought for a moment. "I couldn't do that. She'd call the police."

"What would they do? It's not as if you've stolen the money, you'd just be doing your job and keeping it safe."

"You're a very devious child, you know that?"

Before Kitty could reply to this compliment – if it was a compliment, she wasn't sure – there was a knock on the door and it opened.

"Ah, here you are!" said Billy Cott, "can I come in?"

He looked quite like a pirate, Kitty thought, with his hair tied back in the pony-tail and his stained canvas smock and a red handkerchief round his neck. He had turned his wellingtons down so they looked like old fashioned sea boots. She thought he was very dashing and rather handsome. She got down off the desk and went to draw him into the room.

"Come in," she said, "do you know Melody? Melody, this is Billy Cott, Faith and Charity's brother."

Melody looked at him and blushed. She had plainly never seen anything like him in her office. In his turn Billy took off his woolly hat and turned it in his hands, shuffling his feet.

"How do?" he muttered. Melody said nothing, just stared.

Kitty thought she should take charge of the situation. "Why have you come?" she asked. "I mean, it's nice to see you, just we weren't expecting ..."

"Ah yes, pet," he said, "I came to tell you we can't take you out in the *Mercy* tomorrow. We've a wee problem with the engine, and have to get the spare part from the Volvo place in Newcastle. So we're stuck."

"Oh, shame. How long will that take?"

"Twa-three days, like."

"What does that mean?"

"Can you not speak English, man? Two or three days," he annunciated carefully.

"I can speak English perfectly well, thank you, just not your kind. The trip can wait, it's not a problem. But while you're here, can I ask you something?"

"Of course, pet."

"Why is your boat called the *Mercy*?"

"Ah, now that's a thing. There was a girl called Mercy in our family, a long time ago. It's a sad story, like."

"I asked your Ma but she wouldn't tell me."

"No, she doesn't approve of all these old stories. But she isn't a Cott, you see, she just married my Da."

"So what happened to Mercy?"

"She was a bonny lass by all accounts, and she fell in love with a young fella called Roland. One of the Fossetts, he was, and his family were furious. They couldn't have one of theirs marrying into a common family."

"Well, why am I not surprised? Nothing changes, does it?" Melody said softly. "Sorry, go on."

"Well, Roland disappeared, see? One day he was here in the Castle, and the next he wasn't. The family had spirited him away, sent him off to foreign parts, people said. An' poor Mercy was beside herself, because she'd fallen pregnant."

"Oh dear," Melody whispered. "And her own family?"

"Well, it was different times then, wasn't it? They chucked her out, wouldn't have anything to do with her, called her a whore and other things worse. So by all accounts she drowned herself, just walked into the sea and was never seen again."

"They didn't find her body?"

"Na, not round here, like. The currents run swift along these shores, she'd have been swept far away. Probably wash up down Yorkshire or Lincolnshire, I should think. We just have to hope whoever found her had the decency to bury her properly."

"And what happened after?"

"Nothing happened, that was it. But it was a great shame in the family. Not her getting pregnant, that happens all the time, like, but the family's cruelty putting her out. We've never forgotten it, or lived down the shame. That's why we named the boat for her."

"But she wasn't eaten? Sir Lancelot thought that something ate her."

Billy snorted. "Haddaway, don't be daft! What could eat a great girl? No, she drowned."

Kitty thought about this sad story. She thought she could understand how it might be, suddenly finding yourself cast out from the family that had kept you warm and safe all your life, losing the person you loved most in the world, and a little life growing inside and depending on you when you had nothing to offer it, no food, no shelter, no comfort. The walk over the hard stones of the beach and into the dark water must have been terrible. She had been alone several times in her own short life, but had no idea how to feel desperate enough to let the waves close over your head and choke the life out of you.

"And did Billy mind you choosing the name? He isn't family, is he?"

"Na, never him. He isn't a Cott, but he knows the story well enough and he has a soft spot for our family."

"For some more than others, I imagine?"

Billy chuckled. "Aye, that's right enough. Though he isn't quite sure which one in particular!"

"Because he can't tell one from another? I can. Faith has a brown watch strap and a little mole on her wrist, and Charity has a black strap and no mole."

"Well, no flies on you, are there?" he laughed. "No, true enough, he hasn't spotted that. But it's more than that. One of them likes him and the other doesn't, and he doesn't know which. It's quite funny to watch, really."

"Poor Billy. If he did know, might he be disappointed because it was the wrong one?"

"No, never him. He can't tell one from the other, can he, so whichever one it was he'd be happy!"

Melody stirred at her desk, and cleared her throat. "Look, fascinating though this is, I do have work to do, you know. Could you operate your lonely hearts club somewhere else, Kitty, please?"

Kitty looked at her and wondered if there was more to her words than met the eye. Other hearts can be lonely, she thought, not just Billy Brannicle's. Melody caught her look and glanced away, blushing again.

Billy Cott took the hint, though, and made his farewells. Kitty followed him out of the door.

"Billy," she called softly after him, "why don't you come again? We'd love to see you, some of us." He grinned. "Oh yes? Well, in that case ... you're a bit young for me, mind ..."

"Not me, you fool, find someone your own age!" She dropped her voice. "She's quite pretty, isn't she, Melody? Didn't you think?"

Now it was Billy's turn to blush. "Oh ... yes, I suppose ..."

"Come on, Billy, pretty or not?"

"All right, yes. Right bonny, she is. Don't tell her I said that."

"Of course I won't. You can tell her yourself, next time you come."

Billy Cott looked confused, and walked off down the corridor with a wave of farewell. Kitty followed more slowly, thinking. If anyone dared to interfere in her own life as she did with others, she'd be furious. But when she did it, somehow it seemed all right. Sometimes people needed a shove in the right direction.

Kitty followed Billy Cott in the direction of the village but his long stride soon carried him out of sight. She was heading for Blue-Sky Lovechild's dark emporium, hoping for a cup of tea and a chat, but was arrested by the sight of Professor Crust standing at the grass triangle. He was deep in conversation with a man in a blue boiler-suit whose white van was parked nearby, and Dashwood Belhatchett. This was interesting, she thought. What had an archaeologist to do with the man from the Post Office, or he with him? She drew into a corner of one of the houses, and watched.

The conversation was quite animated, and involved a lot of pointing in various directions, mainly towards the beach and the castle. At one point the blue man produced some plans and they all examined them intently. Perhaps the professor was seeking Belhatchett's local knowledge? To her over-active imagination, it looked more as though they were plotting.

Presently the meeting broke up. The boiler-suit drove off towards the harbour, and Belhatchett strode off to his Post Office. The professor stood looking round for a moment as though not sure what to do, then set off across the grass in the general direction of the castle. Kitty came out of her hiding place and followed him, the visit to Sky forgotten. He took a lane she hadn't seen before, but realised it must go down to the castle and hit the curtain wall about halfway along the land side, where the rock was highest and her tower rose a hundred feet above.

She was right, it seemed, but when she emerged from the bushes on either side of the lane and found herself right underneath the towering wall of rock, Professor Crust was sitting on a bench waiting for her.

"Ah, I thought it was you behind me," he said affably. "I wanted to have a word with you, so this is very convenient. Come and share my bench."

She sat, and waited to hear what he had to say. He didn't speak immediately, but sat beaming round and humming softly to himself. Eventually he cleared his throat and turned towards her.

"I have a confession to make," he said. "I didn't tell you the whole truth yesterday, about my researches. I'm afraid in my ... er, business ... it is often necessary to play one's cards close to one's chest, as it were."

"I understand," she said, "what didn't you tell me?"

"Well, I wasn't straight with you. But when you mentioned the Wyrm of Castle Crayle I was rather taken aback, as it were. I didn't think many people would know about it, never mind the first person I met when I arrived here. That's why I was taken aback. Because ..."

He leaned closer and dropped his voice like a conspirator, "because, my dear, the Wyrm is exactly why I'm here. My purpose is to try and find some evidence of the Wyrm's existence in the ... er ... archaeological record ..."

"I thought it was just a myth?"

"Ah, indeed! That's what most people think, of course. This area is rich in myths and legends and it's easy to believe this is just another of them. But ..." he dropped his voice still lower and fixed her with his eyes, "... what if it weren't? What if the Wyrm had been a real creature? What if its bones still lie under the earth somewhere nearby? What then?"

"Some sort of prehistoric thing?" she said, "like a dinosaur or something?"

"Exactly! A fossil record, perhaps ... and if it were ..."

"This place would be famous, I should think. The newspapers ..."

"Precisely! And that's why it must be a secret, you see, a secret I am sharing with you because I can tell you're a discreet person who knows how to keep her mouth shut! You mustn't tell anyone, see, because if the news gets out that such a distinguished archaeologist as myself is taking it seriously, the village and the Castle will be flooded with treasure seekers and hippies and conspiracy theorists and we'll be unable to continue our work seriously."

There it was again, she thought. That confusion between Archaeology and Palaeontology. Something wasn't right.

"So if you did find something, it would be fossilised, would it? Not real bones, but the fossils of bones. From the Ordovician, perhaps?"

"Mm, yes, yes, quite possibly! The Ordovician or the Silurian, very possible."

"But they were millions of years ago, weren't they? And there weren't any people around then, they hadn't been invented yet. So where would the stories have come from?"

"Ah, well, that's the mystery, isn't it? That's the puzzle, all right!"

He beamed at her, his mouth smiling but his eyes not.

You're lying, she thought, looking at him. I don't know what the truth is, but you aren't telling it. If you were a real archaeologist you'd know that fossils and prehistoric creatures are in Palaeontology. And if you were a real palaeontologist you'd know that there was nothing moving on land in the Ordovician. No animals, no dinosaurs, nothing at all. The dinosaurs were from the Triassic which was many millions of years later on, she wasn't sure how many. That would be in the book she had in her pocket, she could look it up. This man didn't know what he was talking about.

That was a thought; she pulled the book out. His eyes lit up. "Oh, so you've found my little opus, have you?" he said with a twinkle. Kitty thought he was trying to look modest, and failing.

"Do you mean you wrote this?" she asked politely.

He laughed deprecatingly. "Just something I dashed off when I was at university," he said. "I've done much better things since then, but I suppose it was a start."

"Which university were you at?" she asked.

"Oh, a little one, you know. You won't have heard of it. But it had a good Archaeology department."

Kitty said nothing. Archaeology and Palaeontology weren't the same thing. She knew that, and he didn't. This wasn't his book.

"I have to go now," she said politely, getting up, "Miss Trinket wants me to help her with something."

She walked round the perimeter of the castle towards the car park in a rather confused state of mind. She needed to get away and think. Some things were clear enough. The man was a fake. He claimed to be an archaeologist but he was searching for Palaeontology. And he wasn't a palaeontologist because he didn't know his Eras from his Periods. So what was he after? It couldn't be, could it, that he believed the wyrm was real and still alive? That was ridiculous, how could that be? And if it were, did he think he was going to find it and capture it? How would he do that, with a whole castle on top of it?

One thing was plain. She should never have mentioned the wyrm to him. She had been too trusting, and the professor was taking her for a fool. She wondered whether to confide in Melody. She'd be pleased at the idea there might be some unknown fossil creature here, it might make the Castle more famous. But no, she would keep quiet for now. She'd already made one mistake, probably, by talking out of turn.

As she made her way up to the Library, Perkins the cat mewed at her and followed her up the stairs. Once she had settled herself in the window seat with another book, the cat jumped up and settled in her lap, purring. She read happily for a while, stroking Perkins. She had found a book that told in some detail about the Redcaps, Gyests and Boggarts that haunted the folklore of this region. They were nothing to do with wyrms, particularly, but they were entertaining. The Redcaps were short, goblin-like creatures like old men with talons for fingers, and always wore a red cap. If travellers stumbled across the lair of a Redcap, it would throw boulders at them and try to kill them. If it succeeded, it would soak its cap in the blood of its victims to ensure that it retained its crimson hue.

Gyests could also be called Ghests or Bargyests, and lurked in moors and marshes to lure travellers off the path and over a cliff or into a bog. They could disguise themselves as men, horses, huge dogs or even stacks of hay. She wondered about that one. How would imitating a stack of hay be helpful? No one walked past and said "Hey, there's a stack of hay, let's follow it!" Boggarts could also be called Boggles, and lived in people's houses. They were a sort of House Elf from Harry Potter, but wicked, turning the milk sour and making the dogs go lame and stealing things.

"That's our cat," said a voice. She looked up. The Sisters had appeared silently, and she was so absorbed she hadn't seen or heard them come.

She put a finger in the book to mark her place. "I'm sorry?" she said, "I wasn't paying attention. What did you say?"

"That's our cat. And it's sitting on you," said Clorinda.

"... sitting on you."

"... on you."

Kitty looked at the cat fondly. "Yes, she looks lovely and comfortable, doesn't she? She just came and jumped up, I didn't ask her to."

"It shouldn't sit on you," said Lady Drusilla.

"Not on you, no," echoed Lady Clorinda.

"It ought to sit on us, because it's our cat," whispered Pamilia

Kitty was a little nonplussed. "Oh? She can't sit on all of you. And do you think she understands that? Have you told her?"

The six eyes regarded her with a dead, fish-like gaze that made Kitty think of the harbour. This was ridiculous, she thought. No one told a cat where to sit, cats made up their own minds. They were either too stupid to know what was expected of them, or too clever to take any notice.

"You should have known," said Clorinda accusingly. "It's our cat, you shouldn't be touching it."

"... touching it, no."

" ... no ..."

Kitty began to feel irritated. "Actually," she said icily, "I didn't touch her. She touched me. She followed me, and jumped up, and that's all there is to it. If you want her, why don't you call her?"

"We won't do that," came the distant, weary voice.

"No, we shouldn't have to ..."

"... have to, no ..."

Kitty had heard enough. "This is stupid," she said, getting up. The cat didn't seem to mind being summarily decanted onto the window seat, but arched its back and stretched, glaring at the Sisters. Then it jumped smoothly down and scampered off.

"Now see what you've done?" cried Drusilla, "you've frightened it!"

"No I didn't ..." Kitty began, but it was pointless to argue; no kind of sense would penetrate that fog of vague resentment. She would take the book back to her room and read it there. No one would notice. She walked off, followed by fluttering cries of "You shouldn't ..." and "It's our cat, and you've stolen it!" and "A cat thief, that's what ..." that faded as she closed the door gently behind her.

Dinner down in the kitchen was sausages and mash, with peas and onion gravy. There were stewed pears and ice cream afterwards. When she told Ma and the twins about the Sisters, they laughed and said "Haddaway, pet, it's not their cat. That's a kitchen cat, that is, and has been from a kitten like its mother before it! Take no notice!"

But notice was to be taken, apparently, for at the end of the meal Cartilege appeared and summoned her upstairs. His Lordship and Her Ladyship wanted to see her in the dining room. The Sisters had been telling tales. She followed the butler's stiff back up the stairs, listening to his knees creak. This was silly. It was a cat, that's all.

Lady Sybil sat facing the door, her back ramrod straight, her luxuriant grey hair coiled into elaborate shapes that looked hard, as though set in stone. Behind her stood Sir Lancelot, while Melody sat in her usual place looking pale and agitated. The Sisters sat opposite her, twittering and fluttering their hands.

Lady Sybil's tone was icy. "Now look here, young lady, this isn't working. We can't be having this, not after all we've done for you ..."

Kitty broke in indignantly, "Can't be having what? And you haven't done very much really ..."

But Lady Sybil was into her stride now, and would not be interrupted. "After all we've done for you, taken you in off the street although we didn't know you from Adam, no idea who your people were or what you were doing here."

"But you know perfectly well, it was Marcia ..."

"Only to have our charity thrown back in our faces! You've done nothing but cause trouble ever since you arrived, and this is the last straw. You have to go."

"Might be different if you was pretty," muttered Sir Lancelot, looking down his nose. "Quite jolly, having one or two pretty gels around the place. Something to look at, anyway. But you ain't."

"Not pretty at all," breathed Drusilla, and her sisters whispered their agreement.

"Quite plain, in fact ..." added Clorinda.

"Ugly, I'd say. All that red hair," whispered Pamilia spitefully, "and the glasses, most unbecoming ..."

"Yes, I know!" tittered Clorinda. "And she wears those awful clothes, like a tramp or a criminal ..."

Lady Sybil glanced at them, not bothering to hide her irritation. "Nothing to do with looks, you blithering idiots! It's a question of gratitude, and you, young lady, don't seem to know the meaning of the word. You've slept in our beds ..."

"Only one bed ..."

"Slept in our beds, and eaten us practically out of house and home, and disturbed the servants and Trinket ... well, Trinket hasn't been the same since you arrived, completely useless, dithering about and arguing the toss! No, you have to go!"

She spoke quietly and viciously, and the words pooled on the bright floor between them. Kitty felt that if she turned round she would see them sliding wet and sticky down the wall behind her.

"Got to go!" Drusilla bleated, and "Yes, go ..." and "Go, yes ..." repeated her sisters in a dismal chorus like sheep on a distant hill.

"Beat her!" broke in Sir Lancelot, "she needs a good beating, that's what she needs! I was beaten when I was young, and it never did me any harm." His eyes were hot and his mouth slack as he contemplated violence.

"Yes, beat her!" said Drusilla.

"With a cane ..."

"... a whip! ..."

"... there's a carpet-beater ..."

Kitty felt her face flaming and was about to dare them to try anything of the sort. She eyed the remains of the meal on the table, noting the knives and other implements she would snatch up, but Melody Trinket stood and said loudly "Sir Lancelot, you may not do anything of the sort! You do not have that right, it would be completely illegal!"

Sir Lancelot was outraged. His face went very red, and he shouted "Well, really! Whatever next? What business is it of anybody's what I do in my own castle? If I can't beat someone in the privacy of my own home, where can I beat them?"

"You can't, you idiot," said Lady Sybil tightly, "you can't beat 'em anywhere. There are laws, unfortunately. Think of something else, for goodness sake!"

Kitty turned on her heel and stalked out, slamming the door as hard as she could behind her. History was repeating itself. Her cheeks were flaming and her throat was blocked with indignant tears waiting to burst out. The cheek of it, the sheer bloody-minded stupidity of it!

But Melody had been magnificent. Kitty hoped she wouldn't suffer for it. She would really have liked to go to the kitchen and ask Ma or one of the twins for a hug, but they'd have gone home by now, their work finished for the day. It was so annoying, for she was just starting to enjoy this place, she had made some friends and had plenty to occupy her mind. And those stupid, vapid, moronic women had spoiled it all out of nothing but empty-headed spite.

Her head full of plans for extravagant revenge, she went up to bed. Perkins did not appear, but shortly afterwards, Melody did. She poked her head round the door, saw Kitty still sitting up dry-eyed, and sat on the bed. Wordlessly they put their arms round each other.

"Thank you," Kitty whispered, "you were marvellous. And very brave."

"I was, wasn't I? They didn't say much after you stormed out. I don't know what'll happen tomorrow though."

"Well, if you've got any sense, you'll get up early and go and change that password. That'll give you some leverage."

"I'll think about it. You going to be all right now?"

"Yes, I feel better. Here, what did you think of Billy this morning? He's nice, isn't he?"

"What are you up to?"

"Come on, admit it. You did think he was good looking, didn't you? Did you notice his pony-tail?"

"He seemed ... well, a bit rough?"

"No, never, he's a gentleman. He does do a rough job though. I expect there's a bit of a fishy smell too, but you'll soon get used to that."

"Do you mind if we talk about something else?"

"Well, I think I might go to sleep now. It's been a funny day. Thank you again. Don't forget the password, good night."

VII

"Kitty, love," Melody said next morning, "Lady Sybil is still fuming about you. She says you have to work for your keep in future."

"Shan't. She can't make me. I was invited here for a holiday, and that's what I'm going to have, so there."

"Well, I told her it was illegal to use child labour, but she's not listening to anything I say. I think you should go along with it for now."

"Why?"

"She mentioned Social Services. She said you appear to have no parents, no home and no money, so she'll telephone Social Services and tell them to take you into care."

"She can't do that!" Kitty said, alarmed. "Can she? Will they listen to her?"

"Well, she is Lady Sybil Fossett, she's quite well known, so they might. And how could you prove that you're not homeless and have a perfectly good family? Of course you could eventually, but in the meantime they'd probably take you away and make you live with a foster family in Newcastle."

Kitty looked out of the window, where the sun shone and the wind blew and the waves were glinting on the beach.

"What about the police?" she asked. "If I called the police and told them this nasty old woman was trying to use me as an unpaid slave, wouldn't they arrest her?"

"They'd certainly have to investigate. But while they did it, they'd have to remove you from the scene of the crime, and that would mean Social Services again, so you'd be in the same boat."

"What do you think I should do?"

"I suggested you should work with me this morning. I've got a job that will take us quite some time ... look!"

Across the floor were stacked great piles of papers, forms and invoices and lists. They covered half the floor of this large room, and some of the stacks had collapsed into unruly heaps. The breeze from the open window was busily muddling up the heaps, too. "We need to go through all these and sort them into their proper order, one year at a time. The filing system is a complete mess, no one's organised it properly for years. I could do with a hand, as you can see ..."

Kitty thought for a moment. Melody was right, the adult world would have only one solution in the immediate future, and that would see her taken from the Castle and sent somewhere else much worse. Mother would rescue her when she returned home from America, of course, but in the meantime ...

"All right," she sighed, "where do we start?"

"I have no idea, frankly." Melody gazed at the mess. It certainly was daunting. They'd have to examine each sheet of paper carefully and find a date on it. Then it could be put into a little pile with others of the same year. Later each year would have to be put in date order.

"We need some blank sheets, to write the years on," Kitty said, picking up some of the papers and examining them. "I think this lot goes back to the 1980s at least." She rummaged in the drawers of Melody's desk and found a block of printer paper and a big marker pen. She began to write '1980' and '1981' and '1982' on each one while Melody took them and arranged them on the empty part of the carpet.

Before long they were both dancing round the room as though they were engaged in a complicated game, taking an armful of papers and dealing them onto the piles according to their year. Even after Melody closed the window there was still a draught across the room from the gap under the door, and more than once their carefully stacked piles of paper took off across the floor so they both had to dive on them, giggling.

"Oops, there goes 1997 again!" Kitty laughed, chasing the errant papers. "Why are some years more flighty than others? We need some weights to hold them down."

"But then we'd have to lift the weight up every time we wanted to add another sheet," said Melody, diving sideways to grab 2003 before it escaped. "I know, if we moved them all against the wall, at least the draught could only get them from one direction and not both."

It took most of the morning to complete stage one of the task so all the papers were in their right years at least. Melody breathed a sigh of relief, got up from the floor and slumped in her chair. She gazed at Kitty. Her eyes looked a little watery and emotions were chasing each other across her face as though she didn't know whether to cry or laugh or sigh with relief.

"I feel exhausted," she said in a quavery voice. "Thank you. I couldn't have done that without you. I was ... well, a bit of a mess, as you saw. But you cut right through it. You're very clever."

Kitty felt a flush creeping across her cheeks, and looked down at the floor. "It was nothing," she said, "anyone could have ..."

"No, anyone couldn't have!" Melody cried. "I couldn't, for a start! But you could, and you did, and ... I'm not very good at this sort of thing. I don't know how to behave when people are nice. What am I supposed to do? What would your mother do?"

"She'd give me a hug and a kiss, and she'd put the kettle on and get the biscuits out," said Kitty, grinning, "so you could do that."

"Oh!" exclaimed Melody, her hand over her mouth. "Oh, yes! Of course, that would ... come here!"

The hug was a little awkward because Kitty's arms were still full of 2001, but she appreciated it all the same, and accepted a dry little kiss on one cheek. Up close, Melody smelled nicely of lavender and something else, something slightly musky and old. Then, blushing deeply, she got up and went to fill the kettle with something of a spring in her step.

By lunch time they had sorted 1980 to 1994 into proper date order, and felt a sense of satisfaction in a job part done. They had made an excellent start, and Melody announced that she would take Kitty out for lunch.

"We can walk down to the village," she said, "and go in the pub. I've never been there, but I believe they do food."

"Are children allowed?"

"Of course they are. At least, I think they are. We'll find out, won't we?"

On the way, they were passed by two of the white vans. Another stood at the far end of the car park, and two men were fussing over something at the open doors at the back. Kitty was still puzzled. If they were indeed involved in Professor Crust's search for archaeology, they seemed to be doing it in some pretty unlikely places. Were archaeological remains usually scattered so randomly all over a village? Surely it was better to pick the most likely place and keep digging down, not parking in odd corners and pushing long rods into the earth? What did that prove?

The pub was called *'The Dragon'* and had a rather fine sign hanging outside with a curling dragon, smoke coming from its mouth, about to attack a girl in a white dress tied to a pole. As you went in through the door and wiped your feet on the mat, there was a board on the wall that told the story of the dragon. *'Local legend has it that a fierce dragon came out of the sea and was about to devour a maiden named Mavis or Meg, when the heroic Rolph or Roland Fossick intervened and fought the dragon. After a savage battle the hero was killed and eaten, but the maiden escaped. However, filled with sorrow for her brave young saviour, she later drowned herself. The dragon was never seen again.'*

"Huh, that's not right!" Kitty snorted. "It wasn't Mavis or Meg, it was Mercy, and she was a Cott. And she wasn't attacked by a dragon. She was in love with Roland Fossett but he disappeared, and that's why she drowned herself."

"You'd better tell the landlord," Melody said, but Kitty could tell she wasn't serious.

Children were allowed in the pub, it seemed. She didn't like the smell of stale beer very much, but it was nice to see ordinary men and women sitting around and chatting like normal people, not fierce harridans and vague eccentrics like the Fossetts, or vicious lunatics like the Sisters. Kitty ate a meat pie with gravy and peas, and Melody had a salad. They talked idly, Kitty telling of her home at Strathtay in Scotland, with forestry plantations covering the hills and the snow-topped Cairngorm mountains as a backdrop, and the brawling rivers that lined every valley.

Melody spoke of her own childhood in Melton Mowbray, where the famous pork pies are made. "There are more fat people in Mowbray than anywhere else I've ever seen," she said, "I expect they like their own pies too much. How's yours, by the way?"

"Lovely. It isn't a pork pie, though, it's ham and mushroom."

"I used to think I was going to work in London," Melody continued. "I saw myself in a plush modern office in a tower-block at Canary Wharf, working for some international bank, eating tofu and beansprouts for lunch and going for a run every morning. Instead of which I'm in that great draughty room with a wicked witch for a boss, and I don't think Mrs.Cott's even heard of tofu."

"Nor have I," said Kitty, mopping up the last of her gravy. "Do you think anyone will notice if I lick the plate? I went to London once. Mother took us. We went to the Tate Modern, it's an art gallery."

"I know what it is. Was it nice?"

"They had brilliant ice creams."

Melody laughed. "I don't think ice cream is actually the most important thing about an art gallery," she said.

"It is when you're twelve. I've finished now. Shall I take you to say hallo to Sky Lovechild? Her name's Denise Watkins really, but she says she's re-inventing herself."

"That's what I ought to do," Melody said as they went out into the street. "I should re-invent myself into someone radical and confident and able to stand up to Lady Sybil."

"You could try wearing jeans to work instead of that sad business-suit, that'd be a start. You're pretty really, if you'd only let yourself be. At least, Billy Cott thinks so."

"Kitty!" squeaked Melody, "you haven't discussed me with him, have you? Please tell me you haven't!"

"No, no, would I do that?" Kitty gazed at her wide-eyed and innocent. "Look, there's another white van. This one's got something written on it, look, down behind the door. It's rather small, I can't see what it says."

Melody and Sky got on rather well, really, considering how different they were. Sky made them both a cup of herbal tea, and Kitty badgered Melody into buying one of the colourful tie-dye scarves to wear with her jeans. "You could thread it through the loops and use it as a belt," she said, "that'd look very relaxed."

Sky was able to tell them about tofu when they asked. "I looked it up," she said, "it's bean-curds, made from soya beans.

They mix them with milk and squash them into blocks, and you cut it up and eat it. You fry it, usually. It doesn't have much taste of its own so you coat it with other things to make it interesting."

"What's the point, then? Why not just eat something that already tastes nice?"

"Well, it's supposed to be good for you. It has amino acids, iron, calcium for your bones ..."

"I don't need calcium," Kitty muttered, "I've got all the bones I need already ..."

"And it's good for the planet."

"What, the planet eats tofu?"

Sky laughed. "No, silly, but it has a light footprint. Meaning it doesn't take loads of energy to make it, and it doesn't produce global warming gases."

"But I expect the cows do, that make the milk. Cows fart, don't they? So would I, probably, after I'd eaten it."

"Oh, yes. I hadn't thought of that. Still ..." Sky picked up a newspaper from the floor nearby. "... speaking of the planet, I saw something interesting this morning. Look."

Kitty and Melody took the paper between them. It wasn't a normal newspaper, but was called *Global Warming, the Fight to Save Mother Earth'* and had a large headline in heavy type at the top, *'Sea levels to rise fifty feet, experts warn'*. Down at the bottom of the page Sky's pointing finger led them to a brief article headed *'Vandals home in on Northumberland'*.

'In sinister moves to exploit and despoil the dramatic coast of Northumberland ...' they read, *'... major utility companies are eyeing new experimental technology that will allow them to extract coal from vast seams under the bed of the North Sea. In pursuit of profit they are cynically ignoring the risk to wildlife and the well-being of the inhabitants of the coastal area. Environmental experts warn that the potential harm could be immense and render hundreds of square miles of the seabed a virtual desert. Fish stocks would be affected, and with them the lives of seals and otters that depend on them, as well as the livelihoods of inshore fishermen.'*

That'll be Billy and Billy, then, Kitty thought.

'A spokesman for Five Quarter, a pioneer company in the

field, claimed that the process requires no new technology and there is practically no exploration risk thanks to detailed geology reports from the old National Coal Board. However he went on to say that Five Quarter have at present no plans to open new fields in Northumberland.

Global Warming calls upon the government to come clean about this dangerous new development and reveal the extent of the proposed raid upon our delicate environment.'

"That's interesting," Kitty said politely. "Oh! I just thought! Do you think that's what all the white vans are for? Professor Crust told me they were doing archaeology."

Sky took the paper and folded it again. "Well, the thought had occurred, yes. And I saw an archaeological dig once, and it was a field with lots of trenches, and loads of students digging with little trowels. I've seen nothing like that here."

"Have you noticed that some of the vans have writing on the side? Low down just behind the doors? I don't know what it says, though."

"No, I haven't noticed. We should try to find out."

"I might be able to help," offered Melody. "I could have a look on the computer. I can use Google to search for this Five Quarter thing, or stuff about coal under the sea. I'll do it when we get back."

"Good," said Kitty. "While you're at it, could you look up Professor Wilberforce Crust, because I don't think he's quite what he says he is? Now, I think we should go down to the harbour and then home along the beach."

Melody rose and tucked the scarf she had bought into her handbag. "We'd better not take too long, though, because Cartilege will be waiting. I think he has a job for you. I wonder what it is?"

They said their goodbyes and promised to come again. As they took the little lane that led across the marsh to the harbour, another white van swished past and they were able to answer one question, at any rate.

"COGACO, it said," Kitty exclaimed. "Whatever is COGACO? You must look it up on the internet while I'm being enslaved and abused by Cartilege. I bet he's looking forward to it, the old pervert."

"I'm not sure a girl your age ought to know the meaning of that."

"Oh trust me, I've a pretty good idea. Girls talk, you know. And at boarding school they talk a lot, because there isn't much else to do."

At the harbour Billy Brannicle had his head down a hole in the deck and his bottom sticking in the air. Every so often he would say a muffled something and Billy Cott would pass him a spanner or a screwdriver.

"The new water pump came," Billy Cott said, beaming. "We should be in business by tomorrow!"

"Why do you need a water pump?" Kitty asked. "Can we come down the ladder? Melody's never been on a boat before. I have, of course, loads of times, but she hasn't and she's really interested. Why do you need a water pump if you're surrounded by perfectly good water? Can't you just make a hole and let it in? Or are you trying to pump it out? Melody wants to know, she's interested in … stuff like that."

Melody poked her in the back to make her stop, but climbed down the ladder anyway and they both sat and watched the Billies working, though they could only see the bottom half of Billy Brannicle.

"The engine needs to draw seawater in from outside to cool it down," Billy Cott explained, "and that's done by a pump. Ours stopped working, so Billy's fitting a new one. I'm doing the really important work, selecting the tools and telling him what to do, of course."

There was a muffled swearword from under their feet, and Melody put her hand over her mouth to stifle a giggle. Then she evidently decided the grown up thing to do was to show polite interest.

"And what do you catch, please, when your engine is working?" she said to Billy Cott.

He looked at her, and she blushed slightly. "At the moment, it's velvet crabs and lobsters," he said. "then later in the year there's cod and halibut, and Dover sole, whiting or haddock during the winter. There's always something."

"I thought there was a lot of fuss about declining fish stocks?"

"Oh, we do all right. The boat doesn't cost an awful lot to maintain because it's small, and there's only two of us to share the profits, so we don't complain. Further out to sea with big boats and lots of mouths to feed, there's competition from foreign fishers, but our only real worry is the weather."

"My goodness," said Kitty, "you two are having a real conversation. You sound almost like grown-ups!"

Billy Cott grinned at her, and said "We'll take you out, pet, when it's bumpy an' we'll see how grown up you are, puking over the side!"

"I wouldn't," she replied confidently. "I could do it. The one you ought to take out is Melody. She'd like that, wouldn't you, Melody?"

"I don't know. Not when it's rough, no."

Billy Cott looked at her seriously. "Come when it's calm, then. We'll look after you, don't worry," but before she could answer Billy Brannicle emerged from the depths with a great black smear of grease on his nose, and announced that he'd finished. The engine was fixed, and they'd better take a turn round the harbour to check. The girls rose to go. If it wasn't actually fixed and they broke down again, they might find themselves marooned and unable to get ashore, and there was stuff waiting for them up at the Castle.

Walking back along the beach Kitty kept an eye out for the Primeval Porpoise. She told Melody how it had looked at her out of the face of a wave.

"Are you sure it wasn't a seal, or an otter?" Melody said.

"That was what I thought. Well, I didn't think of an otter, but I did wonder about a seal. But Billy says there aren't any around at the moment."

"Which Billy?"

"Your Billy, Billy Cott."

"He's not my Billy, I can't think what you mean," Melody said, but Kitty knew better.

"Well, when you do know what I mean, and he asks you to marry him, will you get married in the Castle and I can be your bridesmaid?"

"Oh really, you ridiculous child, will you stop?" Melody burst out. "I've exchanged about three words with the man and you're trying to marry me off! Just stop it, will you? Besides, I doubt very much if there will ever be weddings in the Castle. It is in my Business Plan, but I can't see the Fossetts accepting any of that."

"I wonder why they won't? Don't they want to make lots of money? Oh look, there's a boat and it isn't the Billies'. I wonder what it's doing?"

A little way out and almost opposite the Castle was a low, black launch with a little cabin at the front. Something bobbed in the water nearby.

"Divers!" she said. "There are divers in the water, look."

As they watched, one of the divers suddenly upended himself and as he disappeared beneath the surface they had a glimpse of air-tanks and bright red swimming fins. In the back of the boat, two other men watched carefully.

"Why are they diving, I wonder? Are they fishing, or looking for treasure or something?"

"People do search for archaeology under the sea, you know. Shipwrecks and so on."

"We'll have to ask the Billies if there are any round here. They'll know. You can ask when you go to see Billy Cott." She fixed Melody with a stern look. "Which you will, or I'll want to know the reason why! How come the Fossetts have the Castle all to themselves? Shouldn't it belong to the Natural Truss or something?"

"National Trust, idiot! It's not a proper ancient monument, you see, that's why. Only the bottom bit of the tower is really old, and most of the south end is actually Victorian or Edwardian, added in the late 19th and early 20th centuries."

"That's the bit where your office is?"

"Yes. And of course the older part to the north is all in ruins, beyond economic repair. There's acres of it, so it would cost millions to rebuild, so even the National Trust aren't interested. And if they were, I don't get the impression the Fossetts would play ball. They prefer things as they are, even if it can't make much money."

Back in the top corridor Cartilege was waiting. Lady Sybil stood glowering in her doorway but said nothing. Kitty's heart sank. The morning had been nice, and they had enjoyed a lovely outing, but now her servitude was to begin.

"About time," creaked the old man. "You come with me, child, there's work to be done. Come!"

He took her arm in his claw and urged her back towards the stairs. Melody scuttled into her office and shut herself in with the orderly years. Kitty shook the butler's hand off, but followed obediently. A lamb to the slaughter, she thought.

Down they went through passages she knew until they reached the great hall with the grand staircase up to the Library. For one moment she wondered if her work was to be something in the Library, sorting books or something. She wouldn't mind that, but he led the way onwards, into a dark tunnel at the far end. They were entering the unknown, for she hadn't explored this far yet. This new corridor had few doors, but right at the end was an impressive portal, oak studded with iron bolts and large plaited iron handles. Cartilege drew out an enormous bunch of keys, rattled through them until he found the right one, and inserted it into the keyhole. The door creaked and seemed to take quite a lot of the old man's effort to open.

Beyond was something like the open cloister she had once seen at a cathedral, a portico that ran round four sides of a square. The one at the cathedral had been a pleasant place where monks might have strolled and sat in the past, with green grass and flowers in the middle. This one was grim, and the space in the middle just flagstones with a few tired weeds poking their heads feebly in the cracks. The other cloister had been sunny, but this one was dark and gloomy, for the walls that shut it in rose for many storeys so only a small square of daylight could be seen far above.

Cartilege led her along two sides of the cloister, then opened another door and ushered her in. In the dim light she could make out long tables on either side, all covered with plates and great dishes, cups and flagons and bowls, dull and dusty.

"The silver," he announced. "Your job, polish silver! There's rags there in that box, and silver polish. Get busy, I'll come back at teatime and see what you've done. Now then!" and he left. He pulled the door to behind him, and Kitty heard his keys rattle. He had locked her in. This was even worse than she had feared.

She looked round her. The room was lit only by a couple of small windows very far overhead. At one end was a great empty fireplace, and in the corners were piles of old furniture stacked all higgledy-piggledy, with spider webs and, probably, large spiders lurking. She didn't like spiders but she wasn't scared of them. They squished easily enough when you stepped on them. The box contained a lot of rags, some clean and some not, and a tin bottle of silver polish. She knew you put the polish on with one rag, rubbed and rubbed until it was bright, then polished it off with a clean rag. What she didn't know was whether she was going to do it or not. What would the old man do if she simply refused? Keep her locked in here until she obeyed? But surely Melody or Ma Cott would miss her and raise an alarm? It had to be illegal to imprison little girls, even awkward, obstinate ones.

As her eyes grew accustomed to the dim light she examined some of the silver. On the side of one chalice she could make out lettering, deeply incised, telling her that it belonged to *'Reginald de Vere Fossett'* in 1892. It was hard to know why Reginald de Vere Fossett would have wanted such an ugly thing. What would he have done with it? It was too big to use as a drinking cup, and too horrible to keep on the mantelpiece. She turned it over, looking for the silver marks. She knew nothing about silver marks, but thought there should be some, little stampings to show it was real silver. But there weren't, or at least she couldn't find them. Perhaps it wasn't real silver then? Perhaps this wasn't quite the treasure-trove it appeared to be, but just a collection of useless old junk? She searched on, picking up item after item, but found very few marks.

She cleared a space on one of the tables by the simple expedient of throwing the silver cups and plates up the other end and not caring where they landed. She brushed the surface clean with one of the rags, then hauled herself up and sat on it. Might as well make oneself as comfortable as possible, she thought, and wished for a cup of tea. Then, finding that just sitting wasn't quite enough, she made a pillow out of the rags and lay full-length on the table with her ankles crossed, staring up at the dim ceiling.

She relaxed, trying to think of all the words that ended in '... ough' and wondering why they sounded different – cough, bough, rough and dough, through and though ... the word 'through' reminded her of the route Cartilege had taken to get here. They had gone mostly straight, she thought. True, there had been a bit of up and down, but mainly they had come in a straight line, and that straight line had led them from the south end buildings, past the entrance to the central tower, and onwards in a roughly northerly direction. And they had walked for as much as five minutes after leaving the places she was familiar with. You could get quite far in five minutes. She was in the North End, somewhere in that great heap of jumbled masonry she looked down on from her north window in the tower, where the pigeons tumbled and clattered their wings. She was in the ruined half of the Castle, beyond repair and dangerous.

She looked round her again. It didn't look all that dangerous. It was dark and dusty and ill-cared for, certainly, but not a stone was out of place, the ceiling hadn't fallen in cob-webbed though it was, the grubby glass in the high windows was intact. This wasn't a ruin at all, it was just dirty. What about the rest of the buildings? Was this one isolated bit, still intact and usable, and the rest was a desert of dereliction? Or was the story about the ruins a lie? She thought about the cloister that had led her here – that had been grim but not ruinous. And the walls that rose above it, shutting out the sky, they hadn't been crumbling at all. So far as she could see, the north end was perfectly habitable with a little work.

So, why would people have been lying all these years? There was probably plenty of room here for all Melody's Business Plans, for the gîtes and the hotel rooms and the wedding venue ... and the supposed ruins was one of the things keeping the Castle from attracting serious money from outside organisations, and preventing the place from being a proper ancient monument ... what was going on? The Fossetts must know, presumably, so what were they playing at?

She lay back again, puzzled, and then started as she heard a soft sound. Sitting up, she heard a little chirrup and Perkins skittered out of the fireplace and jumped up on the table. The cat butted her head against Kitty's knee.

"Why, Perkins, where did you come from?" she said, delighted. "Did you come all this way to find me? That was kind, aren't you lovely?"

The cat nuzzled her and she scratched it behind the ears. It purred and blinked at her, settled on her lap and began to wash itself.

"So, how did you get here? I bet you know your way all through these buildings, don't you? Is this where you spend your time when you're not in the kitchen? What adventures you must have! I suppose you realise I'm only here because of you?"

Perkins didn't care. She preened herself, then jumped down and went sniffing along the table, picking her way delicately between the silver.

"I bet you're looking for spiders, aren't you? Do cats eat spiders, I wonder? They probably do. I wouldn't fancy it myself, but they're probably lovely little crunchy snacks to a cat, aren't they? Do you find the legs get stuck in between your teeth?"

The cat didn't answer, but plopped down to the dusty floor and sauntered back to the fireplace. Kitty got down and followed. Leaning into the great open hearth, she peered upwards. The chimney rose above her, blackened and coated with brick dust, and not far above she could see light. There must be another fireplace not far overhead, she thought, and the cat had used it to find her way down here. The chimney was wide, and here and there bricks stuck out from the wall and made a kind of staircase one could climb easily enough if one were a cat. And not impossible for a girl, she thought, especially a thin one good at wriggling. She stepped further into the hearth and put one foot on a projection, felt above her for a handhold, and raised herself up. Now her head was up the chimney, and only her legs would be visible from the room behind her. She looked down. Perkins sat in the hearth and gazed up at her, blinking. Kitty found the next foothold, and raised herself a little further. Now she was entirely in the chimney, invisible from the room. That would be a splendid trick, when Cartilege came – he would find the room empty, and no clue where she had gone! But then he might leave and lock the door again, and she'd be stuck here all night.

She decided to go just a little further, to see where the light came from, and then get down again. A couple of minutes scrambling and, her hair full of dust and old soot, she found herself looking out of another hearth into a very grand room, long and high, with what must once have been opulent hangings on the wall now dull and disintegrating into lace, and tall chairs with stiff wooden backs along the walls, and another long table down the centre. There was a door halfway along one side, and tall windows opposite it so the room was bright with afternoon sunlight. Dusty motes danced in the slanting sunbeams. At the far end was another great fireplace adorned with carved shields and coats of arms, matching this one. She climbed out into the room and stood on one of the chairs, looking out through the window. Dimly seen because of the grime on the glass, there were roofs falling away below, and then the castle wall, and beyond that the sea, sparkling. Far out was the *Mercy*, butting its way gamely along the coast to the south.

She felt obscurely happy. Here she was in the dim and not-so-ruined secret castle, and out there in the sun were normal people going about their ordinary lives. Behind her Perkins gave another little chirrup.

"I'd better go back down," she told her. "It wouldn't do for Cartilege to come and discover your little secret, would it? Where will you go now? Further up the chimney? Or into that other one? You must show me another day. We'll come again, and have an adventure!"

She got down off the chair, stroked the cat once more, and clambered into the fireplace again. It was harder going down than coming up, because you couldn't really see past your own body to find the next foothold. She managed it although by the time she emerged into the Silver Room she was dusty and dirty and had brick dust and cobwebs in her hair. She cleaned herself up as best she could with rags from the box, and then settled on the table again, happy. Cartilege would be livid when he came and saw she'd done no work at all, but she didn't care. What could he do?

He was livid, indeed, when an hour later he arrived rattling his keys and opened the door.

"You've done nothing! Lady Sybil will hear about this," he grated in his ancient voice, "you'll be sorry for this disobedience, you young harridan! You'll rue the day you set yourself against the House of Fossett, you mark my words!"

'House of Fossett', what do you think this is? she said to

herself. Some gothic fantasy? They're just a nasty old woman and a dotty old man, they aren't a House! She slipped past him and out of the door. She scampered round the great cloister, into the long passage and out into the familiar surroundings of the staircase hall. She would go to her room, have a bath and put some clean clothes on, and then go down to the kitchen and see if it was dinner time yet. Supper time, she told herself, not dinner. I'll play to my own rules, whether they like it or not.

VIII

Expecting to be seized by a vengeful Cartilege at any moment, Kitty crept carefully down to the kitchen next morning, intent on breakfast. There she found Faith and Charity but not their mother.

"She's having a day off," Faith said. "We can cope. But we've had instructions from her upstairs not to feed you ..."

"That's a blow," said Kitty mournfully.

"... but there's a packet on the table with some sandwiches and apples in it. If it just disappears, we probably won't notice ..."

"How can you stand it, working here?"

Charity laughed. "It's all right, most of the time. It's just when trouble-makers like you come and upset things ..."

Kitty grinned gratefully and tucked the packet of food into her pocket. She looked at the twins, so big and bonny and cheerfully confident.

"But isn't there a feud between your family and the Castle? Because of your ancestor Mercy Cott? How can you bear to work for them?"

"Oh, goodness," said Faith, flicking with her duster so at least it looked as though she was still working, "that's all in the past, isn't it? I mean, poor Mercy was treated pretty bad, but half of that was down to her own parents, wasn't it? They kicked her out, poor thing, when she fell pregnant? And her lad, that Roland, he ought to have stood by her, but no one actually knows what happened with him. He seems to have disappeared."

"What do your parents think, though?"

"My mam's not bothered, but then she isn't a Cott, is she? My dad, though - he's another matter. He hates the Fossetts with a vengeance. If it was up to him, he'd burn the whole Castle down to the ground, and Sir Lancelot and Lady Sybil with it!"

"So he must hate you working here, then?"

"He does a bit, yes, but he thinks that one day we're going to spy out something that'll prove they're all criminals, and get 'em kicked out and locked up!"

"And will you?"

"No, probably not. Sir Lancelot's too stupid to make plots, and Lady Sybil's already got everything she could possibly want - money, a castle, nice clothes, servants an' everything, an' people bowing and scraping wherever she goes. Why would she want to get involved in anything dodgy?"

"And besides," added Charity, "it's not for ever. We'll go soon anyway. Faith's going to marry Billy Brannicle and be a fishwife!"

"Oh. Does he know that?"

"Not yet he doesn't, pet, we haven't told him. But he won't put up much of a fight!"

"But what about you? You can't both marry him."

"Oh, me? I'll go and work with me Da. He's a haulier, he's got three lorries and another one coming."

"Can you drive a lorry?"

"I can that. Right good fun, that is!"

"What about your mother?"

"Ah, never mind her. The landlord of the Dragon's been after her for years, to go and cook there. It's a much better kitchen they have."

"Well I hope you won't go off before I do," Kitty began, but before she could explain why, Melody arrived, out of breath and in a hustle.

"Here you are," she said, "I thought I'd find you here! You need to make yourself scarce, her Ladyship's on the warpath! She's spitting feathers, she is, but she's busy at the moment with those men, Medulla and Cockley Knowes. But she'll turn her attention to you soon enough."

Kitty rose and gathered herself. "I will then, but first ... did you find anything on the internet?"

"Yes, plenty. Though nothing about your man Crust. There's no Professor Crust, and no Wilberforce Crust, not anywhere I can find. I tried all different spellings as well. So far as Google's concerned, he doesn't exist."

"I didn't imagine him."

"No, but that might not be his real name. He's not with them this morning."

"He's probably still looking for the Primeval Porpoise. What else did you find?"

"Quite a lot about COGACO, actually. It stands for Coal Gasification Company."

"What's that when it's at home?"

"It's the stuff in Sky's paper, getting at the coal under the sea. I'm not sure yet how they do it, but I'll keep looking."

"But it would explain what they're doing here, poking around, I suppose. Though not why they're so interested in the Castle. Anyway, I'd better get going."

"Will you be all right?"

"Oh, I'm good at creeping and hiding and going tiptoe. I'll be fine. Have you ever thought, if we can tiptoe, why can't we tipfinger as well?"

"No, I haven't thought, and you haven't time to waste on it either. Go on, get!"

Kitty got. She made her way to the beach, planning her route carefully and keeping out of sight as much as possible until she was clear of the castle buildings. Once into the sand dunes she could relax. As she plodded through the soft sandy hillocks where your feet slid at every step, she considered her situation. There were still two weeks until she could go home, which was quite a long time to last out when bed and board seemed to slipping away from her like the sand under her feet. She could knuckle under and take her punishment, of course, but that wasn't in her nature.

It might be thought that she was in a pretty impossible situation, miles from home, alone, unable to contact her mother or sister or brother, with her friend Marcia out of the picture and her reluctant hosts out for revenge for her defiance. Not to mention, she reminded herself, the threat of Social Services which would be dreadful for a short while, and would cause her mother no end of difficulty and embarrassment.

But perhaps things weren't quite as bad for Kitty as it might be for an ordinary girl. She was used to being away from home as she went to a boarding school. She was used to people disapproving of her because she was a wilful and uncooperative child with a habit of antagonising her teachers, and was bossy with the other girls because she tended to know best. And there was an upside – she had this fascinating castle and its seaside environs to explore, and a library full of books she hadn't read. Marcia wasn't much of a loss, as she wasn't the greatest friend anyone could have, being selfish, greedy and rather stupid. And it was still the beginning of the summer holidays and the weather was magical, bright blue skies and fluffy white clouds processing inland and the green sea sparkling and inviting.

She hunkered down in a hollow in the dunes and unwrapped her breakfast. Munching a sausage sandwich still gratefully warm, she watched the white clouds marching towards the coast. One cast its dark shadow on the water, and her heart sank as it raced towards her. As the shadow reached the beach the joy went suddenly out of the day. Everything about her, the dunes and the stony beach and the boats bobbing offshore, seemed smaller somehow, and no longer friendly. She crouched down and gathered her coat round her. The wind felt the same, the gulls still cried and wheeled and stitched through the breakers, the sand beneath her feet felt the same, neither harder nor softer, but she shivered and glanced over her shoulder, feeling that something nasty might be creeping up. A moment ago the sea had been green and happily sparkling. Now it was grey. It looked cold and heaved sullenly, the waves skeined with slimy weed, threatening flood and capsize and somehow much wetter than before. If this had been a real adventure, she thought, in a book or something, she wouldn't have been on her own. She would have had several friends with her, or her older brother and sister and a cute toddler or a dog for laughs. They would have cried "Family conference!" and sat round the kitchen table eating bread and home-made raspberry jam and drinking mugs of cocoa, and worked out what to do next. But this wasn't an adventure. It was just a dismal situation, there was no cocoa, and she was on her own.

But just as she had decided the day was not so nice, that this empty beach was really rather frightening and she'd rather be at home in the castle kitchen with a cup of tea and a cheese scone, the cloud passed. It dragged its shadow inland to frighten the sheep, the day was glorious again and she wondered what she had been worried about. She had friends, hadn't she? She had Melody and the twins and Ma Cott and the Billies and Sky

Lovechild? She wasn't alone at all. And her enemies, though unpleasant, were viciously stupid, few in number and deserved to be stood up to.

Standing up to began sooner than she had expected. At the harbour the jetty was deserted and the *Mercy* was evidently out fishing, so she made her way into the village. As she crossed the grass towards Sky-Blue's emporium she heard running feet behind her. It was the nasty boys from the other day. She stiffened and looked around for a weapon, but it was not her they were after. They had cornered a small boy, who dodged in and out of the parked cars. He was quick, but they were too many for him and eventually he was cornered. She saw raised fists, and heard muffled blows and cries of pain.

Without thinking she ran towards them, stopping to pick up a stick that had fallen from one of the trees. She whirled it round her head and gave an inarticulate shout of rage as she dashed at them. They turned to face her, laughing.

The year before, she had taken some valuable lessons from her friends Lance and Gwennie. Then it had been a short sword in her hand, not a stick, but she knew the same principles applied. Keep moving, turn and slash, round and round with your blade (or stick) in constant movement keeping a clear space around you that your enemy can't penetrate, not stabbing or thrusting but relying on the tip of your fast-moving weapon to do damage as it whirled. The important thing was to concentrate on your feet, because that was where the whirling movement originated, that was what drove your ceaseless momentum, and one little trip or stumble could be fatal if it caused your blade to falter and leave a gap in the defensive circle.

Right now, her enemy had no such experience. They could run and grab, they could punch or wrestle, but they had no concept of such dizzying, vicious speed. There were six of them but they were defenceless against her. The largest took the jagged broken tip of the stick across his mouth and ducked away with blood spurting between his fingers. The next caught a stinging blow round one ear and cried out in pain, while the remaining four backed away. She followed, pinning one up against a car and catching him across the hands he held out to protect himself, and then they were running, fleeing for the safety of the houses, and the little boy took to his heels as well, running full pelt in the opposite direction. She was left breathing heavily, her berserk rage fading. She wished it had lasted longer.

She dropped the stick and walked slowly back across the grass towards the tie-dye shop. As she was about to push at the door, there was a shout from down the street and Dashwood Belhatchett came running heavily up.

"You vicious little swine," he grated, breathing heavily. He reached out one hand towards her shoulder and she tensed herself, twisting away. "My son ... scarred for life, he'll be, what did you ..."

"He was beating up a little boy," she said stoutly. "He's a bully, and he deserved what he got. It was one girl against six boys, did he tell you that? And if he comes near me, I'll do it again!"

"I'll cut your head off, girl, and hang it from the highest tower of that castle of yours!" he yelled, his eyes staring and spit flying from the corners of his mouth. "Your lips will curl back from your teeth, the wind'll blacken your skin, your teeth'll come out and the crows will peck your eyes, moths'll crawl into your ears ... every thought you've ever had will escape from your shrivelled brain and scatter over the dunes ..."

"And I'll gouge your bloody eyes out, and mark you for life, you great lout!" cried a voice behind her, and Sky emerged from the door, her lips drawn back in a snarl and a large pair of scissors grasped in her hand like a dagger. She pushed past Kitty and stood in front of her. "Have you any idea what you look like, you fool, shouting and screaming and threatening a little girl? Are you mad?"

"She slashed my boy's face ..."

"And I'll slash yours! Your son's nothing but a rotten bully who picks on anyone weaker than himself, just like you! But he picked on the wrong one today, and so have you! Now, get off my doorstep before I do you damage!" Sky brandished the scissors in his face and he backed away, then turned and shambled back down the street while she stood and watched him, her face flushed.

Then she turned to Kitty, and grinned broadly. "Quite a turn of phrase he has, doesn't he, for a man who keeps a Post Office? Moths'll crawl into your ears, is it? Who'd have thought he had it in him?"

She pulled Kitty inside. "And," she said as she fussed with the teapot, "who'd have thought you had it in you? Did you actually take on the whole gang?"

"That was easy. They'd never met anyone who could fight before."

"And you can, evidently, I wonder where you learned that? What was it all about, anyway?"

Kitty told her about the little boy they had been beating, a wizened little dwarf of a boy in canvas sneakers and shorts and a grubby t-shirt with flowers on it.

"Oh, I know who that is," Sky said. "I gave him that t-shirt, it's one of mine. That's Nearly Normal Nidd's boy."

"I've met him," said Kitty, taking the cup. It was proper tea this time, with milk and two spoons of sugar. "Those boys were harassing me up the lane and he saw them off. What did you call him?"

"Nearly Normal Nidd. His name's Nidd, see, and round here we call him Nearly Normal because he isn't, really. Normal, that is. He's quite an eccentric. And the little boy's his son, Willy Nidd. He's as wild as his dad is strange, but he's a nice enough little lad really. He just doesn't like going to school, and has a tendency to steal food because his father forgets to feed him."

They chatted for a while, and Kitty told her about COGACO and what Melody had found on the internet. "I liked her, your Melody, I'm glad you brought her. She must come again. She'll be a lovely person once she's just relaxed a bit, and got some new clothes. I've got a tie-dye dress that'd suit her down to the ground. And it's a long one, so I do mean down to the ground! Speaking of which ..."

She bent down and pulled out a sort of smock, tie-dyed in subtle shades of brown and ash like something you found in a wood, something natural and earthy.

"Oh, that's lovely," said Kitty.

"Now you just slip it on, it's yours."

"Oh, I don't ..."

Sky insisted that it was a present. She couldn't sell it because it was too long for a t-shirt and too narrow for most women, the supplier shouldn't have sent it. But it would make a nice dress for Kitty because she was so slim.

"Skinny," Kitty said, and pulled it over her head.

"Slim, I said. That's nice, you keep it on, girl. It suits you."

Feeling nicely camouflaged in her earthy dress, Kitty made her way carefully back to the castle. The car park was filling up nicely, so she waited until a larger group of tourists had paid at the ticket hut, then walked through the gate with them trying to look as though she was just a bored teenager doing what her family wanted. Once inside she slipped away from them and into the private door. She wasn't entirely sure where she was going, perhaps to find Melody or maybe to her room to take her new dress off and put it away safely. There was always the chance the Fossetts might be waiting for her, of course, but they couldn't be everywhere at once and they couldn't watch any one place the entire day just on the off-chance she might turn up. This was an enormous place, she was young and quick and sneaky, and there were only three of them, the Fossetts and Cartilege and they were all quite old. The logistics of the situation were very much on her side.

Reaching the top corridor she paused, kneeling on the top step and carefully putting her head round the corner to make sure the coast was clear. It was; the long carpet was empty, stretching away from her to the windows at the far end. She could hear voices from Lady Sybil's room, rising and falling. She thought she could distinguish Lady Sybil's high-pitched protest, and a quieter voice placating her. Then Sir Lancelot's querulous tone, raised in protest at something, and again that quiet voice, calm and soothing.

She took the passage towards the tower, meaning to go to her own room and use the bathroom, but before she reached the spiral stairs she was undone. When considering the opposition, she had forgotten about the Sisters. They were so vague and insubstantial they could hardly be considered a threat, she had thought, but here they were, fluttering and squeaking towards her with remarkable speed, their dull eyes fixed on her and their claw-like hands outstretched. She backed away but found herself surrounded and hustled into a corner.

"Little sneak, why are you always sneaking around?" said Pamilia spitefully.

"Spying, she is, she's spying on us!"

"Sneaky little spy!" hissed Clorinda, poking Kitty's chest with a sharp finger.

"She should leave," said Drusilla, yanking on Kitty's hair.

"We'll make her leave!" exulted Pamilia, throwing her head back. "We'll tell everyone she's been spying on them," she crowed, "and going into their rooms and stealing things, and then she'll have to leave!"

"Or be thrown off the walls," said Drusilla grimly, "just tossed off, just like that! No one will care. No one cares what happens to a nasty ginger sneak!"

"Ugly ginger sneak," correct Pamilia. "I wonder if she'll bounce? Do they bounce, spies, I wonder? Shall we do it now, the throwing?"

Kitty thought this had gone on long enough. She kicked Drusilla on the shin, wrenched her arm from Pamilia's feeble grip, barged Clorinda rudely aside and marched off down the corridor, her head in the air and her face burning, daring them to come after her. But as she reached a corner there was a sudden bulk beside her and she was seized in a bearlike grip. A great hand covered her mouth, and she was lifted off the ground, kicking helplessly.

"There now," said a silken voice, "I think we have an opportunity to repay our gracious hosts' hospitality!" It was the man Medulla, and the bear that held her was the giant Cockle Knowes. "It's all right, ladies," Medulla called down the corridor where the Sisters watched open-mouthed, "we'll take over now! This is one irritation you won't have to worry about any longer. Please, go about your normal business, you're safe now."

The Sisters hesitated and milled around, but eventually reached an unspoken accord and drifted off up the passage, twittering. Medulla turned to Kitty and smiled.

"Now, young lady, what shall we do with you? You've caused dear Lady Sybil quite a lot of annoyance, haven't you, one way or another?"

Kitty kicked out at him but he was too far away, and the grip that held her was like iron. No amount of wriggling was going to help.

"No, no, young lady, don't bother struggling," Medulla said calmly, "Mr.Knowes is a rock, you know. Once he grips, there you stay – he's famous for it, in fact. Now, what to do? I think it would be an act of the greatest kindness to resolve this problem without bothering Lady Sybil or Sir Lancelot, don't you, Knowes? They've been put to enough trouble as it is, so I think we should spare them any more. Bring her this way, why don't you?"

He set off along the passage towards the Library stairs, and her enormous captor heaved into motion. She was carried helplessly, her feet far from the floor and her lungs gasping for air as the man's great arm wrapped round her chest and crushed. As they walked, he decided to adjust her position, for he twisted and tossed her upwards and she suddenly found herself over his broad shoulder, her legs kicking uselessly in the air and her head hanging down his back. In this undignified position she could see little except the flagstones and his great shoes pounding heavily as they went.

She could tell, though, that they did not embark on the stairs to the Library, but carried on towards the far end of the hall. When the floor beneath her was plunged in shadow she guessed that they were following the same path on which Cartilege had led her the previous day, towards the North End. And indeed she was proved right when they halted and she heard a rattling of keys, and the grating of an ancient lock. How did these men come to have Cartilege's keys, and how did they know their way around so well? Into the gloomy cloister they went, along one side and then a turn to the left and along the next, and halted outside a door she knew. Once more the keys rattled, and she was decanted abruptly to the floor. She sprawled on her back, but the giant Knowes gripped one arm in his beefy hand and hauled her roughly to her feet.

"Careful, Knowes, careful, we don't want to break her, do we? She's only a child, after all. Now, young lady, I think you are familiar with this place? Well, you're going to become even more familiar now."

Knowes pushed her through the door. She turned and looked at them, the looming large and the smoothly smiling small, side by side, crowding out the daylight.

"We're not going to tell anyone where you are, so no one's going to come and let you out. I think you need a period of quiet reflection, and that's what you're going to have. And let's be clear, no one's going to miss you. No one in the village knows you. Your family won't even know you ever arrived here in the first place, because ... look, I have your phone which you obligingly left in your room! I've searched through it and you've called no one since you came. I expect you were too busy poking your pointy little nose into things that don't concern you."

His smile grew even broader. He reached in and began to pull the door closed. "So, you can just stay here. You can die of starvation for all anyone cares. You can scream and shout, but no one'll hear you. No one comes to this part of the castle, and the walls are eight feet thick. You've been a minor irritation, just a tiny itch as it were, and you're scratched!"

And the door finally closed, and the key grated in the lock, and footsteps receded around the cloister.

She stood for a long time in the shadowy room, gazing at the door, shaken and thinking furiously. She believed the sinister little man when he said he wasn't going to tell anyone where she was. But he was wrong, there were people who would wonder about her. And her family did know she'd arrived, because she'd borrowed Melody's phone and called her sister to tell her she was all right. Melody would begin to worry quite soon, and Faith and Charity. Eventually Sky Lovechild might start asking questions, too. Oh yes, she had friends. But how long would it take before any of this began to happen? Might they assume that she was being clever and keeping hidden? It might take days before they became seriously concerned, weeks even. Then it would take more days while they searched, and goodness knew how long before they thought to search in the North End, if they ever did.

How long did it take for a girl to starve to death? The way her stomach was rumbling already, not long. The sausage sandwich seemed a long time ago.

IX

Kitty sat on the table and thought about her situation. She felt she might cry, but decided not to. That was the sort of thing the girls at school would do, and she wasn't the girls at school. Goodness, she'd been hunted by wolves less than a year ago, hadn't she? She hadn't cried then. She felt in her pocket and found she still had one of the apples from the kitchen. That would set the starvation back an hour or two, then. She took a couple of little bites, and tucked it back in her pocket for later. She had to make it last.

I've got one advantage they don't know about, she told herself. I know a way out of here, up the chimney like before. Admittedly I don't know where that'll lead me, but I'm not actually stuck in this room. In the big room upstairs there are windows I can reach by standing on a chair, for instance. Perhaps I could break one. On the other hand I have one disadvantage they don't know about, which is that I'm going to need the loo soon. That's where I was going when they caught me. That's a bit of a problem.

Before she tackled the chimney she went to the box of silver-polishing rags and stowed most of them about her person, some tucked into her pockets, some in her belt and a couple in her knickers. You never knew when a rag might come in handy, and she didn't intend to come back here if she could help it. Then she ducked into the fireplace and began to feel for the handholds she had used the day before.

She had evidently knocked down a lot of the dirt during her climb yesterday, because she arrived at the top rather less messy than before. She got out of the fireplace, brushed herself down and looked round the long upstairs room with its remains of fine hangings and the stiff chairs round the walls. She look into the fireplace again, trying to see if there was a way to go even further up, but all seemed dark. If she was going to try that way, she'd have to do it by touch alone.

The fireplace at the far end of the room was identical. Kneeling down, she peered into the chimney. Looking up, she thought she could just detect the faintest light, nothing more than a slightly lighter black than the rest. Glancing down, beside her knee she noticed a faint smudge in the dust of the floor. She stood up and looked further. Yes, that was it, she was sure. Very faintly, the paw prints of a cat. This was the way Perkins had come for her visit, and that meant there probably was a path to the outside world here, for a cat if not for a girl. This was the way she must go.

Before she tackled it, she went to the long door in the centre of the wall opposite the windows, and tried the handle. Sure enough, it was locked. Still, better to check, she thought, you'd look pretty silly if it had been open all the time. Back at the fireplace she took a deep breath and squared her shoulders. This was it.

At first it was nasty. She remembered reading that in times past little boys had been sent up chimneys to clean them. This was what life must have been like for them, except that they had to do it every day. She gritted her teeth and forced herself to be slow and methodical. First feel upwards for a handhold, sometimes a sort of ledge in the brickwork and sometimes just a brick that projected slightly. Holding your breath and keeping your eyes tight shut, brush the dust and soot off it. Once the dust has stopped falling past your face, open your eyes, grasp the handhold and pull yourself up. Then feel for a toehold to take your weight, and reach up for the next step.

And so it went, for what seemed like a long time but might only have been twenty minutes or so. She didn't allow herself to think what it would be like if she slipped and lost her grip. She would fall down a long way, and probably break a leg or sprain an ankle on landing, and on the way down she would bash herself against every brick and ledge. It didn't bear thinking about, so she put it out of her mind. Just reach up, brush clean, grasp and pull up and look for the next. She kept her eyes shut a lot of the time because there was nothing to see, but when she finally paused for a rest and did open them, she found she could actually make out the wall of the chimney in front of her face. Carefully looking upwards, there was definitely light filtering down, and now she could actually see the handholds and irregularities that would help her climb. On she went.

It was extraordinary, really, that Perkins had found this way to move through the abandoned buildings. She must have to jump between the handholds. Of course cats are wonderful at jumping, that wouldn't be a problem to her, but why would she have gone to all that trouble? Kitty thought she'd probably risen about thirty feet already, six times her own height, an incredible climb up or down for a little cat. Why had Perkins done it? Had she been able to smell something that intrigued her? Did she think there were going to be mice or rats to catch? Or did she just have a powerful curiosity that drove her on?

The light grew stronger quite quickly, but looking up Kitty couldn't see out into another room. Instead, when she finally managed to get her fingers over the top of the climb, she found that she was in a horizontal tunnel that ran across the top of her chimney, stretching away in two directions. With her head sticking up from the vertical flue, she looked both ways. One ran back into the dark, but the other led to daylight. Obviously that was the way she must go.

The cross tunnel or flue was only eighteen inches wide and slightly less than that in height. Bending her body at right angles to get up and round was quite hard, though she fitted all right. Anyone bigger would be in trouble. Goodness, she thought, what have I done to Sky's smock? I've ruined it! I should have taken it off and left it behind. And it was so pretty! Perhaps Faith or Charity might be able to work a miracle with the washing machine? If it isn't actually torn, it might only be dust and grime that would wash out. Using her elbows and knees she wormed her way along towards the light. Soon she reached a place where the tunnel dipped down. As the floor of it dropped away from her face, she wondered if it were going to go down vertically now. If so, she'd be stuck. There wasn't room to turn round so she could go down feet first, and she doubted if she could manage to climb downwards head first like some sort of subterranean animal.

Fortunately the down turn was very short, a couple of feet only, and she was able to put her palms on the bottom and let herself down slowly. Then the tunnel straightened again and became horizontal once more, and a moment later she was looking out of another fireplace into another room. She shuffled forward and down to the hearth and then she was out, rolling onto the dusty boards of the floor and lying on her back giggling with relief.

This seemed to be not one room but a suite, for she could see a low passageway with more light at the end, and a door standing open with another room beyond. The ceiling was low, and sloped. She must be up under the roof. The windows were small dormer windows let into the roof. She went to the first one and was rewarded with a view of rooftops below, and then the castle walls and the sea beyond. This was the very top of the jumble of buildings that made up the North End.

But her need to pee was getting rather urgent now. Where was the loo, didn't people go to the loo in olden days? She answered her own question: no, they didn't, they used chamber pots and then emptied them out of the window or into a gutter. She looked round feeling a little desperate. This room had been a living space, plainly, for there were low chairs and a table, and shelves holding dusty objects, pottery and candlesticks and on one, a crude wooden figure, a child's dolly perhaps. She walked over the uneven boards and looked through the open door into the next room. It was much the same, but the windows gazed out towards the village rather than the sea. There was a small bed in one corner, with the rotted remains of sheets and a pillow that had burst to reveal ancient dry straw.

She left the room unexplored and followed the passageway towards the next source of light. It was narrow, with cold stone on either side, but it led to another much larger space, still under the roof but lit with at least six more dormer windows on the side nearest the sea. There was yet another fireplace at the far end, but little furniture except for several old wooden chests against one wall. She would look inside them later. With a bit of luck there might be some bedlinen she could use, if it hadn't rotted away over the years. Eventually she'd need to sleep, when it got dark. But right now she needed desperately to pee, and it could wait no longer. She could see no chamber pots but there had been smaller containers on the shelves in the first room. Running back, she selected the largest and used it with relief. She put it back on the shelf again, because she could think of no alternative. Hopefully it would evaporate in time, and not be a problem.

Feeling the need to rest, she selected the most comfortable-looking chair – well, she corrected herself, the least uncomfortable-looking – and settled herself, taking a couple more small bites of her apple. It wasn't too bad up here, she thought. It was decently light, and she had a view of the sea. And it felt as though it had been some kind of a home, once upon a time. She wondered about the inhabitants. Had they been castle servants, perhaps? Had there been children up here, who had played with the wooden dolly? Had they been happy, ordinary people, with friends and families who had laughed and played games? Had the whole castle ever been a happy place? It wasn't a very happy one now.

She looked idly across the floor, trying to see if Perkins had been here and left her footprints in the dust, but could see no sign. She yawned, and snuggled down into the chair as best she could, and exhausted sleep overtook her.

When she woke it was dark. She groped her way to the shelves and found her pot, and used it. Then she pulled all the rags out of her clothing and tucked them round her in the chair. She nibbled a little more of her apple, and fell asleep again.

She awoke to the cold light of dawn. She was shivering, and that was what had woken her. She got up and stretched and ran on the spot and did exercises until she felt a little less stiff and cold. While she attacked her apple again, trying to ignore the rumbling of her stomach, she considered her course of action. There simply had to be a way out of here, now that she knew the chimney flues were navigable. But what had the old inhabitants done, with their pots and their bedding and their children? They didn't move round the building by the chimneys, for there would have been fires in the fireplaces and smoke in the flues. There had to be stairs, so where were they?

In the far room, the one with all the windows, she had spotted a door. It wasn't a grand door studded with iron like those lower down, but looked more like a cupboard which was why she had ignored it. But if there were stairs, that was where they had to be. She went to investigate. The door opened towards her with a creak, and revealed a small space like a vestibule. Right in front of her was another door, a more substantial one this time, with a lock and in the lock, a big key. To her left was a blank wall, and to her right the top of a steep stone staircase falling away into darkness. She had been right.

She gathered up her useful rags and stowed them about her person in case they were needed again, picked up the wooden dolly which she had decided to keep as a memento of this place and the people who lived in it, and went to the head of the stairs. Then she paused. There was another room behind that door, presumably, one important enough to warrant a lock. She ought to have a look, otherwise she'd always wonder. She tried the handle, but the door was locked. She tried to turn the key but it wouldn't budge even with both hands. The lock had rusted solid, probably.

Going back to the shelves she searched for a tool of some sort, but could find nothing. Then she thought of the chests. One did indeed contain the powdery remnants of bedding, which turned to dust when she touched it. The second was empty, but the third was a treasure chest of useful things, tools, wooden mallets, a reel of coarse string that broke and shredded into brown fibres when she handled it, and rusty knives and spoons. She selected a mallet and a couple of the largest knives, rusty but still with some solid metal remaining, and took them to the mysterious door. Even when she put the largest knife through the loop of the key, it wouldn't turn. Instead, the blade of the knife bent and snapped off for there was so little solid metal left. She looked at the lock, wondering if logic and patience might achieve what brute force had not.

Which way did the door open, she wondered, away from her or towards her? It was hard to tell. But by looking closely at the lock and the side of the doorway near it, she thought it probably opened outwards, towards her. That meant the tongue of the lock, the bit that came out when you turned the key, was engaged in something in the door frame. She didn't know if it was supposed to be called a tongue, but that's what it looked like. The door frame didn't look all that strong. Could she dig into the wood and cut away the bit that held the tongue of the lock? She started digging the second knife into the wood. The knife was very blunt, but the wood was old as well, and she soon had splinters coming away. Under the surface the wood turned out to be soft and crumbly, and it didn't take her long to jab and prise it away until the could see the tongue nestling inside. With one last stab she broke out the last piece, and tugged at the door. It moved slightly, so she tried again, bracing her feet against the wall and pulling with all her strength. The door creaked and groaned, and moved a little more. It had dropped on its hinges and was scraping on the floor which was why it was so stiff. She put her shoulder under the handle and lifted, and was able to gain perhaps an eighth of an inch, enough to let the door slide towards her a little more. Was the gap big enough? It was a good job she was skinny.

With a push and a shove and a grunt she was in, wriggling through the narrow gap. Once in she was able to put her shoulder to the door and open it another three or four inches, protesting loudly. That was good, she was in and could be sure of getting out. She stepped over the remains of a shattered chair and looked around.

This room was different. It had been richly furnished, and curtained, and the walls were hung with the remains of rich tapestry, now moth-eaten and disintegrated. The large single window looked over the village and the marshes beyond. Chairs and a bench and a small table stood around the walls, and shelves held a multitude of objects which would take a day or two to investigate properly. And wonder of wonders, there was a chamber pot, large and heavy and, mercifully, empty but obviously a chamber pot nevertheless.

But the main event, the chief feature of this opulent room, was a great bed, a four-poster, that stood on one corner but dwarfed everything else. Its hangings, like the curtains and tapestries, were moth-eaten and mildewed, falling away in tatters. On the bed itself there was a great heap of bedding and fabrics that had once been white but were now yellow fading to brown. And as she looked, her eyes slowly making sense of the shapes they saw, there was something in the centre of the bedding, something dreadful that made her want to whimper and run out. She did not, though. She stood and stared, and thought, and clenched her fists to stop herself from fleeing, and gritted her teeth to stop herself from crying, and braced her whole body to keep from shivering in fright.

In one hand she still gripped the old knife, and she held it out in front of her. But she knew this thing wasn't going to attack. This thing was beyond all that. This thing was no threat at all. Disgusting and alarming, yes, but not dangerous. Not any more.

It lay half propped up, its ... legs, yes, they were legs, pointing towards her. They still ended in shoes, old leather shoes that had cracked and curled but were recognisably shoes with little heels and buckles. The upper half was against the remains of pillows which were piled against the wall, and from the depths of the sunken pillows gleamed teeth bared in a hideous grin. Between the feet and the teeth was a mess of rotted clothing and white bones. This person had been very, very dead for a very long time.

She stood for a long time, unmoving. She had seen dead bodies before, during her dreadful adventures a year ago, but they had not been skeletons as this was. Their faces had been peaceful or anguished or angry or terrified depending on their manner of death, but this just grinned and grinned for it had no features left at all, just yellowish bones and the teeth. Kitty moved a little closer. The shoes, she decided, looked like a man's shoes of a bygone age. She thought an expert would be able to tell from the bones whether this had been a man or a woman, and even what age they had been when they died, but she couldn't. But she had a feeling. She had a feeling that this had been a man, a young man, and she had a feeling that his death had been a very sad one indeed.

On the plaster of the wall behind the bed were marks, spidery marks. It looked like writing, and as she relaxed from her shock and gazed round she realised that most of the walls were covered in it. She backed away from the bed, reluctant as yet to turn away for she didn't want it behind her, and sidled up to the nearest wall. It was, indeed, writing. It looked to have been done with black ink, now faded to pale grey. In many places it had faded entirely, and in others the plaster had fallen off or bubbled up, and there was one great greenish patch of mildew obscuring the writing altogether. She peered closer at one section that survived comparatively unscathed.

'... *thiss day no newes of ...*' she read, '... *Avis bringeth whoulsom soupe but doth not ...*'. She moved on. '*My father doth not here my plea ... in thiss place three weeke ...*' . The script was irregular and hard to decipher, with tall loops to many of the letters. '... *begge of Avis to ... newes ... my belovede M ...*'

Avis seemed to feature quite frequently. Was she the man's wife, or some kind of nurse, or even a gaoler? After all, the room had been locked. Perhaps the dead man had been a prisoner. Were there any wars he might have been involved in, a captured enemy who had to be kept confined here? Many of the comments involved food. Kitty thought that if you were locked up all day, meals would become pretty important and loom large in your mind.

'a fricasse of fowle very good this ... possett ... but bred and meat fr ...' Kitty moved over to the far side of the room. Here the writing was a little more intact, and one or two paragraphs seemed nearly complete.

'father most angrie and saith I shalle never be let to marrie save at hys will ... imploureth hym for alle Godde's mercie that he shall rellent hys most ...'

An idea was forming in her mind. She was beginning to think that she knew who this was. If she was right, his death had indeed been a most sad one. She steeled herself to move closer to the bed. The writing here was even wilder and more faded, and of a different colour. With a sinking feeling she wondered if she could guess what it had been done with. It was brown, a rusty brown. Had the man written this with his own blood? She dared to put one hand on the bed and lean closer, keeping an eye on the teeth.

'... sixth day Avis doth not come and ... knowe not if ... father hath decreed my dethe for my most grevious sinnes ...' and a little lower down, *'... grow week and cannott ... Avis hath not ... this fourtnite or ... ye dore but cannot ... Mercie my ...'*

Kitty could read no more. She went back to the centre of the room. She thought she could guess what this was. This poor man had been locked up, and left to languish and die. Avis, a faithful servant, had attended him and brought him food, but one day she did not come, and the day after that, and the day after that. Whether she had been sent away by the master of the Castle, or was just obeying orders, who knew? More likely she was an old woman, and she died and no one thought to take her place. Whatever the explanation, the daily visits ceased, the food came no more, and the young man had paced the room and gazed from the window at the busy village, his former neighbours innocent of his imprisonment, going about their daily business without glancing up at this remote window high in the Castle. Slowly he grew weaker from lack of food, and lay on the bed half conscious instead of pacing. She glanced at the debris on the floor. Just inside the door she had stepped over the shattered remains of a chair which the man had used to try and break out, but the door was stouter in those days, and the lock held, and he was enfeebled by hunger and when the chair broke he gave up and returned to the bed.

And slowly, yearning for his life and his love, he slipped away and died, and lay here alone and unknown for two hundred years or more, and only one person had grieved for him. Kitty knew who had grieved. She knew who had mourned, and wondered, and not understood, and eventually gave up hope and walked into the waves.

This was Mercy Cott's vanished lover. This was Roland Fossett.

X

While Kitty mourned for poor Roland Fossett, locked up long ago, forgotten and starved to death in his remote room, out in the sunshine the life of the village continued unaware. Melody walked blithely down to the village to take yesterday's cash to the Post Office. She glanced down at herself, the bright tie-dye scarf threaded through loops of her jeans for a belt as Kitty had suggested, and her most relaxed chunky sweater instead of the severe business suit. She felt liberated, quite a different person. It was remarkable what a difference the little girl had made. For the first time in her life Melody had someone other than herself to worry about, and worry she did. Kitty had not slept in her bed last night, and had not appeared in the kitchen for her breakfast. No one knew where she was or what she was doing.

Melody had taken one other piece of advice from Kitty. The previous evening after a strange dinner in the dining room with Medulla making polite and inconsequential conversation and Cockley Knowes sitting in massive silence and shovelling food into his mouth, she had shut herself into her office, booted up the computer, and changed the internet banking passwords so that no one but herself could have any access to the accounts. The money belonging to the Castle was in her hands, and hers alone. She wasn't sure that what she had done was entirely legal, but she thought it was. Anyway, she'd done it now, and felt obscurely powerful. If push came to shove, she had leverage.

Dashwood Belhatchett greeted her with a scowl when she pushed through the Post Office door and wished him good morning.

"Nothing good about it," he rasped, taking the plastic wallet with the cash in it. "Where's that little savage of yours? You heard what she did?"

"Sorry, I'm not sure what you're talking about? Do you mean the little girl who's staying with us? What's savage about her?"

He snorted. "Savage, that's putting it mildly! She's a lunatic, a dangerous lunatic. I've a mind to phone the police, except they probably won't do anything. Attacked my boy with a stick, that's what. Slashed him across the face, laid his lip open. He'll be scarred!"

Melody made an effort to keep calm. "Don't forget my receipt, Mr.Belhatchett. I'm sorry to hear there's been ... any trouble. If what you say is true ..."

"True? You calling me a liar?"

"If it's true, I say, my first question is to ask what he was doing to warrant such an attack?"

He tore the receipt from the pad and threw it under the glass at her. "Nothing! Nothing, that's what he was doing! She just picked up a stick and went for him for no reason. And then that dirty hippy woman Lovechild backed her up, threatened me with a pair of scissors when I went to enquire! What are you going to do about it?" He thrust his beard at her, glaring.

"Do? Well, the first thing I'll do is go and talk to Miss Lovechild and find out the facts, Mr.Belhatchett. And in the meantime, I suggest you moderate your language. This is no way to treat one of your most important customers. If it wasn't for the Castle, you probably wouldn't have a business, remember that. Depending what I find out, I may go to the police myself since you seem to be scared of doing so. Good day to you!" and she stalked out, slamming the door behind her.

Well, that went all right, she told herself, I think I dealt with that quite well. But what on earth has Kitty been up to? Where is she, what is she doing?

Sky Lovechild didn't know where Kitty was, but she had things to tell all the same. She drew Melody into the shop and made her sit down at the back, and fussed with the kettle. Sitting opposite her Melody saw a tall thin man in shabby, mis-matched clothes. He nursed his own cup of tea, and nodded and smiled and rocked to and fro, not speaking.

"There, drink that up," said Sky, sitting down. "Now, you want to know about Kitty's battle yesterday ... oh, have you met Mr.Nidd? He knows about it too."

Melody held out her hand, and the man shook it briefly, not looking at her.

"What happened, then? Mr.Belhatchett says she attacked his son, is that true?"

"Well, yes, in a manner of speaking. The son and his friends were beating up Mr.Nidd's little boy Willy. They're a bunch of bullies and they're always hunting him and trying to corner him, and yesterday they managed it."

Mr.Nidd stirred and spoke for the first time. "It's my fault, really," he said. "My boy's a bit ... different, I suppose you should say. I suppose I'm a bit different myself, come to that. He's wild, a truant, and goes his own way, doesn't fit in. So they pick on him. If he'd stay at home I could protect him, but he wanders where he will and does what he wants, and that irritates them."

"So they caught him and Kitty got involved?" asked Melody.

Sky laughed. "Involved, that's one way of putting it! She went for them, the whole gang, with a stick. Who'd have thought she was such a fighter? She got the Belhatchett lout a dreadful swipe and laid his mouth open, then she got a couple of others before they ran for it. They didn't know what hit them, by all accounts, she was so quick! And her not hardly out of breath."

"I'm amazed. I don't suppose she learnt that at her boarding school," Melody said. "She's a very ... unusual girl, I find. But do you know where she is? She didn't come home last night."

"Not a clue." Sky looked at Mr.Nidd but he shook his head sadly.

"I really don't know where to start looking," Melody said, baffled. "She's made herself very unpopular with the Fossetts. They were talking about calling Social Services and having her taken away, but I don't think they have, yet. I'll go back by the harbour and see if the fishers have seen her, and then I'll go and see the Cotts. They might have heard something."

Mr.Nidd rose to his feet, stooping to avoid the cantrips hanging in the ceiling. "I'll go and take a tour of the village, I think," he said, "some of the villagers may have seen her."

"Will they talk to you?" Melody asked.

"Oh yes, they're not all like Belhatchett. I usually try to avoid him – and his beastly son and his friends. But most of the village are all right. They think I'm loony, they call me 'Nearly Normal' which is their idea of humour, I suppose. But they're all right really. I'll see what I can find out," and he made his way through the shop, his head brushing the dreamcatchers and making the chimes tinkle.

Sky asked about Melody's internet searching and what she had been able to find out. Melody explained that her search for the mysterious Professor Crust had come to nothing. As far as Google was concerned, he didn't exist. But COGACO was another matter, there was plenty about them.

"It stands for Coal Gasification," she said. "It's rather like fracking, where they pump water and chemicals down into the ground and get natural gas in return."

"I know about that, it's wicked," Sky said. "It causes little earthquakes, and who knows what other damage. It shouldn't be allowed."

"Coal Gasification is similar but not the same," Melody said. The object was to liberate the massive reserves of coal that lay under the seabed, by pumping stuff down to heat them up and turn the coal to gas, then pipe the gas back to land. It was potentially a huge business because the amounts of coal that might be accessed were colossal. "In County Durham there were coal mines reaching out eight miles under the sea," she explained. "Just think, coal miners travelling out all that way in little trains, and sending the trains back full of coal. It's an amazing thought."

She pulled from her bag an article she had printed out from the internet. '*The coal lies around our shores,*' it said, '*billions and billions of tonnes of coal from Swansea to Whitehaven and from the Firth of Forth to Lincolnshire. That coal is not only there but, thanks to the astonishing evolution of horizontal oil drilling technology, it can also be cheaply, quickly and safely converted into gas and piped ashore. Drilling for oil and gas in the North Sea now is not only exorbitantly expensive, but the odds against any commercial discovery are lengthening to unacceptable levels. Yet our coal and its characteristics are known, as a result of the former National Coal Board's exhaustive attempts to mine coal offshore from the old collieries of Durham and Cumbria.*'

"Who is saying this?" Sky asked.

Melody looked at the bottom of the page. "Algy Cluff, chairman and Chief Executive Officer of Cluff Natural Resources, apparently. I looked him up as well. He's a very big businessman indeed. He used to own the *Spectator* magazine, and an oil-field in the North Sea, and has mining interests all over the world. He's the main proponent of this Coal Gasification thing. He says it's safe because the coal isn't just under the sea, there are great layers of other rock on top so the sea should be safe."

"Well, he would say that, wouldn't he? So he owns COGACO?"

"No, it seems not, they're nothing to do with him. They're a new company, I think, trying to muscle in on the business. Who's behind them I couldn't see, but I did get mentions of Mr.Medulla here and there, the man who's now staying up at the Castle and talking to Lady Sybil and Sir Lancelot. It's not clear what his part is in COGACO but he's definitely involved."

The pair sat thinking for a moment. It was evident that something was in the wind, and that something was almost certainly an attempt to exploit the natural coast here. What they couldn't tell was what effect it would have on the village and its inhabitants.

"It might mean jobs, and money coming into the village," Melody said. "Shops and schools and a doctor ... it could be a good thing."

"Spoken like a businesswoman, I suppose," Sky smiled tolerantly. "My own mind is running on ugly machines and buildings, and great pipes running into the sea, the beach ruined for ever and dead fish and birds ... I know you shouldn't oppose progress and cling mindlessly to the status quo, but when that progress is likely to do such damage ..."

Melody stuffed the article back in her bag, gathered herself together and rose to leave. "Well," she said, "that's for another day, no doubt. There'll be arguments to be had, and public enquiries and all sorts of politics before anything actually happens. Right now, I have a more pressing problem. I don't know where Kitty is, I don't know if she's hurt or scared or stuck somewhere ... and I'm very uneasy about that man Medulla. What's he doing, staying at the Castle? I have to admit I find him a bit scary."

Sky walked her to the door, put a hand on her arm and gave her a peck on the cheek. "Never you fear, she'll be all right, I have a feeling. She's a fighter, that one. Nice scarf, by the way ..."

Kitty was not all right, though, not exactly. She was feeling perplexed and slightly alarmed. The descent of the long narrow staircase from the attic had been easy enough, and interesting for at various levels the stairs opened onto landings with more rooms. She could spend all day exploring if she wanted, but what she was looking for was a route out of here. She was hungry and thirsty. She had eaten the last of her apple, and her stomach was rumbling.

She had a good idea which way was which, because she could remember the windows looking one way out to sea and the other way over the village. She had a strong suspicion that somewhere the stairs must lead down to the cloisters again, and from there she should be able to escape into the main castle provided she crept carefully and wasn't seen. In a way things should be easier, because if the Fossetts and Medulla thought she was safely locked away in the Silver Room, they wouldn't be looking for her anywhere else. She was certain that the twins and Ma and Melody wouldn't give her away when she met them again.

But arriving finally at the foot of the stairs she was faced with a heavy door securely locked. On the other side of it were the cloisters and freedom, she thought, but the door wouldn't budge. She kicked at it and pulled at the handle, but it was rock solid. She sank down onto the bottom step and considered her options. She only had two; to go back up and explore some of the rooms she had seen as she came down, or to go all the way up and take to the chimneys again. She didn't want to do that.

She was woken from her reverie by sudden voices, and footsteps.

"... told me it was taken care of!" she heard. Lady Sybil, shrill and angry. Kitty could hear only a dull grumble in reply, but the footsteps were getting louder. They were coming her way, walking round the cloister. They would pass right by this door, only feet away from her.

"So where is she?" demanded Lady Sybil. "You said she was locked in there, and she isn't! What have you done with her?"

Another rumble. They had discovered that Kitty was no longer in the Silver Room.

"You haven't harmed her? I'll not be party to anything criminal!" Lady Sybil was becoming even shriller. She sounded rattled. "She's an annoyance and I'll be pleased to be rid of her, but I draw the line at ..."

"No, no, dear lady," came Medulla's silken tones, "perish the thought! She's obviously found a way out, a secret door perhaps, or a window we knew nothing about. She's wandering around in here, lost and frightened, that's all."

"I don't care how frightened ..."

"So nothing's changed, has it, Lady Sybil? She's out of the way and harmless. What does it matter if she wanders around until she drops? She's no food and no water, she can't last very long."

That was right enough, Kitty thought, crouching with her ear to the door. What if she called out? Might they unlock the door and let her out, and give her something to eat? But what she heard next convinced of the wisdom of staying quiet.

"Yes, I suppose ..." Lady Sybil was saying, "and if some time her body is found, what will people think? She explored somewhere she shouldn't, and got locked in by mistake, and died. A tragic accident, they'll say, very sad and all that, but hardly our fault. She'd been told not to come in here ..."

"Exactly, dear lady, a tragic accident and no one's fault at all, except her own. One dead girl, hardly a major international incident, I think? Now, I suggest we forget her and concentrate on the matter in hand."

The footsteps began to recede. Kitty listened intently. What was the matter in hand, exactly, if it wasn't her?

"... mustn't say anything to Sir Lancelot just yet. He would be horrified at the idea. His family have been here for over three hundred ..." but the voices were fading and she could hear no more.

She relaxed and sat on the bottom step again. What mustn't they say to Sir Lancelot? What could be so dreadful that he would be horrified? There was something extraordinary going on, some plot or plan, and it was something far more important than the fate of one little girl, apparently. That puts me in my place, she said to herself, I'm supposed to starve to death like poor Roland upstairs, and I'm just a sideshow to the main event ... whatever that is. She allowed herself a moment to mourn poor Roland again. Had he stared out of the window at the village, and seen Mercy walking in the street? Had he called out to her in vain, for she was too far away to hear, and thought he had run away and abandoned her and her unborn child? Had he wept then, because he loved her and knew he would never see her again?

She sniffed and dashed away a tear that threatened to trickle down her cheek. Get a grip, she told herself, that's past and can't be helped. Now, what are you going to do? The rooms or the chimney again? It had to be the rooms first, she decided, and got to her feet.

At the first little landing, so not very far up and still a long way below the attic, she found that the stairs opened into a long passage running, she thought, from east to west like the rest of the building. Rooms opened off it, all intact but strewn with abandoned furniture and containers. Some of the containers weren't exactly historical. There were cardboard boxes full of junk, and wooden tea chests, a great pile of them in one room, almost up to the ceiling. Everything was dusty of course, and there were more cobwebs here than upstairs. Evidently these rooms had been used as storage within living memory, and that must surely mean there was a way out to the open air. And the abundant cobwebs meant the same thing, because spiders ate flies, didn't they, and there must at some time have been a lot of flies in here for them to eat. And flies have to get in from somewhere.

Almost the last room provided the answer. One entire wall was covered in dead ivy, stiff bristly branches, thick and twisted, fanning out from the broken window where they had entered seeking more wall to colonise and not realising they were heading indoors where they would find no rain or sun. The tall window that had let them in was completely smashed, glass and wooden bars strewn across the floor, and dead leaves and other debris were piled high against the wall in every corner. Against the wall on the inner side, near where Kitty had entered the room, was a pile of boxes and old furniture including the sad remains of an old piano, most of its keys missing. At one end of the room was yet another deep fireplace with elaborate carved pillars on either side.

She walked over to the window and looked out. She was

almost at ground level. There was another building in front of her, but directly outside her window was a narrow strip of grass and tall weeds. Beneath the window a pile of debris offered a way to the ground if you were careful and fairly agile. Here was her way out of the castle at last – she was free!

Before she made her final escape, she took one more glance round the room. The pile of furniture by the old piano had an odd look, almost as though it had been carefully constructed rather than just accumulating over the years. She strolled over to take a closer look. Someone had been at work here, and there were signs of habitation. Several plates were stacked neatly on one chair, and a book lay open and face down on what was, when she leaned closer, quite a modern mattress. Rolled neatly at the head of the mattress were some blankets. It was a nest, she realised, someone had made themselves a cosy nest in here, and had slept in it. Who could that have been?

She picked up the book and examined it. It was a book of natural history, *'The Wildlife of the Northumberland Coast'*, and was in perfectly good condition. She turned the pages and looked at the coloured photographs.

"Put that down!" said a small voice. Kitty froze, a chill running up her back. She bent her knees, ready to run. "Put it down, that's mine. What are you doing in my room?"

Silhouetted against the light, the face in shadow, a slim figure stood on the window-sill, holding on to the window frame with one hand.

"I said, what are you doing here? You're trespassing, this is my place!"

Kitty relaxed. "It isn't, actually," she said, "actually it belongs to Sir Lancelot, so it's you that's trespassing, not me."

"You're not Sir Lancelot, though," said the boy, jumping to the floor, "so you are too. I know you, you're that girl with the stick. Cor, you can't half fight! Where d'you learn to do that, could you teach me?"

Now she could see him more clearly, she recognised him. She remembered the shorts and the canvas shoes and the flowery t-shirt from Sky's shop. "You're the little boy they were roughing up, aren't you? Were you hurt?"

He grinned at her. "Not me. Well, a few bruises, like, but I'm used to it. They're always doing it, or trying to. They mostly can't catch me because I'm too quick for them."

He strolled forward, holding out a hand. "I'm Streaky Nidd," he said. "It's Willy really, but they call me Streaky because I'm thin like streaky bacon, and because I can run fast. I expect you know my dad, Nearly Normal. Everyone knows my dad."

She took his hand and shook it. "I'm Kitty," she said. "But you didn't run fast enough yesterday, did you?"

"No, they caught me napping. I was careless. Kitty's a funny name, you sound like a cat. I've got a cat. Would you like a biscuit?"

From somewhere in the chaos of his furniture nest he pulled out a biscuit tin and offered it to her.

"Can I take two?" she asked. "Actually, can I take quite a lot because I'm starving? Have you got anything to drink?"

It was pleasant lying on Streaky Nidd's mattress and seeing the sunlight outside though the room itself was in deep shade. Feeling a lot better with Streaky's biscuits inside her, and half a plastic bottle of water, Kitty relaxed. She had a way out. Things were better.

"You turn left out of the window," he said, "and right in front of you there's a high wall so you think there's no way out. But right in the bottom corner, there's a little archway hidden in the weeds. It goes right through the wall, and when you get to the other side, you're in the ditch that runs round the bottom of the rock. Only you have to wrap your head and hands in something when you go through the arch because it's full of nettles. That's why no one's found it, except me."

"Thank you," she said. "Now, in return for that and the biscuits, you said you wanted a fighting lesson. Have you got a stick or something we can use?"

An old chair leg was just the thing, and she showed him how to turn in circles, slowly at first and thinking entirely about the feet, never crossing your legs but moving smoothly and keeping a wide enough base that you were stable and wouldn't lose your balance. He tried, but kept trying to stab the chair leg at his imaginary enemies.

"No, no, never stab!" she said. "Only slash, and keep your

blade moving all the time. Once it stops, they can grab it and snatch it from you, and you're defenceless. It's the movement of your blade that keeps you safe because they can't get past it without being hit."

"Where did you learn this?" he asked, circling and circling.

"Oh, not so far from here, actually. In a Roman fort on Hadrian's Wall."

"Were there Romans there?"

"Er, no ... how could there be?"

He shrugged and whirled again.

"Now, try to keep moving always in one direction. You can reverse, but if you had a real sword it would be heavy, and stopping it and then starting again in reverse will tire you out."

"Have you got a sword?"

"Not any more. A stick works all right though." She went on to tell him how you must practise and practise, getting faster and faster until there was an impenetrable ring of steel around you. Well, an impenetrable ring of chair-leg, anyway, but at that moment Streaky got his feet in a tangle and sat down rather heavily. The cat had appeared suddenly and run between his legs.

"Hallo, Blackie," said the boy, stroking it, "aren't you a lovely boy?" It arched its back against his hand, and purred.

"She's not Blackie, she's Perkins and she's a girl cat," Kitty said. She didn't add 'and she's my cat, not yours,' because Perkins didn't really belong to anyone. She was her own cat. This didn't stop her from feeling rather jealous as they sat down again, the fighting lesson forgotten, and Perkins sat on Streaky's lap instead of Kitty's, and purred loudly as he stroked her.

"He comes most days, if I'm here," Streaky said, looking down fondly at his lap. "Only I don't know how he gets here. He must have ways of getting around in here, but I don't know what they are."

"I do," said Kitty smugly, but decided not to tell Perkins' secret.

Suddenly the cat turned her head and stopped purring, looking towards the fireplace.

"Uh-oh," muttered Streaky, "there it goes again!"

"There what goes?"

"It. Listen, just listen."

Kitty was silent, straining her ears. From the direction of the fireplace came a faint sound, a sort of moan but very far away. The cat jumped off Streaky's lap and walked a few paces towards the fireplace.

"What is it?" she asked, but Streaky shook his head and held up his hand.

"There it is again," he said. "I keep hearing it, the last couple of days. I don't know what it is, but I don't like it."

She listened again. There was another sound behind the moaning, a sort of flapping sound as though someone were beating a wet blanket on a rock in the far distance. The moan rose and fell. She felt the hairs on her neck standing up which made her shiver.

"I think it's a ghost," the boy whispered, his face pale. "I don't like it." He got up.

"There's no such thing as ghosts," she said quietly. "At any rate, the cat doesn't seem to mind. In fact, she looks as though she wants to go and see it."

Indeed, Perkins had run gently towards the fireplace and stood listening again. She looked over her shoulder at Kitty and Streaky, then returned her attention to the fireplace. She seemed to Kitty to look like a cat that has just heard a friend calling in the distance, and was wondering whether to respond. Once again the eerie sound rose and fell, and more of the slapping noise.

"I'm off!" said Streaky suddenly. "I don't like this. You coming?"

"Not just yet. I think ... look, I don't think it's anything bad, or the cat would be worried. And she isn't, look."

Perkins had advanced into the fireplace, empty except for a few brown wind-blown leaves, and sat staring up the chimney. She looked as though she might be about to start her tortuous wanderings again. As Streaky moved lightly to the window, the cat glanced over her shoulder at Kitty, as if to say "You coming, or what?"

Kitty rose to her feet. "I may be making the most ridiculous mistake of my life," she said slowly, "but I think I'm going to see what that is. It doesn't sound very frightening to me, and if Perkins isn't bothered, why should I be? I can always turn round and come back. I know how to get out now."

"You're mad, you are," said the boy, his voice shaking. "I'm going home, I am. You should come."

"No, I'll just ..." Kitty said quietly. Streaky stepped up onto the window-sill and disappeared.

She pulled Sky's smock over her head, folded it carefully and draped it over one of the chairs in Streaky's nest. No point making it any worse than it was. In her skirt and t-shirt she went to join the cat.

"I hope you know what you're doing," she said, touching it behind the ear, "because I don't. Go on, then."

Perkins gathered herself on her haunches and sprang lightly upwards into the chimney. Kitty ducked inside and felt for her first handhold.

XI

In some ways it was better this time. It was never quite pitch dark, for one thing. Every so often the flue would open into a fireplace and the dim light filtered up and down. Once Kitty's eyes had become accustomed to the gloom, she could make out the way without difficulty. In places the flue was blocked by clusters of sticks and dead leaves which she had to kick out of her way, presuming they were the remains of old birds' nests. In one or two of them the birds still lay, long dead and dessicated. And Perkins seemed to take her responsibility quite seriously. She led Kitty upwards with odd little chirrups and mewing sounds, and every so often came back to see how she was getting on, and butted her head against whichever bit of her was nearest, which was comforting.

But in another it was much worse, for once they had climbed up into the first chimney, the way soon turned downwards, a nearly vertical shaft with side-shafts opening off at intervals and leading into other fireplaces, presumably. And going down was very awkward. Perkins was happy enough, dropping down softly from one projection to another, beautifully balanced with four feet and her tail. But Kitty had no tail and two feet fewer. She had to clamber clumsily, peering dimly down past her own chest, holding on with her hands and feeling with her feet for the next toehold.

As she climbed she listened for the ghostly noise below. It was still there once in a while, with long silences between, but it didn't seem to be getting any nearer. Kitty thought they had come fifty or sixty feet down, and the walls of the chimney were no longer brick but stone now, larger and larger stones as they descended. She thought they were probably reaching a level where the castle was older. It also got cleaner as they went, because the chimney had served fewer fires down here. But it was narrower too, and she began to feel uncomfortably aware of the mass of the buildings above. She had reached a spot where the flue kinked this way and that, giving her the chance to lean against the wall and rest for a moment. She was in the heart of a thousand tons of masonry, lying back with stone a few inches in front of her nose and stone close on either side. She only had to move a finger to touch it. The cat stopped a few feet below her and began washing itself, unconcerned. "It's all right for you, cheeky monkey," she said, "you're little, you can nip through here easily. You might show a little concern for me. Don't you know how scary this is? Where are you leading me? And will I be able to get back when we've been there?"

The cat didn't reply, but stopped washing and winked both eyes at her. Then it sauntered up and rubbed its head on her knee. She scratched it under the chin and was rewarded with a brief purr. The faint moaning floated up the flue, and Perkins turned her head and mewed. It plainly meant something to her. She knew what it was.

"Come on, then, puss, let's get on with it!" Kitty said, and started climbing down again. She thought the light was increasing as they descended. They had reached a much wider flue, with plenty of footholds where the stones were carelessly cut, offering what felt almost like a ladder down which she let herself slowly with soot under her nails and in her hair. Presently her feet reached solid stone, and she found herself standing in a great open fireplace with welcome daylight dazzling her eyes. She stepped out into the day and stood on a broad pavement with a wall behind her and an arcade of graceful arches in front. Why should there be a fireplace out here practically in the open air? It was an enormous one, too, far bigger than anything she had seen before. Did they have barbecues in medieval times?

Looking over the balustrade she caught her breath, for in front of her and below was a startling panorama of stone and brick and tiles, a confused assembly of buildings and windows and staircases, deserted and silent. This was a part of the Castle she had never imagined, one which seemed completely unknown and forgotten. Along this broad covered pavement she pictured lords and ladies slowly parading in gorgeous silks and satins and lace, accompanied by the soft fluting of minstrels, solemnly smiling and bowing to each other as they passed. There was no sight of the outside world, for the grey walls rose over the great enclosure and shut off any glimpse of the sea or the land, though dark clouds scudded overhead and the wind could be heard to moan far above. Down here not a breath stirred the dust and desertion and the ghostly lords and ladies could pass undisturbed.

Perkins had gently leapt up onto the rail of the balustrade and sat admiring the view, blinking her eyes at the sudden light. Then she dropped to the paving and trotted serenely on with her tail in the air. Kitty followed.

A quarter of a mile to the south and nearly one hundred and fifty feet higher up, Melody stood looking out of the window of her office. She gazed unseeing at the grey sea and the scudding clouds beyond the castle wall. A few tourists strolled in the grounds, huddled in anoraks and woolly hats. She was thinking about Kitty, and the conversation she had had with Charity and Faith early that morning. She had gone to the kitchen hoping for news of the missing girl.

"No, nothing," said Faith, "we were hoping you might know. She didn't come for her breakfast this morning."

Charity was worried. "Do you think something's happened to her? She might have had an accident."

"Or she might just be hiding out in one of the outbuildings, keeping a low profile," said Ma Cott, bustling in. "She'll be hungry, but she'll be all right, just you see."

"Has Mr.Baggott said anything? If she's somewhere in the grounds, he'd probably know."

But Baggott knew no more than anyone else, they said, or he'd have told them. He was all right, Baggott.

"Perhaps we ought to go down to the harbour and see if Billy knows anything?" Faith suggested.

"I'll do that," Melody said quickly, and didn't see the amused glance that passed between the Sisters. "I meant to go and see Sky Lovechild later anyway, so I can go round that way."

She started and turned away from the window, hearing voices in the corridor outside. "Trinket? Trinket! Drat the woman, where is she?" It was Lady Sybil.

Where do you think I am, you fool? Melody said to herself, where else would I be at this time of the morning?

The door opened abruptly. "Ah, there you are, did you not hear me calling?" snapped Lady Sybil. "Why must I hunt around for you? You need to buck your ideas up!"

Melody went to her desk and sat down, stirring the computer

mouse into life. "Was there something you wanted, Lady Sybil?" she asked politely, thinking of the banking password.

"Of course there is, you fool! Why else would I be shouting myself hoarse? I need another five hundred from the account. See to it, would you?"

Melody looked at her calmly. "What do you need it for, please? You had a thousand pounds only the other day."

"What's it to you? Mind your own business!"

"But it is my business, Lady Sybil. Sir Lancelot put me in charge of the business accounts, so I have to keep accurate records of all income and expenditure, that's my job. So can I have the invoices and receipts for what you spent this week?"

Lady Sybil leant forward and slapped her hand on the desk, making the computer screen jiggle. "How dare you? Just remember who I am, and who you are, you worthless object! This is my home and it's my money, and what I spend it on is none of your damned business!"

"But that's exactly what it is, Lady Sybil. It isn't your money, it's the Castle's. This is a business, and it must be run on proper business lines. You can't just dip into it whenever you feel like it."

Melody forced herself to appear calm and confident. She sat back in her chair, hoping that she looked like an efficient executive interviewing a candidate.

"Now, the receipts, please?"

Lady Sybil stared at her, her mouth working. "You idle, worthless piece of garbage," she ground out through gritted teeth, "I'll have you out on your ear by the end of this day if you dare to defy me! You have no idea who you're dealing with, and you have no idea what disaster I will bring crashing round your ears if you ..."

But Melody had heard enough. "Lady Sybil, I'm an employee here," she said, rising from her seat. "I'm employed by Castle Crayle Limited to manage its affairs, and the company's funds are not your private pocket money. Unless you can provide me with evidence that you are spending money on the company's behalf and for the company's benefit, I will no longer release any funds for your future use. I hope that's entirely clear, Your Ladyship? Now, if you'll excuse me, I have work to do," and she sat down again and fiddled with some papers on the desktop.

There was a long silence. Lady Sybil stared at the top of Melody's bent head as though she was about to pick up a chair and smash it over her. Then she recovered herself. She placed both hands on the desk, leaned forward and hissed "Then I shall just take the money, and see how you like that?"

Melody smiled at her and said pleasantly "You can't. You have no access to the bank account, remember? You can only go through me, and I'm not going to help you. And by the way ..." she stood again, and echoed the older woman's stance with her hands on the desk. "... where is our little guest, Kitty Younger? Do you know? Because she hasn't been seen since yesterday, and there are concerns for her safety."

Lady Sybil was taken aback by this directness. "How should I know? She's probably taken herself home. Yes, that's it, she's had what she wants from us, so she's gone to sponge off someone else! For two pins I'd call the police. She's bound to have stolen something."

"For two pins, Lady Sybil, I'll call the police myself. A child is missing here. That's police business, isn't it? Someone needs to start searching for her, and that's the job of the police. So if you know anything, you should say so, so I can pass it on to them."

The woman glanced from side to side. "You're to call no one," she said shakily, "I don't know anything about the wretched girl. If you dare speak to the police, my husband will sack you on the spot. You hear? On the spot, I say." She raised her voice again, her confidence returning. "We won't be needing you much longer in any case. You'll see, you'll be out on your ear, homeless and jobless, characterless and penniless. Just you wait and see!" and she turned and strutted out with as much dignity as she could muster.

Melody sat down and leaned back in her chair. She felt elated. She had stood up to the dreadful woman, and it had worked. And, of course, it had to work because she alone controlled the bank account, though Lady Sybil didn't know that yet. That was a card she would save up her sleeve for when it was needed. Now, she would do as she had promised, go out and see Billy Cott and Sky in case they had any news. But as she gathered herself together and shut down the computer, she paused. There was something ... what had Lady Sybil said? 'We won't be needing you much longer in any case'? What did that mean? Had her ladyship accidentally let slip something she shouldn't? What was she planning? It had to be something to do with Medulla, she thought. This would want watching.

Kitty, meanwhile, was not having quite such a good time as before. Perkins had led her briskly along the broad pavement, round a corner and into a wide passage with an elegant tiled floor that led away from the light into the bowels of the building. On either side were locked doors – Kitty snatched at one or two door handles as she passed, but none would move – and overhead were festoons of cobweb. They turned a couple of sharp corners and then the light increased as they entered another long gallery open on one side to the air. Here there was some damage to the building though, the ceiling had fallen and and the way was blocked by jumbled stone and rubble. Perkins didn't stop, but jumped lithely onto the balustrade and then down into a void.

Kitty ran to the rail and looked over, alarmed. Three feet below her, the cat stood on a ledge, perhaps twelve inches wide. As Kitty watched, she moved off along the ledge, oblivious to the drop. Kitty looked all round, but found no alternative. Her heart in her mouth she climbed on to the rail and let herself gingerly down to the ledge. She faced the wall, her nose touching the rough stone, and spread her hands along it keeping as close to it as she could, then sidled slowly along, one foot at a time. She dared not look out or down, but somehow knew that behind her was a forty-foot drop into a deep triangular well in the centre of the castle, sheer walls below falling to a dark and jumbled floor, sheer walls rising above, windowless, to a little triangle of bright sky far overhead.

Luckily it didn't last long, but she was almost weeping with fear by the time Perkins slipped into an empty window aperture, and Kitty was able to follow, dropping to a safe stone floor shaking with relief. Then off they set again, always downwards. There were broad elegant staircases an inch deep in soft dust, and narrow precipitous stairs with uneven treads and a handrail long ago crumbled to shreds, and once they went through a long room with tiny windows high up near the ceiling, and long stone tables on either side. She couldn't decide if it had been a refectory or dining room, a study area for monks, or a place where once long ago some alchemist had carried out his arcane experiments. In this room the soft moaning from the depths echoed and reverberated and once again she heard a sort of slapping noise, something soft and wet against stone, she thought.

Out into another hallway they went, with another floor of homely red tiles, and suddenly with another little chirrup, Perkins disappeared. Only by getting on her hands and knees was Kitty able to look about and work out where she had gone. In a corner there was a small arched aperture less than two feet high. The tiles sloped down towards it. It looked for all the world like a drain. Peering in, she could see two green eyes regarding her steadily.

"What's this, puss?" she said quietly. "This isn't a chimney, is it? Where are we going now?"

But this evidently was the way they were to go, because from the black night behind the cat rose that mournful howl again, not exactly loud but louder than it had been before. It sounded sad rather than savage. Something or someone was not happy.

The little tunnel was dry, and big enough to start with. Its floor was fairly smooth and sloped gently down. At intervals other tunnels joined it on either side, bringing a little light with them. Ahead, Perkins' black fur was mostly invisible, but every so often she would turn to make sure Kitty was following, and her green eyes shone in the darkness. She made encouraging little noises as she trotted onwards and down. She plainly knew what she was about.

Kitty found it tiring, crawling on all fours. In places the tunnel or drain – for she had decided that was what this was, a drain although it didn't smell much, just a hint of the sea perhaps – was lower and she had to wriggle forward on her elbows.

"Oof! Wait up, puss!" she gasped after one particularly exhausting wriggle, "I need a rest. It's all right for a cat, but I'm not one, am I, I'm a girl?"

This was true, though Perkins may not have appreciated the difference. Kitty was a lot bigger than a cat, and less bendy. Cats didn't seem to get soot and brick dust in their mouths and eyes, and they didn't have a grazed knee. A cat didn't have to worry which way she went forward. She always went head first because she knew she could land softly. Kitty sometimes went feet first in which case her skirt rode up round her waist and her legs got scratched, or she went head first and risked knocking herself out if they came to a sudden drop. And a cat didn't cry and find her cheeks were streaked with dusty tears. It was a lot better being a cat, where labyrinths of tunnels and chimneys were concerned.

As they got deeper into the labyrinth, the tunnels or drains – she was certain now that she was in some sort of elaborate drainage system – got smaller and progress slower. There was still a little light from time to time as side tunnels joined, but she realised with dismay that where they did so, there would not be sufficient room for her to wriggle round into one of them and aim for the light. She could only go onwards. There would be no escape.

The stone was touching the back of her head most of the time now, and she was reduced to wriggling on her stomach for there wasn't room even to crawl. She humped along slowly, and Perkins had to stop and wait for her more and more often. The cat seemed very patient, though, and showed no sign of wanting to hurry forward into the darkness and leave her behind. Although the drain did not smell very drainy and was perfectly dry, there was a stronger smell of salt sea and seaweed now. They must be approaching sea level, she thought. Perhaps this was the source of the cat's fishy smell at night. She wondered if she would suddenly find herself faced with water, and no way to back up again. But no, a cat wouldn't lead her into water, would she? Cats weren't over-fond of water, salt or fresh.

Humping along, listening to the mournful howling ahead and still no clue what was making it, she banged her head. She lay and waited until the wave of pain subsided, then peered in front of her. There was still just a little light from the last junction, and she thought there was a little light up ahead too, for she could make out the shape of Perkins silhouetted against it. The cat had hunkered down and sat waiting for her, looking like a blancmange on a plate and blinking her eyes patiently.

A stone just in front of her hung lower than the rest and made a kind of bottleneck. She reached forward with her hands and tried to judge whether there was room to pass. There was not, she thought. She might get her head through by turning it to one side, but the rest? What bit of her body would stick up most, her shoulders or her bottom? She wasn't sure, her bottom, probably. But she was squashy there, wasn't she? Perhaps she could force her way past. Further on where Perkins waited, the drain looked bigger. In any case, she knew she would never be able to go back.

Slowly and with infinite patience she undid her belt and wriggled her skirt down over her feet, then managed to pull it up to her face. She pushed it forward past the obstruction. Then she did the same with her knickers, and then her t-shirt. Then she lay for a long time, the stone cold against her bare skin, gathering her courage. She could die here, she thought. If this didn't work, she'd be stuck and helpless. What was worse, to be discovered naked and dead, or just dead? She thought she liked just dead better. But it was academic, wasn't it, because no one would ever find her here. No one came here except one small cat and whatever was making that noise up ahead. She would never be found, and even if she were, she'd be a skeleton so the lack of clothes wouldn't matter.

How incongruous, to be stuck down here, naked in the bowels of the earth! She thought of her friends. Melody wouldn't be naked. It was hard to imagine her without her clothes, probably trousers and a fitted jacket. Sky would be swathed in bright tie-dye shawls and a long skirt, and big boots. And her family – Jake would be wearing a few clothes, probably, rolling around on a rugby field getting muddy and having a lovely time. Ellie would be wearing her uniform, unless she was swimming. And her mother would be having a meeting in a skyscraper somewhere, telling people what to do and definitely fully clothed. And here was Kitty, stuck in a drain and completely bare except for her socks and shoes. Her shoes, she thought with a start! Suppose her shoes got stuck? Her socks would follow wherever her feet could fit, but her shoes might not. She reached back, wriggled them off and pushed them in front of her.

Then she gathered her courage and pushed forward with her fingers and toes scrabbling at the stone. She turned her head sideways and inched forward. Her hair caught on the rough stone, and then she felt her shoulders brushing against it. A little respite while her slim waist came through, and then came the crunch. She felt her skin rasping on the stone and pressed her stomach against the floor as hard as she could, and wriggled and wriggled until some part of her gave and she was through. Her legs followed, then her heels. She could do nothing with her toes, but was able to grasp ahead of her with her fingers and find something to pull on. An inch, and then another inch, and she was past the obstruction and found space around her, big enough to sit up. She laughed with relief, and set about dressing herself again.

The cat got up and sauntered back to her, wondering what the hold-up was. She petted it, and it butted her and purred as if to say 'Well done, I'm proud of you!'. Then it turned and led onwards. The moaning and flapping were louder now, much louder, and inside it she thought she could make out speech though the words were indistinct. That was good, she decided. If it had words, it probably wasn't a dangerous monster, but a person. It might be a nasty person – there seemed to be a few of those round here – but it probably wouldn't eat her. She got down on her stomach and began to crawl again.

"Nearly Normal Nidd came this morning," Sky said, "to tell me he's asked all round the village and no one's seen her. Is that tea all right?"

"Oh yes, thanks. I never knew you could make tea with beetroot."

"You probably can, but that's echinacea, sage and blackberry. Do you like it?"

"It's … interesting. I went to the harbour and the Billies haven't seen anything either."

They sat in companionable silence for a moment.

"I had a row with Lady Sybil this morning," Melody said. "I think I won. I should have stood up to her long ago, she's just a stupid old woman who doesn't begin to understand running a business."

"I expect she threatened you with the sack, though?"

"Of course she did. But I'm a lot less worried about that than I ought to be. I've got some leverage. I expect I could sue her for breach of contract. There's something going on up there though, something I don't know about."

"What is it?"

"Well, I don't know about it, do I?" Melody laughed. "Some plot, though. Not against me, so much, but something to do with the Castle. She said I was going to be out of a job soon."

"They're going to sell the Castle, perhaps? Can you sell a castle?"

"I expect you can, if you can find someone daft enough to buy it. It's not as if it's an official ancient monument or anything."

"That could be a good thing, though. Someone else might let you run it properly."

Melody smiled and put her cup down. "One can but hope," she said. "I'd better be getting back. Don't want to give her any excuse to kick off. It's always her, you know. Sir Lancelot isn't much bother, he wanders around in a daze most of the time, his head full of moths."

"Moths? You mean he's dotty?"

"Well, he is. But they're real moths, did you not know? He has one of the largest collections of dead moths in the world, or so he says. I think he might be working up to organising another of his moth-hunting expeditions, because he asked me to look up French Guyana on the internet for him. He'll get a shock though, because I won't release the money for it."

"Can you do that?"

Melody grinned at her. "I can, actually. Oh yes, I certainly can. Bye bye!"

They kissed, and Melody made her way out into the street. The grey clouds were breaking up and sped inland, leaving a watery blue sky behind.

Kitty was making better progress now, able to raise herself up and crawl on hands and knees. In front of her Perkins scampered, pausing now and then to make sure she was following. The noise was getting closer, a rolling monotone that rose and fell, sometimes contemplative and almost tuneful, then relapsing into something that sounded a lot like swearing though she could not make out the words. It was when the swearing started that the slapping noise could be heard. She wondered what was being slapped, and by whom.

The drain grew steadily wider and higher, and was slanting downwards more and more steeply. She was able to rise to her feet and go forward at a crouch. The cat was having no difficulty, but Kitty found it harder and harder to keep her footing, digging her shoes in to stop herself slipping. Once or twice she did slip, and fell on her bottom, grabbing at the walls with her hands to stop herself and sending a shower of small stones and debris down in front of her. Perkins stopped and looked back at her as if to say "Would you stop chucking stones at me like that? Just use your tail, silly!" but Kitty had no tail and was two feet short of a full set. It was harder for her.

The light was stronger now. There was clearly a large space in front of them and below, but the drain was falling away almost vertically and Kitty was losing her grip. She tried to turn on her face so she could control her slide with her hands, but she was moving too fast. She sensed Perkins leaping nimbly out of the way as she slid past in a shower of stone fragments, shrieking into the void. There was a broad space, and a broad floor beneath, and a row of lights far above. Then something struck her head, and everything went black.

XII

"What a rotten piece of luck, I seem to be completely stuck ..."
Kitty heard. Were those words in her head? Had she imagined
the soft voice, the words clear but somehow mangled as though
spoken by a mouth containing more tongue than usual? There
was a pain just above her ear, and space above her. She opened
her eyes, then shut them again. Stone, she had seen, wide acres
of stone up above, vaulted and dimly lit. She moved her arm,
and put her fingers to her face. Yes, that was her face all right.
Her lip was swollen, and hurt when she touched it.

She tried the other arm. That moved too. Her back ached, and
she seemed to be lying on something rough. Little spikes of pain
stabbed her when she wriggled. She lay back and began an
inventory of her limbs. Right arm, yes, there it was. Left arm,
and all the fingers seemed to work. Right leg, bent at an angle
but intact. Left leg straight out. She lifted her head, feeling a
lightning stab of pain as she did so, and peered down the length
of her body. Stomach, okay. Shoes down there in the distance,
scuffed and dirty but still present.

There was the voice again, "I need to get away and go, to
where the kelp sways to and fro ..." Kelp, she thought, that was
seaweed, wasn't it? "Because I'm getting very hungry, and ...
tumpty, tumpty, tumpty ... what rhymes with hungry? Tumpty,
tumpty, bungry, mungry, I am getting very ... is there someone
there?"

Yes, there's someone here. It's me, she thought. I'm here, and
I'm imagining poetry, how weird is that? She made a great effort
and rolled onto her stomach. Her chin rested on flagstones, and
the floor stretched away in the dim light. The light, where was it
coming from? She rolled back again and craned round.
Overhead there was a sudden clatter and a pigeon fled across
her vision. It settled somewhere up in the roof, and another
pigeon welcomed it with a coo. So there was a roof, and birds
could get in. That was good. She was still in the Castle, but
where birds could get in, perhaps she could get out?

Where was Perkins? Perkins had led her here, so where was
she? Was she all right? Was Kitty all right herself? She rolled

over again and sat up, her head pounding. Yes, she decided, she was all right. She shivered slightly. It was cold down here. Down, she thought, that was something. She was down. This place felt deep, deep down, right at the heart of things. She was somewhere right at the roots of the great castle. They had gone down, down the passages and staircases, down the chimney flues and the drains, and now had reached the very bottom of things.

As if on cue, Perkins appeared beside her. She put her front paws on Kitty's knee and looked up at her face, as if to ask "Are you OK? I was worried about you!"

"Yes, I'm all right, thank you," Kitty said, and stroked her. "I think I must have got knocked out for a minute. Banged my head or something. But I'll do. Come on, let's try and get up!"

"Is someone there?" asked the voice again. Kitty stood, feeling still a bit shaky, and looked round. This was a large space, not particularly high but wide and long. Overhead was a shallow vaulted ceiling of stone, ribbed and fanned. Along one wall, very high up, was a row of apertures, not windows for there was no glass, just holes. The light that came in was green for the apertures seemed to be partially covered with leaves, ivy and ferns that reached in and hung in festoons down the walls. Distantly she could hear gulls crying, and the pigeon clattered across the vault again and slipped out through one of the apertures.

The floor was largely unobstructed but in places under the walls there were piles of fallen masonry, pale scars on the wall showing where the stone had crumbled and slipped. In one corner was a heap of other debris, baulks of timber and branches dessicated and broken, and smaller white sticks she did not care to investigate too closely for they made her think of poor Roland, far above in his forgotten room. "Is there someone there?" said the voice again. "Oh drat and blast it!" She turned her attention to the centre of the room.

The floor sloped gently down to the middle, which made sense to Kitty. If the path she had followed to get here had been an ancient drainage system, it made sense that any water it carried should flow down and be collected. Presumably there was a way for it to run out to the sea, eventually. She told her feet to walk for the first time, and obediently they led her down to the centre of the floor. Here was a long dark shape, a fallen statue she thought at first. Its surface was delicately carved in little diamond shapes, and it curved and flowed sinuously along the length of the room. It was rather beautiful in a sinister way, but what was the point? She followed it along. It was quite three feet high and rounded. At its end there was something that might have been a head, a blunt shape with a bulging eyelid and a wide mouth, closed. It wasn't a fallen statue, she realised, but was supposed to be here on the floor. Was it the enormous figure of a snake? And if so, whatever was it for, down here where no one would see it?

It seemed ridiculous, to carve a great snake and leave it down here in the dim dark, unseen and unappreciated. Who would do that? It must be very old. She gave it a little kick.

"Ow," said the voice, "what did you do that for?"

Kitty leapt back, tripped over her own feet and landed on her bottom. One carved eyelid had snapped open, and she found herself the object of a black, bulging, liquid gaze.

"I wanted to see if you were alive?" she said hesitantly.

The creature stirred slightly, all along the length of its great body. "Of course I'm alive, you silly creature! How could I be speaking to you if I weren't alive?" The voice, like the eye, was liquid, and she could see the mouth working, and a glimpse of a thick black tongue within. But no teeth, so far, she thought thankfully. "I'm alive all right, only I are stuck," it said.

"I am stuck," she said without thinking.

"What? You too? This is serious!"

"No, no," she laughed, "I was just correcting you. You're supposed to say 'I AM stuck', not 'I ARE stuck'."

"So you're not stuck?"

"No. Well, except that I don't know how I'm getting out of here. That's a sort of stuck, isn't it? We're both in much the same boat."

"What's a boat?"

Kitty knelt up and looked at it. Somehow she was no longer frightened. This creature was big, and strange, but there was no threat in it. If anything, the large eyes – for as the head turned she could see the one on the other side too – were rather sad, large and luminous, brimming with tears.

"I've seen you before, haven't I?" she said, getting up and moving closer. "That was you, wasn't it, down on the shore the other day, looking at me?"

"My dear young creature," it said airily, "why would I do that? Why should I be looking at you? Is there something particularly interesting about you, is that it?"

"No," said Kitty slowly, feeling uncomfortable. "No, not really. Except I've got arms and legs, and you haven't. I suppose that might seem a bit unusual if you're not used to it."

Kitty immediately wondered if that had been a bit too rude. She knew that a little bit of rudeness can always be dismissed as "direct speaking", but occasionally one went too far and caused offence. The creature rolled its eyes and looked at her out of the corners. For someone with almost no facial expression, it seemed to be rather good at suggesting disapproval and scepticism. It had taken no offence, however.

"Arms and legs?" it said without rancour. "I suppose you mean those sticky things you keep waving about. What are they for, exactly?"

"They're for moving about, and picking things up. Look!" She walked up and down a little, and picked up a stick from the floor and tossed it into a corner.

"Huh!" it said, "looks a bit unsafe to me. Don't you ever fall off them?"

She had to admit that occasionally one did fall over, yes.

"There you are, then. Why don't you just get down on the ground and crawl like a civilised being? You can't fall off the floor."

Kitty was about to protest, and explain the advantages of running and jumping and throwing things, but the creature was not to be stopped.

"That little creature that comes ... you know, the little black one that's soft and winds itself all round you ..." it asked.

"Do you mean the cat?"

"Cat, is it? All right, the cat. It seems to have these limbs, like you have. But the cat's limbs all point downwards most of the time, which is at least consistent and makes it harder to fall off. Yours go all over the place. You look quite dangerous to me."

As if on cue, Perkins scampered up to say hallo to the

creature, butting her head against it as though it were an old friend. There was a short silence. Kitty was thinking that she knew perfectly well what this was. This was the famous Worm, or Wyrm. This was the thing everyone said didn't exist, but it did exist, and here it was, talking to her.

"I notice that you talk English," she said. "Oh, and do you have anything I could eat? I had some biscuits a while ago, but they've worn off."

"What's English? No, I've nothing in here. I'm pretty hungry myself. Sorry."

How remarkable, she thought, a savage legendary monster and it's apologising to me! Out loud she said "English is the words you're using. They're the same ones I use myself, so I can understand you."

"Are there other words, then? These are the only ones I know."

"But how did you learn them?"

"I don't know. They're just there in my head, I think. How did you?"

Kitty was silent for a moment. How had she? No one ever sat you down and said "Now this is Enlgish, and I'm going to teach it to you," did they? Miss Hevesham was the English teacher at school, but everything she taught depended on you knowing the words to start with.

She decided to change the subject. "It was you, though, wasn't it, the other day? You were looking at me out of the water?"

It admitted that sometimes it might swim quite close to the shore, "just following a particularly juicy bit of seaweed, you know, or the scent of a whelk."

"Why, what do whelks smell like?" she asked politely.

"Like themselves, of course. Why should they smell like anything else?" He sniffed. "Do you smell like something else, or is that all you?"

"I don't think I smell like anything," she said. "Soap, perhaps."

"What's soap when it's at home?"

"It's stuff we put on our skin to make it clean."

"Oh, really." It thought for a moment. "I just rub myself

against the sand, that usually does the trick. Not that I get very dirty, being in the sea so much. Why don't you rub yourself in the sand?"

"I don't think that would be very comfortable. I have soft skin, you see, not nice hard scales like you. What's your name?"

"Name? What's a name?"

"Everybody has a name. It's what you call yourself."

"Oh. I call me 'me'. That's my name, 'Me'."

"Or 'I', I suppose?"

"Or 'I', yes. Wait a minute, you just called yourself 'I' as well. We can't both have the same name. That would be too much of a coincidence."

"Yes, it would. A name is another word that people call you. My name is Kitty, for instance."

"Kitty, yes, that's a nice ... er, name. What other people, though? I don't see any people, only this thing here, that just sits and blinks. No one comes and says 'Hallo, Herbert, how are you today?' or 'Hey, Christabel, what do you think just happened?' Those are names, aren't they, Herbert and Christabel?"

"Yes they are. I don't think either of them are very suitable for you, though. How do you know about those words?"

"Don't know. They're just there, in my head, like all the others."

"And Christabel's a girl's name. Are you a girl?"

"I don't know. Am I?"

"Well, have you had any babies?"

"Do you mean have I laid any eggs?"

"Or that, yes."

"No, not that I recall."

"Well you must be a boy then. And I think you're a wyrm. I'm a girl, Perkins over there is a cat and you're a wyrm. I think that's what your name should be, 'Wyrm'."

"All right. My name is Wyrm. How do you do?"

"Very well, thank you. We ought to shake hands, but you don't seem to have any. Have you got anything else we can shake?"

"I have a tail, but it's occupied at the moment. It's stuck in that hole."

Kitty walked down the length of Wyrm's body. It tapered gradually, but before it could come to a point she reached the end wall of the chamber. There was an arched entrance here, about four feet high. Evidently this was how Wyrm came and went. Presumably the archway led to the sea. There must be a tunnel first, though, under the castle walls and the dunes. She wondered who had built it. It must have been a very long time ago, for its existence to have been so forgotten.

But she saw immediately what the problem was. As Wyrm had been coming in, probably to rest and sleep after a trip out in the sea, part of the arch had fallen in. Perhaps he had brushed against it, and finally dislodged some of the decayed masonry. Several of the stones of the arch had slipped down and lay across his tail, gripping it. They were large stones, each a foot or more across, and they still clung together to make a heavy stone beam, trapping him.

"You see?" he called, "you see what the problem is? I've been here for ... well, days, I think. A long time, anyway. I can't budge it, look!" and he suddenly broke into frenzied movement, his long body forming huge coils and thrashing this way and that. His scales beat against the flagstones, making the slapping sound she had heard on her way down, and his voice rose in a wordless howl of frustration.

"Stop! Stop!" she shouted, flinging herself out of the way before she was struck and hurled to the floor. "Stop, you'll hurt yourself. And me, probably!"

Wyrm lay still, his head curled round, looking at her from one sad eye. "See?" he said. "I'm trapped. Oh, bother, what am I going to do?"

Kitty got to her feet again and walked closer. She leaned over his tail and grasped the end of the stone beam, but it was far too heavy for her to shift. What was needed was a lever. She remembered the jumble of rubbish in the far corner and walked towards it.

"Have you any idea what this place is?" she called as she passed his head. "Do you know what it was built for?"

"How would I? It was old when I found it, and that was ... I don't know, a very long time ago. It was quite a Godsend, too, a good place to lie in the winters when the storms are out and the sea's too rough to feed. In the Autumn and Winter there's a nice little stream out of that hole you came through, and I can lie in that and be comfortable. I don't like it too dry."

Approaching the pile of rubbish, she could see that the white things she had recoiled from before were just what she'd feared – bones. Whether they were human or animal she couldn't tell, and didn't care to look. Instead she spotted a large beam of timber propped up against the wall. It looked just small enough that she could move it, but stout and not rotten. She tumbled it to the ground and then spent a long time lifting one end, dragging it a few feet and then resting before starting again. When she managed to get it to the broken arch she left it on the ground and went back. She needed something to rest it on, a fulcrum. She could see plenty of stone blocks that would be perfect, but she couldn't move them. At last she settled on two more lengths of timber, thick and heavy but short and just about moveable.

In all it took her an hour or so, she estimated, to assemble her lever. She managed, with much pushing and shoving and grunting, to get the end of the timber under part of the fallen stonework, with the smaller blocks underneath it, one on top of the other. The tail part, that she would push down on, was long and the part that was under the stones was short, that was the right way. She remembered some of this from Science lessons at school.

She rested for a while, and tried to explain to Wyrm what she was planning to do, though she thought he didn't really understand. Then she made her first attempt. She stepped up onto the tail of her lever, one hand on the wall to keep her balance, and gently bounced up and down. The lever held and did not snap, as she had feared. Its short end ground against the stone above it, and she thought there was a little movement. One or two fragments broke free, a trickle of stone slivers, but the main mass held firm. She stepped off and had a rest.

Her second attempt also failed, even though she threw caution to the winds and jumped vigorously up and down on the end of the lever. She just wasn't heavy enough. She needed help, something much heavier. She looked round, and couldn't see anything she could use, nothing she could manage to move anyway. Then she had a brainwave. Wyrm! Wyrm himself! He must be terribly heavy, he was almost twenty feet long, wasn't he? He must weigh ten or fifteen times as much as she did.

"Dear Wyrm, I need your help," she said, walking towards his head, running one hand along his scaly side. He felt warm, just a little, like a living thing under the scales. The scales gave off little glimpses of colour under her fingertips, and she realised what it was that Sky had given her, and what she had found herself on the beach. The pretty little diamonds were Wyrm-scales, scraped off by the sand or just working themselves loose to be washed up by the surf. Looking more closely she could see places on his side where scales had come away, and there beneath them were new ones, small and soft and pale and evidently growing. He could afford to lose a few, then, if he could grow new ones.

"What I need you to do, Wyrm, is to turn yourself round and bring your head up to your tail. Can you do that? I don't know how flexible you are, but can you try?"

He did try, and proved to be very flexible indeed. He followed her back towards the arch and his own tail, wriggling and shuffling easily.

"Now, can you lift your head and put part of yourself on top of this bit of wood? And when I say, I want you to bear down as heavily as you can, and at the same time wriggle your tail?"

"That's an awful lot of things at once," he grumbled, but did as she asked. Once a great loop of his body was resting on top of the lever, she used it to haul herself up as well, and sat on him. "If the girls at school could see me now," she thought, "I'm basically sitting on a live dragon! How cool is that?"

She settled herself, looked round to see that Perkins was well out of the way, and said "Now, Wyrm! Push down one end and wriggle the other! Come on!"

It went beautifully. Well, fairly beautifully, in that it did work. As she had planned, the weight of Wyrm's coil pressed the lever down, the other end of the lever lifted the stonework a couple of inches, and a violent wriggle of his tail freed it. True, she had to leap for her life as the stone beam slid sideways off the end of the lever and threatened to crush her. She landed spread-eagled on the flagstones, bruised but elated. And true, as the stonework fell it landed on Wyrm before sliding off and crashing to the floor with a great thud, making him bellow. But it did work. He was free and the tunnel was open.

"Ow, ow," he complained, "that's the second time I've been hurt since you arrived! You're a very bad influence!"

She got to her feet and patted his long back. "Now, don't make a fuss. You're free, aren't you? You're not stuck any more, look!"

"Oh yes. Yes, that's good. But I've taken all the scales off my neck, look! All my beautiful scales, scratched and torn off. It'll take ages to grow them again."

"Well, you've got ages, haven't you? Just be patient. Now, before you slither off to do whatever it is you do out there, can we just sit a little and try to think how I'm going to get out of here? Perkins can get back the way we came, but there's no way I can, so we have to think of something else!"

She let herself slide down his neck and sat leaning against it, his great black soulful eye just beside her. It felt quite companionable. Perkins, pleased all the excitement and thrashing about was over, came and sat on her lap.

"I don't understand how you did that, though," Wyrm said. "Was it magic?"

She laughed. "There's no such thing as magic," she said.

"How do you know?"

She thought. "Actually," she said slowly, "I don't, not really. I mean, I'm leaning against a mythical creature, so I ought not to be too dismissive. But no, it wasn't magic. Even if magic exists, I don't know any. It was something called a lever. If you put weight on one end of a piece of wood, it'll lift the same amount at the other end. And if you make the wood uneven, with a long bit one side and a short bit the other, it'll lift much more. Some old mathematician said that if he had a lever long enough, he could lift the world."

"Lift the world? What for, why would anyone want to do that? Think of the mess if he dropped it!"

"I don't think he meant to actually do it, he was just saying he could."

"What's a mathematician anyway?"

"Someone who does really hard sums."

"Like one plus two?"

"That isn't a hard sum."

"It is in my world. It makes three, which is the biggest number I know."

"What happens if you have more than three things, then?"

"I've never had more than three things."

"What sort of things do you have, usually?"

"I don't. Mostly I have no things." He thought for a moment. "Yup, that's it. Look around you, what do you see? Any things? No, that's it in a nutshell, I have no things."

"You probably don't need any," she said, "you're lucky. Things are more trouble than they're worth, on the whole. Now, how do I get out of here? Because it's been lovely to meet you but I need a bath. And I'm more hungry than I've ever been in my life!"

XIII

"You could have knocked me down with a feather," Ma Cott said. Faith, Charity and Melody stood open-mouthed. "Standing there on the back doorstep she was, filthy dirty and dripping wet as though she'd been swimming with all her clothes on, the lamb. And all she said was 'Is there any breakfast? Or is it dinner? I'm not quite sure what time it is?'"

"But where had she been?" said Melody.

"She wouldn't say. I brought her in and sat her by the range, and made her take all her sopping things off and wrap herself in an old coat of Baggott's, and she ate three sausage sandwiches and a bowl of cornflakes with half a pint of milk."

"Where is she now?"

"She slipped off up to your bathroom. She's probably basking in a hot bath right now, I would hope!"

"I'll go up," Melody said, and darted out.

Kitty was indeed wallowing in a hot bath. She grinned when Melody walked in.

"Hallo," she said, "did you miss me?"

"Child, we've been so worried! Wherever have you been? And are those bruises?"

"Probably," Kitty said, pulling the plug and standing up. "Could you pass me a towel?"

As she wrapped herself in the towel and stepped out of the bath, Melody caught sight of more bruises, and a grazed knee and another long weal on her back.

"You've been in the wars!" she said. "Who did this to you?"

"No one. I did it all myself. I went exploring, and there was some climbing. And falling, actually, I banged my head, look! Now, I'm still not sure what time it is but I think I'd like to go to bed for a bit. I'll clean my teeth when I get up."

"Shall I bring you some cocoa?"

"That would be lovely, thank you. And could you ask Ma Cott for some biscuits? I'm still a bit peckish. And when you come back, I've got something to tell you, something lovely. But you have to promise – it's a secret!"

"A worm?" said Melody faintly a few minutes later. Kitty sat up in bed looking clean though slightly battered, but happy. She cradled the hot cocoa in both hands and crunched on the remains of her third biscuit.

"Not a worm, a wyrm. The one and only Wyrm, in fact."

"You mean some sort of monster?"

"Well sort of. But he's not dangerous, he's rather nice, actually. He'd got his tail stuck in a hole and I helped him get out. But you're not to tell anyone!"

"Why not?"

"Because he's lived down there for a long time, and he doesn't get any visitors. So I don't think he'd cope very well if people started coming to look at him. He'd probably run away. Or swim, rather, he's very good at swimming. Now, I think I need to have a sleep now, would you mind? I'll tell you more when I wake up, but you've got to keep it secret for now, all right? Thanks for the cocoa. Could you leave the door open a bit, in case of Perkins? Goodnight!"

Wyrm certainly was a wonderful swimmer. Kitty had clung to his tail as he towed her through the tunnel, breathing deeply in case she had to hold her breath.

"But how will I breathe?" she had asked when he told her what he meant to do.

"Is that when you suck air in?" he asked.

"Yes. Do you do that?"

"Yes, occasionally I do. Do you?"

"Yes. Quite often actually."

"I'll try and keep on the surface as much as I can. But the end of the tunnel is always under water so you'll have to hold your breath then."

And so it had proved. The tunnel went gradually down and down and the roof had got nearer and nearer to the water's surface. Eventually she sucked in the biggest breath she could manage, and ducked her head under. The speed of his passage was so quick that it was hard to hang on, and her fingers hurt. She could feel the muscular tail vibrating under her hands, driving them forward, and then the light changed and they were out in the sea, among the breakers that divided the outlying rocks from the shore.

Here he rose to the surface, but the combination of his rapid movement and the heaving waves undid her, and she lost her grip. She went under, then trod water gasping for air as the breakers smothered her in foam, but he had circled quickly and was already passing by her. She grabbed for his scaly side, reaching up and trying to find something to grip and hold, but he was slick and slippery with salt. Then one flailing hand found something rougher, a little nubbin on his back about a third of the way back from his head, and her other hand found another one, a hard projection she could grip, and soon the water grew smoother as he turned out of the breakers and parallel to the beach. He ran on, his body making great sideways undulations that drove him swiftly through the water, before turning in towards the shore.

When she felt the sand beneath her feet she stood up and let go, and staggered gratefully up the beach. She turned and watched and waved as he rolled in the little waves for a moment, then slid back and disappeared. She hoped he was going to find something to eat, he must be almost as hungry as she was. She took her shoes and socks off and carried them in her hand as she began to walk back towards the castle. After so long confined in clammy stone and dark, the wide world with a blue sky and the soaring gulls was wonderful, but despite the warm sun she shivered as her wet clothes stuck to her skin.

Going to her office the next morning after checking on Kitty, who was still sleeping peacefully in the tower, Melody found that something was going on in the top corridor. Outside Lady Sybil's sitting room, Cockley Knowes stood, massive, with his arms folded. As she passed him his head moved and his eyes followed her impassively, but he said nothing and did not reply to her muttered 'Good morning'. From inside the room she heard low voices, the soothing tones of Mr.Medulla, a querulous complaint from Sir Lancelot, and a sharp retort from Lady Sybil, but as she paused Knowes shifted his feet slightly and she knew that she was not to linger. She went into her room, but left the door open while she settled herself at the desk and booted up the computer.

While she clicked on the internet to look at her emails, she heard shuffling footsteps from the corridor and looked up to see Cartilege approaching the sitting room with a tray hanging in his hand. He looked as though he had come to clear away coffee cups, but Knowes did not move. He looked down at Cartilege and made a small movement of his head. Cartilege took the hint and shuffled away again. If it hadn't seemed so ridiculous, you might have wondered if Mr.Medulla and his giant bodyguard weren't holding the Fossetts prisoner in their own sitting room.

She shrugged, and turned to her work, but a moment later was disturbed as Medulla himself came into the office with small silent steps. Behind him Knowes still kept his vigil outside the Fossetts' door.

"Miss Trinket, I want you to do something for me, if you please," Medulla said. "I need the title deeds to the Castle. Do you have them?"

Melody closed the email she was reading, trying to be calm. "I've never seen them," she said. "They may be here, but it will take me some time to search. Did you ask Sir Lancelot where they would be?"

"Of course, but he was ... a little vague about it. As he is with most things, I expect you find?"

Melody did not reply. He was right, of course, but it was hardly professional for her to discuss the shortcomings of her employer with a stranger. "Can you tell me why you need them?" she asked. "Did Sir Lancelot ask you to get them?"

Medulla smiled without warmth. "Of course he did. We need to ... consult something about the boundaries. Perhaps you would find them for me and give them to Mr.Knowes?"

Melody ducked her head as though to give assent, and he turned and went quietly back to the sitting room. She had no intention of even looking. She knew where they weren't, and that was in any of the drawers of the filing cabinet or her desk. They'd be old, centuries old probably, and if she'd ever seen them she'd surely remember. They would probably be written on rolled parchment and very distinctive. She would tell him, if he asked again, that she had searched and found nothing. Let Sir Lancelot worry about it. Besides, she worked for the Castle, not for Mr.Medulla or COGACO.

At mid-morning she went up to check on Kitty again, and found her gone, probably down to the kitchen in search of food. She decided to walk into the village and pay yesterday's door money in at the Post Office. As she left the Castle and looked across the car park, she found that something had changed. Where yesterday there had been nothing but tourist cars and a couple of white vans, down at the far end there was now quite an assembly of machinery, more vans, and two or three yellow JCBs with their long digging arms neatly folded, and several dumper trucks with great buckets for debris and the drivers' seats high up at the back. While she watched, an enormous lorry ground its way down the car park with a huge red bulldozer hulking on its back, squat and sinister. She knew nothing about all this, and she should have done. She was the administrator for the Castle, surely, and if its car park was to be used to store heavy machinery she should have been notified. Was this part of the strange goings-on upstairs?

As she approached the Post Office she found Dashwood Belhatchett standing in the doorway, watching a second lorry bringing another bulldozer towards the Castle. It ground slowly up the hill, overhanging the pavement and almost scraping the houses on the other side.

"Shouldn't something like that have a police escort?" she asked him, pausing to see it pass.

He shrugged. "How would I know?" he said truculently. "It's nothing to do with me. I'm just glad to see something happening up there. It's high time you people got sorted out, lording it over the rest of us."

"I don't lord anything over anybody," she said obstinately. "Now, are you going to come in and take this money off me?"

With poor grace he shouldered past her and led the way to the back of the shop.

"What about the little hooligan?" he asked, shoving her receipt under the glass. "You got rid of her yet?"

"No, and we won't be. What did the police say?"

He didn't rely, his head down, fiddling with something in a drawer.

"You didn't call them, did you?" she pursued. "Why was that? Were you afraid they'd find out what your son was doing?"

"I'm not afraid of anything. You're the one should be afraid, from what I hear. You'll get your comeuppance soon enough, Miss High and Mighty!"

She looked at him for a long moment. "You're a very unpleasant man, you know," she said quietly. "I think the Castle might take its business elsewhere. I have a car, I can always drive to a Post Office somewhere else, somewhere they have decent manners!"

"Why don't you do that?" he snapped, and walked into the back room, closing the door loudly.

Lunch in the dining-room was very strange, Melody found. All the usual people were there, Lady Sybil and Sir Lancelot, the Sisters, and Medulla and Knowes, while Cartilege hovered at the sideboard, serving omelette and cold meats and salad. There was no conversation at all. Sir Lancelot sat with his head down and seemed to be sulking. The Sisters twittered occasionally, but were otherwise silent, glancing at their brother from time to time with worried looks. Lady Sybil stared straight ahead.

"Lady Sybil, I was thinking ..." Melody began, but Lady Sybil silenced her with a quick shake of the head. The Sisters picked at their food as usual. When Cartilege came to collect their plates he would find them disarranged but still basically complete.

Medulla and Knowes alone ate normally, though in silence. Medulla ate with small neat movements, taking small mouthfuls and chewing each one for a long time with little movements of his jaw, like a rat nibbling. Knowes shovelled great forkfuls in and swallowed them with a grunt, hardly chewing at all. His plate was empty in seconds. At the end of the meal, everyone sat silent and unmoving until Medulla rose. Knowes heaved himself to his feet, and this seemed to unlock the rest of the family for they got up and scuttled out, still in silence.

Melody was last to leave. She turned back to Cartilege who was clearing the plates,

"What's going on, Mr.Cartilege? Why is everyone behaving so strangely?"

He shrugged and ignored her.

"And where is the little girl Kitty?" She knew of course, but she wanted to know what he knew about it.

Again he shrugged, but seemed disturbed. With his head down, not looking at her, he muttered "I never ... it's nothing to do with me, I've no part in it, it's them, they done it ..." but would say no more.

Kitty herself, full of a very late breakfast and feeling much restored from her adventures, reasoned that as everyone who liked her was sworn to secrecy and could be trusted, and everyone who wished her harm thought she was safely locked up in the North End somewhere, it was probably safe enough to move round the castle provided she was careful. Obviously she couldn't go up to Melody's office any more, but the Library should be all right unless Sir Lancelot and the Sisters were there. She pattered down the corridors in her socks, carrying her shoes in one hand, and paused at each corner, peering round and listening intently before stepping out.

The Library was deserted. There was no sign of Sir Lancelot or the Sisters, and they plainly hadn't been in for some time. There were no little collections of dead moths on the table, ready to be pinned to their cards, and on the *chaise longue* there were no lace handkerchiefs or pieces of embroidery or other accoutrements of idle ladies of a certain age.

Kitty searched quietly until she found a book entitled *'English Defensive Architecture, 1189 onwards; A Brief History'*. Like most of the books here, it was far from being brief, but was a weighty tome, bound in fine leather now starting to dry and crack. It was sparsely illustrated with nice line drawings and rather awful photographs. She browsed through, scanning the pages rather than reading them properly, turning over rapidly. She found no mention of Castle Crayle. It seemed to be more general than that, and frequently had sentences that said *'... one example of this may be seen at Dover Castle ...'* or Warwick or Hurstmonceaux or Alnwick or a host of other names, *'... where So-and-so built such-and-such in 1356 ...'*

She did, however, halt eventually, arrested by the word *'oubliette'*. She knew from French at school that 'oublier' meant 'forget'. This struck some sort of chord. She read the page more carefully. *'Many castles contained oubliettes in their foundations. Otherwise known as a bottle-dungeon from their distinctive shape, these were spaces to which the only access was a trap door in the roof. Prisoners were lowered, or dropped, through the trapdoor and left to languish in darkness, often until they died of starvation'.*

Well, that fitted up to a point. What concerned her was certainly a place where men (or, in her case, girls) might be walled up and forgotten. But it wasn't bottle shaped and had no trapdoor. In fact it had no access at all, save the drain high up at one end, and the tunnel to the sea at the other. It was difficult to see what purpose it might have served for its builders. But then there were the bones, of course.

She shrugged. It didn't matter really, it was just a question of the right name, and if she chose to call it an *oubliette*, what was to stop her? She wondered if it could have been built, centuries ago when the castle was still new, on purpose for a wyrm to live in? It was ideal for the purpose, being secret and deep down in the rock, with a supply of cleansing water most of the year round, and convenient access to the sea. But why didn't the Fossetts know about it? Had no one mentioned it when the family bought the Castle? She imagined a sixteenth or seventeenth century estate agent saying "Oh, by the way, there's a dragon in the basement. He's no bother, though, and you don't have to feed him ..."

She closed the book, returned it to its shelf and left the Library. She knew she had one really important job, and it was time she started. She slipped down the broad stairs, but stopped near the bottom. Near her, facing away with the coloured light from the stained glass in his white hair, stood Cartilege. She had not realised he was there, because he did not move but stood quite still, staring mutely at the passage into the North End of the castle down which he had taken her to polish the silver. He had a duster in one hand. She wondered if he was going to clean the silver himself, since she had refused.

She must have made some small noise, or perhaps he sensed her breathing, because he suddenly wheeled round and saw her. His eyes widened, and his mouth worked but no sound came out. The duster fell from his fingers. He shook, seeming to be in the grip of some strong emotion.

Kitty saw no point in running away. He couldn't catch her

whatever she did, he was too old. She decided to brazen it out. She stepped towards him softly, put her finger to her lips to indicate silence, then pointed the same finger at his face, as if to say "Keep quiet, or I'll come after you!" He nodded frantically, making little squeaking noises, then stooped to pick up the duster and shuffled quickly off, glancing at her fearfully over his shoulder as he went. Either he was feeling very guilty and ashamed, or he took her for a ghost. Either way, he would probably keep his mouth shut.

Feeling unconcerned by this encounter, she went to the kitchen and begged a couple of sandwiches and an apple, and took them out by the back door into the castle grounds. Sitting in the sun on one of the benches, she ate her sandwiches and looked carefully at the panorama of the North End buildings, grey and austere with sightless windows, wondering which ones she had looked out of during her adventure. There were so many and the buildings were such a jumble, it was hard to make sense of them. She looked particularly along the base of the buildings where they rose from the rock. Somewhere there must be the row of apertures that lit Wyrm's home, but she could see nothing that looked useful. It would take a more detailed investigation.

Stuffing the apple in her pocket for later, she walked towards the rocky outcrop, glancing from side to side for clues. She tried to imagine the route of the tunnel out to the sea, for that might give her a clue. They had come out in the rough water between the outlying rocks and the shore, so the tunnel must be in line with the rocks – that was a start. She found one of the stairs that led up to the top of the walls and climbed it. There were tourists walking along the walls, looking out to sea and holding their hats on against the fresh wind. She could see the rocks clearly enough. She walked along the wall until she thought she was directly in line with them, then looked back at the castle. Where did that leave her?

It left her, she thought, opposite a patch of rougher ground that Baggott had not tamed. Areas of coarse grass gave way to small bushes, gorse and brambles, then larger shrubs and small trees, the ground beneath them choked with undergrowth which ran right up to the stone walls. Somewhere in there, she thought, she would find the apertures, but it would be hard going for a girl in a skirt. She ought to have stout boots and trousers to guard against the nettles and brambles.

"So, found your wyrm yet?" called a cheery voice. Professor Crust was approaching along the top of the wall.

"No," she said. "It's hard to know where to look, really." That wasn't totally a lie, she told herself. She certainly was finding it hard to know where to look, and she hadn't found the wyrm. Not today, anyway.

"That's a shame," he said blithely, settling himself on a bench and beaming at the mass of the castle in front of him. "Down there somewhere, though, is he, do you think?"

"I don't know. It might just be an old fairy story."

"Ah, maybe, maybe. It's always nice to get to the bottom of things, though, isn't it?"

It was, she thought. And the bottom of things was certainly what she had got to, though she wasn't going to tell him that. "What would happen, Professor, if we did find the wyrm?"

He looked at her sharply. "Ah, that would be the question, wouldn't it? What would? I'll tell you what I think. I think there'd be the most awful fuss! I think we'd have the newspapers and the television, for a short while. Then the scientists, eminent men from universities wanting to dig their own holes and find their own fossils if we wouldn't show them ours. Then the National Trust, probably, wanting their share. They've taken no interest in this old pile all these years, but that'd soon change if they thought there was money to made and influence to be wielded. Then the loonies would arrive – conspiracy theorists hoping to find signs of alien invasions and stuff like that, and environmentalists looking for any excuse to set the world back a couple of hundred years. American millionaires, offering colossal sums of money for relics to add to their collections ..."

His voice tailed off. He looked as though he might relish an American millionaire or two, whatever he actually said. He was saying all this to warn her to keep quiet, as if she needed telling. But she was wise enough to know that any secret wouldn't be safe with him. It was odd: although he presented himself as an important scientist, he was really rather a shabby character. There was a shifty look to his eyes, like those of the men you saw sometimes hanging around at railway stations or outside betting shops. And his clothes were not new, his trousers were bagged at the knees, his raincoat hung open and had lost its belt, and his shoes were run down at the heel and clearly hadn't been cleaned in living memory. But then, perhaps he was an eccentric professor who cared nothing for such things?

"Why did you come with Mr.Medulla?" she asked. "Is he just a friend, or do you work for him? Is he keen on Archaeology?" She looked at him innocently, trying to give the impression of an artless child.

He hesitated for a moment, and she thought he was taken aback by such direct questioning. "Oh, ah ... no, he has no interest in Archaeology so far as I know. But he knows I have, so he invited me to, erm, assist him with advice and suggestions, you know. Yes, that's it, I'm here in an advisory capacity."

"But what about? What is he here for, that needs your advice? Is it to do with things under the sea?"

"Under the sea? Goodness, my dear, I don't think so!"

"But there were divers the other day, and a boat."

"Were there? I didn't see them. Now, I ought to be ... erm ... getting on, you know. Things to do, things ... erm, yes, things ..." and he held his raincoat round him and walked off along the wall rather quickly.

Curious, she thought to herself, he wants to talk and then he doesn't. He's a colleague of Mr.Medulla but he isn't. He's an archaeologist but I already know he isn't. And he calls himself a professor but I don't believe he's anything of the sort. Altogether curious! She waited for some time, to make sure he really had gone, then went back to ground level and walked towards the trees and bushes where she hoped to find what she was looking for.

It was just as hard as she'd imagined, forcing a way through the bushes and brambles towards the buildings. Even after she'd gone to find Mr.Baggott and borrowed a pair of shears and a little saw, it took hours of hot, back-breaking work to hack and cut a way in. She tried to do as little damage as she could. Although it was necessary to create a path through the undergrowth, she didn't want to leave any sign of where she had come, so she left enough growth to close behind her and conceal her passage.

By the time she approached the walls of the buildings above, she was dirty, sweating and tired. The afternoon was well advanced, and her hands and legs were covered in scratches, her hair in a tangle and her skirt torn in several places. The sun reflected off the stone walls in front of her, and so close to the tall buildings the wind was not to be felt. Big black flies swarmed in the heat, and little stinging things sought her out. And when she eventually did penetrate through the tangle and could lay her hands on the rough stone of the castle wall, there was no sign of the apertures she sought. She wiped the sweat from her eyes with the tail of her skirt and looked around. To her right a buttress rose, supporting the lofty wall of the building, while to her left the ground seemed to be falling away. She reasoned that as what she sought lay at the very bottom of the castle, down to her left was the way to go.

The going got a little easier, as the undergrowth was thinner. As she clambered and stumbled downwards into a sort of pit against the bottom of the building she was in deep shadow which discouraged the ordinary bushes and trees, but encouraged ivy and moss and climbing things. There were always masses of nettles, though, those hardy things that will grow wherever there is space, and she got thoroughly stung as she used the shears to cut a path. There were stones in the ground, tumbled boulders coated in moss and slippery so she was in constant danger of turning an ankle. What would she do if she hurt herself? No one knew she was here.

After almost an hour of stumbling and sweating and swearing, she thought she had reached the lowest point, cleared a space in the nettles and sat wearily with her back against the ivy that clothed the wall. Craning her head back, she could see the walls of the North End soaring straight up to the sky which was now grey, with clouds threatening rain before long. The sun had gone, but nothing discouraged the flies and gnats which swarmed round her face, attracted by the sweat. She closed her eyes, feeling very downcast. She had felt so sure this was the place.

Just as she was gathering her courage to start retracing her steps, a sudden noise startled her. A couple of yards to her left there was a sudden commotion among the undergrowth, and a clatter of wings, and a pigeon shot out of the leaves and flew up and away. She pulled her feet under her to leap to her feet, but one foot slipped on a mossy stone and shot from under her, and she fell back. Instead of hitting hard stone, she felt stalks and branches giving way underneath her and grabbed wildly at anything she could reach, stinging herself badly. Just in time she managed to stop herself, and realised that all along she had been sitting with her back to one of the apertures. Only by a hair's-breadth had she saved herself from falling through it, to plunge twenty feet onto the flagstones and once again be imprisoned in the *oubliette*.

She crawled forward and parted the leaves. There in front of her was the dark, damp hole, and poking her head cautiously in, she found herself looking down at Wyrm's home. There was the pile of debris in the corner, there in the dim green light was the runnel down the centre where Wyrm would lie when he was home, there were the shattered remains of the broken arch and the black hole from which Wyrm would emerge. Now all she had to do was think of a way to get down there.

"A rope ladder?" Billy Cott said. "What do you want a rope ladder for, pet?"

"I can't tell you. Well, to climb up and down, obviously. But I can't tell you more than that."

Kitty sat beside Billy on the edge of the jetty, their legs dangling over the water. Down below was the *Mercy*, where Billy Brannicle was tidying crab pots and coiling rope. She felt damp, for it had indeed rained on the way down the beach to the harbour, a fine rain driven on the sea breeze. She was not cold, for the evening sun had made a welcome reappearance, slanting low over the derelict boats and the shacks on the shore, but she was tired and sore and scratched all up her legs and arms.

"How long do you want it?"

"About twenty feet, I think. I'm guessing. But twenty feet should do it."

"What's all this?" said Billy Brannicle, vaulting from the *Mercy*'s rail onto the jetty. "Now then, bonny lass, you're looking a bit paggered!"

He sat down beside her. "I don't know what that means," she said, grinning at him. It felt nice, to be sat here in the gentle sun between two handsome pirates with their sun-tan and their big boots.

"I mean, you look as if you've been in the wars. What have you done to yourself, pet? You're all scritched? You been in a fight again?"

"No. Well, yes, with some brambles."

"Who won?"

"It was a draw."

Billy Cott leant across her. "Lass wants a rope ladder, now. What have we got in the locker, in the way of cordage?"

Billy Brannicle thought. "We've no rope ladder, that I do know. But there's a whole coil of half-inch that would make the side ropes. What sort of weight are we talking about?"

"Just me, I think," she said.

"So that would do fine, and we could tie the rungs with small stuff, the orange poly, provided we seal the ends to stop them unwinding. When do you need it, pet?"

"Tomorrow morning?"

They both laughed, then stopped. "You're serious, aren't you? Rope ladders don't make themselves, you know, there's hours of work."

"Drinking time lost, then. We'd need compensation!"

Kitty got up. "Stop complaining," she said. "You can do knots and drink beer at the same time, can't you? It's called multi-tasking. Women do it all the time. I bet Melody does, and Faith. Or Charity."

Billy Cott smiled at her. "It'd go a lot faster if we had, like, some encouragement. Do you think yon lassies'd come down and lend a hand?"

Kitty started off down the jetty. It was time for a bath and supper. "No chance," she called over her shoulder. "You men don't need any distraction. Multi-tasking two things is probably the best you could manage!"

XIV

There was a lot of giggling outside the kitchen door the next morning when Melody and Billy Cott brought the rope ladder from the harbour in Melody's little car. Kitty hadn't heard Melody be silly before, and hoped this was a good sign. The rope ladder, however, was bulky and heavy and she wondered how she was going to get it round to the other side of the North End and through the bushes. She could only just lift it, but she could hardly ask anyone to help. The way down to the oubliette had to be kept a deadly secret.

In the end she went and borrowed a wheelbarrow from Mr.Baggott, and used that to take the ladder round, tipped it out and hid it in the bushes. Then she went in search of Streaky Nidd. In a burst of inspiration she had decided that anyone who could operate a secret hide-out in the North End and not get caught, must be very discreet indeed. She would just have to trust him. He owed her a favour, after all.

Sky told her where the Nidds lived in a tall, shabby house at the back of village, and it was there that she found Streaky kicking a ball round the yard. When he saw her watching, he started performing tricks, kicking the ball into the air and catching it on the back of his neck, then twitching it off and catching it in mid-air to slam it with his foot through the open back door of the house.

"That's really clever," she said, "you must do a lot of practice. Have you practised your fighting?"

"I have, miss," he said with a grin. "I can whirl for five minutes without falling over once. D'you want to see?"

"Later perhaps. Right now, I need you to help me. I have a secret. Can I trust you?"

"'Course you can. You haven't told anyone about my camp, have you? Hey!" His eyes widened when he remembered. "What happened after I left? Did you find out what was making that noise? Was it a ghost?"

"No, it wasn't. I didn't really find anything," she lied, "but I'm pretty sure it wasn't a ghost. Now, are you going to help me or not?"

He was, and together they ran to the North End and round to the bushes. There she revealed the rope ladder, and he helped her manhandle it through the undergrowth to the wall. Then he showed her how to pull the grass and nettles across the path to hide their tracks.

"So where are you going with this?" he asked. "Is it anything to do with the ghost? I mean, with the noises?"

"Streaky, do you mind if I don't tell you? It has to be the most deadly secret, and if I don't tell it to you, you can't be forced to give it away, can you?"

"Who's going to force me? I'm tough, I wouldn't tell!"

"Not even if they tortured you?"

He laughed uncertainly. "No one's going to torture me. Are they? They're not, are they?"

"They won't if you don't know anything. Ignorance is bliss, after all."

He thought for a moment, then saw the logic of her argument. "All right, I'll go and leave you to your secret," he said. "I expect you'll tell me one day, when the secret's worn off a bit. Will you come again?"

She said she would, and he crept off, promising to conceal the path on his way. She breathed a sigh of relief. She knew, though he hadn't spotted it, that her argument hadn't been the least bit logical. Still, it had worked. She set about tying the tops of the rope ladder to the stonework of the aperture, using the best knots she knew. Then she pushed the whole ladder into the void, turned round and pushed her legs in, and began to feel for the rungs with her feet.

"What do you eat?" she asked, leaning back against Wyrm's scaly side. He was still a bit wet from being in the sea and was making puddles, so she'd had to find a piece of wood to sit on.

"Kelp, mainly."

"What's kelp?"

"Seaweed. There are lots of different seaweeds, but kelp's best. It grows in great tall fronds, really long so it's easy to suck in. It's very good for you, it's got all these ... er, things in it, that are good for you. Which is just as well, because the taste is awful."

"I thought you were supposed to be a ravening monster, and eat maidens? That's what it says in the song."

"I never heard the song, sorry. And my ravening days are long gone, these days I don't raven at all. Actually, I'm not sure I ever did. Are you a maiden?"

"Mm, I suppose I am."

Wyrm looked at her down his nose, or down where his nose would have been if he had one. "Huh! Wouldn't get very fat on you, would I? All skin and bones, you are."

"So where did you come from? Did your mother bring you here?"

"I don't think I had a mother."

"You must have, you wouldn't be here otherwise."

"Don't remember one. What do mothers do?"

"Well, they ... oh, I know! I expect you came from an egg. Your mother laid an egg, and you hatched out of it and here you were."

"How do you know? Can you make eggs?"

Kitty giggled. "No, silly, I'm a human. We don't lay eggs, we have live young."

"Live? I find that hard to believe, frankly. It sounds a bit squishy to me. Look, can we talk about something else?"

Kitty looked round happily. It was nice down here in the dim, talking to her new friend, so long as she didn't have to go near the bones in the corner. And it was doubly nice to think that when she had to go home, there was a stout rope ladder up which to climb, instead of the tunnel and the breakers and the rocks.

"What do you do all day, lying down here with no one to talk to?" she asked.

There was a long pause. "Well ... hrrm! Actually I ... well, I make things up, you know. With words."

"What sort of things do you make up?"

"If I tell you one, you promise not to laugh?"

She sat up and turned to look at him. The idea that he might be embarrassed was ... not something she had anticipated.

"I promise," she said. "Go on, tell me."

He cleared his throat again, and declaimed rather proudly:

"A clever young Worm in a castle
Wrapped seaweed up in a parcel.
It might be too wet
But he won't give up yet
And it's a convenient way to store it until he's hungry."

"Oh my goodness!" she said. "You're a poet!"

"What's a poet?"

"Someone who makes up poetry. Which that was, more or less. Only I'm not sure about the last line. Shouldn't it end with something that rhymes with 'castle'?"

"Oh, I didn't realise I was speaking to an expert on poetry," he said scornfully. "Say some of your own poems, then, if you're so clever!"

Kitty blushed, feeling insulted. "I never claimed to be an expert, and I don't write poems," she said hotly, "but we do study poetry at school, so I know what's poetry and what isn't, and that wasn't!"

Wyrm was silent for a long moment, and then to Kitty's horror a large tear welled from each eye and trickled down, leaving a shiny path on each cheek.

"Oh goodness, I'm sorry, I spoke without thinking," she said hastily. "Please don't cry. I'm sure it was a lovely poem in Wyrm language," and she stroked his scaly head, which was surprisingly warm to the touch.

"I don't know about Wyrm language," he said mournfully, and sniffed. "I only know one language, and that's what we're speaking now." It's large watery eye rolled towards her, imploring. "It wasn't that bad, was it?"

"Oh no, no, it wasn't, some of it was very good indeed - nearly all, in fact. It's just the last line that needs a bit of work."

This seemed to cheer him up. "Shall I tell you another one?" he asked, and launched into verse without waiting for an answer.

"I think that I shall never see
Anything half as nice as me,
Such glossy scales, such flowing curves,
Are more than any normal person deserves."

"It rhymes beautifully," Kitty said to be encouraging. "'See' and 'me', 'curves' and 'deserves', just right. But aren't there too many words in the last line?"

"Too many? How can you have too many words? Words are the finest thing in life, you can't have too many of them!"

"I just think it would sound better if it went *'Such glossy scales, such flowing curves, Are more than anyone deserves'*."

But Wyrm dismissed this literary criticism out of hand. "No, no," he said airily, "you may rely on it, the way I have created it is the way it was meant to be created. Us artists know such things by instinct. Now, I did this one last week ...

Munching bladderwrack and kale,
Rocking in the waters torrid,
I accidentally crunch a snail
Which makes the seaweed taste horrid.

... how about that, fussy-pants? Too many words again?"

"Not enough, this time. It needs one more syllable in the last line, and then it'll be perfect."

"Syllable?"

"Don't worry about it. Look, I think I ought to be getting back. They worry if I'm gone too long." This wasn't entirely true, but she thought it sounded plausible.

"Who worries?"

"The other humans. My friends."

"You have other friends besides me?"

"Of course I do. You have another friend, don't you? Having lots of friends is a really nice thing."

"Who's my other friend? Oh, I get it, you mean the little ... what was the word you used? Cat, that was it! You mean the cat."

"Yes, Perkins the cat. Has she been today?"

"Not yet. She usually turns up later on. She's very regular, but she doesn't have much conversation. In fact she doesn't have any at all. She just rubs herself against you, and blinks, and sits for a bit, then goes away."

"Well, that's cats for you. But at least she's reliable, that's very important. Now, I'll see you tomorrow, and you can tell me some more poetry."

On the triangular green in the centre of the village someone had erected a large board. When Melody arrived on her way to see Sky Lovechild, a group of villagers were gathered round, looking at it. Most seemed bemused by it. Joining them, Melody saw that it was a big drawing, not quite a plan and not quite a picture but a stylised representation of roads and houses, each building shown as a block with a pitched roof and a door but few other details. Across the top was the legend *'New Crayle – new homes for a brighter future!'*

The little block houses were shown grouped round a triangular village green just like this one, with a couple of roads radiating off it. A larger complex of buildings was labelled *'New Crayle Health Centre, medical practice, dentist's surgery, Citizens' Advice etc.'* Another was called *'New Crayle Village Hall'* and a third was *'New Crayle Primary School'.* Down one side was a blue area for the sea, with a fringe of yellow to indicate the beach. In a couple of places there was a block of very plain buildings behind the beach, just simple red cubes with a legend *'Gas Reclamation Facility'.*

"Have you noticed?" said a soft voice at Melody's shoulder, "the road layout looks awfully similar to the village as it is?" It was Sky in her bright colours, with a tie-dye scarf wrapped round her dreadlocks. "I mean, there's a triangular green here, isn't there? And that little lane goes off to the harbour and this other one back towards the Castle. But where's the Castle? The plan doesn't show it. So is this the old Crayle or a completely new one somewhere else and they've made it as much like the old one as possible?"

"But why is there any need for a new one?" asked another voice. "I don't think we've finished with this one, have we?" The speaker was a short elderly woman with a sausage dog on a lead. She wore a paisley square on her head, and her eyes were bright and combative. There were murmurs of agreement from others standing round. Quite a little crowd was gathering.

"A doctor would be nice though," said one. "And we've never had a village hall here. We could have whist drives ..."

"Christmas party for the old folk ..."

"Scouts and Guides ..."

The suggestions came thick and fast.

elody kept quiet. It wasn't really any of her business, was it? She was a newcomer, and her job here might not last all that long. What was her business, was the Castle, and it was very unclear where that fitted in with this grand plan. Why was it not shown at all on the board? Were you just supposed to take it for granted, because it was there and always had been and always would be, so it didn't need any clarification?

"So, ladies and gentlemen, how do you like our little idea?" said a loud voice. Dashwood Belhatchett strode across the grass.

"Local councillor," whispered the lady with the sausage dog to Melody. "Very self-important!"

The villagers gathered round Belhatchett, peppering him with questions. "Of course it's just an idea at present," he was saying, "there's a long way to go before any of this becomes a reality. There'll have to be consultations and public meetings, and the deliberations of the County Council Planning Committee and so on. But we have to start somewhere."

"But why do we need a new Crayle at all?" asked the old lady. "What's wrong with the one we've got? And where will it be?"

Belhatchett turned to her, beaming but with little warmth in his smile. "Well, a doctor's surgery and a dentist ... a new Village Hall, a brand-new primary school run on the most modern lines ... what's not to like, dear lady? And some modest industrial development that will bring much-needed employment to the area so our young people don't have to go to Newcastle to find a job? It'll be a new era, one of lively prosperity ... I can tell you that the developers are thinking of cutting a new road through to the A1, so we'll find the world on our doorstep at last. Think, Newcastle in less than an hour ... commuters bringing wealth and new life to the village ..."

Melody noticed that he had ducked the last part of the lady's question, about where the new village would be built.

"But we already have jobs here, don't we? There are fishermen, and people who work at the Castle, and we have two shops as you well know since one of them is yours ..."

"Ah, but not enough jobs for all those that need them, surely?" said Belhatchett. "We'll give them better jobs at the plant. And if that isn't what they want, they can go elsewhere. It's their decision. We're not tyrants - this is a democracy after all!"

"Plant? What plant?"

"Why, the modest industrial development I mentioned, of course. Where do you think all this new money is going to come from? It's the perfect arrangement – we welcome ... er ... this commercial concern to come and build their new facility here, and in return they bring all these wonderful benefits! Everyone wins!"

"And what will this modest industrial development do for our environment?" Sky stepped in. "We have to live here, remember, both while all this work is going on, and afterwards. Lorries coming and going at all hours, noise and pollution ... and what will it do to our tourist business? People won't want to come and look at a factory, will they, they come to see the Castle and the beach and the countryside?"

Belhatchett turned on her with strange look on his face, almost a snarl. "Oh yes, I expected that you'd be the first to raise objections! We all know where your sympathies lie, the poor little foxy-woxies and limp-wristed hippie garbage about your holy environment ... you don't care about the ordinary lives of hard-working people who need to move forward and make a better life for themselves!"

This created quite a stir among the company, growls of agreement from some, but shocked gasps from others.

"Tourists don't mean squit to us ordinary folk," said one man, "all they bring is queues of traffic through the village and money in the pockets of the nobs up at the Castle. How does that benefit the rest of us, exactly?"

"Aye, we just sit in our front rooms and watch the cars go past and the money pouring into the pockets of them Fossetts!" said another.

The old lady wasn't going to stand for this. "Chester Draws, your mother would be ashamed to hear you!" she snapped. "I knew her for a hard-working woman who struggled all her life to put food on the table for you and your brothers, and she'd be mortified to hear you talking about just sitting in your front room all day! When are you going to get out and find an honest job?"

"I'll get an honest job at the new factory, won't I? Mr.Belhatchett said ..."

But a new voice joined the fray. Shouldering his way to the front was the tall figure of Nearly Normal Nidd, at first glance a figure of fun in his wellingtons and colourful trousers which were, now that Melody had the chance to look closer, almost certainly made from old curtains. But his height gave him an air of authority and his voice was firm.

"If the village doesn't profit from the tourists, it only has itself to blame!" he said loudly. "Where are visitors supposed to park if they want to stop before they go home? Where's the car park for them, with a sign telling it's there so they can find it? These few spaces along the green aren't enough. So they just keep driving, and there's an opportunity missed!"

There were one or two looks of surprise. No one had heard Nearly Normal make a speech as long as this before, or one that made as much sense.

"And if they do manage to park, what is there for them? Where do they go to buy ice cream for the kids, or mementos to take home with them? They've money to spend in their pockets and we don't take it from them. The Post Office is the only place that sells ice cream, and Miss Lovegood is the only person selling trinkets and stuff, why is that? Where's the enterprise?"

"Quite right!" cried the old lady. "You should stand for the council, man, you talk more sense than ... well, you talk sense, anyway. I'd vote for you!" There were one or two murmurs of agreement, but she wasn't finished. "And what about food? The only place in the village where people can eat is the Dragon. It's all right, but it's not all that big. Where's the fish and chip shop? There's room for two or three little cafés here, I should think, and no one has had the gumption to start one!"

"A snack bar down at the beach, that'd be welcome," said another woman.

"Boat trips!" exclaimed a man. "No one does boat trips out round the island. There are seals there sometimes, people'd pay to go and see them!"

Belhatchett evidently felt he was losing ground and needed to intervene. "But all these ideas need capital, don't they? Lots of people might like to run a snack bar, but it takes money to set it up and if you don't have the funds to start with, just having the idea won't help. But the developers are offering just that, don't you see, an injection of cash into the village? And if you want a snack bar that just makes a profit for its owner rather than a village hall that benefits everyone, well, that's all well and good, but we need to be wary of these daft, airy-fairy schemes ..."

"Who are you calling daft, Dashwood Belhatchett?" said the old lady, squaring up to him. "You may be able to browbeat and bully some people, but it won't work on me! I remember when you were an ill-mannered little lout running round in short pants, loud and rude and idle, and the way your mother despaired herself into an early grave on your account. And your boy's no better, a proper little bully he is ..."

Melody felt she had heard enough. This was plainly the beginning of a long argument, one that would rage for weeks, probably. Patting Sky on the shoulder, she pushed her way out of the crowd and set off for home. But as she walked, what she brought away with her was a great puzzlement. What she had noticed and no one else had, was that in the band of blue sea on the drawing, the rocks were shown as little black triangles sticking up. Unless they were planning to move the rocks, this wasn't a new village down the coast a bit, it was THIS village. So were they planning to knock all the houses down and build new ones? Where were the people supposed to go?

And the most glaring question of the lot – in all these grand plans and schemes, where was the Castle?

"There's a fine old ding-dong going on upstairs!" hissed Charity, slipping into the kitchen where Kitty sat at the table with Ma Cott. "Cartilege is hiding in the dining room and daren't come out. Her Ladyship's kicking off something awful, and Sir

Lancelot's having none of it. And that Mr.Medulla's in there, and he keeps saying something and Sir Lancelot shouts him down, and that just makes Lady Sybil worse. Oh, there'll be bloody murder done up there before long, you mark my words!"

"And that man Knowes, is he up there?" asked Ma. "If there's to be a murder, it'll be him as does it. I have a very bad feeling about that man, he'd crush you into little bits without a second thought! I ... oh, where's she gone?" for Kitty had slipped from her chair and out of the door.

"Gone to see the fun, I expect," Charity said. "I hope she's careful!"

Kitty was indeed being careful, running in her stockinged feet quietly up the stairs. At the top she paused and put her head round the corner, ready to run if anyone was coming. The top corridor was empty, but from the sitting room she could hear raised voices. She crept along and stood against the wall near the door. Opposite, the door to the dining room was ajar but she could not see Cartilege.

"Are you out of your mind?" she heard. Sir Lancelot's voice had a strangled quality as though he could barely squeeze the words out of a throat strangled with rage. "Three hundred years my family have ..."

"And so what, you old fool?" This was Lady Sybil, shrill and scornful. "Where has it got us? Bills and more bills and worry and stress, that's what it's brought! And now these people are offering a way ..."

She was interrupted by the smooth tones of MrMedulla, still so soft that she could only make out the odd word. "Dear Sir Lancelot ..." she heard, "... our offer stands ..."

"Offer, he calls it! Sheer bloody blackmail is ..."

"... our offer stands and you'd be foolish ..."

"Get out! Get out or by God I'll ..."

There was a deep rumble, and Medulla said sharply "No, Knowes, leave it! Sir Lancelot will ..."

Lady Sybil cut in. "Put the poker down, you silly old man! What are you going to do, you feeble ...

think of it, man, millions of pounds! A villa in the South of France, a flat in Paris ... if you're still so besotted with your moths you could mount a dozen expeditions, in fact I wish you would so I don't have to put up with you bumbling uselessly around ..."

"But what about the servants? Some of 'em have worked here all their lives. Are we just going to kick 'em out without so much as a by-your-leave?"

"In a word, yes, we won't need them any more. And it's our castle, not theirs. We'll do what we like with it."

"Well, technically it's not our castle, it's mine. It's been in my family since William and Mary, while your people were grubbing a living on some poverty-stricken smallholding in Dumfries. And what about the moths? Where will I put my moths?"

"Who cares about your moths, you fool? They're just an excuse to fritter your time away up there instead of doing anything useful ..."

"... national importance! They're a unique ..."

"National fiddlesticks, they're worthless junk ...!"

But there was movement now, a shifting of chairs and shadows on the glass of the door. Knowes's massive arm appeared, holding the door open. Mr.Medulla turned in the doorway and said in measured tones "I think I've heard enough. My offer stands, but it won't stand for ever. The machinery's waiting ready. You only have to give the word and hand over the deeds, that's all. But ..." he stepped back into the room a pace or two, and his voice sunk to a menacing hiss, "... I warn you, my patience is running thin! If you don't come to your senses very soon and do the sensible thing, I have to warn you ... you will regret it very much. Now, think on!"

As the door began to open more widely, Kitty crept hastily back down the corridor and took to her heels before she was seen.

"There's something going on," Kitty told them back in the kitchen. "I don't know what it is, but it's Lady Sybil and Mr.Medulla against Sir Lancelot. And it's something really big, to do with the castle, but I don't know what."

"I might know something about it," said Melody, who had arrived moments before Kitty rushed in full of excitement.

"There's a big billboard up at the village green with a plan of something called 'New Crayle' with new buildings marked on it, a village hall and a school and a doctor's. And Dashwood Belhatchett is trying to convince everyone it's a good thing, and they don't all believe him."

"And what does it say about the castle?"

"Nothing. No mention at all. So ... no, nothing."

"So we're not much further forward, then."

"No. But I have to say, child, you took a dreadful risk going up there. What were you thinking of?"

"Oh, pooh, I was safe enough. There was only Cartilege to see, and he won't say anything."

"Why won't he? I asked him where you were when you were missing, and he was really strange. He seemed guilty, somehow."

"Well I've sorted him out!" Kitty laughed. "I met him on the Library stairs, and he looked as though he'd seen a ghost. I think he does believe I'm actually dead. I say, that's an idea, I'll take a sheet off the spare bed and go around in it! Then if anyone sees me ..." she lowered her voice into a sinister whisper, "... I will be a small pale figure flitting across the end of a corridor, the dead girl still haunting the scene of her dreadful murder ..."

XV

"Blow sandstone and granite and gravel and soil,
The wind's in the sand-dunes, the surf's on the boil!"

Wyrm declaimed sonorously from above Kitty's head. He had raised the front half of his body up from the flagstones. She felt that if he had any hands, one of them would be posed importantly on his chest. Or where his chest would have been, if he had one.

"Oh goodness, you've made some more poetry!" she exclaimed, delighted. "Sorry, I interrupted. do go on." She sat on her piece of wood and listened attentively. He started again ...

"Blow sandstone and granite and gravel and soil,
The wind's in the sand-dunes, the surf's on the boil,
The breakers are roaring, the air's full of spray
And the seagulls lament as they're blasted away;
Wriggle and coil, wriggle and coil,
The wind's in the sand-dunes, the surf's on the boil."

"Oh Wyrm, that was wonderful! You're so clever!" she breathed.

"Right number of syllabubs this time?"

"Syllables. Yes, pretty much. It was lovely, is there any more?"

"There is. I seem to have been on a bit of a roll yesterday."

He closed his eyes and recited ...

"The breakers are roaring, the air's full of spray,
But under the water the kelps gently sway;
Silver scales flash as the little fish swim
And play hide and seek in the green and the dim;
Wriggle and coil, wriggle and coil,
For under the water the kelps gently sway.

Silver scales flash as the little fish swim
And play hide and seek in the green and the dim;
Above, the storm rages, the fishing boats toss,
And fisher-folk watch for their ruin and loss,
But we'll wriggle and coil, wriggle and coil,
As we play hide and seek in the green and the dim!"

Kitty clapped her hands and gave a cat-call. "Whoo-hoo! That was marvellous, Wyrm! You're so clever, it has a chorus and everything. I'm so impressed I can't tell you!"

Wyrm lay his head down beside her, doing his best to look modest. "Just a little thing I tossed off in the small hours, you know," he muttered. "I didn't expect you till this morning and the cat had been and gone, so I'd nothing else to do."

Kitty thought to herself that self-pity was an unattractive quality and not to be encouraged. "Perkins must be a great comfort, though?"

"Oh yes. Not much conversation, as we said. But he's company, you see."

"Something to look forward to," Kitty suggested.

"Something forward to which to look," the Worm muttered, "no, that doesn't sound right."

"I think Perkins isn't a he, he's a she," Kitty said gently.

"Is he? I mean, is she? What's the difference?"

Kitty thought for a moment. This was the second time the issue of gender had come up, and she was finding it hard to explain. "Nothing significant," she said, "nothing for you to worry about, anyway. It's just words."

"Ah, but words are important. And now I have another friend - you. You may be an odd, sticky, tottering sort of creature, but at least you talk. The only thing that could possibly be better is if you made any kind of sense, but I suppose that's too much to ask."

Kitty chuckled lazily. We all make sense to ourselves, she thought. Not Marcia, of course, there was an exception to every rule. Marcia was inexplicable. But when you cut to the chase, most people made sense. What was the past tense of 'cut'? It was 'cut', wasn't it, how silly?

"What are we sitting in, anyway?" she asked out loud, watching a dribble of sea water run down Wyrm's side and begin to trickle downhill. "It's a drain, I think?"

"Mm, could be," said Worm. "Some sort of conduit, perhaps?"

"Conduit? How do you know all these words, if you've spent all your life down here in the dark? You didn't go to school, I don't suppose."

"Not sure. Where do words come from?" he said thoughtfully. "They're just in my head, that's all I know, sitting there in case they're needed."

There was a short silence. "I know what you mean," she said, "I have loads of words in my head too. Some of them don't make sense at all. I mean ... 'snoot'? What does that mean?"

"Well, what does it mean? You said it, you must know what it means."

"I don't though. Perhaps there are some words that don't have meanings yet. They just sit around waiting to be needed. And when something crops up that hasn't got a word, they attach themselves to it, and that's what they mean."

"What, like these little lumps on my back? I don't have a word for them."

"Oh, those?" she said, scrambling to her feet and leaning across him. "I noticed them the other day, when you pulled me out of the surf. They were the only thing I could grab hold of. What are they?"

"Snoots, probably. They itch. And it's been worse since you manhandled them."

"Girl-handed them, you mean. I'm sorry about that, I was a bit desperate at the time. Let's have a look."

She reached across him and touched the little black nubs gently. There were two, side by side, rough little places where something broke through the smooth scales.

"That felt nice," he said. "I don't know what you did, but could you do it again?"

She touched them again, rubbing with the tips of her fingers.

Wyrm gave a little shiver. "Aah, yes! Go on, do it harder!"

She used her fingernails this time, catching at the roughness. She hoped she wasn't doing something a girl ought not to do, it seemed a bit personal somehow. But no, silly, of course it wasn't. It was just like scratching Perkins' ears, wasn't it, except that Perkins couldn't talk or make poetry? Wyrm was obviously enjoying it, for little waves of excitement were passing down his body, the rows of scales rippling sinuously. She scratched harder. This was an act of kindness, wasn't it, for it was something he could hardly manage for himself, having nothing to manage it with. Perhaps he could roll over and wriggle his back against the floor?

"Look, Wyrm," she said, "how long do I have to do this for? It's tiring!" He said nothing, but groaned with pleasure. "Perhaps you could teach Perkins to do it? She's got claws, she'd be good at it."

He craned round and looked at her with one sad eye. "You think?" he said, shuddering again. "How would I explain it to her?"

"Not sure. Ooh, what was that?" Something had given way under her fingers. A small piece of black slid down his scales and skittered along the floor. She looked closer. There was something poking out, a little black frond, spiky. She touched it gingerly, and it twitched slightly. This was weird. Then it hit her. He was a dragon, wasn't he? He was called a wyrm, but that was just the local name for a dragon, wasn't it? All right, he didn't have legs and claws and he probably couldn't breathe out fire, but he was roughly the right shape. If you spent a lot of time in the sea, breathing fire probably wasn't a practical option. Another piece of black crust was sticking up and breaking away now, and inside another little frond quivered, on the far side this time.

"Oh, silly, I know what they are," she cried, "they're wings! They're just baby wings that haven't grown yet!"

"Not snoots, then? I can't call them snoots?"

"No, wings, not snoots. Definitely wings. Try flapping them."

Worm shut his eyes and concentrated. "Anything happening?" he asked.

She looked closely. "Do it again. Oh yes, there! One of them sort of twitched a bit!"

"It didn't flap?"

"No. I expect you need to practise. They're ever so tiny at the moment, but maybe they'll grow now they've started. Look, I have to stop now. My fingers are worn out."

She got down and sat beside his head again. "Thank you," he said, "I enjoyed that. Will you come and do it again?"

"Well, I will, but you have to do something in return. You have to practise twitching them. Really put some work into it, you know, concentrate hard and get them moving. Try it now."

He closed his eyes and frowned. She craned up and looked to where the little fronds stuck up. First one and then the other gave a little twitch, and another piece of crust slid down.

"That's it, it's working!" she said. "Now, I'm going to go home and leave you to it. Every half hour, you have a little practise and I expect it'll get easier and easier, like when I learned to fight."

"What's fight?"

"Oh, just something we humans do. And in between, you make me another lovely poem like the last one. *'Wriggle and coil, wriggle and coil, As we play hide and seek in the green and the dim!'* - that was so good! 'Bye now!"

She looked back as she reached the foot of the rope ladder and put her foot into the first rung. He lay with his eyes shut and an expression of extreme abstraction on his face, his wide mouth pursed into a little knot of concentration.

When she got back to the kitchen she found Ma and the twins in a rare old bate, banging round and scowling.

"What do they think they're doing?" Ma said crossly. "All of a sudden, no discussion, just 'do this!', 'do that!' with no warning?"

"What's going on?" Kitty asked. Faith took a moment to lean on the back of a chair and answer.

"It's her bloody Ladyship!" she said. "Sent orders down with Cartilege. All the best crockery to be packed up, wrapped in newspaper and put into boxes! It's all to be sent away to Newcastle and put into store."

Ma sniffed. "All that lovely Coalport, with the pretty tree on it. Years, we've been using that, and never broke a single plate!"

"And the stuff with gold edges," put in Charity, "the Minton, I shall be sad to see that go."

"And that's not the half of it," Ma went on. "Cartilege is up there now, packing away all the silver, That's to go as well. And all the decent cutlery."

"So what are they going to eat off?" Kitty asked. "Or with?"

"They can eat with their fingers for all I care," said Ma, banging a cardboard carton on the table. "Perhaps she expects us to serve the food straight onto the table, is that it, and they'll just scoop it up with their fingers? The very idea! We've always done things properly in this house, and now it's all going to pot!"

"There's other china," Faith explained, "cheap stuff you know, like we use for ourselves down here. But Ma's always taken pride ..."

"Pride?" Ma snapped, "I'll give 'em pride! If she won't allow us to do things right, I'll go somewhere else! The Dragon might not be posh, but it's honest. I'll go down there and be an honest cook, not someone pretending to be posh but serving up in any old bucket that comes to hand!"

Kitty wondered if this didn't have something to do with the row last night, up in the sitting room. Were the Fossetts planning to move out, was that it? Or did they fear some sort of attack, and wanted to protect their more vulnerable things? She spent an hour helping to pack bone china, taking one pretty plate at a time and wrapping it in layers of old newspaper and putting carefully into a box. The little teacups were delicate, you had to be careful of the thin handles, stacking them one inside the other with the handles all pointing the same way into a corner of the box. When one complete set was done and the box taped up, she slipped away and went up into the castle to see if she could discover anything more.

She hadn't yet taken a spare sheet from her other bed to wear for a ghost, but she practised flitting wraith-like along corridors and across landings, running softly in stockinged feet and ready to give a ghostly moan at any moment if someone came. No one did. She padded up the Library stairs and crept quietly inside. Hiding behind the shelves, she made her way by gentle stages towards the far end where Sir Lancelot's moths lived.

Peering through the very last bookcase, looking over the tops of the books on the third shelf, she could make out Sir Lancelot himself. He sat at the table, but was not doing anything with the cards and pins and little jars of dried moths. He sat staring at the fireplace, his mouth moving, talking softly to himself. On the *chaise longue* the Sisters sat in a row, screwing their handkerchiefs up in their fingers, watching him with anxious faces.

"No, no, it won't do!" he was muttering.

"No, it won't do ..." echoed Lady Drusilla.

"... won't do ..." whispered Lady Clorinda, and "... no, no ..." sighed Lady Pamilia like the wind under the door.

Sir Lancelot started at nothing, jerking his head up, and said sharply "They shan't have it! Damn them, it's mine, they shan't have it!"

"... shan't have it ..."

"... have it ..."

"... have it, no ..."

"William and Mary, it was! Been in the family ... my father, and his father before him, and his father before that ... they shan't have it, I won't let 'em!"

"... let 'em! ..."

"... let 'em ..."

"... let 'em what?"

No one answered Lady Pamilia, and she dropped her head again and concentrated on screwing up her handkerchief.

Sir Lancelot stood up suddenly and began to pace back and forwards, shaking his head from side to side and waving his arms. The Sisters sat up and shrank back, alarmed. "Fight!" he shouted, "I'll fight 'em! I'll fight ... fight ..."

"... fight ...", gasped Drusilla and Clorinda.

"... fight who?" asked Pamilia faintly, looking round for the enemy but seeing no one. Kitty ducked as the empty gaze swept past her bookcase, but Pamilia was only looking, not seeing.

Sir Lancelot appeared to grow calmer, and sat at the table again, his chin on his hands, still muttering to himself. The Sisters once again fixed their anxious gaze on him. It must be strange and unsettling, Kitty thought, to be so wrapped up in someone that just staring at him was your main occupation in life. Had they been like this when they were children, following their big brother round like three little shadows? She imagined them, pretty little creatures, cooing and twittering and holding each other's hands as they tripped after him in mindless worship, cosseted and protected and never an original thought beneath their ringlets. They had never grown up, not really. And why should they have? What had ever happened in their lives that was real or challenging? What had they ever had to learn or experience? They had hardly been alive at all.

Her thoughts turned to Wyrm, lying in his cool dim place at the very root of the castle. He had never met anything real or challenging either, not to him. The sea was no challenge to a creature that could swim without thinking, food was no problem to someone who could live off the plants that grew so abundantly under the water. His only challenge, ever, had been getting stuck in the tunnel. He hadn't dealt with that very well, but then why should he?

Yet he was not a useless, vapid creature that floated through life with no aims or ideas of his own. He was something the Sisters had never managed to become, he was a being with a personality, who thought for himself within his own narrow experience, who loved words and made poems and could hold a conversation, who looked at his small world with a little more than mere vague amazement. Kitty felt a vast contempt for the Sisters, and even though she told herself this was unworthy and she should control herself, she could not because of the empty-headed spite they had shown her.

Plainly there was nothing more to see or learn up here, so she crept silently between the bookcases until she reached the door. As she opened the door she thought of leaving with a ghostly wail to startle them, but decided against it. Furtive caution was becoming a habit. But thinking of ghosts reminded her that she had not yet claimed her ghostly sheet, so she scampered along the corridor and up to her room. Either Faith or Charity had been up and tidied and made the bed, but otherwise it was just as she had left it.

She pulled the top sheet off the spare bed, the one that would have been Marcia's if not for the mumps. What a different holiday this would have been. She would never have discovered Wyrm, for a start. And how cool was that, to be the only girl in the world who had a dragon to talk to? No, it was much better that Marcia wasn't here.

The sheet wasn't very successful. She tried it draped over her head, but when she moved it fell off unless she held it all the time with one hand. She wrapped it round her shoulders like a cloak, but the same thing happened. Then she tried to wind it round her, tucking it into itself which looked a bit like an Indian sari. One of the girls at school had said it was racist to dress up in the costume of another country. Kitty thought this was rubbish, but was not keen on this solution anyway. She tried passing the sheet up between her legs and tucking it into her waist, but it looked as though she was wearing a nappy. Even a ghost had to have some self-respect.

In the end she gave up on the sheet idea, and sat down at the mirror looking at herself, wondering if some make-up would give her a ghostly pallor. Perhaps Melody would be able to lend her some? She presumed that ghosts didn't usually have freckles. The mirror stood on top of the chest of drawers and was in three parts, hinged so that you could move the outer sections. If you thought about it carefully and contorted yourself, you could even see the back of your own head. She found it rather disturbing, though. If you got the angles right, you could see the reflection of your own reflection in the other mirror, and then another smaller one, and another, and another receding into the distance. A host of shiny spectacles gleamed back at her, little circles of light getting smaller and smaller, and a million freckles getting more and more tiny. And right in the furthest, darkest distance where the spectacles were mere pinpricks and the freckles were like dust, was there not something that looked over her shoulder, something that was not her, something other? She shuddered, moved the mirrors to break the spell, and got up. It was, as Ma would say, far too nice a day to be frowsting in here, even if you were dead. She should go out and let the wind blow the shadows away. She would walk down to the village and see the 'New Crayle' plan for herself.

Melody had already been to the village, and now sat at her computer in the office. She had talked with Sky and Nearly Normal Nidd, and while they were chatting at the rear of the trinket shop the old lady with the sausage dog had turned up.

She was called Heather Law, and was plainly a force to be reckoned with. She described herself as 'a tough old bird' and had lived in Crayle all her life. What was needed, she said, was a campaign to save the village from the developers. Someone had to take a stand, and there in that room were just the people to do it.

They tossed ideas around. Sky was particularly interested in the environmental aspect of the scheme, and Melody from her internet searching was able to shed some light on this.

"They'll pump steam and oxygen through pipes down into the seabed," she told them. "When it reaches the coal seams, it heats them up and they give off methane, hydrogen, carbon monoxide and carbon dioxide. They bring those back to the shore in other pipes, and use them to generate electricity."

"So they'll have a sort of power station on the shore, then?" said Nearly Normal. "And they'll need pylons and cables to carry electricity away to the rest of the country. That won't be pretty."

"And where will the power station be? It would have to be quite big, wouldn't it?"

"That's right. And the plan they've put up doesn't show any of this. The little red blocks called 'Gas Reclamation Facilities' would be the pumping stations, presumably, where the steam is pumped down and the gases pumped back. But where the electricity is to be generated they're not letting on at all."

Heather Law banged on the table. "So dishonest!" she said. "Such a fraud, the whole thing! They're planning a major industry here right in our midst, and all they've told us is the nice doctor's surgery and a primary school! Do they think we're idiots?"

"Well, we're not idiots ..." said Nearly Normal slowly. "What we need to do is publish this information somehow, so they have to either confirm or deny it."

"Two approaches, then," Melody suggested. "One would be to go to the local newspapers and try to get them interested. The *Northern Echo* would be the main one. I don't want to do that bit, because I work at the Castle and I have a nasty suspicion the Fossetts are involved somehow. I don't want to lose my job just yet. Apart from anything else, Kitty's still up there and I need to be sure she's safe. Once she goes home I don't mind so much."

"I'll do that, then," offered Heather Law, "I've nothing to lose, I don't mind anyone knowing what I think. You'll have to get me the right addresses to write to, though, or the phone numbers."

Melody said she could do that easily enough from the internet. "But the other thing I suggest is a lot of flyers, distributed round the village and the surrounding area, explaining what we think is going on so everyone knows. Just little paper sheets, you know."

"I can do deliveries," said Nearly Normal. "People are used to me walking about all over the place, and I expect my boy'll help. He'd rather do that than go to school. And I dare say there will be others offering, once the news starts to get out."

Melody thought Nearly Normal Nidd was turning out to be a bit more than he let on. For someone who looked and lived like a tramp, he was remarkably well spoken and seemed educated. Round the billboard on the green, people had listened to him with respect.

Sky offered to do the deliveries closer to home, round the centre of the village, and also to try and intercept any tourists who came past. There was no harm in spreading the message a bit wider.

"The hard part is actually writing the flyer, and then getting them printed," said Melody. "I could write it on the computer in my office, no one will know. But I daren't try and print them out there. We have a printer and a supply of paper, but if anyone sees what I'm doing I'll be out on my ear and that doesn't help anyone."

"Ah, well that's where I come in," said Heather Law. "You know Mr.Cott's garage up at the crossroads on the road to Glororum, where he runs his lorries from? My nephew works there, in the office. And they have a computer up there, and a printer for invoices and that sort of thing. Quite a modern boy, he is. He'll do it, no question. He's got a soft spot for his old auntie!"

"And if Mr.Cott finds out?"

"I should think he'd be delighted, actually. He hates the Fossetts with a passion, he does, and if he sees a chance to do them damage, he'll be on it like a ferret up a drainpipe! You leave him to me, anyway, we're old friends."

So the meeting had broken up, with a feeling of satisfaction at some decisions taken and a course of action clear before them. Now Melody was at her computer with a document in front of her, writing her account of the bits of the New Crayle plan that had not been included on the billboard.

'Undersea Coal Gasification is a process that has yet to be used successfully in this country,' she typed. *'A mixture of steam and oxygen is pumped under the seabed to ...'*

There was a sound outside and she quickly hit a key. The screen disappeared, to be replaced by a spreadsheet of income from the ticket hut for the last year. The door had opened slowly, and the vast bulk of Cockley Knowes made the room a little darker. He peered round the room, running his eyes over the filing cabinets and the charts on the walls.

"Yes, can I help you?" she said brightly.

He said nothing, but stood in the centre of the room, still gazing round massively. Then his eyes lit on the desk. He walked slowly round behind her, the floorboards squeaking under his feet, and leaned very close over her head. She smelt an odour she did not recognise, something unwholesome. His laboured breathing was in her ear. Then he reached a ponderous hand over her shoulder and prodded a key on her keyboard. On the screen in front of her a column of figures disappeared.

He grunted and stood up. Still without a word, he walked to the door. As he left, he turned for a moment and regarded her impassively. Then a ghastly grin spread across his broad face, and he closed one eye in a hideous wink before withdrawing, closing the door softly. She realised that she had been holding her breath almost since the moment he entered, and let it out slowly. What had that been about?

Shakily she closed the spreadsheet without saving, then opened it again. The column of figures reappeared, undamaged. As her breathing returned to normal she clicked over to the document she had been writing, and saved it with an anonymous-sounding name that no one would suspect. She would finish it later, when she felt a bit steadier. Then it would be a matter of copying it onto a memory stick and getting it to

Heather Law somehow. The scent of the man was still in her nostrils. She got up and opened the window to let the fresh sea air in.

"Kitty, I have a job for you," she said, sitting on the bed that night. "I need to get something to a lady called Mrs.Law, but I can't go myself. Could you do it?"

"Of course. But I don't know Mrs.Law, who is she? Where does she live?"

"She's just a lady in the village. And I don't know where she lives either, but Billy Cott will know. So what I want you to do is, I'll give you a computer memory stick at breakfast tomorrow, and you take it to the Billies and tell them to deliver it for me. They'll know her, and where she lives, and no one'll think anything of them going around the village because they live there."

"Why can't they tell me where to go, and I'll do it?"

"Because I don't think you should be seen round the village too much. You're dead, remember? Sooner or later someone might see you and the news'll get back to the Fossetts that you're still alive. Or to Cockley Knowes." She shuddered, still hearing his heavy breath in her ear.

"OK!" Kitty said brightly, "that makes sense. Leave it to me, the Kitty Express always delivers! Any message for Billy, then? Any little endearment, a scrap of verse or a piece of ribbon in a significant colour?"

"Oh goodness, will you give up? What's a significant colour, anyway?"

"I don't know. Pink, probably. Do you think Billy Cott's got nice muscles?"

"Kitty, you're incorrigible!"

"Yes, I am rather, my headmistress said that. She also said I was rude, defiant and a disruptive element, which I thought was a bit over the top. Would you kiss me goodnight?"

Melody did, and let herself out of the door. Before she could close it behind her, Perkins slipped inside with her tail in the air. Actually, he does have nice muscles, she thought as she went down to her own room.

XVI

The next couple of days were highly entertaining for Kitty. Melody's plan had worked – Kitty had taken the memory stick to the harbour, the Billies had carried it to Mrs.Law, and before the end of that day the leaflets started to appear, poked into people's letterboxes, or thrust into their hands as they walked in the street. A whole bundle of them were pinned to the billboard on the green, which someone had defaced in large black letters, *'Save our village, stop the vandals! No frottling in Crayle!'* Kitty thought 'frottling' was a rather nice word, and wondered who had coined it. During the next night someone tore the whole billboard out of the ground and left it lying in smithereens on the grass. Plainly feelings were running high.

They ran even higher that evening when Tyne Tees Television included a short report in their North East News programme. They used the term 'frottling' as well, but said that no one from COGACO would come and answer their questions. The following morning the subject of frottling in Crayle was the headline in the Northern Echo newspaper. The campaign was off to a flying start. During that day a couple of shabby-looking vans appeared at the green, and people got out and milled around. The people were as shabby as their vans. There was a lot of tie-dye, dreadlocks and beards, big boots and ancient waxed jackets. Some of the strangers wandered over to Sky's shop and disappeared inside.

Meanwhile Kitty occupied herself with Wyrm. She found him rather pleased with himself. He had been practising as she said, every half hour or so when he was not out feeding, and the little wings were now six inches long.

"Mmm. They aren't very big, are they?" she said, not wanting him to be too satisfied and let up on his efforts. "I think they'll get much bigger if you keep trying."

"Well, they're about ten times bigger than when you saw them last," he said loftily, "what do you expect? Rome wasn't built in a day! ... erm ...I've no idea why I said that."

"No, it was perfectly appropriate. Rome was ... a very big

thing, and certainly took a long time to build."

He brightened. "Anyway, look what I can do! Watch this!" He closed his eyes and pinched up his mouth, and looked rather strained. A low-pitched hum arose. At first Kitty thought he was singing in his throat, but then realised the noise was coming from the wings. The pitch of the hum rose higher and higher, and looking at his back all she could see was a blur. The wings were not flapping ponderously as she had expected, but were vibrating rapidly like the wings of a bumble bee, almost invisible and giving off this ear-splitting drone.

"Wow!" she laughed, putting her hands over her ears, "that's remarkable! All right, you can stop now!" The hum got lower and lower, and eventually stopped. The little wings folded themselves against his back neatly. Looking closer she could see that they were not feathered, but shiny and hard, dark grey but veined with intricate patterns of black. They were taking on a distinct curve so that she thought they would fit neatly against his scaly back when they were grown.

"They're not what I expected, quite," she said. "I thought they'd flap like a bird's wings, but they're more like a dragonfly or a bumble bee."

Wyrm sighed and said humbly "Those are things of which I have very little experience. Of."

"That's one too many 'of's," Kitty said.

"Sorry. Delete 'of'."

"Better. They're very impressive, though. You should be proud. I'm sorry I brought up bumble bees, I probably shouldn't expect you to talk about things you have no experience of."

"I don't have much choice, do I? I've very little experience, when you think about it," he said sadly, "just kelp and ... well, just kelp, mainly. The occasional scallop."

Then he brightened. "I did make up another poem," he said, "shall I say it?"

Without waiting, he drew himself up into his declaiming pose, and announced ...

"Laricky lumpkin, suet and lard,
Making up poetry isn't so hard.
You take a few words and a phrase that appeals,
String 'em together and see how it feels!

Cheerily, cherrily, chicken and chips,
My words are a treat for the tongue and the lips.
I bet you're enjoying this marvellous verse,
So witty and twitty and pithy and terse!

Umpetty, bumpetty, bacon and ham,
Oh what a wonderful poet I am!
Diggerel, doggerel, metre and rhyme,
I think I'll start talking like this all the time!

Pidderley, podderley, parsley and sage,
But what shall I do at the end of the page?
Shall I turn over?
Go back to the top?
Shall I continue?
Or shall I just ..."

"Stop!" cried Kitty, giggling. "Coo, that's impressive, you just made a joke! How do you know about chicken and chips, anyway?"

"I don't, they're just words. I seem to know an awful lot of words that mean nothing to me, but I like the way they sound."

She told him that there were human poets who specialised in inventing words and turning them into poetry, and recited most of *Jabberwocky* to him:

"'Twas brillig, and the slithy toves
Did gyre and gimble in the wabe;
All mimsy were the borogroves,
And the mome raths outgrabe.

Beware the Jabberwock, my son!
The jaws that bite, the claws that catch!
Beware the Jubjub bird, and shun
The frumious Bandersnatch!"

He laughed at that, a deep rumbling chortle she hadn't heard before.

"That's wonderful!" he said, "I could do that ... see ...

I have no need to blart and shout,
I've not the slightest bindlesnitch
Just what this verse is all about,
Except it makes my snarkles itch!"

She clapped her hands and complimented him. Inwardly she thought 'What have I done? I may have created a monster here. Except he was a monster to start with, I suppose.'

But Wyrm frowned and became serious. "There's something I forgot to tell you," he said. "I saw something this morning, something I don't understand."

"What was that?"

"Well, you know those things that sit on top of the water, and humans are in them?"

"You mean boats?"

"Yes, that's it, boats. There was one the other day, and this morning when I went out to the rocks for my breakfast, I found something on the seabed. Long thin things, black. They weren't there yesterday, so the boat must have dropped them."

"Long thin things? How long, and how thin?"

"Oh, very long. They point in towards the shore and out to sea. Many times as long as me. But much thinner, only about as thick as you. I'd have picked one up and brought it back to show you, except I haven't got anything to pick it up with, have I?"

"How many were there?"

"Three. Well, more than three, I think, but I don't know any more numbers."

"And where, exactly?"

"Just to the south of the rocks, and not as far out as the island."

Kitty thought. Long things running from the shore out to sea, sitting on the seabed? Could this be pipes, something to do with the frottling? That was quick. She'd better tell Melody.

"Don't worry about them," she said. "I don't think they can do you any harm. But I'll talk to my friends about them, and see what they think. In fact, I'll go and do it now. I'll see you tomorrow. Keep practising!"

"I will," he said. "I rather enjoy it, actually, I like the noise it makes. It satisfies my bindlesnitch!"

She took to her rope ladder, and clambered away through the bushes with the rising hum behind her. She wondered where Melody would be. If she was up in her office, Kitty could hardly go and find her, she might be seen. Perhaps she should go and consult the Billies instead, and ask them about what Wyrm had seen?

But as she set off across the grass towards the little wicket gate to the beach, there was a shout and Professor Crust appeared, hurrying after her. She wondered whether to run for it, but instead turned and waited, ready to brazen it out.

"So, not so lost after all?" he said cheerfully, puffing from his exertions. "I thought you were supposed to be shut up somewhere, dead to the world? But here you are, out in the sunshine, large as life and bold as brass and twice as pretty! Poof, I shouldn't run at my age. Let's sit down a minute, shall we, and have a nice chat?"

Reluctantly she followed him to one of the benches and sat down. He unbuttoned his raincoat and stretched his legs out, resting his shapeless hat on the bench beside him.

"You see," he said, turning towards her with that smile that sat on his lips but not his eyes, "they told me you were lost, and no one knew what had happened to you. So ..."

"Who told you?"

"Why, my colleagues, you know. Mr.Medulla and Mr.Knowes. They said you were probably locked in the ruins or something, perhaps fallen down a crater or crushed by fallen masonry or some such accident. Very sad, but not surprising when people will go poking around in things and places that don't concern them."

"But here I am," she said, wondering where this was going.

"But here you are," he agreed, "here you are indeed. And that makes me wonder, you see. I wonder where you've been and what you've been up to? Have you ..." he leaned closer and looked into her eyes, "... have you found something? Have you found our wyrm, perhaps? Found it, and weren't going to tell me?"

"No, I haven't," she lied, keeping her face blank.

He looked at her for a long moment. "You wouldn't lie to me, would you?" he said softly. "You wouldn't lie to your old friend? I thought we were friends, wasn't that it?"

"You said that, I didn't!" she answered boldly. "And if I had found something, why should I tell you?"

"Because if you didn't ..." he said, leaning towards her and putting his hand on her knee, "... if you didn't, that would be unfriendly, and I might think twice about telling what I know." His grip on her knee tightened. "I might feel bound to tell my friends that you are not safely locked up as they thought, but are free and running around in the daylight, getting up to mischief! What do you suppose they'd say about that?"

"I'm not sure," she said, and stood up, knocking his hand away. "I'm not sure what they'd say, and I'm not sure what it is you think you have to tell them, and I'm not sure what it is you think I might have found." She began to back away. "What I am sure about is that we are not friends and never were. You're a fraud and a cheat. You're not a professor, and you're not an archaeologist and you're not a palaeontologist as you claimed. You're something else, and I'll have nothing to do with you!"

She turned and walked very quickly away, along the path under the curtain wall and towards the wicket gate and the beach. When she had put a good distance between them, she glanced over her shoulder. He was not following, but still sat on the bench, gazing after her with a little smile on his face.

At the harbour she found the Billies down in the cockpit of the *Mercy*. Billy Cott was bent over a small primus stove and a frying pan.

"Hallo!" he said when she called down from the jetty. "Want a bacon sandwich? There's plenty!"

Kitty had enjoyed a hearty breakfast with Ma Cott and the girls that morning, but she could always manage more. She climbed down the ladder and sat with the Billies in the sunshine, eating a thick bacon sandwich with a tin mug of sweet tea.

"This is lovely," she said. "Are you going out? Because I've got something to tell you ..."

She explained about the pipes on the seabed, but did not say how she knew.

"So, where are they exactly? Do you know?" asked Billy Brannicle.

"They run out from the shore towards the sea, just south of that rocky outcrop. But they don't go as far as the island with the little white house on."

"And you know this how?" said Billy Cott.

Kitty was silent for a moment. She had known this would be awkward, but didn't feel she had any choice but to tell them what she knew. "I can't tell you," she said. "Someone told me about it, but you'll just have to trust me."

The men looked at each other. "That's not very satisfactory," began Billy Cott, but Billy Brannicle wasn't worried.

"Look, Billy, we can trust Kitty, can't we? We're all on the same side here! We know that Melody trusts her, and we trust Melody, so we have to go along, don't we? And if we go out and have a look and it turns out to be not true, what have we lost? A couple of hours and a couple of gallons of diesel, that's all. I'm up for it."

"And speaking of Melody ..." said Kitty.

"Ha! Now that's a useful coincidence," smiled Billy Cott. Melody herself had just arrived at the foot of the jetty. Kitty clambered up the ladder and ran to meet her.

"I'm glad you've come," she said, "come on, we're going out on the boat! By the way, Billy says what are you doing tonight, because he thinks you're very pretty and he wants to come over and kiss you?"

Melody laughed. "No he didn't, you wretch! Your headmistress was right, you certainly are incorrigible! Just you wait until you get a boyfriend of your own!"

"So he is your boyfriend, then?"

"No. Change the subject. Have you seen these new people that have come? The ones with vans?"

"Yes. Who are they?"

"People Sky knows, I think. She calls them 'radicals' and 'truth-seekers'. There've been some interesting discussions, though. They're talking about barricades and blockades, something they call 'active resistance' ... I'm not sure how the villagers are going to like strangers coming in and taking over their fight. I'm not sure how I feel myself."

"Whatever gets the job done, I'd have thought," Kitty said. "You don't think COGACO would mess about, do you? Nor should we! Come on, I just had a bacon sandwich, if you smile very sweetly at Billy he might make you one!"

It was lovely, sitting in the cockpit with the engine chugging and a white wake streaming behind them as the gallant little boat butted its way through the small waves. The sea was brilliant blue, and the land behind the castle was green, fading to pale purple at the inland horizon where the higher hills rose beyond the A1 road. The castle looked almost gay, with a flag flying on the stumpy mast on top of the tower, and another one at the gatehouse. Tourists moved along the walls, little dots of bright red and blue and yellow in their anoraks. Kitty wondered if they were looking out to sea, wishing they could be rocking in this little boat, or if they wondered where it was bound. A gentle breeze from seaward lifted a lock of hair on her cheek.

Where they were bound, of course, was the other side of the rocks. They passed forty yards off, watching the waves breaking over them and sending spray high in the air, flashing in the sunlight.

"Not a good place to be in rough weather," Billy Brannicle told them, "boats have been lost here, over the years."

"What's the little white house on the island?" Melody enquired.

It was, Billy Cott explained, just an empty shell these days, though in past days a hermit had made his home there, only able to launch his boat and go for supplies in very settled weather. He'd be marooned for months at a time in winter, Billy said, and survived on seabirds' eggs and the seabirds themselves, and keeping warm with a tiny fire of flotsam and dried seaweed. The villagers would look out and see the tiny spark in the stormy darkness, and wonder that he was still there.

"But no, no one comes out there these days," Billy said. "Once a year some of us go ashore when the weather allows, and give the place a fresh coat of whitewash, because it makes a useful mark to look out for when you're approaching the coast searching for the harbour entrance. But otherwise it's deserted now."

Billy Brannicle throttled the engine back to an idle, and called from the deck-house. "Just south of the rocks, you said, pet?"

Kitty nodded.

"Right, Billy, then we'll just go back and forwards with the grapple and see what we come up with, shall us?"

The two men set to work, tying a cross-shaped grappling iron to the end of a cable. It had four sharp points to catch on anything it came across. Billy Cott fed it over the stern while Billy Brannicle drove the *Mercy* slowly ahead. "Wouldn't do for the rope to get near the propeller," he explained.

Melody leaned closer to Kitty. "I don't understand, though. I know we're looking for these pipes, Billy said, but how do you come to know about them? Who told you?"

"Oh, just someone I met," she said airily. "No one you know. Tell me more about this 'active resistance' thing?"

"I see, you want to change the subject. Fair enough, then. Well, it's what I said, putting up barricades and trying to make things as difficult as possible. There's talk of people lying down in front of the bulldozers, that sort of thing. And one or two have mentioned trying to get into the castle and occupying it."

"That wouldn't be hard, I don't think. I could show them ways to get in."

"You're not to get involved, you hear? Some of these people are rather sinister, I think. Not above a bit of violence and criminal damage, I shouldn't wonder. And there are a lot more coming, by all accounts."

The *Mercy* was now travelling quite quickly parallel to the shore. When she came level with the rocks, she turned and went about in the opposite direction so they were making a series of passes across the area Wyrm had identified. On the third or fourth pass Billy Cott, standing in the stern, gave a shout and raised his hand. The boat stopped and rocked quietly, and Billy Brannicle left the wheelhouse and went to join his friend at the stern. The rope disappeared into the water, taut and dripping. The two men hauled on it, hand over hand. It was hard work, and they made little progress.

"Something big anyway," said Billy Cott, moving to the big winch that sat in the back of the boat. "Not just some old lobster pot, then." He wound the end of the rope round the big drum of the winch, made the end fast, and began to turn the winch handle. Gears went round, and the rope creaked, and the boat moved backwards a little. Slowly the rope came in, Billy Brannicle leaning over the stern to see what was on the end of it. Eventually he held his hand up.

"Well, our bonny lass is right enough, come and see!" he said.

Just breaking the surface of the water, heaving up and down as the boat rose and fell, was the grapple. Securely caught in two of its tines was a black plastic pipe about nine or ten inches across. It was plainly very heavy from the sluggish way the rope moved, and the fact that the boat was pulled backwards every so often by its weight. It must be slightly flexible, for it bent over the grapple and disappeared into the murk on either side.

"Much too long for us to raise," Billy Cott said. "We'd need much more equipment."

"And a bigger boat?" Melody said, standing very close behind him.

"Aye, probably a bigger boat. We'll have to let it go for now. But we know it's there all right."

"That could be very useful. I mean, if COGACO have started work before getting planning permission, we might be able to use that."

"I expect they wanted to get pipes laid while the weather was kind. Another couple of months and it might be too rough. A big pipe-laying vessel wouldn't worry about a bit of a blow out at sea, but this close inshore it's another matter."

The two Billies busied themselves with rope and boathooks, manoeuvring lighter lines round the pipe to take its weight off the grappling iron, then releasing the winch and letting the grapple fall away from the pipe, hauling it inboard and finally allowing the pipe to sink again. In a moment it had vanished beneath the waves, and the *Mercy* revved its engine and set off for home. Kitty sat back, pleased to have been vindicated. And pleased, too, that Wyrm had thought to tell her about this important event in human affairs that must be of no importance or interest to him. Remarkable really, she thought, wasn't it, that a creature who hatched from an egg and had never talked with a human being before, somehow knew the meaning of friendship?

Kitty made her way up to her bedroom in the tower that night in a very satisfactory frame of mind. It had been a good day. She'd had two breakfasts, had an excellent visit with Wyrm, been pleasantly rude to Professor Crust and enjoyed a lovely boat trip – and been proved right, as well. Altogether, a day of reward and accomplishment.

And, she remembered, she had gone and stood with Billy Brannicle in the wheelhouse on the way back to the harbour. He had let her stand in front of him and steer the *Mercy*, almost all the way back and up to the jetty before he took over. The reason she had gone to the wheelhouse was because Melody and Billy Cott were standing rather close together in the stern, talking softly, and she hadn't wanted to cramp Melody's style.

Mission nearly accomplished, she thought. Now, what could she do about Billy Brannicle and the twins? And which twin was it to be? That was the nub of the problem. How could even an accomplished match-maker function properly if she didn't know who she was supposed to be matching? She wondered if a quiet word with Ma Cott might be the way forward.

She pushed open the door of her room, and smelt something. She sniffed. Yes, there it was, it was something she had smelled before, but what? She felt her way across to the bed and reached for the candlestick and the box of matches that sat on the bedside table. The tiny flame of the candle crept up the wick and grew brighter, casting long shadows on the walls. As she sat on the bed to remove her shoes, one of the shadows moved and she remembered where she had smelt that smell before. A great hand covered her mouth and eyes and she felt herself lifted effortlessly into the air.

XVII

"Look at that!" snorted Lady Sybil, standing at the window. "There are people all over the lawn, some of them have even lit a bonfire! Lancelot, what are you going to do? We're supposed to be closed, so how did they get in? And I hardly think they've paid. What are you doing about it, man?"

Sir Lancelot grunted, and went to stand beside her. "Mm ... not sure what ... good grief, isn't that one of the park benches they're burning? The police, that's it, yes, we'll call the police ..."

Kitty sat in one of the deep armchairs, so deep that her feet didn't reach the floor. It was bad enough that Medulla stood with his back to the fireplace, smiling slightly and saying nothing, or that Cockley Knowes loomed over her, ready to seize her from behind if she moved. But to have to sit with your feet sticking out in front of you and not even being able to touch the floor was the ultimate indignity.

On a sofa opposite sat the Sisters, twittering among themselves. Occasionally they would glance at her, their eyes full of empty spite, and nod their heads together and mutter about her. They were enjoying this. Behind them Professor Crust paced, his hands behind him, trying to look calm but actually radiating tension. At the door Cartilege waited for instructions, his head down, staring at the carpet.

Mr.Medulla shifted his feet and cleared his throat. "I don't think the police, dear lady," he said, "not just yet. Things haven't reached quite that pass yet. We don't need the police."

Sir Lancelot turned, bristling. "Whose castle is this, pray? Since when do you make decisions ...?"

"Quiet, you idiot!" snapped Lady Sybil. "You've never made a decision in your life, not when it mattered. You always leave it to me. If it's deciding which moth to pin where, or whether to go off wasting money in some benighted corner of the globe just to bring back a few more dead insects ... but when it comes to anything important, I make the decisions, not you. So be quiet!"

Sir Lancelot turned scarlet and drew a deep breath. "Sybil, I ..." he began in a strangled voice, but Medulla interrupted.

"Dear Sir Lancelot and Lady Sybil, pray let us not fall out at this juncture. There's far too much at stake, for you as much as for any of us. Millions, remember, millions and millions ... all waiting on a simple yes or no."

"Cartilege, wait outside!" snapped Lady Sybil. "I don't care to discuss such things in front of the servants!" Cartilege stirred and let himself quietly out of the door, looking relieved.

"What about in front of children?" muttered Sir Lancelot, aggrieved. "That's all right, is it?"

Lady Sybil turned from the window and eyed Kitty malevolently. "Yes, that's right, children. One child in particular. One nasty, sneaking, idle little spy, demanding shelter under our roof and then doing all she can to cause trouble .... what do you suggest we do about her, Medulla? It was you and your ... man ... who said you'd taken care of her, and you didn't. And now you bring her back, large as life, well-fed and defiant, and leave it to me? How dare you! All this time you told me it was done with, and she's been eating me out of house and home, corrupting my servants and turning them against me, no doubt, sleeping in my beds – and you had no idea, had you?"

Medulla smiled lazily. "No," he said, "that's true enough. I had no idea at all, until my esteemed colleague here told me." He nodded towards the Professor, but didn't seem at all troubled by the thought of his own failure. He was sleek and confident.

"It seemed the right thing to do, your Ladyship, once I discovered her," Crust said, bowing slightly to her. Kitty thought if he'd still been wearing his hat, he'd have taken it off and swept the floor with it.

Lady Sybil wasn't impressed, it seemed. "Who are you again?" she said rudely. "I don't remember who you are. What are you doing here, exactly?"

"Professor Crust is my colleague, dear lady," said Medulla. "I did introduce him. Professor Crust is an eminent geologist who has been helping me, advising me on matters pertaining ..."

Ha, thought Kitty, so that was it. Not an archaeologist, not a palaeontologist, but a geologist. She knew that geologists study rocks. Not the remains that lie in them, but the very rocks themselves, and the other rocks that are hidden beneath them, and the ones below that, all the way down to the centre of the earth. And, of course, the coal and oil and gas that are trapped in them. It all made sense at last.

"Good grief, there are tents, now!" exclaimed Sir Lancelot from the window. "Look, they're putting tents up! The sheer bloody nerve of it! What do they think this is, a camp-site? Who the hell are they?"

"They're protesters, Sir Lancelot," said Medulla. "They turn up all over the country, professional rabble-raisers, determined to oppose progress wherever they find it. They're set on preventing honest businessmen from making a living, and if they ruin the lives of ordinary people that's of no consequence to them because they don't have to live here, they can always move on to the next squat or caravan-park. They're scum, and we'll obliterate them soon enough, once you have signed. Just sign, Sir Lancelot, and you won't have to worry about them any more. Knowes and I will take care of them in no time, and you won't be troubled in the least."

Behind Kitty, Knowes stirred from his massive immobility. "Baseball bats!" he sniggered, "half a dozen big men with ..."

"Quiet, Knowes!" snapped Medulla. "These good people don't need to know the nitty-gritty, the unpleasant exigencies of our profession, do they? They only need to sign the papers and get on with their untroubled lives. Now, Sir and Lady, can I direct your attention to the most pressing matter of the moment? What do you wish to do about Miss Younger, who I understand has been causing some irritation?"

"Give her a good whacking!" grunted Sir Lancelot, "that's what I said before. Tan her hide and see how much trouble she feels like making after that! Should have done it days ago."

"Not an option, I fear, Sir Lancelot. The times have moved on, have they not?"

Kitty wriggled forward in her chair, put her feet on the floor at last, and stood up. Knowes made a move behind her, but Medulla stopped him with a gesture.

"Why not lock me up in the ruins, like you did before?" she said defiantly. "You locked me in with no food and no water, and left me to starve, didn't you? What will the police say about that, I wonder?"

"They'll say nothing about it, my dear, because they won't know about it. They won't know about it because no one's going to call them." He looked around to make sure he had been heard and attended to. "It was an unfortunate accident, of course. When we went to release you and give you your tea, you had got out and gone on your adventures somewhere, so what were we to do?"

"Well, I'll call them if you won't," she said bravely. "You're in a bit of a pickle here, aren't you? You don't want the police because you've got too much to hide yourselves. If I call the police you'll all be in trouble for kidnap and attempted murder. So you don't have too many options, do you? Either keep me a prisoner and worry about it in case I escape again, or ... what? Kill me? Are you up for that?" She glared round. Sir Lancelot looked cowed, Lady Sybil was ashen and seemed about to pounce and tear her to shreds, Professor Crust looked seriously alarmed, and the Sisters had stopped twittering and sat mutely staring in amazement. Cockley Knowes was impassive, and Medulla seemed faintly amused.

"Rather melodramatic, I think, but admirable spirit all the same. I congratulate you, young lady, you've put it in a nutshell, indeed you have. It's not quite that simple, of course. I might be able to think of other options. You might disappear to the other side of the country, for instance. Or Knowes here might keep you for a sort of pet. He has some unpleasant character traits, true, but he does love to play with small things. So no, it's not quite as simple as you think."

"But I have friends here. They'll want to know where I am. So it's not quite as simple as you think, either."

"Mister Medulla, will you stop this?" barked lady Sybil. "How long will you allow this little criminal to keep answering back and wasting our time? Just do something, for God's sake! Get rid of her! Get rid of her for good!"

Medulla was unfazed. "I don't mind her wasting my time, your Ladyship. She has a certain spirit which I appreciate. What I do mind, rather a lot, is having my time wasted by you and Sir Lancelot here. I have the money sitting in the bank, I have the machinery and the manpower sitting idle, while you procrastinate. One little girl is the least of my worries, to be honest. I'm tempted to let her go, actually."

"Let her go, man? Are you mad?"

"No, not mad. Not even close. What harm can she do? She sleeps in a bed, she eats some food, she reads in the Library – oh yes, young lady, I know how you spend your time! She talks to the servants, she annoys the butler, she goes exploring in places she shouldn't, but at the end of the day, where's the harm? What do any of us have to fear from her? She's a little girl, when all's said and done."

"Not so little," Kitty said boldly. "I know what you're doing, remember. I know about the village plan, I know how you're bribing the councillors with promises of village halls and stuff, I know about the pipes in the sea ..."

"Oh, really? How do you know that, pray?"

"... and I know about frottling, the damage it'll do ..."

"And you're going to tell who, exactly? There are already protesters out there, and more on their way no doubt. They're far more experienced than you, though I'm confident that Knowes and his men will take care of them. Who's going to take notice of a little schoolgirl? And, Miss Younger, I caution you to take care. At the moment, I see two options: either we let you go, or we give you to Knowes and leave it to him, with his little ... hobbies. Which would you prefer?"

Kitty looked round. Sir Lancelot and Lady Sybil stood rather close together, evidently cowed by this little man's glib confidence. Professor Crust looked guilty, possibly regretting that he had betrayed her. The Sisters were blank. This might be Sir Lancelot's castle, but it was Mr.Medulla and COGACO who were calling the shots.

There was a scuffle outside the door, and Cartilege appeared. "You Ladyship, there's Miss Trinket and some of the servants and ..."

But he was barged aside by Melody, with both the Billies backing her up and looking ready for a fight. Behind them was Ma Cott, and Faith and Charity with their sleeves rolled up, beefy forearms and a light of battle in their eyes.

"I've come for Kitty," Melody said boldly. "I'm taking her with me now, whether you like it or not. Now then!"

"You're fired!" snapped Lady Sybil hotly. "All of you, get your stuff and leave now! You're all fired!"

But Melody glanced at Billy Cott for support, and smiled. "Not that easy, I'm afraid, your Ladyship. How are you going to manage, exactly? Who'll make your food and clean up after you? Cartilege, on his own? And what'll you do for money?"

A look of intense interest came to Medulla's face. If anything, he seemed slightly amused.

Lady Sybil drew herself up. "Money, you idiot? What do you mean? There's plenty of money, what are you talking about?"

"But how will you get it? There's the Castle bank account, but can you get to it?"

"Why, I'll go to the bank! There's plenty ..."

"There isn't, actually. And what there is, you can't get at. I've changed the account so only I have access to it. I am the administrator here, after all. All legal and above board, I promise you. It's in my job description, *oversight of all fiscal affairs including appropriate steps to ensure accountability and security ...*'

"I'll call the police!"

"There's been no crime. There's nothing you can do."

Ma Cott had heard enough. She shoved the Billies aside, and stood truculently in front of Lady Sybil. "As far as I'm concerned, madam, you can shove your job! Me and my girls'll be off at the end of the week. We've made other arrangements!"

"Oh, splendid, splendid!" said Medulla softly. "But in the meantime, dear Mrs.Cott, may I say that I've enjoyed very much the excellent food you have provided. I hope that while you work out your notice, you'll continue to do so, for my sake if not for anyone else's? And shall we say, four weeks' salary for all three of you, as a token of good will on your sad departure? Lady Sybil, may we say that? I'm sure Miss Trinket can make the necessary arrangements."

Lady Sybil said nothing, but stood transfixed, her eyes bulging and her mouth working. Medulla turned to Kitty and said "Young lady, please accompany your friends, and feel free to continue to enjoy the hospitality of the Castle for a few days more? And you, Miss Trinket, I applaud your decisive initiative. You are plainly a businesswoman after my own heart. If you should ever find yourself in need of alternative employment, do get in touch. Knowes, kindly see the ladies and gentlemen out?"

Kitty went to Melody's side, resisted the temptation to stick her tongue out at Lady Sybil, and followed into the corridor. Behind her, the Sisters came out with a hasty rustle of organdie and scuttled off towards the stairs without a single twitter. Kitty realised that she had no idea whether they had a room or rooms of their own, or where they went when they weren't with Sir Lancelot. Did they all sleep in the same bed, side by side in their lacy nighties, turning over in unison and twittering softly in their sleep?

They reached the stairs. She felt for Melody's hand and held it, then glanced sideways and saw that with her other hand Melody was holding on to Billy Cott. She grinned to herself, and looked for Billy Brannicle. Was he closer to one of the twins than the other? But Faith and Charity both grinned at her rather meaningfully. They were still keeping both her and Billy guessing, and finding it rather a game.

As night began to fall, Kitty went out to the front of the castle to see what was going on. It was a strange sight. The incoming protesters had set up quite an encampment on the grass on the seaward side, protected from the sea breeze by the castle wall. There were twenty or thirty tents, and several bonfires burning with figures moving round them. There was the sound of talk and laughter, and someone was playing a flute or recorder.

Nearer to the castle and right in front of the entrance gate was a small crowd, some of the incomers but also a good number of villagers, marching slowly round in a big circle holding placards on sticks, that said *'Leave our beach alone, vandals!'* and *'No fossil fuel in Crayle'*, *'Crayle's not for Sale'*, and *'COGACO frottle off!'* . One said *'Elvis lives!'* but she thought that was just a joke. Watching them were a couple of policemen in yellow vests.

Other people were moving about, with clipboards and microphones, approaching the protesters and asking them questions. She saw Mrs.Law in the centre of a small knot of reporters, talking confidently. The reporters were smiling at what they heard, and jostled for her attention with many questions. As Kitty watched, a large van drew up with *'Tyne Tees Television'* on the side. Some men got out and began taking equipment out of the back. She wondered where the BBC were.

"So, liking what you see?" said a voice. It was Nearly Normal Nidd in his colourful trousers. Beside him was Streaky, who nodded and grinned at her.

"Yes, I think I do," she said. "The campaign's certainly taken off, hasn't it? You must be pleased."

"I am. It was Sky's idea to involve these others, the professional protesters. I don't approve of them, but in the circumstances it was probably the right thing to do. We couldn't have mounted a show like this on our own. Not everyone in the village is on our side, a few of 'em are seduced by the offers of village halls and so on."

"Bribes."

"Exactly. If the village really wanted a village hall, it should have got its act together years ago. Plenty of other places have. Goodies that fall in your lap from the sky usually aren't worth having in the long run."

"What'll happen now?"

"Nothing for a bit." Mr.Nidd went on to explain that there was always a period of stalemate in these affairs. The protesters would stop any more machinery from getting in by lying in front of it if necessary. They were acting illegally of course, but any attempt to remove them had to be approved by a court and that took time. In the meantime the police would act to stop any breach of the peace, but that was all they'd do.

Meanwhile, Kitty knew but did not say, there was stalemate upstairs as well. Lady Sybil wanted to go along with Medulla's plans, whatever they were. Sir Lancelot was holding out because he was worried about his moths. Eventually she thought Lady Sybil, or Medulla, would win, but in the meantime things were just as stuck indoors as they were outside.

"Of course, you know what this is all about, don't you?" Mr.Nidd said softly.

"Yes, it's the frottling thing, getting gas out of the coal under the sea, isn't it?"

"Yes. But that's not all. Look over there ..." he nodded to the far end of the car park. The area had been fenced off with tall wire mesh panels, and some security men in dark uniforms were moving slowly with torches. There were the two enormous bulldozers, and the yellow JCBs with their digger arms, and the string of dumper trucks for removing debris. But right in the centre was something new, a tall crane with a big cab at the back, and caterpillar tracks for moving about. The security guard walking past it didn't even come up to the top of the tracks.

"I see that big crane," she said, "what about it?"

"Look what's hanging from it."

She looked. Hanging near the ground on the end of a long chain suspended from the top of the crane's jib, was a massive steel ball the size of a small car.

"You know what that is, do you? That's a wrecking ball. The crane turns round and swings it against things to knock them down. It takes time, but that'll go through walls, whole buildings, anything ..."

Kitty took a breath. "You mean ...?"

"Yes. They're planning to knock the whole castle down, smash it into a heap of rubble, and build their power station in its place."

She went to her bed with a heavy heart. She knew Nearly Normal Nidd was perfectly right. It all made sense now. This was what Medulla had been planning all along. The COGACO scheme needed a place to build a power station to turn the gas from under the sea into electricity. The power station should be as close to the beach as possible, so the gases didn't have to be piped any further than necessary. And where was the one place that was not either shifting sand dunes or marshy bog? Where was the one place that had a stable platform of solid rock on which to build? Why, the castle of course, Castle Crayle which had been built in this exact spot for the exact same reasons. This was the plan, to buy the castle from the Fossetts who would pocket several million pounds and fly off to a comfortable life abroad, while the bulldozers and wrecking balls would smash the ancient castle to smithereens and build a power station instead.

And under all this destruction was Wyrm, dozing in his conduit, talking to his friend the cat and making up his poems, innocent of his doom. She had to tell someone. She had to stop it.

But if she told anyone she had found a wyrm, a living dragon, probably the only one anywhere in the world for hundreds of years, what would that mean? It would stop the destruction of his home under the castle, certainly. But there would be newspapers and television, tourists and scientists, studies and experiments, a convoy of boats permanently moored off the coast to catch his every movement, closed circuit TV monitoring his private life in the oubliette ...

Oh yes, she could save his life all right, if she told someone. But the very thing that saved his life would also ruin it in one fell swoop. And either way, it would be entirely her fault, because she was the only one who knew.

XVIII

When Kitty approached the bushes next morning, looking round carefully to make sure she was unobserved, she could hear Wyrm even before she had parted the first clumps of grass. As she pushed her way through the nettles and under the low-hanging branches of the trees the air was filled with a drone, rising and falling but strong and all-pervasive. This was going to be a problem, for there was a good chance of people hearing him and wondering where the sound was coming from.

As she pushed aside the nettles and ivy at the ladder the sound was nearly deafening, and she felt battered by it as she let herself down to the dim floor. Wyrm lay in his usual place, the look of concentration on his face, and at his back a blur of powerful movement. The wings were almost invisible, they were moving so fast, and the draught nearly lifted her off her feet. She crouched on the flagstones at his head and tapped him on the nose.

Immediately the drone faltered, then fell lower and lower in pitch. Finally it stopped altogether, and the wings folded themselves neatly against his back. They were much longer now, nearly as long as she was, and with a start she realised that there were actually four of them, two on each side, neatly nested together, overlapping slightly. His eyes opened, and he gazed at her rather proudly.

"What do you think?" he said. "Impressive, or what? I've been doing a lot of practice. I think I've scared the cat off."

"I can tell. Haven't they grown? I wonder if they're going to go on getting bigger, or is that it?"

"Not sure. They got bigger last night, but there was not much change this morning. Perhaps this is it, they're as big as they're going to get."

"So, any more poems?"

"No. I've been busy. Look, you might know. These wings ... they're fun, I really like them, but ... what are they for, exactly?"

Kitty looked at him for a long moment. "Wyrm," she said slowly, "they're for flying. You use them to fly in the air."

If she had asked him to balance on his head or juggle a few

boulders he could hardly have been more outraged. "Fly?" he shrieked, "are you out of your mind? It's all right for you, you go around on top of those stick-things ..."

"Wyrm, they're called 'legs', I've told you."

"Whatever, you're used to it, you sway around in the air all the time. Me, I like the ground, nice and safe and secure. It feels comforting under your belly. Nothing worse than a draught round your belly. No, I can't fly. Perish the thought!"

What irony, she thought. A flying creature who's afraid of heights! "But Wyrm, you're a dragon. I know they call them wyrms round here, but that's what you are really. Dragons are famous all over the world, and everyone knows they fly. It's one of their most distinctive qualities, flying."

"Show me one. Come on, bring me a dragon that can fly!"

"I can't. You're the last one. All the others are gone."

"And that's the way I intend to keep it. I shall go on being the last one, because I'm not taking any risks, all right? Flying ... the very idea!"

She leaned against his warm side and closed her eyes. This was going to be difficult. Best take it slowly. "Do birds know they can fly, or do they think they're swimming?" she mused. Perhaps she could capture his interest. "Alternatively, do fish know they're swimming or do they think they're flying? Wyrm, when you go under water and into the kelp, do you fly or swim?"

"I eat, mostly."

"But how do you get down there?"

Wyrm thought. "I never thought about it. Just wriggle, I think. I just point myself downwards, and wriggle."

"You're a bit of a disappointment, you know that? An actual dragon, the like of which hasn't been seen anywhere in the world for hundreds of years, and you just point yourself downwards and wriggle, is that the best you can do?"

"Sorry. Nothing I can do about that," he said loftily.

"No one taught you how to swim, or wriggle, or whatever, did they?"

"No. I just knew how to do it."

"So ... perhaps you already know how to fly, you just haven't realised it yet."

"Not going to happen. Forget it. I am an earthbound creature. I am an earth wyrm."

She giggled. "You're not an earth worm. They're pathetic creatures, they just wriggle about and if you cut one in half, the halves don't realise and keep wriggling."

"You cut my cousins in half?"

"Not your cousins. They're nothing to do with you, it's just an unfortunate coincidence of names."

"Oh. So no one's going to come and cut me in half, then? That's good."

"No, don't worry. No one except me and Perkins know you're here, you're safe enough. But ..." she sat up and looked him in the eye, "if someone did try, you know what you could do about it? You could fly, then they couldn't reach you. See, there's safety in flying!"

"And quite a lot of danger of falling off. You can't fool me."

"Oh come on, Wyrm, you chicken! Just give it a try, just for a moment. You can always stop if you don't like it!"

"What's chicken?"

"A bird. It flies. Not very well, but it does fly. You'd do it better."

Wyrm was silent for a long moment. "I can always stop, can't I? And if I aren't very high up, I can't crash, do you think?"

"No, I think that's right. Come on, just try a little hover to see what it feels like. You like your wings don't you, they make you feel good? So perhaps you'll like how it feels when you use them properly."

"Why do I feel I'm being bullied into something I know I shouldn't ..." he began, but obediently closed his eyes and started to concentrate. The wings stirred into life and the droning rose higher and higher. As its pitch became painful to the ears, Kitty moved away from him and stood with her back to the wall. With a tight frown he made an extra effort, the drone rose to a scream, and the middle of his body rose off the flagstones. After a moment he relaxed, and the wings slowed until they became visible again, and his belly slumped down.

He opened his eyes. "What happened? I felt odd, did anything happen?"

"Yes, yes it did!" she laughed, clapping her hands. "You nearly did it. Next time, keep your eyes open, and your neck stiff. Go on, have another go!"

Obediently he pursed his mouth and the drone began again. This time the pitch went almost straight up to the painful level and once again his body stirred and lifted six inches. And this time he kept his body straight so everything except the very tip of his tail went up. He drifted slightly sideways, then relaxed and came to rest on the edge of his ditch.

He looked round at her excitedly. "I did it, didn't I? Did you see, did you?" he said.

She clapped again. "You did, you really did! You're so clever!"

"But, the thing is ..." he became serious again, "I felt myself slipping to one side, you know, so I stopped. But how do I control it? I mean, going up and down is all very well, but I need to go along as well, don't I?"

"I have an idea about that. When you go into the sea, how do you make yourself go down or up, or turn to the left or right?"

He thought for a moment. "I told you. I just point myself where I want to go, and I automatically go there. That's what I've always done."

"Exactly! You don't think 'Oh, I want to go down so I'll raise my tail a bit and drop my head and wriggle to the left and then to the right ...' I mean, you probably do all those things, but you do them without thinking. So perhaps it's the same for flying?"

"But how do I stop myself thinking about it? You can't stop yourself thinking, can you?"

"Distract yourself. Recite a poem, and concentrate on that. Or I'll recite one, and you listen to it while you fly."

"All right. Let's try it. It'd better not be a funny one, though. I don't know what'd happen if I laughed in the middle."

The drone rose again, and Kitty stood up and declaimed ...

"The common cormorant or shag
Lays eggs inside a paper bag."

The drone reached a scream and Wyrm rose like a stately galleon, two feet off the floor.

"The reason you will see no doubt,
It is to keep the lightning out ..."

With his eyes fixed on her, he began to slowly move forward. This time even his tail was off the floor.

"But what these unobservant birds ..."

He leaned slightly to the right and his body began to turn.

"... what these unobservant birds
Have failed to notice is that herds
Of wandering bears may come with buns,
And steal the bags to hold the crumbs! Wyrm, you did it, you did it!"

She shrieked and halloed and jumped up and down, for Wyrm had performed a stately figure-of-eight, two or three feet off the ground, and ended up hovering where he had started. She ran to his head which was now level with her chest, and gave him a big kiss between the eyes.

"Oh Wyrm, my love, you're such a clever old ... reptile ... erm, insect ... oh, I don't know, you're such a clever dragon!"

The draught from the humming wings was colossal. She could sense the power there. He could do much better than this.

"Try going a bit higher, Wyrm," she suggested.

He looked at her with a rather jaundiced expression, and peered down at the floor. "I think I'm quite high enough here, thank you," he said. "I'd better not try and run before I can walk. Which is rather a silly expression, in the circumstances."

"Oh go on, another foot or so won't hurt!"

So Wyrm gave in with a show of reluctance which Kitty knew was mostly fake, for he was just as excited with his new-found skill as she was, and as proud as punch. For the next half hour he droned and hummed and turned and circled. By the time he felt tired and decided to stop, he had performed several circuits of the oubliette at heights of eight or nine feet and only hit the wall once. The sight of him gliding in stately solemnity overhead brought tears of pride to Kitty's eyes, and she finally said goodbye to him in rather an emotional state.

How could they? she thought as she pushed through the undergrowth and pulled it back behind her to cover her tracks, how could they even think of bringing the house down on this wonderful creature? And how was she to stop them? She was going to have to tell someone, that was clear. They wouldn't be allowed to demolish the castle after that. But then the real, long trial would begin, the interest and the enquiries, all peace and privacy at an end.

Once he had really mastered the flying, she wondered if she could persuade him to run away? Could he not find another home somewhere else, a cave or grotto with some kelp beds nearby? Not far to the north were the Farne Islands, for instance, fifteen or twenty of them with odd names like the Wideopens and the Wamses, Big Harcar and the Longstone. Might he find a place there to lie and feed undisturbed? Then she wouldn't need to tell anyone anything, he would be safe regardless of what happened here.

She wondered if the Billies were familiar with the Farnes, did their fishing trips extend that far? But in order to ask them, she might have to say why. Their expertise and local knowledge might be crucial. Oh goodness, she thought as she jogged towards the front of the castle, decisions, decisions, what to do? She longed for a friend, someone she could confide in. But then, she had such a friend, hadn't she? She could trust Melody, couldn't she? Melody had saved her from Lady Sybil and Mr.Medulla, Melody had bravely marched in and put herself on the line. Yes, she could trust Melody, and Melody could persuade Billy Cott ... but could she convince her? When she'd talked about Wyrm before, she got the impression that Melody was only pretending to believe her, and privately thought she was telling a schoolgirl story, a fantasy.

This was important, so important that it was worth a risk. She needed Melody, and Melody was probably in her office. Kitty didn't want to go to the top corridor again, but needs must. After all, Medulla had told her she was welcome, hadn't he? He seemed to have a bit of a soft spot for her, considering he had made a serious effort to kill her a few days before.

She ignored the protesters at the gatehouse, still circling and chanting. There were a lot more of them now, and another two police cars with quite a little knot of officers in their yellow jackets. The BBC had arrived, finally, and set their cameras up a discreet distance from their poor relations from ITV. Inside the private entrance she trotted up the stairs, then along to the Library to check where Sir Lancelot was. Easing open the door she could see him at his table as usual, and could make out at least one sister on the end of the *chaise longue,* so that was them safely out of the way. She hadn't forgotten Sir Lancelot's desire to beat her with a stick. She went out again, and made her way to the top corridor.

All was quiet, but Melody was not in her office. As Kitty came out and returned down the corridor, there were voices on the stairs. Medulla and Knowes were coming, and she thought she heard Lady Sybil's voice too. She nipped into the dining room and pulled the door almost to. She would wait until they had gone into Lady Sybil's sitting room. But horror of horrors, they did not go into the sitting room, but headed straight for her own door.

"Let's go in here, we may want to spread the plans out," she heard Medulla say, "the dining table's big enough!"

Without another thought Kitty ducked and slipped underneath the table. She pulled her legs up and made herself as small as possible, and resigned herself to an uncomfortable wait until they went away again.

"No, Crust, don't sit down!" ordered Medulla. So Professor Crust was there too? "Offer that chair to her Ladyship, won't you? Where are you manners?"

A chair was pulled out and Lady Sybil sat down. Her knees were barely a foot away from Kitty's face. Kitty wondered what would happen if she suddenly buried her teeth in the horrid woman's leg. It was tempting, but not very grown up and probably dangerous.

Overhead there was a rustle and a sliding noise, as some large plan or diagram or map was laid out on the table top. The feet of the three men moved around and kept changing positions, the neat highly polished black shoes of Medulla, the gigantic boots of Knowes and the down-at-heel brogues of Professor Crust.

"Now, I think I have this all straight in my mind," said Medulla, "but I do like to have it down pat so I never need to refer to any documents but keep it all in my head."

"... as I said in my report," began Crust importantly, but Medulla snapped "Shut up! Don't interrupt me!"

Finally he grunted in satisfaction, and his feet moved back from the table.

"Yes, your report, Professor," he said. "Since you mention it, a remarkably poorly written document, I thought. Even an ignorant businessman like myself knows how to spell 'gneiss', but not you, apparently. And 'schist' usually has an 's' in the middle. At which august seat of learning did you win your professorship, remind me? Bangalore, was it, or Pondicherry? Or Luton Polytechnic, perhaps?"

The Professor said nothing. Kitty imagined him gaping, searching for words.

"To be frank, Professor Crust," Medulla continued, "the only reason we employed you was because some of the Board of Directors still have a childish and sadly misplaced trust in the wisdom of academics. Now that they have made all the right decisions, we have no further use for you. Knowes, the Professor has reached the end of his employment with us, don't you agree? He's becoming a little irritating. He's served his purpose, so why don't you get rid of him?"

Crust gasped and began to move, trying to speak but only managing a strangled cry. Kitty ducked her head as low as she could and peered out sideways. Looking up, she caught a glimpse of Crust's face, pale, his mouth open to protest, as Knowes shot out an enormous arm and grasped him by the front of his coat, twisting so it bunched up under his throat and prevented him from speaking. His face turned from pale to puce and he tore ineffectually at the arm that held him, his eyes rolling desperately.

Knowes lifted him effortlessly off his feet and carried him out of the room with his legs kicking. A moment later they heard a cry, and a crash, then Knowes' heavy tread in the corridor.

"Bit of an accident, tripped and fell down the stairs," he said calmly.

"How unfortunate," sympathised Medulla. "Mind you, it was

bound to happen sooner or later. He did drink rather too much, the sad man."

"Accident waiting to happen," smiled Knowes, "and it happened. Dear, dear."

"Have you phoned for an ambulance?"

"Sent Cartilege."

Medulla drew himself up. "Well, good, I'll send some flowers to the hospital. Or then again, perhaps I won't. But that's enough of that, we have business to transact, do we not, dear lady? We don't need to debate the pros and cons yet again, you know what you have to do, so don't waste my time. Have you managed to win Sir Lancelot round yet? And if not, when are you proposing to do so, exactly?"

Lady Sybil did not reply, but made a sort of gobbling sound in her throat. Beside Kitty, her knees were shaking. Medulla's neat shoes moved closer, and Kitty sensed that he was leaning over Lady Sybil's shoulder and speaking venomously into her ear.

"I'm out of patience, lady. I'll give you to the end of the day to sort it out, and then I'll ... make my own arrangements. And I can't promise you'll like them very much! Now, Knowes, it's time we made our visit to the site. Are your men waiting? I think we need an escort. Don't want to get too involved with that rabble outside," and their feet carried them to the door, neat step and heavy tread, and off down the corridor.

Beside her, Lady Sybil's knees were still shaking, and above the table there was a sort of muffled snort. Kitty realised that Lady Sybil was weeping.

How are the mighty fallen, she thought. Miss Hevesham had said that to her once when she managed to find a spelling mistake in one of Kitty's compositions and marked her down from an 'A' to a 'B'. The next lesson, one of Marcia's jaffa cakes had managed to find itself onto Miss Hevesham's chair and she had to walk round the whole day with chocolate on her bottom. Maturity was a wonderful thing, but sometimes childishness gets the job done.

She clambered out from under the table and sat down on the chair next to Lady Sybil.

Lady Sybil started. "What are you doing in here? How dare you ..." she spluttered, but Kitty could tell her heart wasn't in it.

"I was looking for Melody, Miss Trinket I mean, and I heard most of that," said Kitty. "You've got yourself into a bit of a mess, haven't you?"

Lady Sybil sniffed. "None of your business," she said, and wiped her nose with a scrap of handkerchief.

"Probably not. That doesn't usually stop me, though. Do you know where Miss Trinket is?"

"I told her ... I suggested that she put some extra notices up, to keep those people outside."

"Oh goodness, that won't work. I s'pose you're used to being Lady Sybil and everyone doing what you say without question, but the world's moving on, that won't work any more."

Lady Sybil looked up at her over the handkerchief. "Yes, I've noticed. Starting with you."

"Do you want to talk about it?"

"No."

"All right, I will. They're making you sell the Castle, aren't they, only Sir Lancelot won't sign the papers. Is that right?"

The woman nodded, sniffling into her handkerchief.

"What are you getting out of it?"

"Money. Rather a lot of money. We can go and live in the South of France, and be free of this damned place!"

"I think it's a lovely place."

"No it isn't. It's damp and draughty, the cold in the winter is unbearable, in the summer it's overrun with tourists staring about and making comments ... there's never enough money, the servants are unreliable and you can tell they're looking down their noses, my husband is never here ... all he's interested in is those damn insects, and those three half-wits forever trailing round after him ..."

"Mm, I can see how annoying ..."

"And it takes an age to get anywhere halfway civilised ... all one wants is decent service in nice shops, and proper restaurants that don't serve chips with everything, and theatres and concerts and afternoon tea with polite people ... why am I telling you all this? I don't even like you!"

"That's all right, Lady Sybil," Kitty said, getting up. "I don't like you either. I suppose you're going to work on Sir Lancelot

240

now, are you? Good luck with that. It isn't going too well so far."

"Oh it will," the woman said bitterly, screwing up her handkerchief. "You'll see, I'll fix the senile old idiot ..."

But Kitty had heard enough. It was hard to feel sympathetic towards someone you'd heard saying she'd be happy to starve you to death. And she had problems of her own to solve, hadn't she, far more important problems? She still needed to find Melody.

She found her in the courtyard below, putting up notices she had printed on her computer, saying *'Private, no public admittance'* and *'Danger, keep out'*. Melody said she was worried about the protesters getting into the castle and occupying it. If they did, she hoped to persuade them to keep to the public areas and not invade the top corridor or the Library. But, she admitted, it was a forlorn hope. No one was going to take much notice of a few warning signs.

"Isn't it a bit odd that Mr.Medulla doesn't seem very worried about the protesters?" Kitty said.

"He doesn't, does he? I think he has a lot of confidence in Cockley Knowes to deal with anything that arises."

"Yes. We don't know what he's capable of, do we?"

"I should think he's capable of quite a lot, actually. None of it good."

Kitty didn't reply. She had lied, in fact, she'd seen what he was capable of with Professor Crust, hadn't she? Melody regarded the sign with her head on one side. It said *'Strictly no admittance. Castle staff only'*. "It isn't straight," she said plaintively, "I've put it up so it slopes down to the left."

"Let's have a look," said Kitty, coming to stand beside her. "No, it's all right. The sign is straight enough, it's the world that slopes."

Melody turned, confused. "What? What do you mean, the world slopes?"

"Well, you know the earth is round, don't you? So there's a thing called the curvature of the earth, so we can't see things that are too far away because the earth is sloping away from us?"

"Mmm ... yes, I suppose ..."

"Well, there you are then! If the earth slopes away from you, it must slope in all the other directions as well. It slopes behind you, and it slopes to your left and it slopes to your right. Simple!"

"Oh, I get it!" A slow smile crept across Melody's face. "You're pulling my leg, aren't you?"

"That's my job, it's there to be pulled," said Kitty, grinning. "Yes, the sign's crooked, so what? You can still read it all right, can't you? Not everything in life has to be perfect. But listen, I have to tell you something important. You remember I told you I had found a wyrm under the castle?"

Melody smiled. "Oh yes, but that was just another leg pull, wasn't it?"

"No, it wasn't. This is serious. I have to make a decision, and I don't know what to do so you have to help me."

"Of course, whatever is it? I thought we ..."

But she was interrupted by a sudden burst of shouting. Medulla and Knowes had emerged from the gatehouse to be met by a group of burly guards in blue uniforms. They all started walking across the car park, but the parading protesters gathered round them waving their placards and shouting. This was a signal for fresh groups of protesters to come running from their encampment, and instantly the group of guards were engulfed in a crowd of yelling hostility, pushing and shoving and poking with placards. The security guards pushed back and began to bludgeon their way through the crowd. Fists flew and at least one protester was knocked to the ground.

The policemen came running and fought to get between the two factions, and press photographers hovered, running round the outside of the melée and snapping with their cameras. Television men shouldered cameras from their stands and advanced, swinging round to capture all the action. For a while the outcome was in doubt, but the security guards were more organised and more ruthless. They had no point to put across, they did no shouting, they were encumbered by no placards, so they simply kept close together in a flying wedge that drove through the crush and eventually broke free. With Medulla and Knowes in their heart, they marched off towards the other end of the car park where their machinery waited.

Behind them, the scene was like the aftermath of a small war. Several protesters sat on the ground nursing sore heads, the gravel was littered with placards torn and trampled underfoot. The policemen talked urgently into their radios, and the photographers and cameramen withdrew to their cars and vans to examine their footage. There was a noise of sirens and several ambulances swept up the drive with their blue lights flashing. Kitty thought they must have been parked nearby to have got here so quickly. Plainly someone had been expecting trouble.

Shortly the security guards returned, walking on either side of a small lorry which drove slowly up to the gatehouse and stopped. The guards began to unload it, lifting down more of their steel mesh fence sections and erecting them across the front of the gatehouse. Evidently they were aware of the possibility that the protesters might try to get into the castle itself, and were determined to make it as hard as possible.

"How are we going to get back in?" said Melody.

"Not a problem, I'll take you round the outside to the kitchen back door," Kitty said.

"You had started to tell me something? Something about pulling my leg?"

"Oh yes ... look, it'll wait. I think it's going to kick off again. We need to get out of the way."

But it didn't kick off, not quite. While the guards busied themselves with the new fence, some of the professional protesters interfered. They were plainly used to this sort of thing, for they offered no violence but just hung onto the mesh to hinder the guards who found it impossible to move a fence panel that had three or four men or girls clinging to it. The whole thing was quite good-natured really. The guards and the policemen would prise a laughing protester off, who then ran round to the other side and attached himself to the next panel. One or two of the guards were rough and had to be cautioned by the police, but otherwise it was almost like a game, one which the guards and the police would win in the end but not before the protesters had given them a lot of grief and wasted a lot of their time and effort.

And even when the fence was complete, the protesters hadn't quite finished. It was mainly the villagers who got involved this time, and soon the new fence was elaborately decorated with flowers and streamers and placards, giving the photographers and cameramen plenty to film. The first battle of this war had ended in stalemate, predictably, but there were plenty of people on the campaign side who felt they had won a victory of a sort. They still held the field, and the enemy would be embarrassed once reports of violence reached the evening news on TV and the newspapers next morning.

Kitty went to the oubliette very early the next morning, slipping out of the kitchen back door before the sun had risen over the seaward wall. The lawns were pearled with dew, and there was no sign of movement among the tents of the protesters although, like true professionals, they had left a picket on watch round one of the bonfires. One of the watchers was Sky, wrapped in a filthy old great-coat. She had evidently thrown in her lot with these people. As Kitty passed she waved and smiled, and held up a mug to ask if Kitty wanted to join them, but she signalled 'no, thanks!' and passed on. Behind her back she knew that Sky was telling her friends who she was.

She was determined to speak to Wyrm as soon as possible. She needed to warn him that if anything untoward happened, if he heard any noises he didn't recognise or saw any movement in unexpected places, he should get out through his tunnel and stay well out of the way. He would be safe in the sea, she would tell him, whatever might be happening on land.

But when she pushed her way through the dripping bushes and reached the rope ladder, all was silent and still. She peered in through the aperture, waiting until her eyes got used to the dim light. The oubliette was empty. Wyrm had evidently gone out early to the kelp beds, and was happily browsing. So her message couldn't be delivered. It would be nice if she could have left him a note, but she had no paper or pencil, and she didn't think he could read anyway. She would have to leave it now and come back later on, hoping that nothing bad would happen meanwhile. She scrambled back through the undergrowth and ran round to the kitchen, hoping there might be some breakfast.

There was breakfast, and she ate it gratefully. Who knew? It might be the last one, if Medulla had his way. She told Ma and the twins what she and Nearly Normal Nidd had realised last night, but found they were not as surprised as she expected. The same conclusion, that COGACO meant to demolish the castle altogether, had evidently occurred to others round the village and in the protest camp. It was obvious, when you thought about it – the coal was here just off the shore, and right here was the only piece of solid rock foundation where a major industrial building might be built. It didn't need a university degree to work that out, and many people had. That was good, she thought, for surely they wouldn't stand for such an audacious piece of vandalism? They'd close ranks, and make a fuss with MPs and the County Council, and the whole scheme would founder and fail, wouldn't it?

But when she finished her breakfast and went round to the front of the castle to see what was going on, she found that Mr.Medulla and COGACO didn't share her faith that everyone would see the great crime that was being committed, and act accordingly. At the far end of the car park the wire fencing had been opened up, and with a roar and clouds of black diesel fumes the bulldozers and JCBs were bursting into life. Men in orange hard hats moved around and clambered over the machines, and the first of the monsters began to grind slowly through the gaps in the fence and across the gravel towards the gatehouse.

There was a small contingent of protestors standing vigil in front of the gatehouse, having maintained a watch there by taking turns through the night, and as soon as the machines started to move figures could be seen sprinting one way towards the village, and the other way to the encampment. The alarm was being raised. Three police cars had been parked nearby all night, and now their doors opened and yellow-jacketed officers got out, rubbing their eyes, putting on their caps and lighting cigarettes. Sky and another girl from the encampment appeared, bringing them cups of tea on trays. Good relations with the constabulary were always important.

Two columns of vehicles had now formed up across the car park, JCBs in front, then the massive bulldozers, and behind them a rank of dumper trucks. They sat with their engines rumbling, looking sinister. The men in hard hats perched on them and in them, smoking patiently and calling quietly to each other, while a squad of blue security guards formed up in front. They too wore white hard hats now, and Kitty thought some of them had sticks or baseball bats tucked unobtrusively down beside their legs.

Up the winding drive from the village, people were pouring in ones and twos and larger groups, some with placards and some with their own hard hats though none with weapons that could be seen. A brief 'whoop!' from a siren made them move out of the road to let a little convoy of white police vehicles pass, a car and two minibuses with burly policemen looking out of the windows. Sky's tea ladies were going to be busy.

Protesters were also swarming from the encampment, and a sizeable crowd now spread across the front of the gatehouse, facing the bulldozers. Some people walked forward and lay down on the ground in front of the JCBs to prevent them from moving. One or two of the security guards fidgeted and looked as though they wanted to start getting involved, but a sharp command stilled them. From between the vehicles Mr.Medulla emerged, walking calmly with Cockley Knowes looming huge behind him. Medulla wore no hard hat, but a neat overcoat and scarf, and looked as though he was on the way to a business meeting, not a battle. He strolled among the guards, saying a few words to one or another, and calling up to the hard hats in the cabs of the vehicles, a general going among his troops.

On the sidelines, watchful and ready, waited a phalanx of policemen. Kitty saw Dashwood Belhatchett come hurrying up. He went to the policemen and began talking urgently to them, waving his arms. Evidently the local councillor wanted more positive action from them, but they remained unmoved. A senior officer with silver buttons down his tunic took Belhatchett aside and spoke earnestly into his ear. Belhatchett didn't look as though he liked what he was hearing.

Presently and for no particular reason that Kitty could see, the engines of the enemy began to rev. Exhaust pipes rattled and belched black fumes, and one or two of the drivers released their clutches repeatedly, making their machines rock as though eager to get into the fray. At this, more people ran out of the crowd and prostrated themselves on the gravel. Others began to tug at the wire fence behind them, evidently trying to clear a way into the castle. It was going to take the police and the security men a long time to pick the lying figures up and move them out of the way, and of course more would come and take their places. The only solution for the invaders was to hope that the police would start arresting protesters, locking them in the vans and taking them out of the struggle so there would be fewer and fewer left to fight. But this would take time, and there were still more people toiling up the drive from the village to join the fun.

Kitty was just thinking that Mr.Medulla must be on a hiding to nothing and could not possibly win, when a large black car swept up the drive and came to a halt beside the police vehicles. Out stepped a couple of men in dark suits, with briefcases. They consulted swiftly with the senior policeman, then walked with him to the front of the crowd. One pulled some papers out of his briefcase, took a loud-hailer from the policeman, and addressed the crowd.

"Good morning," he said, his voice sounding metallic through the loud-hailer and echoing sharply off the wall of the gatehouse, "my name is Masseter, and I'm a solicitor from the firm of Ardle, Masseter and Clint from Newcastle, and represent Coal Gasification Company Limited otherwise known as COGACO. I have here a Court Order issued yesterday afternoon! It requires all persons to cease and desist immediately from interfering with or hindering the officers of the Company from going about their lawful business. Any attempt to do so will be a criminal offence and I have asked the police to treat it accordingly. That is all I have to say, thank you. Please disperse now, and let these men go about their business in accordance with the law and the decision of the court!"

There was a moment of stunned silence as he closed his briefcase and walked calmly back to his car. Kitty looked around for someone to explain what this meant, Melody or Nearly Normal or someone. One or two of the prostrate protesters started to get up, but most stayed down, resting up on their elbows and staring round them. The crowd shifted its feet and muttered, but made no attempt to move. The senior policeman looked uncomfortable, and shrugged apologetically. He raised the loud-hailer to his mouth and said, "Sorry, folks, but you heard the man! I must ask you to disperse."

No one moved. But the frozen silence was suddenly broken by a screech as a figure appeared behind the protesters, a bizarre figure, tall and thin in combat trousers and a frock coat, with an old helmet on its head and an antique sword in one hand. Sir Lancelot pulled at the wire fence and moved one panel aside with a squeaking noise and squeezed through the gap. The crowd parted and let him through. Behind him staggered the Sisters, tripping and snagging their dresses on the fence and getting in each others' way. Sir Lancelot came to a halt facing the bulldozers, and the Sisters clustered round him, peering round, fluting and twittering in alarm.

He raised the sword in the air. "Stop this!" he said in a high voice. "I am the Lord of this Castle, and I say this must stop! No one shall pass! This is my place, and my property, and I have not agreed to this. I will not agree, and never will!"

Behind him rose a sullen growl of support. This ridiculous figure was not alone, daft as he looked and sounded.

Once again he waved the sword above his head. "Be gone!" he shrilled, "you shall not pass!" Someone cheered, but mostly the crowd stood sullen and silent, looks of determination on their faces. But one small voice called "Look! It's on fire!"

Everyone turned. From the roof of the castle, a skein of smoke curled, wreathing close to the slates before being whipped away by the wind. As they watched it grew stronger, black and dense. Kitty gasped. The castle was on fire!

Sir Lancelot had also seen. "The library!" he cried. "My moths, oh, my moths!" and he turned and pushed his way back through the crowd, between the parted sections of the fence, and ran stiffly across the cobbles followed by the Sisters, making for the private entrance and the stairs.

Behind him Mr.Medulla stirred into action. "Knowes!" he snapped, thrusting some paper at the giant man, "take these! Follow him, make him sign!" Knowes snatched the papers, shoved them into his pocket and took off across the gravel. He trod on more than one of the prostrate protesters and crashed through the crowd, using his bulk to toss them aside as he ran, unstoppable. At the fence he did not bother to find a gap but launched himself at the centre of one panel and bore it to the ground with his weight, stamped over it and thudded over the cobbles in hot pursuit.

As he disappeared through the little door, Kitty gasped "Lady Sybil! She's still in there! And where's Melody?" She took to her heels, dashed round the back of the startled crowd and across the courtyard and into the door. Up the steep stairs she pounded, hardly thinking, desperate. As she neared the top and reached the top corridor she could smell something, smoke and something else, something familiar ... she had a sudden picture of her mother filling the Land Rover from a can – petrol! That was it, she could smell petrol!"

She ran along the top corridor and crashed into Melody's office but it was deserted. Back again, and into Lady Sybil's sitting room, calling "Lady Sybil, you have to get out, there's a ... oh! There's no one here." Out into the corridor, and turn right towards the great hall and the Library. There was smoke now, hanging near the ceiling in evil coils. She could hear voices, a crackling sound and shouts up ahead. She burst out into the hall with the staircase and found a desperate tableau.

At the head of the stairs, wreathed in smoke and silhouetted against the flickering light from the Library, stood Lady Sybil with something in her hand. Halfway up, staring aghast at her, was Sir Lancelot with his sisters clustered behind him. At the bottom of the stairs was Cockley Knowes, about to start up towards them.

"There! There, you senile old fool!" crowed Lady Sybil in triumph. "I've burned your damned moths, they're going sizzle, sizzle and pop! What are you going to do now, you idiot?" She advanced down towards him, a mad smile on her face. She was streaked with soot and her hair was coming down. "Now will you sign the bloody papers? There's nothing to stop you now, is there, so sign and let me out of here! I never want to see you or this place again, you hear? Sign!"

Behind her there were dreadful noises, a loud crackling as books and bookshelves caught the fire. The grand glass-paned doors were blistering and some of the glass popped, shards tinkling down the stairs. "My moths!" cried Sir Lancelot, "what have you done, you bitch? My moths, my moths!" and he sprang forward, brushing her aside, and through the doors into the flames. "... moths! my moths!..." chorused the Sisters and followed him. Lady Sybil ran down the stairs as the Sisters disappeared into the crackling flames, passing Knowes who was thundering up in hot pursuit. He paused at the top, put his arm over his face and pushed inside. Flames licked through the top of the door and raced up the wooden panelling towards the ceiling, vaulted in timber high above, ancient and dry.

Lady Sybil reached the bottom. "Lady Sybil," cried Kitty, "you have to get out. You've really done it now, haven't ...?" but the woman ignored her, pushing her out of the way and running back towards the top corridor. As she ran she was waving the thing she held in her hand, and Kitty realised it was a petrol can. She was spilling petrol as she ran, deliberately, leaving a shining rivulet on the bare boards. Kitty paused, uncertain what to do. The decision was taken for her, though. With a crash the doors of the Library sprang open for the last time, for they were coated in flame and blackening. Out staggered the massive figure of Cockley Knowes, wreathed in fire. From his outstretched hand fell the ashes of the contract, burned to a crisp. He staggered down a couple of steps, lost his balance, grabbed for the balustrade and missed, and fell with a thud onto his face, then slid heavily down the length of the staircase with a grunt at each step. As he reached the bottom there was a splitting noise and a groan high above and part of the ceiling slowly peeled away from its fastening and began to fall. Blue flames now clothed every part of the vault and black smoke was descending in choking clouds. The debris hit Knowes full across the shoulders, a great heavy beam of smouldering oak, and floored him.

As he howled in pain and began to gather his limbs under him to shrug the beam off and get up, Kitty took to her heels.

Outside, all was confusion. The idling engines of the waiting bulldozers were turned off, the prostrate protesters got up and stood staring at the smoke billowing from the roof of the castle, while the senior police officer snapped orders into his radio. A line of policemen spread themselves along in front of the wire fence to prevent anyone from entering the gatehouse, while the crowd milled and gaped. A string of ambulances appeared up the drive with their sirens wailing, and parked while their crews opened the doors and prepared equipment to receive casualties.

Some of the crowd wanted to cheer at the burning castle, but enough of them were villagers and the cheers soon died. People began to drift away to the sides to watch and wait, as it became obvious that hostilities were suspended.

"Kitty, where did Kitty go?" Melody said desperately to Ma Cott who had appeared at her side.

"I haven't seen her since she had her breakfast. Girls, have you seen Kitty?"

Faith and Charity came hurrying up. Charity had Perkins in her arms, and the two Billies were close behind them. No one had seen Kitty, though.

Melody went to one of the policemen. "There's a child," she said, "I think she may have gone back inside. She lives here."

"Don't know anything about that, pet. Our orders are to see that no one tries to go in. Fire engines'll be here soon enough, they'll search. Listen, you can hear them now!"

It was true, there were more sirens and a large red fire engine heaved into view and was waved on by other policemen, straight in through the gatehouse where desperate hands had pulled down the fence and wooden gate. Heavy smoke filled the courtyard, and was gushing from the private entrance. High above, flames were now to be seen above the roofs. The fire had a firm hold.

"If she is in there, she knows her way around," said Billy Cott, trying to be a comfort. "Where might she make for?"

"The North End, perhaps," suggested Melody. "She spent some time there, and I think it's nearly all stone so it'll take a long time before the fire gets to it."

"How can we get in there?"

"I don't know. She does, but I don't."

"I do," said a high voice. Melody looked down. Streaky Nidd had arrived, with his father in attendance. "I know how to get in, I can show you," said the boy again.

Melody looked at the Billies. "We have to try, don't we?" she said.

"Aye, pet, we do," said Billy Cott, and with Streaky and Nearly Normal in front they set off round the seaward side of the castle, but Melody suddenly stopped.

"Wait!" she said. "I just thought! Suppose she's gone up to her bedroom? That's in the tower, and that's all stone, isn't it? She might be safe there?"

"Aye, could be!" agreed Billy Cott. "We ought to tell someone - one of the firemen? Billy, you go on with Mr.Nidd and try and get to the North End, we'll see what we can do here!"

The last thing Melody noticed as she took his hand and

started to run towards the fire engines, was a large black car that came from behind the bulldozers, bounced over the grass and sped away down the drive. At the wheel, staring fixedly through the windscreen and not looking to right or left, was Mr.Medulla.

Kitty ran, her feet seeming to hardly touch the ancient floorboards of the corridor. She sped past the room with the sliding table, and felt a pang of regret that she had never tried the game she had imagined playing with her friends. She'd lost the chance now. Glancing behind, she saw a little tongue of blue flame rising from the floor. Lady Sybil's trail of petrol was alight. But before she could wait to see any more, the bulk of Knowes filled the corridor, his clothes smoking, black against the flames in the hall behind. He gave an animal bellow and began to shamble after her, unsteady on his feet and bouncing off the walls. At his feet raced the blue light as the trail of petrol ignited, overtaking him and bursting into tall yellow flame through which he came like a creature from hell.

"The tower!" thought Kitty. "The tower's all stone, isn't it? And if I close the door at the bottom of the stairs ...?"

She ran, with Knowes's heavy shambling tread behind her, and fled through the narrow door that led to the spiral stairs. She pulled the old door behind her and heard it latch, then in almost complete darkness began to climb. The steps were narrow, very narrow at one end and wider at the other, and unevenly worn from centuries of feet. Turning always to the right she climbed, her breath heaving, tripping and slipping in the dark and bruising her knees. She reached the bathroom but did not go in, for she heard a crash and a splintering of timber as the door below was smashed aside. Knowes was still coming. She wasn't sure why he wanted her, but wasn't about to stay and find out. Perhaps he was crazed with pain, burned and sore and confused, and would lash out at anything he could reach.

She passed the door of Melody's room. It was open, and a quick glance with her hands on the high step was enough to convince her that it was empty. She climbed on, and reached her own bedroom door. It was here that she realised her mistake. The tower was all built of stone, true enough, and here she was climbing round and round in the very heart of its thick stone wall, and stone doesn't burn though there was smoke around her, blowing past her rather fast as the hot air rose up the stairs which acted like a chimney. But the beams that supported each floor were wood, weren't they? And the floors, they were of stout oak planks, ancient and dry? When she had lain in bed, staring up at the ceiling, what had she seen? Oak beams, gnarled and twisted and strong, and above them planks of more oak, shiny with use above and clad in cobwebs beneath. Once the flames got in, the centre of the tower would become an inferno, smoke and flames funnelling up into the sky above.

But behind her she could still hear Knowes, grunting in pain at every step and swearing steadily under his breath, so she turned and fled upwards, uneven step by uneven step, nimble and light but full of dread. She ignored the unused room above hers, and came at last to the door onto the roof. Frantically she fiddled with the lock until it gave and the door shot open. Gasping and tearful she rolled out onto the lead of the roof.

What was the roof made of, she asked herself? It was lead sheets, wasn't it, laid flat and clenched into waterproof seams. But under that? Why, wood of course. And wood will burn and lead will melt. As if to confirm her worst fears, she heard a sullen roaring beneath her feet, and little wisps of smoke began to appear. And from the stairs was the grunting of her pursuer and the heavy pounding of his feet. He was moving slowly now, confused and wracked with pain, but still coming.

She crawled across the lead sheeting on all fours, remembering wistfully the last time she had been here, the glory of the storm and the wind and the clouds. Now there was wind but no glory, and the clouds were of thick black smoke that rose from the roofs below and choked her. Under her crawling hands and knees the lead was warm, then quickly became hot so she rose to her feet and ran the last few feet to the parapet. Peering over she could see people swarming around like ants, and running figures, and more fire engines arriving, their sirens sounding puny against the great roaring of the fire below her feet.

There was a bang, and looking back in panic she saw Knowes fling back the door and roll out of the stairwell onto the roof. He writhed to and fro, then began to gather himself to get up. She knew he would seize her and fling her helplessly into the void and there would be little she could do about it, just fly tumbling through the air and crash to the ground and there would be an end to it. Probably he'd jump with her, for there was no sanity in his savage eyes as he glared at her and began to crawl across the roof. She drew her legs up and huddled in the stonework, transfixed.

But the fire was booming underneath them now, and as she watched a part of the lead sheet split, and curled downwards, and turned suddenly silver and disappeared. Below was a burning hell of orange flame and noise, and Knowes turned a despairing gaze on her before he lost his grip and slid slowly into the void without a sound. He was gone, and the roof was gone. She was finished.

She turned in her narrow perch of cool stone, and looked out and down, to the world that lay green and unburned below her. She hoped that Melody was all right, and the twins. And Perkins, where was she? And Wyrm, had he realised he was in danger and taken to the waves? The roaring of the flames behind her rose higher, with a deep thrumming that told of immense heat. Would the very stones begin to glow red and crack apart? Would the tower stand, at least long enough for her to gather the courage to jump and end it all? The deep thrumming was louder now, almost drowning out the roaring of the flames, an intense drone that filled her ears. She put both hands on the stone, getting ready to jump, and Wyrm rose ponderously into view, his great wings a blur. He slid sideways, over-corrected and slid back the other way, his eyes starting out of his head.

"Quick!" he hissed, "I'm not sure how long I can keep this up!"

She told herself not to look down as she climbed through the gap in the parapet and launched herself onto his back, kicking him on the nose as she did. She ended spread-eagled on the back of his head, facing backwards and clinging on with desperation. The thrumming wings almost touched her and she had time to notice that they seized the black smoke and tore it to spiral shreds as Wyrm slid sickeningly sideways and down, then turned to face the beach and let himself fall in a headlong flight towards the south, a flight that was only just controlled, muttering to himself ... "You're all right, don't panic ... you have wings, you can fly .... look, it's just the same as swimming, only higher ... oh goodness ... it's all right, you can't fall off. Well, you can, but you've got wings ..."

XX

A mile to the south, where the beach is stony rather than sandy so few people come, and a little-used coastal road runs just behind it, Wyrm set gently down in the shallows and Kitty slid off his back. His wings folded neatly and were silent.

She stood by his head, and kissed him between the eyes. "Darling Wyrm," she said, trying not to cry, "you're a hero. You're the greatest dragon in the world!"

"I thought you said I was the only dragon in the world?" he said with a mischievous look in his eye.

"That too. How did you know I was stuck up there, and needed you?"

He was silent for a moment. "I don't know," he said slowly. "I just did, somehow. Evidently I have abilities I don't know about yet."

"I'm sure that's true," she said. She leant against him, stroking his pretty scales.

"What's going to happen now?" he asked.

"I'm not sure. I think I'll have to go away. There's no castle to stay in, and I only had another week or so anyway. And you ..."

She explained that it would be dangerous for him to go back to the oubliette. There were far too many people around, and were going to be for quite a long time. Even if COGACO went away with their plans in tatters, which they probably would be now, there would be fire investigators and the press, and then builders to put it all back together ... the castle was no place for a reclusive wyrm any more.

"You need to find a better place," she said as encouragingly as she could. "A cave perhaps, on an island?" She told him about the Farne Islands. "You could try there."

"But you won't be there, will you? I won't be able to see you. I'll have no friends, and I was just getting used to it. Who's going to listen to my poetry?"

"You'll just have to make some new ones. Have you thought about seals, at all? They tend to lie about on the beach all day if they're not fishing. Perhaps they'd like to listen to your poems? They always seem very patient to me."

"Mm. I do see them occasionally. Wonderfully agile creatures, very quick in the water."

"They can't fly, though, can they?"

"No. No, I suppose they can't!" he said, brightening.

She heard something in the distance. "Look, you need to go, I think there's a car coming. Keep safe, darling Wyrm!" She kissed him again. "But listen, keep away from humans, they're not good for you. But if you see the *Mercy* ..."

"What's that?"

"It's a boat. It's blue, and has a little yellow house on it, and a chuggy sort of engine. And in it there are two friends of mine. One's called Billy Brannicle and one's called Billy Cott. And if you see them, just pop your head out of the water and speak to them. Mention my name."

"Do they use the same words as you? English?"

"More or less. And they're safe, they'll be glad to see you, and they won't tell anyone."

The noise of the car was louder now. As well as the sound of the engine she could hear the swish of its tyres, and it gave a little hoot.

"You must go. Go on!" She gave him a shove, and he gazed at her with one moist eye, wriggled round and slid over the pebbles. Just before he disappeared below the gentle breakers she was sure she heard him mutter *'I ask myself how it would feel, To say my verses to a seal?'* and he was gone.

The car pulled up, and Melody and Billy Cott got out. Kitty brushed away a tear and watched them coming over the pebbles towards her, holding hands.

Melody was crying. "Kitty, how did you get here? What happened? We saw you up on the tower, and then ... there was so much smoke ... Kitty, were you flying?"

Kitty gave her a hug, and then gave Billy one for good measure. She forced a smile to her face and said blithely "Flying? I don't know what you mean. I can't fly!"

That was going to be her line, she decided. Complete denial and there's nothing anyone can do about it. Melody looked very dubious, but Billy smiled at her, a kind and slightly knowing smile, and said "I expect that's it, it was a trick of the light.

There was a lot of smoke, after all."

"But what about that?" Melody said, waving her hand at the breakers. "There was something ... it went into the sea, didn't you see?"

"No, no, I thought I saw something, but it was just the waves humping up and falling down, look, there's nothing there now. Forget it! Trust me, I'm a fisherman, I've seen a lot of waves and they can trick you if you're not careful. Let's get this child home and find her some clean clothes. She's all wet and sooty."

Melody tried to insist, asking how Kitty got so far down the beach and why she was all wet, but Billy soothed her and Kitty thought her advice to Wyrm about the *Mercy* had been wise. There was more to Billy Cott than even Melody knew, who loved him.

"I'm not sure where we can go, though," said Kitty. "I mean, we've got no rooms and no clothes and no anything any more, have we, either of us? I don't even have my train ticket home, that was burnt as well."

"We'll manage. I still have my credit card," said Melody. "Actually, I can remember the passwords for the Castle account, and there's no one left who knows how much is in there apart from me. So we won't go short. And I have my car. We can go to Billy's to get cleaned up, and borrow something to wear, and then I'll take you home."

"There's no one there. I know how to get in, but Mother won't be home for a week at least."

"I'll stay there with you. I'll look after you, and you can look after me. Just until your mother comes. It's not as if I have a job any more, so I might as well have a little holiday in Scotland."

Kitty felt pleased. It would be fun. "Can Billy come too?" she asked, "he could sleep in Jake's room."

Melody blushed, and Billy looked at the ground.

"I'd like that," he said softly. "But I have to stay and help Billy. He can't manage on his own, that's a two-man boat."

"I'll be back, though, as soon as Kitty's mother's home," said Melody, looking at him shyly.

An hour or so later, with Kitty damp from the shower and brushed and enveloped in an odd assortment of clothes from

Faith and Charity, they headed inland towards the A1 and the road north to Pitlochry. The castle was still burning, and Melody had to pull into the bank several times as more fire engines swept past with sirens wailing.

She said "Once we get north of Berwick we'll find somewhere to stop, and have lunch. I expect you can eat Macdonald's, can't you?"

Kitty nodded. "I don't believe you, you know," Melody continued. "I know when my leg's being pulled. I'll drag it out of you before I've done, young lady."

Kitty relaxed in her seat and craned round for a last glimpse of the castle with its plume of smoke. "Good luck with that," she thought.

About the author

David Bramhall is a former musician, composer and teacher, and a choral conductor of some distinction. His book *Training Your Young Choir* sells slowly but steadily all over the world, as do two classroom text-books on music.

An acerbic and irreverent commentator on political and social matters, for many years he ran the popular website *GrumpyOldSod.com*, and a collection of articles is still in print and entertaining, though sadly no longer topical.

In recent years he turned to writing novels and is currently working on his tenth. An occasional poet – though he prefers to describe himself as "a versifier" and refuses to take the form very seriously – in 2020 he won the King Lear Prize for Poetry with "*Snape Maltings, the Concert Hall at night*".

He lives in the East of England with his wife, also a musician, and plays with historic steam locomotives in his spare time. He's written a book about them, as well!

If you enjoyed *Kitty in the Castle*, you might also like *Kitty in the Winter Wild* and *Kitty at the End of the World*.

All the books in the *Greatest Cape* series and the three *Kitty* novels are available in paperback from your favourite book retailer, or on Amazon or from Smashwords.com.

www.davidbramhall.com

Training Your Young Choir
Composing in the Classroom Opus 1
Composing in the Classroom Opus 2
How to Own a Steam Engine
Captain Grumpy's Book of the Road

The Greatest Cape

1 The Black Joke
2 The Bernadette
3 Rio Sagrado
4 Turnstone
5 Patience and the Pyrate

The Kitty Novels

1 Kitty in the Winter Wild
2 Kitty in the Castle
3 Kitty at the End of the World

The Honeyplot

www.davidbramhall.com

Printed in Great Britain
by Amazon

31163007R00155